Heads You Lose

Heads You Lose

Martin Samuel Cohen

Ekstasis Noir

Ekstasis Editions

National Library of Canada Cataloguing in Publication Data

Cohen, Martin,
    Heads you lose.

    Novel.
    ISBN 1-896869-93-1

    I. Title.
PS8576.O778P74 2002   C811'.6   C2002-910160-0
PR9199.3.M657P74 2002

Published in 2002by:
Ekstasis Editions Canada Ltd.   Ekstasis Editions
Box 8474, Main Postal Outlet   Box 571
Victoria, B.C. V8W 3S1   Banff, Alberta ToL oCo

THE CANADA COUNCIL | LE CONSEIL DES ARTS
FOR THE ARTS | DU CANADA
SINCE 1957 | DEPUIS 1957

BRITISH
COLUMBIA
ARTS COUNCIL
Supported by the Province of British Columbia

Heads You Lose has been published with the assistance of a grant from the
Canada Council and the Cultural Services Branch of British Columbia.

For Arne Silverman

with gratitude

Author's Note

As this is a work of fiction, all the characters portrayed in this book are products of my imagination. The Bible stories, on the other hand, are mostly authentic.

M.S.C.
Mission Viejo, California
January 2, 2001

I

It was so unbelievably hot in the motel room that even sleeping naked didn't do much to help, but these were desperate times…and it really must have been hot enough to boil water in that damn room. Mind you, I didn't love walking around completely bare-ass with the kid snoring in the chair just inches away anyway. I mean, it was bad enough that I had taken the bed for myself in the first place—not that I didn't deserve it, mind you, since I was the *shmuck* who was paying for the room without asking the kid to contribute anything more than some sullen conversation I practically had to beg for—but still, it seemed a bit *intimate* just to walk around like that in front of a kid I hardly knew.

Anyway, it was something like five in the morning so it didn't really matter what I was wearing because the kid was fast asleep and the only reason I was up in the first place was that I had had the dream—the one with the heads—again. I mean, I knew what the dream is all about, but it still wasn't that easy to deal with. I guess it's pretty transparent when you get right down to it, but that didn't make me any less drenched with sweat when I woke up in the middle of it—unless, of course, you want to attribute my sweat to the fact that I was sleeping in a oven with no air conditioning, no breeze coming in through the window and not even any really cold water in the tap to wash my face with rather than to the contents of the dream at all. No wonder eight hundred dinosaurs crapped out in the national park right down the road from there—they probably couldn't take the heat either.

Believe me, I knew how they must have felt.

So I'll tell you about the dream if you want, but you'll have to promise not to whine about how poor your knowledge of the Bible is. It's irrelevant—even if you *had* gone to Sunday School or Hebrew School or some damn school where they teach the Bible, they wouldn't have taught this particular story anyway. Not a chance.

Anyway, the dream begins just after this guy Jehu has just seized power from poor dead King Ahab's wimpy son Joram. Now it's true that this Jehu guy wasn't exactly acting on his own—the prophet Elisha, the one with the trained she-bears, Elisha had already ordained him king over Israel—but the story isn't really about Jehu or Joram as much as it is about the sickness of the servile soul and the corruption of power. So anyway, once he was anointed king, Jehu had to seize his kingdom, which he managed the old-fashioned way: by shooting Joram in the back and having his man Bidkar pick up Joram's bloody corpse and fling it into the field of Naboth that his mother—Joram's mother, I mean, that quintessential bitch Jezebel—that his mother once stole as a little gift for his father just to say she loved him. Then, just for good measure, he—Jehu—has King Ahaziah of Judah shot too, basically just for having had the bad luck to be hanging around when the arrows started flying.

Anyway, none of this is actually in the dream. But the next part is. Jehu has to move quickly to consolidate his power. So he sends over to Samaria, where the elders of the city have taken charge of Ahab's seventy sons. (The commentaries all want to make them into relations and descendants, but I figure a king of Israel could have seventy sons if he wanted to. I mean, Queen Jezebel would have had to be pregnant for about fifty-four and a half years to give birth to them all herself, but I figure a king like Ahab would have had plenty of concubines and lesser-status girl-friends on the side…and it would have only taken him about two and a half months to father seventy kids, I figure. Less if he was a twice-a-night kind of guy. Who knows—maybe even a lot less.) Anyway, these seventy sons of Ahab are being held in Samaria and Jehu needs to test their loyalty to the new regime.

So this Jehu guy writes to the elders of Samaria and asks them to send along the heads of the sons' attendants so he can question them about the boys and the likelihood of their giving him problems down the line. Only there's a little misunderstanding…and the elders, almost (almost!) pathetically eager to do their new master's bidding, take him a little too literally and send along not the heads of the boys' attendants, but the little boys' own seventy heads. Each in its own little basket. Without the little boy attached.

Now the book reads that this messenger guy comes up to Jehu the next day and tells him that the heads of the kings' sons have arrived and the next thing we hear is Jehu giving instructions that the heads should be piled up in two heaps at the gates of Jezreel, the city where he had been staying when all this happened. That little hole in the Biblical text, the one between the guy telling Jehu the kids' heads have arrived and him telling his servants to stack 'em up like grapefruits at the city gates, that's where my dream starts.

So it's like this. I'm right there in the thick of it all wearing this Biblical sort of loincloth-and-terry bathroom outfit complete with some filthy dishrag on my head and a wooden staff in my hand. And I'm standing right there when the guy comes in and tells Jehu that the heads of the sons' tutors have arrived. Now Jehu isn't such a bad guy, at least not in my dream. He looks a little like a chubby Dustin Hoffman, except with lighter hair and less good teeth. Anyway, Jehu is thrilled that his instructions have been complied with so quickly and he orders that they be brought right in to him.

You can imagine the scene when the doors open and, instead

of the tutors coming in, the servants start shlepping in these wicker laundry baskets.

"What is all this crap?" Jehu asks slightly distractedly, clearly not wanting the room cluttered up with anybody's wetwash during his meeting with Ahab's kids' tutors.

The servants think he's kidding, so they just put down the baskets and clear out. And I'm still right there taking it all in, even if no one seems to be noticing me. So Jehu opens one of the baskets and almost loses his lunch. Then he looks in another and it's just about then that he catches on to the fact that they brought the kids' heads instead of the kids' head tutors. So Jehu has this royal fit—screaming and yelling and insisting that this wasn't what he wanted. No one really has any idea what to do to calm him, but eventually he somehow quiets down on his own and orders me—who he thinks I am, I don't know, but I'm just sort of there and he seems to accept that—anyway, he orders me to get the baskets taken to the city gates and organize the heads in two neat pyramids of thirty-five each on either side of the archway so he can stand between then when he makes his next speech. I mean, it wasn't precisely what he had planned, but he's prepared to make the best of the situation. A politician!

Segue to the city gates. We get the baskets over there, get the heads out of the baskets and get 'em stacked up. The scene is pretty gross—some of the heads have this brain stuff oozing out of the base of the neck and others of them don't even have necks and some of the eyes are open and others are closed. One or two even have their mouths frozen in this sort of creepy-as-hell smile, but most of them look pretty damn somber, if you ask me. Anyway, we get the job done, me and some of the servant guys that came along to carry the baskets, and then Jehu appears and launches into some endless speech about how he was doing some sort of sick *mitzvah* by murdering Ahab's kids and how he's looking forward to finishing the job someday if any other formerly royal offspring should ever be stupid enough to materialize in his vicinity. I myself am standing off by the side and sort of half listening and half looking at the heads and suddenly I realize that I recognize one of the heads. Or rather that it recognizes me.

At first, I'm not sure if I'm dreaming or not—I mean this whole thing is a dream, but inside the dream I dream of myself wondering if I'm dreaming, if you can seize the difference—anyway, I'm really not sure if I'm dreaming or hallucinating or have some sort of weird vision or what, but I can see that one of the heads is sort of winking at me. It's the third or fourth over in the second row from the bottom of the left-hand pyramid, but I don't really care *which* of the heads is alive, just that one is and that the one that is seems to be trying to get my attention. Now this is the weird part. It winks once or twice, then blinks both its eyes, then opens its mouth once or twice and closes it right up. And no one seems to notice but me.

So anyway, I'm obviously interested in knowing what this is all about—how the head can be alive if it doesn't have a body and why it's chosen this minute to start blinking and winking and opening its mouth and why it's chosen me to blink and wink to, assuming that I'm something more than the purely random object of its attentions, and what it's trying to get across—but I don't feel like I can just walk over in the middle of Jehu's speech and strike up a conversation with the head. I mean, Jehu has just said for the eighth time how he's going to murder anyone who gets in his way and I'm not precisely about to volunteer to see if he means that literally or not, which I'm half sure he does anyway, so I just sort of stand there and try to figure it out from a distance.

At any rate, this particular head looks like the person it was originally attached to must have been about eighteen or nineteen years old. It's got straight black hair and nice, sort of friendly eyes—I always notice the head's eyes for some reason—and it's clean shaven, which is a bit unusual. I mean, some of Ahab's kids weren't even old enough to shave, but most of the older ones had beards. Mostly goatees. Some Van Dykes. A couple of full-length quasi-hasidic jobs. Even an Amish beard-no-moustache or two. But this head has no beard and not even a moustache. And then I realize why the head looks so familiar. It's not one of Ahab's kids' heads at all—it's my brother's. Wil's head. The head my folks refused to let those body-freezers from California sever from his body for reanimation in the twenty-fourth century like Wil had wanted. It's true that he was pretty demented in that last year, but he seemed okay to me when he first told me about the idea. And he pursued it pretty seriously, phoning up this place in San Diego all by himself, making the arrangements, hooking up with the local firm that handles things like that for the mother company in California. He did it all himself, but he didn't really talk it through with our parents and, when the time came, neither of them would allow it.

The rabbi had a stroke when I broached the topic with him. My parents wouldn't *even* talk about it. The guy at the funeral home asked me—this is for real—he asked me if I was taking drugs when I approached him about honouring the wishes of the deceased even in the absence of his parents' approval. I mean, Wil was thirty-three years old when he died, so he hardly needed his Mommy or Daddy's blessing to make whatever plans he wanted for his own body. And I thought—naive fool that I obviously am—anyway, I thought that his wishes would be considered like this absolutely sacrosanct trust that no one would dare ignore. Yeah, right…it took them about four seconds to decide that he must have been crazy even to think about wanting something like that and that what he really wanted was for them to do whatever they felt like with his body, not what he himself had said completely clearly was what he wished them to do with it.

Anyway, I stand there and wait and wait and wait until Jehu finishes this unbelievably long speech about Ahab and Jezebel and he's shlepping in Omri and Zimri and Basha and making it into half an *apologia pro vita sua* and a half a lecture on his Favourite Israelites Who Assassinated Sitting Monarchs and it's like sitting through the speeches at some sort of Stalinist birthday party and there's no end in sight. And on top of that, it's hot that day in Jezreel. Unbelievably hot. The hawks are circling overhead, presumably because they know somebody is going to drop dead in this heat before Jehu finishes yapping. And the heads are already starting to get a little high and the stench of rotting flesh is rising a bit—actually that's probably what the hawks are on to, come to think of it—anyway, it really feels like we're sitting in a furnace and Jehu is going on and on and on with no end in sight. Only he does end eventually—he must have started to bore even himself—and everybody disperses and he sort of signals to me to shovel up the heads and dump them somewhere. I mean, he's finished with the use he figured he could put them to and he can't just leave them there—I mean, he could just leave them, but the hawks would carry them off, one by one, and I guess Jehu figured that would be a bit much, even for him—anyway, he signals to me, tells me to pitch the heads in some ditch outside town, to leave the site unmarked and come back and tell him when the job is done.

So I'm grossed out by the prospect of starting in again with the heads, but I want to get to Wil's and see what that was all about, so I start with the pyramid on the left and begin tossing the heads into some wagon one of the servants has produced and then I finally get down to the row with Wil's head and I pick it up by its hair and look into its eyes. It seems completely inanimate now and I'm just convincing myself that I really must have been hallucinating when it opens both its eyes and looks right into mine.

"Saul, you *shmuck*," it says, "you let me down."

II

They say you never really learn anything in a dream you didn't already know and I guess that must be true. But sometimes you do hear something that you might have known, but hadn't actually owned up to previously even if you maybe really did know it, and I think this was probably one of those dreams. I mean, the scene with Jehu standing between the two pyramids of heads and giving forth on this or that has been in a lot of my dreams, but this was the first time I had noticed Wil's head in the heap and it was certainly the first time it had spoken to me. In fact, it was the first time any part of Wil had spoken to me since he died. But whether this was a vision from the beyond (which I highly doubted) or just me telling myself something I knew but hadn't quite been ready to deal with, the bottom line was that Wil's head was entirely right. I was a *shmuck*. And I did let him down. I guess that was what this whole stupid trip was really all about if you want to know the truth—me running away from Wil in a pathetic, poorly thought out attempt to feel slightly better about having let him down.

But I'm getting ahead of myself. I knew I was never going to go back to sleep—it was really hotter than hell in the room, so much so that I couldn't imagine how the kid could have been sleeping so peacefully—so I didn't even try. I got up out of the bed, pulled on some boxers that had actually been Wil's a million years ago and considered my next move. I wanted some coffee, but I had no idea what time the McDonald's down the road from the motel opened in the morning. Were any of them open all night? I didn't think so, but who knew? I decided to wait until six, then give it a try. Who knew any damn thing anymore?

The kid was asleep in the only chair in the room, so my only real options were to sit in the dark on the bed or to close the toilet seat and sit in the john. I've always been slightly afraid of neon light, so my first inclination was to head back to the bed. I stripped the sheets off the bed, took off the boxers and lay back down flat on my back in the dark. I thought about Wil's head in that heap and tried to remember what it felt like holding it aloft. It was less creepy than you'd think, if you want to know the truth. I mean, there I was in this ancient dung heap of a town holding up my own brother's head by its hair and instead of being completely creeped out, I was sort of enjoying being with Wil for one last time.

I lifted my hands to my own head and lifted it slightly off the mattress. Did my head feel like Wil's had felt in the dream? I didn't think so, but it was frankly hard to say.

I must have lay there with my head in my hands for about ten minutes. And then, when I couldn't stand it any more, I changed my mind about waiting 'til six and got up again, pulled the boxers back on plus a pair of purple plaid walking shorts and a Canucks t-shirt, then slipped some rubber thongs on my feet and headed out the door. I was afraid to get in the car—the owners wouldn't have cared if I drove off because I had already paid the bill, but I didn't want the kid to think I was skipping out on him if he woke up right when I was driving off—so I set off on foot. At any rate, it was already getting hot outside, but the outdoor heat wasn't anything like what it had been like inside the room and although I was depressed, alone, worried and slightly crazy, I was still basically happy to be outside. I considered whistling a merry tune as I walked, then thought better of it.

I started down the road towards the McDonald's thinking about my dream, and about Jehu and Wil, and wondering what the hell I was actually doing in my dead brother's boxer shorts looking for coffee at such an ungodly hour in Barstow, British Columbia. With an underage hitchhiker asleep with my gear in a $23 a night motel room I had paid for with money I didn't really have to spend. And no plans for the rest of my life.

Helene and Lena were…well, I guess I didn't really know where they were at that particular moment. Probably settled into their new life of luxury in California with their new husband and stepfather, a man I hadn't ever actually met and for whom I harbour, even now, what I'd describe as entirely rational loathing since he was basically doing my wife for three years without me knowing or even thinking that we even had a problem in our marriage, let alone one of that kind of magnitude. It all happened so fast, you see—her leaving and Wil dying and my folks going into the home and me getting fired (or rather downsized, as that moron Lefkowitz insisted on calling it even after they canned him too) and the return of my bad friend—to use the delightful name Dr. Schwinger (another dunce) actually wanted me to use to refer to my depression before his wife shot him through the head and left me as shrinkless as I had just previously become wifeless and kidless and brotherless and jobless—and me sticking it out on my own for as long as I could take it—about six months—before starting out to find myself on this enormously pathetic odyssey of self-discovery that I had undertaken in a car that now seemed to me like a relic from my previous life to some undisclosed destination where I would either find some damn meaning in my damn life or else end up, most likely, shooting myself and (thereby) joining Joe Schwinger in hell.

McDonald's was open. There was a bleary-eyed teenager at the counter who barely managed to look up when I came in.

"Coffee ready?" I asked in as friendly a voice as I could muster that early in the morning.

"Yeah," he answered without looking up.

"Can I have a cup?"

"Sure."

As he tore himself away from the sports page of the previous day's Province to get my coffee, I found myself wondering what he would look like with Wil's head on his shoulders. It didn't take long: he would have looked like Wil, except a little taller and less broad-shouldered. As he handed me my coffee, the tips of my middle and index fingers touched his hand along the contour of the warm paper cup. It struck me that I hadn't had any physical contact with another human being since I had set out on this little trip to nowhere. As I reached my other hand into my pocket to dig out some change, I considered that thought, then dismissed it as unsettling and probably irrelevant. But, as Dr. Schwinger, may he rest in peace, would have said—and as I knew all too well anyway— having had a thought in the first place is what counts, not how quickly you can dismiss it as inconsequential or meaningless.

Did you ever ask yourself what happened to King Saul's head? The Biblical text is tantalizing in its unclarity and I fell into that familiar reverie as I headed into the men's room to take a leak, then came back out and sat down on a plastic chair bolted to a plastic table and looked out at Route 17. As far as I could tell, there had been a nuclear holocaust while I was in the can and the kid behind the counter and I were the only humans left in the world. If the kid in my motel room had survived, I obviously couldn't say. I hoped he hadn't.

Old Saul was basically screwed from the word go. He had the stuff of greatness in him—he was a head taller than any other Israelite, after all, not to mention being the most comely of any of Kish's other boys—but he screwed himself over and over by being crazy and depressed and by being stupid and vain and by getting the witch to raise up Samuel from the dead when Samuel being dead was actually the best thing that ever happened to him.

Anyway, he's dead on Mount Gilboa with three of his sons and the Philistines, who don't even know that he killed himself rather than risk the possibility of the Philistines taking him alive and "making sport of him"—which even my dog knows what that means—anyway, he's dead and then, the day after the battle, the Philistines show up to strip the dead of their armour and their swords and whatever else there might be to steal and they find him.

So what do they do? They strip him naked and chop off his head and send the head and the king's weapons on a tour of Philistia so everybody can see what great heros their guys were and what pathetic wimps the Israelites were. Anyway, everything gets accounted for: the weapons get installed as some sort of permanent display in the Temple of Astarte somewhere in Philistia and the body gets nailed to the walls of Bethshan along with the bodies of the three of Saul's sons who died with him. So the inhabitants of Jabesh-Gilead—who owed Saul big—they hear about it and send their best guys to march all night and get the bodies back, which they accomplish nicely, then bring the royal corpses back to Jabesh, cremate them, bury the bones under the tamarisk of Jabesh, whatever that was, and then fast for a week to atone for having gazed on the king's nakedness or whatever else they figured they needed to undo with a week of not eating.

End of story. Except for the head. Another Biblical author tried to come up with some sort of explanation of what happened to the head, but the real story, the basic story, the *original* story leaves the whole issue unexplored: the weapons end up at Astarte's temple and the bodies, or what's left of them, end up buried in Jabesh—at least until David retrieves them later on and buries them somewhere else—but the head is never heard from again. I mean, didn't the Jabesh-Gilead guys notice that there was something really important missing from Saul's cadaver? Or is that why they cremated the bodies—to cover up the fact that they had screwed up royally (hah!) by failing to locate the part of the king that wasn't nailed to the walls of Bethshan when they got there. I've always felt a certain tie to Saul, you know. And not just because of the name thing, although that might be part of it. He's just...I don't know, so pathetic and so brave and so noble at the same time he's so completely screwed that something about the whole ensemble of his qualities, positive and negative, just calls out to me. I don't wish I was him. But then again, I don't really wish I was me either. And what precisely do you suggest I do about that?

Anyway, the coffee was lousy. I know some woman (or rather, some litigious, self-righteous, self-appointed defender of the rights of the clumsy) somewhere in the States sued McDonald's for serving her coffee so hot she scalded herself with it when she spilled it—what are they supposed to do, post "Do Not Spill Coffee On Your Lap" signs on the wall of each restaurant?—but every cup of coffee I've ever had there has been luke warm. And weak. But I was hardly in the mood to start searching for a more elegant coffee bar and I drank my coffee quietly without complaining, then headed back to the motel.

Barstow was not exactly gearing up for rush hour. In fact, I didn't see one solitary soul on the road as I walked back to the motel and pondered the fate of Saul's head. Probably, the thing about sending the weapons around to the towns of Philistia was just something you did when you killed some foreign monarch. And nailing the king naked to your city walls was also probably sort of de rigeur in those days, sort of like hanging Mussolini by his heels or something like that. But why would they have cut off his head? I mean, without the head, how precisely did anyone really know that the body was Saul's? And even if they took it on faith, then didn't they all wonder where the head was? Now the text is a bit ambiguous...it says they cut off his head and stripped off his weapons and sent them off on a road show of Philistia, but then it only notes that the weapons themselves ended up in Astarte's temple. So we're back where we started: with the headless body nailed to the walls of Bethshan and the weapons on display in the temple and the head…somewhere else.

Maybe they had it stuffed and used it as a football. Or maybe they had it stuffed and had it mounted on some palace wall somewhere. Maybe the whole thing is just as simple as the fact that the Biblical author didn't know what happened to Saul's head and was hoping no one would notice that he hadn't followed up that particular line in the story. Who knows? Wil's head on the other hand, I knew just where it was. I still do, actually.

When I got back to the motel room, the kid was sitting up in his chair wearing a pair of white jockey shorts and watching the Today show with the sound turned off. He had obviously had a shower—his hair was still wet and I could see the wet towels on the floor just behind him—and looked like he was just sitting there waiting for something to happen. For me to come back. For the motel to burn down. For something.

"How come you have the sound off?" A plausible question, despite the fact that I had promised myself not even to try to engage the kid in more conversation than absolutely necessary after trying unsuccessfully to get him to talk to me in the car the previous afternoon and over dinner the previous evening.

"It's boring."

"So why are you watching at all."

"I dunno. Because."

For some reason, that answer reminded me of my old high school pal Danny Zucker ("rhymes with sucker") who, after trying to get into bed with one of the identical twins in our class for almost a year, managed one day finally to end up in the sack with the other instead. I asked him the next day—every boy in school had heard of his accomplishment about eight seconds after it happened—I asked him why he had risked his relationship with Dee-Dee ("the smart one") for the sake of bagging Allison and he had given me roughly the same three-word answer. I, whose major sex partner at the time was my other friend David's older brother's collection of Playboys, was impressed, of which the proof is that this was about twenty years ago and I still remember the conversation. I sometimes wonder what ever happened to Allison and Dee-Dee. Dan's in jail, I think, which is probably all for the best.

Packing up took about a minute. I brushed my teeth, put my tooth brush and tooth paste, both of which I suspected the kid had used while I had been gone, back in my toilet kit and that was basically that. The kid was travelling even lighter than I was. He pulled on his jeans and the same t-shirt he had been wearing the day before, took the ashtray off the top of the television and threw it as hard as he could onto the floor (presumably to see if it would break, which it didn't), then walked out into the morning heat to wait for me by the car.

I must have been crazy—or at least really, really desperate—but we hadn't been driving for ten minutes before I started to tell the kid about my dream.

"You ever hear of Jehu before?" I asked idiotically, knowing perfectly well what the answer was going to be. Who the hell, after all, ever heard of Jehu? I was careful to say his name properly (to rhyme with quaalude, except without the d at the end, and with a y instead of a q in the beginning and without the l in the middle), but it didn't appear to register.

"Who?" the kid asked.

"Yay-hoo. This guy in the Bible."

"Sounds like a search engine."

I had to laugh. Here was a kid hitchhiking from nowhere to nowhere with nothing more than the clothes on his back and an empty wallet in his pocket, but that didn't mean he didn't know his way about the 'net well enough to know how to search for web sites. For all I know, I thought to myself, he's probably slept with identical twins too. At the same time. Which is more than I can say for myself. A lot more.

We drove for about an hour. When I stopped for gas in

Humboldt House, I bought the kid a Jolt and one of those super sweet Hostess apple pie things for breakfast. He didn't say thank you, but I could sense his gratitude. I asked him if he needed to use the washroom before we left the gas station, for which I earned a quizzical look that was half of a put-down and half something else. It wasn't eight in the morning and my shirt was already wet with sweat. The kid looked pretty cool, but there are people who just don't sweat and he was probably one of them. Off we went.

I turned on the radio. They were playing Don MacLean's "American Pie" on the CBC and talking about how simply unbelievable it was that it had been twenty-five years since the song first came out. The kid appeared unimpressed.

"I know what every reference in the song means," I said, shocked to realize I was trying to impress him.

"Wow."

"The day the music died is a reference to Altamont. Satan is Mick. The father, son and holy ghost are…."

"Mick?"

"Jagger."

"Chloe listened to the White Album when she was giving birth."

"Chloe?"

"On E.R."

It was the most involved exchange we had had in the thirty-six hours we had been in teach other's company and I felt vindicated, at least slightly, to have elicited it. He had no idea who Mick Jagger was, or else he did but was just confusing him with John Lennon, but he had apparently once lived in a house with a computer and a television. His defences were falling. I was being let into his world.

"It's a good album. It's actually two good albums. The Beatles."

"Yeah. My dad used to listen to it all the time to calm down after he was finished whaling the crap out of me or my mom. Or my brother."

"You're running away?"

"I'm nineteen."

"Where's your mom?"

"Dead."

"Your dad kill her?"

"No."

"So how did she die?"

"She drowned herself."

"You're sure it was on purpose?"

"That's what the note said."

I had picked him up about halfway between Barrymore and Stanhope. He had been standing on the side of the road with his thumb out sort of watching the cars go by but without making eye contact with any of the drivers. That obviously killed any chance he would have had to get a lift from most people, but he also had some weird kind of adolescent insouciance to him and that, for some obscure reason, appealed to me and I stopped to pick him up. He looked clean (if a little dazed) and he was carrying an empty paper cup and nothing else. I thought there might be some sort of intelligence lurking somewhere behind his blank expression, but it was hard to say. We drove until about seven, then had dinner in some roadside diner place—vegetable soup, toast and ice cream for me, fried eggs, hash browns and coffee with four sugars and no cream for him—then I asked him where he wanted me to let him off and he said he was trying to get all the way through to Winnipeg so he could stay with his mother's mother for a while. I hadn't anticipated having any company on this journey of self-exploration (read: flight from reality) I was undertaking, but somehow the idea of sharing the road with a sullen nineteen-year-old who liked sweet coffee and whose mother had drowned herself appealed to me. I told him I was stopping for the night in the first motel past Yokomo that cost less than $25 for a room and that he could share my room with me if he wanted. He nodded, then dozed off to sleep.

And now it was the next day and we were about eight miles east of Humboldt House heading towards Koolkopak, B.C. I drank a Jolt Cola once and was up for two days, but the kid apparently had a very high tolerance for caffeine and was asleep before we even got to the outskirts of Koolkopak. I stopped on the east side of town to buy another coffee from some Indian coffee bar called the Navajavaho Teepee House (although the band that runs it are about as Navaho as I am), but the kid didn't wake up and I didn't bother waking him. It actually suited me fine that he was asleep, since there are about two hundred miles between Koolkopak and the B.C.-Alberta border and I planned to drive them slowly, taking in the scenery and trying to come to terms with my brother's death, the dissolution of my marriage, the loss of my daughter and the senescence (to use the polite term) of my parents, both of whom were already so ga-ga when I went to say good-bye that they appeared to me already to have forgotten Wil was dead. I figured all that would take about two hundred miles worth of driving, then I could spend the rest of my trip listening to Don Maclean on the radio and wondering about Saul's head. Man, was it hot.

IV

When I was a kid, the last damn thing I would ever have expected of myself is that I might become a teacher. I hated teachers. In fact, I hated school. It wasn't that I had something particularly against knowing stuff, it was just that the schools I attended always seemed to have a lot more to do with making you raise your hand properly if you had to go to the boys' room than with the transmission of wisdom. A lot more.

I can, however, still name each and every one of my teachers from elementary school. They were a prize lot, those saggy-tit biddies, each of them devoted to scarring their pupils for life in a slightly different way. There was Miss Sorensen, for example, who actually used to make the little Jewish children stand in the hall while the white kids said the Lord's Prayer.

And there was Mrs. Petuchowski, who used to inquire if we were going to make Number One or Number Two when we asked permission to leave the room so she could inflict the Ultimate Punishment—a black check in her little notebook—on excessive washroom dawdlers. (You could always say Number Two to gain a few extra minutes, but she was too smart for that—if you had too many Number Twos in what Miss Petuchowski considered a reasonable amount of time, you got sent to Nurse Sawlicki for bowel regulation therapy. Believe me, it wasn't worth it.)

And then there was Miss Swee, the Queen Bitch of Brightonham Elementary, who used to inspect her little charges for head lice daily, allowing her nicotine-stained fingers to linger just a little too long, if you ask me, on the heads of some of the girls and who used to ask my parents in all seriousness if they knew what a handicap it was going to be for me if I got out of elementary school without accepting Jesus in my heart. (My mother, bless her, had a great line the first time Miss Swee brought up the topic. When the Swee asked her if I had ever heard about Lord Jesus, Mom looked her straight in the eye and said, "Who?" Maybe you had to be there....)

I grew up hating school. I vowed never, ever to set foot in a university and it was really only because of parental pressure, of which there was plenty, that I even finished high school. I mean, I was plenty smart enough to do well (as my father reminded me every eight seconds), but it just all struck me as such total garbage that I couldn't bear the idea of bending over and surrendering to a system that tolerated a black hole like Miss Swee at its centre. Maybe that's not quite the right metaphor to say how I felt, but I couldn't stand school and that's the truth.

Anyway, I did end up graduating high school and I went to university anyway. I applied because I think they sent in your application automatically if you had a certain average and even with my intense reluctance to do homework or to study for tests, my grades were well above the required mark. So they sent it in and I got in and my parents (who didn't quite realize that I hadn't applied voluntarily or even consciously) were thrilled and I figured it beat working for four years instead and that, more or less, was that.

To my amazement, I loved university as much as I had loathed high school. My parents almost had heart attacks when I told them I was majoring in English—they had been hoping for something more on the lines of pre-med or, if it turned out I wasn't smart enough for medicine, then pre-law—but there was no talking me out of it. I was going to be a writer. I was going to win the Nobel Prize for Literature—at least! I was going to be famous and make them proud. And no, Dad, I couldn't pursue my writing while I was going to med school on the side. It was my way or the highway and my parents eventually fell in line and let me be.

I don't think we even owned a Bible when I was a kid. If we did, it was buried in those boxes of crumbling books my mother had inherited (if that's the right word) from her parents that she kept stored in the basement in the little storage room just behind the furnace. So it came as a bit of a surprise (even to me) when I ended up writing my senior's thesis on irony in the Book of Job.

I don't remember who suggested the topic, but I had taken a few Bible As Literature courses (little did I know…) and the topic sort of suggested itself to me. I don't know, maybe Bergmann actually came up with the idea first. (My thesis advisor was this pathetic toad named—I swear this is true—Eduardo Bernardo Alfredo Bergmann. Not a bad name for a guy born and bred in Red Deer, Alberta. What his parents—both Polish Jews with no ties at all to Latin America or to Spain—had in mind, I can only imagine.) Or maybe he didn't suggest the topic—I really can't remember and he never claimed credit for it afterwards—but somehow the topic spoke to me and I ended up going all the way with it. The results were good, so good that we ended up entering a scaled-down version of my thesis in this contest the Canadian Literary Society runs every year to encourage young people to consider the study of literature as something reasonable to devote their lives to. I personally didn't give much of a fat rat's ass about the contest itself, but I did feel that winning $500 was something more than reasonable enough to get me to edit the paper (which I did in two days with time to spare) and spring for the postage. I certainly didn't expect to win. Or to get the paper published in the society's journal. Or to get an unsolicited offer to pursue graduate studies at the MacMillan Institute in Toronto on an almost full scholarship. The joke is that it's been a decade since I won the prize and it's only now that I've come to realize that there isn't any irony at all in Job. It's all as true to real life as fiction comes! And Job didn't really have it so horribly bad either—at least his wife stuck with him instead of running off with their gardener's turd of a brother. God, I wish Helene was dead. But I'm getting ahead of myself again….

Anyway, I was hooked. Toronto itself sucked—there's never been an uglier, duller city more in love with itself than Toronto, except maybe Montreal—anyway, I hated the smugness of the place and I hated the people and I hated the TTC and I hated my apartment and I especially hated my roommate, this guy named Morey they practically forced on me in the Housing Office whom I actually had to tell to close the door to his room when he was indulging in his favourite pastime, which he did about eighteen times a day.

Anyway, I hated where I was living and I really, really hated Toronto, but I liked—and believe me, no one was more amazed than I was—I really liked my studies. I read Milton. I read Shakespeare. I read Blake. I read John Donne. In fact, I can still remember the first time I read through Donne's translation of the Book of Lamentations. It was about a million degrees below zero outside and the apartment was so cold than even Morey had gone to the gym (no doubt to seek out some place—probably the men's sauna—where it was warm enough for him to take his gloves off). Anyway, it was unbelievably cold outside and I was sitting at our kitchen table drinking coffee and leafing through this really nice edition of Donne that Marilynn Cohen (that's another story I'll tell you another time), this book that Marilynn had given me for my twenty-third birthday. Anyway, I was sitting there and reading and trying to keep my mind from dwelling on the fact that I was about to die I was so cold and suddenly I had this…I don't know, this almost spiritual experience. The words were individually so fantastically beautiful and the whole ensemble of them all together was so moving that I actually burst into tears and had to wipe my eyes before I could continue reading. Thank God Morey was off abusing himself in the gym that day instead of at home or I'd never had heard the end of it.

Anyway, I was really hooked. And I saw the direction I wanted to take my career in—or maybe it's even more accurate to say that that was the moment that I first realized that I was going to have a career in letters at all. I mean, I had wanted to write for years. And I had wanted to publish. And I already had my Job thing out and had received some flattering comments here and there from people who read it. So I was sort of on my way, but I hadn't really, really thought of myself as having a career in the field until right then, I think. I don't know, it sounds so pathetically Hollywood to have a moment like that in a freezing kitchen in some disgusting student apartment on seedy, run-down, dilapidated Huron Street, but there you have it: my private satori, my turning-point…right there on Huron Street for you to step right up to and laugh at. Anyway, that was when I began the rest of the my life.

I learned Hebrew, Greek and Latin. Hebrew was the worst—the classes were filled with these yeshiva drop-out types looking for an easy A who practically felt obliged to wear the loathing they felt for their goyish teachers (all of whom spoke a far better Hebrew than any of them, if you ask me) on their sleeves. Greek was slightly better, but the teachers were all these creepy guys who tried to shake your hand eighteen times in the course of a twelve minute conversation. Latin was easiest—I had, after all, had twelve years of French—but since it was the one of the three I expected to have the least use for later on, it was also the one I devoted the least time to. My Latin is still lousy, by the way.

I had the idea of expanding my senior thesis into a real doctoral dissertation, but my advisor advised against it for fear that people who weren't going to read either would assume I was—John Cassingham actually said this, which I don't blame you for not believing, since I can hardly believe someone could say this with a straight face myself—anyway, he actually said they would assume I was a Johnny One Note scholar who couldn't get past his own obsession with Job and who, therefore, couldn't really be very bright at all. I took his advice with a grain of salt—Cassingham's own claim to fame is his single book on brother-sister incest in Shakespeare which he's published in eighteen different forms as though it had any value or interest in the first place—anyway, I took his advice and came up with the idea of writing about Christopher Smart's 1765 translation of the Book of Psalms and trying to prove that the author, who was basically insane during the years he was working on his translation of the Psalter, had apparently had access to certain documents of ancient Near Eastern literature that scholars prior to my work were insisting were only discovered towards the end of the nineteenth century. It was a bit of a daring thesis, but I actually found some fragments of a Greek translation of some of the works I was positing Smart must have had available to him buried in a manuscript the British Museum had acquired in 1749 and that made all the difference and, lickety-split, I was at least semi-famous. Or at least I was in the tiny world of Bible As Literature types. My dissertation was accepted with almost no revisions required and my discovery (made, I should add, with the help of two of Cassingham's former advisees who had ended up working in London at some British research institute) was actually announced in an article in the Globe and Mail. I was a doctor. Big whoop!

Actually, it was a bit of a big whoop in that the hoopla surrounding the publication of my discovery got me two unsolicited job offers. One, the one from MacMillan itself, I turned down immediately since it would have meant staying on in Toronto. The other was from Corlingham College back in Vancouver and, after I turned down Toronto, it was all that I had to choose from. My folks were thrilled. Wil was thrilled. I took the job. I moved. I met Helene the second day I was in B.C. in the cafeteria at Corlingham and she moved in with me about three months after that. She was pregnant about five minutes after unpacking and we ended up getting married. I liked teaching. I liked Helene. I found it easier to publish than I had thought it was going to be. We bought a house in Richmond, then sold it and bought another in Burnaby. Helene got pregnant again, then lost the baby. I brought out a book of poetry, then a novel, then another novel. None sold too well, but they all got pretty good reviews and I was thrilled. I published some essays on Job, then a series on Isaiah, then a third series on the stories of Genesis. My Bible As Literature courses were full and the school deemed itself lucky to have me. Everything was actually going great...and then it all fell apart. Almost all at once. It was like I was Job *redivivus* or something, a thought that only struck me as mildly ironic once I had sunk into the depression I ended up trying to get rid of the old-fashioned way: by running away from it as fast as I could travel in a car that really should have been sold for scrap years earlier.

V

The precise order it all happened in is this. First, Helene mentions one night over dinner that, incidentally, she's been sleeping with this guy for three years and that, if I really want to know, he wasn't the first either although I don't have to worry because she knows Lena is mine, but the point is that she's sick and tired—as though this were some awful thing I had done to her—anyway, that she's sick and tired of sneaking around and having to hide what she's doing as though she were ashamed of it—not that she can imagine why she should be ashamed of betraying her husband and ruining her marriage and guaranteeing that her little girl is going to grow up in some other house than the one her father lives in—but anyway, she's sick and tired of all the *duplicity*, so she's decided to bring everything out into the open and if I didn't mind, would I move out of our house so she could be free to *shtoop* her new little friend without having to suffer through any more *duplicity* than absolutely necessary in the process.

That was in the middle of last December, just about a week after the end of the semester. Now that I think back on things, I must have been crazy. I didn't yell back. I didn't run to find a lawyer. I didn't even ask for the name and address of her new friend so I could castrate him and cram his balls down his throat. (Besides, what did it matter where he was living at that particular moment? Soon enough, he'd be living in my house and sleeping in my bed.) Anyway, that's pretty much how it happened. And I found his name out soon enough anyway, as it happened. It was

Gary and he was our gardener's brother.

Can you imagine? I mean, it's one thing to have your wife leave you—although I somehow ended up being the one doing all the leaving—anyway, it's one thing to have your wife leave you for some fabulously wealthy stud, but to find out that you've been replaced by some creep who works—this is the best part—who works as a part-time janitor for the school board when he works at all, that's a damn insult. And I took it that way. But I left anyway. I don't know what everyone thought when I packed up and moved out, but the truth, the real, plain, honest truth, is that I was so absolutely enraged at Helene for being such a lying, *entirely* duplicitous bitch that I just couldn't imagine living under the same roof as her one day longer, much less sleeping with her in the same bed. When it came right down to it, I was glad to go.

Leaving Lena was awful. She was only five then—five and a half, really, since her birthday is on Canada Day—but she was plenty aware enough to know what was going on and she didn't like it one little bit. She cried. She moaned. She whined. She begged me—me!—not to move out. It broke my heart. In fact, my heart was still broken months later and this trip I'm telling you about was probably more about Lena than it was even about Wil, if you want to know God's truth. But, in the end, I went. I had to…if you *really* want to know the truth, the truth is that by the time I left, I had no choice. I mean, I could have killed myself—I thought of it—but I couldn't stand giving Helene the satisfaction of seeing all her problems solved that easily. ("There, you see Gary—he really was crazy!") And then there's the awareness problem. I mean, the great thing about suicide is that all your problems are over. But the thing about it that sucks is that you're not around to know that they're over. I mean, who knows what the hell you think when you're dead. Probably nothing.

Anyway, that was at the end of December. Two weeks later, on the tenth of January, I got fired. I mean, they don't *just* can you—they call you into the dean's office so they can tell you what a genius you are and how much you've added to the school during the years of your service…and then they mention that you're canned like it's this irritating detail that pains them even more than they're sure it's going to pain you. Sure, they can be big shots—you're the one who has a contract that basically lets them can you at will with a little notice and few months' severence and they know perfectly well you can't sue them for wrongful dismissal or even make much of a stink about having to pack up and get gone. But they also know you were intending to work there for the rest of your life—I mean, how many colleges and universities do they think there are out there that even offer Bible As Literature courses anyway?—and the whole contract system is just there to give them a way to dump you every couple of years if you start to make too much money or too much noise or if they think you might be coming on to too many campus co-eds. So Eddy Grant calls me up one day and asks me to drop by Dean Zaremba's office the next day at ten o'clock if I'm free—as though I could ever be stupid enough to say that yeah, I'm way too busy to drop by my boss's boss's office even though the semester is over and my grades are all in already—anyway, I agree and the next day I'm there at ten o'clock sharp.

So I knew I was going to buy the farm when I opened the door and saw the chairman and the vice-chairman of the English department sitting there on this little love seat Zaremba has off to the side of his desk just under the window and they're just sort of sitting there and not talking and watching me walk in and shake Zaremba's hand, which I will regret eternally having done now that I know that that hand was about to slit my throat, and sit down in the chair in front of his desk.

"Thanks for coming, Saul," the guy says, all friendly and collegial like he's my best buddy and he's about to beg me to agree to fill in as dean while he's off on sabbatical leave next year.

"No problem," I say, trying to sound like I have no idea what's about to happen.

For a few painful minutes, he gives forth on my service to the school. I'm the absolute pedagogue of pedagogues, he says. My students all love me. My research papers are fantastic—he's even read a few himself even if his own field of specialization is French poetry (which I'll give you my teeth if he's opened a book of which in the last thirty-five years) and he could logically be expected not to have much interest in what I write about. And even my colleagues think I'm the best thing since sliced white bread, which most of them consume at least a loaf and a half of every single day of their pathetic whitebread lives.

That lasts about eight minutes and then he's ready to lower the boom. "Look," he says, delicately (albeit rather counterpro-ductively) averting his eyes from mine, "I'll be blunt. We've got to cut back. The government is cutting our funds and that means we have to cut back our course offerings. So what it comes down to is that we're not renewing your contract, Saul. You're a good teacher—believe me, this has nothing to do with your skills as a teacher or as a researcher—but we just need to cut back and we're starting with people who teach courses that could conceivably be offered in other departments…."

His voice sort of trails off as though he's said his little piece and is now willing me to thank him for his time and leave with-out saying anything embarrassing. Grant and Nepomnishke are just sitting *shtum* under the window and presumably hoping for the same thing as Zaremba.

I don't know what to say. "I don't know what to say," I start out, hoping I'll think of something really, really quickly.

"There's not really anything to say," Zaremba counters, sounding as though he had actually spent some time thinking of all the things I might say and had a handy response ready for each of them. "We'll have a file full of letters of warm recommendation ready for you with your pay cheque on the 31st, which will cover this month plus two months severance. That's what they say we owe you for breaking a contract in the middle of the year—if you bother to read through the contract, it actually says that in it, you know—and you can feel free to embark on a job search now without any ties to here to hold you back." Said like I'm supposed to be thrilled to have been canned so neatly and politely and with such near surgical precision. Thrilled? I'm delirious.

So what did I do? I didn't do anything. I packed up my office, took my stuff to my new little apartment that I had moved into so that Gary Adultery-Is-A-State-Of-Mind Bouvier (no kidding—just like Jackie O!) could *shtoop* Helene in my bedroom without her orgasm being ruined by negative, life-force-robbing sensations of *duplicity* and started looking for a new job. That took about five hours—I called the two and a half universities in the province and the dozen or so colleges where I had some contacts and confirmed what I had already known: that professors of English were basically $.68 U.S. a dozen and I was, equally basically, shit out of luck.

The best line of the day came from the chairman of the Humanities division at Livingston College in Nelson who suggested I spend my new leisure time—that's actually what that heartless bitch called it—that I take my new leisure time and try to turn some of my essays into screenplays. Might she be interested in buying one herself, I asked entirely seriously. No, she answered with this horse laugh that made it sound like this was the funniest thing she had ever heard, she didn't make movies. But she was sure—I swear she actually said this part without laughing out loud—she was sure that I'd sell one easily once I got to it. My work on Job was, she assured me, very well known. Had she read much of my stuff? She began *Irony in Job*, she allowed, but had had to return it to the library before she got to the end. She was going to borrow it again as soon as she got down there.

She was really sorry. Bringing me to Nelson would have been great if she could have swung it. I wasn't to forget about the screenplay idea. I was to recall, she said almost forcefully, how well Archie MacLeish—she actually called him Archie, by the way—how incredibly well Archie had done with J.B. and wasn't that all about Job and his friends too? And no, she didn't expect any credit if I managed to sell something to Spielberg, which she was certain I would just as soon as he got a look at my work. She was happy just to be a friendly cog in the wheel of destiny....

I got through the rest of January basically by drinking vodka and lime juice and looking forward to my triple pay cheque coming on the 31st. It came. I deposited it. I felt hopeful, then depressed. And then Wil killed himself on the first of February. Things were not looking up.

VI

I think you could reasonably say the first of February that winter was the worst day of my life, but it actually started off rather ordinarily. I woke up in my swinging bachelor pad all by myself, then showered and shaved while a pot of coffee percolated on the stove. I hadn't gotten around yet to arranging for the paper to be delivered, so I drank a couple of cups of coffee while I leafed idly through a secondhand copy of *The World of Learning* I had bought the week before at MacLeod's to inform myself about the demand for English teachers who specialize in Bible As Literature courses in Borneo, Sri Lanka and Chile, all places I thought I'd probably enjoy spending the rest of my life. The book was about eight years old, but I figured things couldn't have changed that much in Borneo in just eight years. And besides, I told myself, I could always get some ideas from my copy and then check them out in an up-to-date edition at the library before actually starting to pack.

I was just asking myself where Borneo actually was when the phone rang. My first thought was that it was the bank calling to say the college's cheque had bounced or something like that. But it was too early for the bank to be open and I had only deposited the cheque in one of the ATMs after hours the day before anyway, so they probably hadn't even processed my final pay cheque from the school I had considered my professional home for lo these seven years, much less determined if it was any good. I don't think I had another idea who might be calling before I picked up the receiver. God knows I didn't have any friends, at least not any who had bothered to phone me since the separation to ask if I was still breathing.

It was Constable William Wu of the Royal Canadian Mounted Police on the line.

Was I Saul Jacobson?

I was.

The brother of Wil Jacobson?

Ditto.

Was I home?

Obviously, you moron. You phoned me.

Could the constable drop by? He had some information he wished to share with me personally.

In retrospect, it seems amazing that I hadn't a clue what this was all about. I mean, he actually asked me outright on the phone if I was Wil's brother, but either I wasn't listening or I wasn't thinking clearly (or both), but I somehow completely failed to guess that this had something to do with Wil. I guess I was so damn self-absorbed at that particular moment in my tragic life that I just couldn't imagine anything bad happening to anybody but me. I don't know—maybe I was already half crazy, even though I would certainly have bristled then at the thought—anyway, I really can't explain how I can have failed to intuit at least some of what Constable Wu had to say, but the truth is that I had no idea at all. Sure he could come by, I said, absurdly (okay, pathetically) happy for some company.

He'd be right there.

Constable Wu, as good as his word, was knocking on my door no more than four minutes after I hung up.

"Saul Jacobson?"

"Constable Wu?"

"May I come in?"

"Why not?"

I stepped back to let him in, then looked at his face and that's when I knew Wil was dead. I mean, it could have been any-thing—either of my parents, something about Helene or Lena, the car—but I knew it wasn't any of the above. And I knew, even before the constable said another word, I knew that Wil was dead. I don't know how I knew. But I knew…and the rest of Wu's visit was just a chance to fill in the details.

It's funny, but in all the months of dealing with Wil's disease, it never really struck me that he might take matters into his own hands and bail out of the game before he lost it the old-fashioned way. I mean, when he first told me about being HIV-positive, I was astounded. Was he gay? It hardly seemed likely, given the fact that he had basically been giving the time to an almost endless series of women since he was about seventeen. Was he a secret drug abuser? That seemed even less likely—Wil didn't even smoke, let alone drink, and it was more or less impossible for me to imagine him nursing a private addiction to intravenous drugs that no one knew anything about. When he finally did tell me how the infection came about, it was almost a relief, although the story itself was as unlikely as I finally concluded it was probably true.

Wil spent three years between college and medical school teaching English in a United Nations school in Uzbekistan, then still part of the almost collapsed Soviet Union but already func-tioning more or less like the independent country it was on the verge of becoming. He lived in a series of youth hostels and tem-porary U.N. shelters, but he spent some nights in hotels and ended up one single time, he told me, in bed with a German tourist whom he had taken for a woman while they had been drinking vodka in the hotel bar, but who had later turned out to be more or less a man. He had been more surprised than repulsed, he reported a bit shyly, but he hadn't gone into any fur-ther details about what happened next and I hadn't asked for any. It was a potentially awkward moment, but we had both seen *The Crying Game* and we both just ended up laughing at how life occasionally really does imitate art and that, we both thought, was that.

We laughed considerably less heartily when Wil got a call from the Red Cross about a year later after he had given blood in one of the med school blood drives. They said—you'll love this—they said there was "a problem" with his blood, but that they weren't permitted to say what it precisely was. He should get his blood checked and discuss the problem with his personal physician.

Checked for what? Wil asked slightly surreptitiously.

HIV, the woman said entirely openly, as though she had been hoping the Doomed Donor would have the brains to ask her the question in precisely the way Wil had chosen.

Anyway, he had his blood tested, then tested again. We got the results, disbelieved them, had the test done a third time, then a fourth. By then, we all had the idea down pretty clearly, Wil included. His girlfriend—a redhead named Nancy Jane Krohn with enormous breasts and no character—left him. His friends mostly deserted him. The medical school—Wil made a point of going to the dean to inform him of the situation, a move I thought of as even more unnecessary than foolish—anyway, the medical school dropped him almost as fast as Nancy had. No, it wasn't their habit to discriminate against anyone at any time in any manner whatsoever, the dean had said twenty-eight different ways as though he were already positioning himself to testify well in some projected law suit he obviously half expected Wil to bring against the school. But, really, what point was there in training someone for a profession he could never ethically work in?

Weren't there HIV-positive doctors functioning out there? Wil asked.

The dean smiled.

Wil got the idea. He was gone by the end of the day.

He got a job working in the same hospital he had hoped to

do his residency in. He did well, rose up the ladder and ended up as one of the higher-paid hospital administrators. He was liked. He made good money. His health was holding. Things were okay.

Then he got sick. Even now, even in this relatively intimate setting, I can't quite bring myself to recount the details of Wil's illness in all their various details. Besides, the nature of his condition was that he kept succumbing to different sorts of diseases, some relatively benign and others virulent to the point of being almost unbearable. He was dying and he knew it. There really wasn't much else to say or do. He quit his job and moved in with Mom and Dad. I was around a lot. He made some new friends and spent some time with them. A couple of gay guys on the block who had lost more than their fair share of friends to AIDS befriended him, which was more than I could say for any of my folks' other neighbours. He went on AZT, but it didn't help him. We more or less got used to our new reality. Even Helene was nice to him, at least before she walked out on me. And Lena was great…loving him and playing with him and taking him for the great guy he was without knowing or caring that he was sick. He really, really loved it when she came over and we made sure that was as often as possible. Some of Mom's friends were appalled that we even let her live in the same province as Wil and were almost shrill in their insistence that we all "consider the child" a bit more carefully. Mom was okay in dealing with them on her own, however—she just told them that she always made sure Lena and Wil never had to share a syringe when they shot up and felt that more or less precluded any possibility of the child becoming infected.

So Helene walked last December and I got canned last January and things weren't going too terrifically great chez Jacobson. Wil knew all about everything, but I was so pathetically caught up in my own woes that I failed to notice that my brother was standing at his own crossroads.

He was getting weaker and less healthy, but he could still walk around and was still able most of the time to come and go as he pleased. I mean, he had his days in bed, but he also had days when he felt more or less okay—but those days when he felt he could go out on his own were becoming few and farther between and I knew—or rather I would have known if I hadn't been so rapped up in my own misery—that the day was coming when Wil wouldn't be able to do much of anything without help.

He knew it too. And it weighed on him, I guess. I mean, he never really said anything about it to me, but I know that he hated the idea of losing his freedom more than anything. In some weird way, the whole thing was that much harder because he actually looked okay. I mean, he used to wear this knit cap when he went out until someone told him he looked like Tom Hanks in that ghastly AIDS movie he made a few years ago, but he—Wil, not Tom—didn't look that unhealthy even without it and eventually he stopped wearing it altogether. He was skinny and frail, but he…I don't know, maybe I'm dreaming here, but he just didn't look that bad or that sick to me. I mean, he didn't look great, not by a long shot. But he didn't look to me much different from any skinny guy with bad skin you might see walking down the street. And it wasn't just me, you see…when we'd be out together, I'd always be on the look-out for people staring or watching us and no one ever seemed to be paying us any unusual attention at all. I guess we looked like two regular guys walking down the street more than the depressive, unemployed cuckold and doomed AIDS patient we actually were. I really loved my brother Wil.

Anyway, Constable Wu didn't hang out too long. Really, there wasn't that much to say. Wil had summoned up whatever strength he had and hanged himself in the basement of the medical school that had turfed him out when he got sick. He had been dead for a few hours when some of the first-year students heading for the locker room in the basement found him. They called for help and the brave doctors who answered the call cut him down and tried to revive him, then eventually recognized him and backed off lest they be rewarded for their efforts with his cooties. An ambulance was called, but he was D.O.A. at St. Paul's. He was thirty-three. There was no note. What was there to say, really?

The couple of days that followed are pretty hazy in my memory. I went to my folks' house alone and told them—Constable Wu offered to come along, but I thought it would only scare them to see me come up the walk with a police officer in tow—then told them about Wil's plans for his head. We had some fight—they were crying and screaming and I was yelling and losing it myself, but the upshot was that they weren't going to let anyone cut their kid's head off no matter what he himself had wanted and that, they both insisted like their own lives depended on it, was going to be that.

I went to the rabbi to enlist his support, but he was totally useless. My brother was suffering from AIDS-induced dementia, he explained (leaving out how he was able to make this remarkable diagnosis without ever actually having met the patient) and that—this is my favourite part—and that therefore *ignoring* his expressly stated wishes would actually be a way of *honouring* his memory. He was spouting pure nonsense—and that's the polite term for it—but he was adamant that he wasn't burying most of Wil without the rest of him and he wasn't even sure the whole concept was legal in Canada (which it certainly is) and he could hardly ask the Burial Society to handle a headless corpse anyway—which is what it really came down to, if you ask me—and that was going to have to be that. He was everything I hate the most about clergymen—self-righteous, opinionated, self-absorbed and so firm in his beliefs as to be almost incapable of honest dialogue—but I needed him to do the funeral and I needed his Burial Society as well since Mom and Dad would have both had heart attacks if I came home to inform them that we were having Wil's funeral at Shady Happy Restful Peaceful Gentile Lawns or some other goyish cemetery or chapel instead of the proper Jewish funeral they obviously were envisaging for their second son.

I was beaten and I knew it. I figured that Wil was dead and what really mattered was keeping Mom and Dad happy. I told myself that the whole cryonics things—you know, where they freeze your head and store it in the hopes that someone will figure out how to clone the rest of you back five hundred years from now when they'll have a cure for AIDS or whatever else ails you—I told myself that was all a load of hooey too, just so much stupid fantasy garbage someone in California (didn't that just cinch it?) had invented to relieve the terminally ill of whatever wealth the health care system had somehow failed to bleed out of them first…and whatever hope they may otherwise have had of coming to terms with the finality of death. I even told myself the rabbi wasn't such a pompous idiot after all, that what he said made good sense, that it was important to cling to tradition at times like this.

In other words, I crumbled under the weight of my own grief and let Wil's wishes die with him. I failed him and I knew I was failing him and I did it anyway. I just didn't have the strength to fight with anyone. I was unhappy, miserably unhappy, and I just didn't have the energy to go up against my parents and the rabbi and the burial society and the R.C.M.P. and every other person in the province who seemed dedicated to keeping me from fulfilling the one favour my brother asked of me before he died.

I screwed up big time and can't even claim that I didn't know what was going on as it all happened. Anyway, Wil got buried two days later.

My parents didn't take it well. They were wrecks at the funeral, but everyone kept telling me they'd be better once they got home. Then, when we were all home, everybody started saying how much better they'd feel once a few days would pass. Then, after a few weeks had passed, people stopped saying much at all. For their part, Mom and Dad weren't difficult or self-destructive, just useless. They didn't eat unless I fed them. And they didn't wake up in the morning unless I came by and roused them, made some breakfast and hung around long enough to do the breakfast dishes and make sure they were both washed and dressed. Then I'd go out—I didn't have a job or a kid or a wife to look after at the moment, but I sure as hell wasn't going to spend my days sitting around with them—anyway, I'd go out and they'd basically sit there in their chairs in the living room until I came back to serve lunch.

I'd clean up lunch, then turn on the television and they'd sit there and watch Oprah or whatever crap was on until dinner time. I'd show up everyday about seven, either cook something or order in—mostly the latter—serve it, clean in up, turn the television off and send them off to bed. It was like being a counsellor in a summer camp for retarded seventy-five-year-olds. And things were getting worse.

I noticed the decline in a thousand ways. Toilets that weren't flushed. Hair that wasn't ever brushed. The same cake of soap lasting for weeks on end until it dawned on me that nobody was using it to wash. The unmistakable odour of decay and decline setting in throughout the house.

We kept it up for almost five months and then, towards the end of May I realized that the situation was beyond me. I was tired. I was lonely. They were miserable. The house was filthy and getting seedier by the minute. My mother must have lost forty pounds and my dad wasn't far behind. They both looked half dead and, to tell you the truth, I don't think I looked so good either. I put them on a few lists for nursing homes, but didn't say anything. Then, a few weeks later, a double room semi-miraculously opened up at the Brier Home. I came over that evening with pizza and broached the topic with them. They were thrilled. Mom started to cry, but I could see that they were tears of relief, not unhappiness. My father didn't seem to understand.

"You're going to live in a new place," I told him.

"A new place?"

"Yeah," I continued hopefully, "a new place. A nice double room in a hotel where there are lots of nice people, good food, nursing care if you need it."

"Who will live in our house?" I was surprised Dad had that much insight into the situation even to ask.

"Well," I said as though this thought hadn't ever occurred to me, "you could sell it. Or you could rent it out. Or I could live here."

They were even more thrilled by that thought than by the idea that they were being shipped off to Siberia in the first place. "You would?" Dad asked pathetically. "You'd live here so we wouldn't have to worry about the house?"

Yes, I said, I would be prepared to make that sacrifice. Besides, I told myself, with Wil gone, they only have one heir, so what did it matter if I moved in now or later on? Besides, I figured, if they gave me the house now, then it wasn't going to end up as cash they'd eventually owe the home.

They both started to cry and I started crying as well and, for a while, we all just sat there over the uneaten pizza and cried out eyes out. Then it was like someone threw some sort of switch. We all stopped crying. We had dinner. I cleaned it up, they went to bed, I went back to my soon-to-be-former apartment and the next day I moved them into their new home and myself into mine.

VII

We crossed over into Alberta about two in the afternoon. I had planned to drive until about dinner time, but by four I was so sleepy that I figured we had better stop for the night, or at least for me to nap behind the wheel for a few hours. Although he had slept in the car for almost four hours, which was pretty amazing after a full night's sleep the night before, the kid was awake by then and, since we were both hungry and I was feeling exhausted, we decided to stop. We should have stopped in the mountains—I once knew somebody whose sister owned a motel in Canmore—but I had hoped we'd get a lot further than we were actually going to get and by the time we stopped, Canmore was a hundred and fifty miles behind us.

I decided to take our relationship—the kid's and mine—to a new level of intimacy.

"So what's your name?" I asked.

He looked over at me, apparently surprised to realize that we hadn't even gotten that far in meeting each other.

"Dave," he said.

"I'm Saul."

"Cool."

The next turn-off took us onto Route 73 in the direction of a place named (I swear this is true) Elk, Alberta. It looked like it had a population of maybe thirty-five, but there was a Best Western on the eastern end of the main street that I presumed was there to cater to the families of guys working in the nearby oil fields—or rather, to wives in town for conjugal visits—and we decided to sleep there for a while, maybe even for the night. I got us a room (and a raised eyebrow from the clerk who hadn't expected the answer he got when he asked if my son wanted a separate key) and we settled in. I went into the bathroom for a shower and a shave—it had really been days since I had shaved and I was starting to look even worse than I felt—anyway, I went in for a shower and shave and when I came out, the kid—I knew his name was Dave now, but I still thought of him as the kid—anyway, he was stripped down to his jockeys and fast asleep on one of the double beds in the room. I had thought we'd eat something, but he was already asleep and I was suddenly so inexpressibly tired that I figured food could wait. I put my trousers back on and lay down on the other bed. I was asleep in about eight seconds.

I woke up about ten o'clock to find the kid sitting up and watching the television with the sound off.

"You hungry?"

"Yeah."

"Want to get something to eat."

"You don't have to pay for me. And I can't pay for myself."

"So what are you going to eat?"

"Your leftovers."

"And if you were alone?"

"If I was alone?"

"Yeah. What would you eat if you were alone right now?"

"The truth?"

"Sure."

"Well, I'd score a couple of chocolate bars from the 7-11, then get some guy to buy me a couple of beers or some coffee in a bar somewhere and try to get away before I had to do anything you can get AIDS from."

"Oh."

The coffee shop in the motel was just closing when we got downstairs, so we ended up in the Harvest Restaurant, an all-night eatery housed about eight hundred yards away in the Husky Station at the other end of town. To my surprise, we weren't the only patrons. In fact, the place was half full. It was this real Alberta late-night scene at the Harvest—guys in cowboy hats and boots and these real religious-looking girls with long sleeves and long hems, some of them wearing these bonnet things on their heads, and native Indian types and oil worker types and some regular looking guys (like Dave and me!) and some truckers and some bikers and a table of cops and a couple of hookers wearing these identical Calgary Flames t-shirts and black jeans to match their eye shadow. The place actually had an okay feel to it and I ended up feeling more at home at the Harvest than I had felt anywhere for quite some time.

We ate dinner pretty much in silence. Dave had fish and chips followed by raisin pie and a chocolate milk shake and I had a Greek salad and two Cokes. The food was okay—Dave said his pie was great, actually—and I paid the bill and left a tip that was about twice as generous as the service had actually been worth. I remember thinking that our evening was drawing to a close.

But when we went outside to walk back to the Best Western—Dave had wanted to drive to dinner, but I said it was pathetic not to walk such a short distance—anyway, when we left the Harvest, one of the girls in the Flames t-shirts was standing in the parking lot and, it appeared, waiting for us. If you want to the know the truth, I was more flattered than anything else. Even now it impresses me to think that I was capable of assuming she was hoping to connect with an overweight mid-thirties type like me rather than with the nineteen-year-old guy I was with.

She looked like a native person, but I wasn't entirely sure she wasn't at least partially non-Indian. Her name was Patsy, she said, and although she wasn't especially pretty in any sort of conventional way, there was still something attractive about her that I found myself picking up on. I don't know, it may have been her pasty complexion or her black eye-liner, but something about her spoke right to me. And, I hear you ask, what did it say? What did it say? It said "Do Me" is what it said. I couldn't wait to get her back to the Best Western. I hoped that heartless bitch Helene was having a pleasant evening too.

Dave was a different story. He looked nervous and uncertain, but he didn't run away or anything and I could tell from the spring in his gait that he was either excited about the prospect of getting lucky the very same evening that he had eaten his first piece of raisin pie (he had mentioned this to me during dinner) or else he had to take a powerful leak. These were not, of course, mutually exclusive possibilities.

I explained to Patsy that we didn't have a car with us and that we were going to head back to the Best Western on foot. She scribbled down the room number on the back of a book of matches, got into her car and drove off in the general direction of the motel. I remember asking myself what kind of person couldn't remember a three-digit number long enough to drive over to where we were staying, but I was also sort of pleased to have a few minutes to discuss the sudden shift in our evening's plans with Dave.

"You been with a lot of girls?" No reason not to get right down to it, I thought.

"Two."

"At the same time or separately?"

"Both," he said quietly. I thought of asking him for more details, but then I thought better of it and didn't solicit any further explanation.

"How'd it go?"

"Okay, I guess."

Ninety minutes later, I was lying back on one of the double beds in the room, Patsy's awful question ("Are you almost through?") still ringing in my ears. I was still naked as I lay in the semi-darkness and tried (mostly unsuccessfully) to mind my own business while Dave was busy giving old Patsy the time to the best of his energetic adolescent ability. In the dim light—the Flames t-shirt I had admired in the restaurant was now draped over the only lamp in the room that we had turned on—I could see that Dave still had his jockey shorts stretched between his ankles as he banged away at her, his hands clamped down on her breasts like they were handles and his head thrown back as though he were intent on experiencing some sort of paroxysm of sexual intimacy instead of just getting laid.

Anyway, I lit a cigarette and leaned up against a pillow and watched idly on. The underpants between his ankles attracted my attention for some reason and I found myself focusing on them as he began to accelerate his deep thrusts while maintaining a complete quiet I found both eerie and a little bit frightening. I mean, I'm personally a big moan and groaner, but watching Dave give it to Patsy in absolute silence was a bit like watching a porn video with the sound turned off and I must have found it pretty unsettling because it's been almost two years since this all happened and I can still remember how weird it was. Not that I had ever seen another guy getting laid up real close before. Except in porn, of course.

I must have begun to doze off, but I woke up soon enough when Patsy set to pulling her panties out from under my left shoulder where they were lying without me even realizing it. By that point, it was almost midnight and things ended up in a strangely business-like manner with her getting dressed, telling us to have a nice day (despite the fact that it was the middle of the night) and leaving with her head held high. I was impressed. I'm not sure what else I expected other than her putting her clothes back on and leaving—I had paid her as soon as we got to the room, so there wasn't any reason to expect any haggling over money on her way out—but it somehow made an impression on me that she was able to maintain such a high level of personal dignity as she gathered up her things and headed for the door in the style more of a chambermaid done making up a room than a whore who gives it to strangers for money. I should also mention that her rates even by rural Albertan standards (I guessed) were actually quite reasonable and the best part was that she gave us a volume discount and only asked for thirty-five bucks instead of the forty she would regularly have charged if we had engaged her separately.

That left Dave and me alone in the room. He pulled his shorts back up, but I stayed naked for a while, chainsmoking Marlboros—I've always favoured American cigarettes for some reason—and sitting up in one of the armchairs while we discussed our experience like two urbane men of the world who had just shared a delightful midnight treat.

"You use a rubber?" An unexpected question from as guy whose sense of hygiene didn't extend to travelling with a change of underwear. Or a toothbrush.

"No."

"Think she's got AIDS or something?"

"Gee, I hope not."

"It's not funny."

"You use one?"

"No."

"So why not?"

"I didn't have one."

"She gave me one from her purse."

"She gave me one too."

"So you did use one?"

"She made me."

"You said you didn't"

"I was lying."

"So what did you think?"

"About the rubber?"

"About Patsy's skill as a love machine."

"I don't know. Okay, I guess."

"You don't have to guess…you were there, son."

"Don't ever call me 'son', okay?"

"Okay, okay, no offence meant."

"It just spooks me, okay?"

"Sure."

I waited for a second, then asked if he wanted to hang out in Elk for the night or hit the road.

"The truth?"

"Sure."

"Split."

"You're not tired?"

"I'll sleep in the car."

"What about me? I can't sleep and drive at the same time, you know."

"So let's stay."

"I sort of want to go."

"So let's go."

VIII

"Tell me a story."

"You want me to tell you a story?"

"Yeah."

It was about three in the morning and we hadn't passed another car driving on the Trans-Canada in either direction in at least an hour. I was feeling wired and weird, but Dave looked more relaxed than he had since when I picked him up two days earlier. We really should have stopped to sleep another couple of hours somewhere, but I sort of liked the idea of driving through the night. I had the vague idea that we'd drive until lunchtime, then stop somewhere for the night and keep going the next morning. As plans go, it wasn't much. But it was a lot cooler at night than it had been in the daytime and I felt awake and anxious to keep on going. I kept driving.

"What kind of story?"

"I dunno."

"You mean like a kid's story? Like Snow White or something like that?"

I expected him to take offence—I had asked him if he wanted a story like Snow White precisely because I wanted him to take offence, although I couldn't precisely say why that was—anyway, I had thought he'd hate the fact that I was obviously thinking of him like an overgrown child whose idea of post-coital fun was a good bedtime story, but he didn't react that way at all. In fact, to my absolute amazement, he loosened his seatbelt, adjusted his seat so that the back part was tilted as far back as it could go, clasped his hands behind his head and closed his eyes.

"Sure," he said. "Whatever."

There weren't any lights on that stretch of the highway, but I could see him pretty clearly in the moonlight. I glanced away from the road two or three times to look at him and, for the first time, he looked like the child he obviously was. A little boy whose Mommy was dead. A boy whose father used to listen to the White Album to calm down after whaling the crap out of his kid. A boy whose cool-as-ice outer demeanour was belied by the fact that what he really wanted after sex was to be told a good bedtime story.

"Well," I began a bit tentatively, "once upon a time, there was this guy named Saul."

"The story is about you?"

"Not me, pal...the other Saul. The king of Israel. The guy David replaced."

"My name is David."

"So what?"

"No, really."

"Really so what?"

"Come on...you said you'd tell me the story."

"David isn't even part of the story I was going to tell."

"Whatever. So can I hear it?"

"If you'd shut up, I'll tell it to you."

"Cool."

I don't know where it came from, but I felt this weird sort of shiver working its way down my spine and settling into the cleft of my buttocks. It didn't hurt—it didn't feel too great either, mind you—I mean, it wasn't painful or particularly pleasurable, but it was just sort of...there. I noted it, shifted around in my seat, tried to banish it to neuron hell or wherever those things go when you manage to get rid of them, but it didn't budge. It was like...I don't know what it was like, just that there was this sense that I was…I don't know. Forget the whole thing.

Anyway, as the Bible says, I picked up my story and began to speak.

"So there was this guy named Saul and he got himself killed in this big battle against the Philistines."

"Who were they?"

"Don't interrupt. They were this warlike nation that kept screwing with the Israelites. Anyway, he got himself killed together with three of his sons in this big battle, but…."

"What were the sons' names?"

"Look, you're really going to have to stop interrupting if you want to hear the story. Their names were Jonathan, Malchishua and Abinadav, but that doesn't matter. In fact, all that matters for my story is that Saul was killed. Okay?"

"Sure."

"Anyway, he was killed and his sons were killed, but there was this other son, this guy named Ishboshet. I mean, that's not really his name—his real name was Eshbaal—but he sort of got known as Ishboshet because it was just too shocking for some of the Biblical authors to think that the first king of Israel had a kid named after some foreign god. Anyway, there was this one surviving son and he turned out to be this major *shlemiehl*, the kind of guy who couldn't pour piss out of a boot if the instructions were written on the heel. But he was more than just your average sad sack, mind you—he was a world-class sad sack, a Greek tragedy waiting to happen. You know what I mean?"

"I guess." Dave pushed his hair off his forehead with his right hand, then put his hand back behind his head. He still had his eyes closed and it struck me that he must have spent his whole pathetic childhood hoping someone would take the time to tell him a story. It was a weird sort of scene, but not a really bad one. To tell you the honest truth, I sort of needed someone to tell a story to too.

"Anyway, after Saul died, his kingdom sort of split in two. David got himself acclaimed king at Hebron, but Saul's big general, this guy named Abner—he was also Saul's first cousin, by the way—anyway, he took Ishboshet and he made him king somewhere else. So the kingdom was effectively split in two with David trying to get himself established at Hebron while Ishboshet tried to reign in this other place. But it wasn't much of a fair contest. Ishboshet wasn't a kid any longer—he was forty years old when Abner made him king—and he was sort of this lumbering doofus in most people's eyes. I mean, he must have had his followers. Maybe he even had some admirers, but for the most part, his was what they used to call reflected glory and the only real claim he had to any fame was that he was his father's son."

"That sucks."

"Big time."

"So what happened to him?"

"So I'm trying to tell you. So anyway, there was this war for years between Ishboshet and David. Or rather, between their commanders, Abner (on Ishboshet's side) and this other guy on David's who was David's nephew named Joab. His name doesn't matter that much, but the basic idea is that they were at war for years with the northern half of the country basically behind Ishboshet and the southern half more or less behind David.

"Until one day, Ishboshet started giving Abner a hard time because he was giving the business to one of Saul's women—not a real wife, but a concubine, sort of halfway between a wife and a live-in—anyway, it turns out that Abner is giving the time to this chick named Rizpah who used to belong to Saul, his former boss."

"That a weird name."

"Rizpah means 'floor' in Hebrew, no doubt where she liked to do it the best. On the floor, I mean."

"How could her parents have known that?"

"Her parents?"

"How could they have known she'd end up liking to do it on the floor when they named her?"

"I guess. Anyway, Abner started up with her and Ishboshet heard all about it. So he calls him in and starts giving him this hard time and Abner accuses him of treating him like a dog that's allowed to be endlessly loyal, but which has to check with its master before it's allowed to take a dump or mount some bitch or eat a dog biscuit or anything like that. So Abner gets really, really pissed—Scripture doesn't quite say why he just didn't laugh in Ishboshet's face and keep on bedding old Rizpah—but he really takes it to heart and the next thing you know, he's over with David in Hebron discussing switching his allegiance over to the other side.

"So it turns out that was his big mistake, because of one little detail that he had conveniently forgotten…."

"Which was?"

"Which was that David's commander-in-chief, this nephew of his named Joab, he had had a brother named Asahel whom Abner had killed. It's actually a complicated story—this is really stories inside of other stories—anyway, Abner hadn't even wanted to kill Asahel, but he—Asahel—wouldn't stop chasing after him and finally Abner just had no choice but to stick it to him, which he did. In the belly. So hard that the dirk came out through the guy's back. And he died there in that place and Joab swore he'd have his revenge one day. And now that day had come."

"So what happened?"

"So Joab killed him—Abner, I mean—he stabbing him through the belly in precisely the same way Abner had killed Asahel."

"Did the blade come out of his back too?"

"Yeah, I think it must have. Anyway, the point is that this was really, really bad news for Ishboshet."

"Even worse than Abner defecting in the first place?"

"Good question! Yeah, much worse. I mean, with Abner alive, he could at least have hoped for some sort of reconciliation. But now that he was dead, old Ishboshet was really screwed and he knew it."

"So what happened?"

"So there wasn't enough time for anything too much to happen. These two brothers who had been working for Abner saw their big chance and they took it. They dressed up like household servants and stole into Ishboshet's house one day while His Majesty was having his afternoon nap."

"And they killed him?"

"Worse. They cut off his head and brought it right to David, figuring that he'd be thrilled that his rival was dead."

"What did they do with the body?"

"Who knows? They probably pitched it into some latrine ditch or else they just left it lying there like the carcass of an old moose after you've had the head stuffed and mounted."

"Cool. So was David thrilled? With the head, I mean?"

"He was delirious. No, really—he was furious that Rechab and Baana—those were their names—anyway, he was so royally pissed with these guys that he had their hands and feet cut off—the feet that had brought them to Ishboshet's bedside and the hands that had cut off his head—anyway, he had their hands and feet cut off and put on display so that everybody in Hebron could see what happens to people who behead reigning monarchs in Israel."

"Did they die?"

"Bled to death on the spot."

"And what happened to Ishboshet? To his head, I mean."

"Well, that's also a good question, but you could also ask about the rest of him. His head, David had buried in Abner's grave. But no one knows what ever happened to his body...."

"What do you mean, no one knows?"

"I mean that no one knows. Ishboshet's head was buried in Abner's tomb in Hebron, but the Bible doesn't mention what ever happened to the body."

"This story is from the Bible?"

"Sure."

"I went to Sunday School for a year or two when my dad was in the army and we were stationed in Nova Scotia. My mom took me, but when we came back here, we stopped going. But I don't think I ever heard this story before. All they ever told us about was how Jesus did this or that miracle and then they killed him but he didn't really die and how he's still around looking after everybody and worrying about everybody and how he knows if you're being naughty or nice and stuff like that. But I don't remember anybody cutting off any one else's feet or head or hands. You sure that's from the Bible."

"Positive."

"Wow."

"You hungry?" It was about four in the morning, but we hadn't eaten since dinner at the Harvest the night before. I personally was starving.

"There won't be any place open at this hour."

"You never know."

IX

I had to drive another two and half hours before we found a place to get something to eat. Dave dozed off about a half hour after telling me we'd never find an open restaurant and I was left alone with my thoughts. Just what I needed, I recall thinking to myself—some time to myself to think....

I passed the time driving in the dark and wondering if Wil was in hell. I mean, if there is a hell, then people who kill themselves are supposed to go there, only the rabbi—you already know what I think of him—he said that you're supposed to assume that the victim—that's what he called Wil, although it wasn't clear whose victim he precisely thought Wil was—anyway, he said that you're supposed to imagine that people who kill themselves repent themselves of their heinous sin in the nanosecond between pulling the trigger and connecting with the bullet or, in Wil's case, between jumping off the chair and having the life breath squeezed out of you, and that gives you the right to ignore the fact that they actually killed themselves and behave as though they died as a result of some tragic accident so you can bury them in a Jewish cemetery and give them a traditional funeral. Now that's just the kind of Pharisaic casuistry the *goyim* are always so exercised about, if you ask me. I mean, if it's a sin to kill yourself, then Wil has to be guilty as charged. And if it's not a sin, then who cares?

Anyway, Wil was such a great guy I still could hardly believe he was dead even though it was already a good six months since he had hanged himself. I can still see him—you won't believe this, but I'm getting all upset even telling you about this, so you can imagine how it felt actually to go through it all—anyway, I can still see him wearing his stupid Tom Hey-I'm-Just-Acting-Like-I'm-Gay Hanks knit cap and sitting up in bed while he drank a cup of tea. We knew he was sick. We knew he was dying. We knew every damn thing and we still couldn't believe it. And now he's been in the ground for more than two years and I still can't quite get it through my skull that he's really gone.

So Wil was this great guy, the kind of brother guys like me always have in the movies, except that this wasn't a movie and I really did have a brother like him. He was funny. He was clever. He was really, really good looking. He was great at baseball—he played third base for years in the Little League, then pitched for a year in high school until he broke his ankle and had to quit at the beginning of grade eleven—and good enough at football not to make a fool of himself when he played, which is a damn lot more than I can say for myself. He was really good with girls too. I mean, I was the older brother, so I was supposed to be the one who explained about girls and sex and stuff like that to him. Only he was the one with all the experience and all the success and, in the end, it was him who more or less explained things to me. And the thing of it is that he never made me feel stupid or failed just because I was three years older than he was…just that he knew this or that thing that he thought I probably didn't and he'd tell me and instead of being pissed at him for being so damn good at everything, I'd really appreciate how much he cared and how much he didn't want me to be the geek he must have known I sort of was. And the really amazing thing is that it never really bothered me to let him know how much I liked him. He was just this really terrific guy and I think I'll miss him forever. I'm getting all teary just writing about him, if you really want to know.

Anyway, it took up until just after six before I finally saw a place that was open for breakfast. I had headed back to the Trans

Canada even though I didn't really want to drive on highways any more than I absolutely had to because I thought it would be easier to find some open restaurant or gas station or something, but there just wasn't anything at all, open or closed, on that stretch of the road. I estimated the drive from Elk to Regina would take about nine or ten hours and that sort of suited me—it was already past six and I figured we could stop for an hour to eat, then continue driving east and get where we were going before lunch and I could sleep for a while. Not that we were actually going anywhere, mind you, but still…it appealed to me to behave as though we were headed somewhere specific.

The sign said that we were pulling into the Smile Cafe, but no one inside looked too exceptionally merry if you ask me. There was one sullen looking waitress leafing through a newspaper and two truckers seated at the counter when we came in—I supposed they were truckers because there were two big rigs outside—but they weren't talking to each other or doing much of anything other than staring straight ahead and waiting for their food and neither of them looked even remotely like he was smiling. The waitress didn't look like she was in any imminent danger of cracking a smile either. In fact, they all looked pretty damn miserable, to say God's truth.

Anyway, we ordered the Breakfast Special—orange juice, oatmeal, two fried eggs, toast and coffee. As she took our orders, the waitress sort of spat out at us that we could get three pieces of bacon each for an extra buck, but we both declined. I remember liking that she actually wrote "No Bacon" on her order pad like she had so much business that she couldn't possibly remember who did or didn't want this or that. Her name ("Debbie") was embroidered onto her uniform, but she didn't even smile when I thanked her by name for taking our order. Just what I needed at six in the morning—another sullen bitch in my life to be unfriendly and rude to me. Well, I told myself, this was destined to be a short lived relationship, so why make a federal case out of it? Besides, she wasn't really rude, I consoled (or rather, defused) myself by insisting, just gloomy.

Somewhat despite myself, I found myself wondering what her breasts looked like as she bent over to pour our coffee and gave us both a peak at her cleavage. I mean, you'd think giving the time to old Patsy would have cured me of that kind of thinking for at least twelve hours, but it had somehow had just the opposite effect on me. Did I mention that my twelve minutes with Patsy had been my first encounter with a woman in almost four weeks? After Helene pushed me out of my own house so she could give it to the gardener's brother in my bed without having her fun ruined by feeling excessively *duplicitous*, I had set to proving to myself that I could satisfy at least some women in bed and had endured a series of dates and encounters with women that had mostly self-destructed somewhere between five and thirty-five minutes after orgasm. There were some stretches where I must have gotten lucky every evening for nine or ten nights in a row, but I had eventually lost my taste for that kind of thing—not for sex itself really, but just for that whole kind of elaborate dating thing where you spend a whole evening sipping red wine (which I can only stand if it's drier than you can usually get in the dives I used to take these ladies to) and listening to some chick drone on for hours and hours on the chance you might end up getting her into bed. I mean, I like sex—who doesn't?—but it just wasn't worth it. After all, I had at least some dignity left. I might have been through the self-esteem wringer, but even Helene hadn't managed to take every scrap of pride when she pushed me out of my bed and my house and my life.

Dave was apparently all talked out and we ate more or less in silence. When we were on third cups of coffee, however, the silence broke.

"You wanna pick up another chick tonight?" I couldn't

believe I was speaking like that to a minor. Or are nineteen-year-olds considered adults when it comes to pimping for them? I didn't really know, but it wasn't like I was offering him a filly from my personal stable or anything like that—I was just suggesting that if we ended up still together by that night and if the opportunity presented itself, then would my young friend like to repeat the experience we had shared the previous evening?

His response was classic. "Sure," he said.

"Maybe we'll find a chick who will let us do it to her at the same time."

"You can't really do that."

"Sure you can."

"Are you sure?"

"Why not?"

"Where would the other guy stand?"

"There's a way."

"What is it?"

"I'll tell you later."

By a quarter to eight, we were back on the road. It was a beautiful morning. The month of August is always gorgeous on the prairies—the skies are big and blue and the fields are green and lush and the sense you have is of being in this endlessly enormous garden where everything grows free and wild and there aren't enough people in the world to make a difference or to crowd you in. The sun was already pretty high in the sky as we approached the Saskatchewan border and I was feeling better and more in touch with myself than I had in a lot of long, dark months. I guess it was a combination of having some company—I had been pretty terminally reclusive in the last few months while I tried to sort out my life—and the caffeine and the sugar in three cups of coffee and the release of having had sex with someone who didn't make me drink red wine for hours first and the sense—still mostly inchoate, but getting to be slightly perceptible for the first time—that I was maybe going to get over Wil's death and Helene's betrayal and losing my job and turn back into a productive, useful member of society. I don't know—it felt like a miracle, but I was actually feeling a bit hopeful. And you can't imagine what it felt like to sense even a smidgen of hope after feeling as awful as I had when I finally decided to get in the car and drive either for as long as it was going to take for me to find some peace in the world or until I maxed out all my cards and needed to sell the car to buy a bus ticket back home.

We got to Regina about eleven in the morning, but we only stopped for gas (at the Petro Canada station owned by Dick Assman, the guy who earned his fifteen minutes of fame by letting David Letterman ridicule him and his name in front of twenty-five million people for a couple of weeks) and coffee (at a place called Land O' Donuts which was basically filled with a particularly unappealing selection of male and female delinquents, hookers and other assorted ne'er-do-well types) and kept on going. I don't know…I had thought we'd hang out for the day in Regina and spend the night there too. But somehow when we actually got there, I didn't want to stay. Dave was asleep as we approached the city, but after our snack at Land O' Donuts, he agreed that we should press on. It wasn't the smartest move of my life, but who knew?

X

Having passed up the pleasures of Regina, we got to Endoz, Saskatchewan, at about two in the afternoon and crashed there instead. As far as I could tell, there were two possible places to stay in town, one scarier looking than the next. We flipped a coin and ended up taking a room at the Al-Mar Bed and Breakfast, which was basically an enormous (and enormously dilapidated) private home run by this fat, slovenly couple named (you guessed it!) Alvin and Marlene who, I thought, must have been thrilled to have someone who wanted a room for the night rather than for an hour or two. They gave Dave and me a long look when we came in—no doubt wondering what a guy like him was going to cost a guy like me for the night—but this time I had the brains to say he was my son and they appeared either to believe me or not to be interested enough in the whole situation to challenge me on it.

The room they gave us had one double and one single bed. I took the double for myself—it was me who was paying for the damn room, after all—and we both crashed for hours. When we got up, it was already nighttime. I didn't imagine Endoz boasted a wide range of fine dining establishments, but I was still surprised when Marlene told me that the only places to eat in town were her kitchen—the price of our room included breakfast, but she'd serve us pea soup and a meatloaf dinner for a reasonable price if we wanted—and a Denny's about four miles north of town on route 21. The Denny's, Marlene admitted sort of sourly, had a salad bar, but she couldn't vouch for the freshness of the vegetables and Alvin once ate there with a friend who got sick in the car on the way home. If we chose that option over her home cooking, she said with slightly menacing logic, we were "on our own." Given the cleanliness level of the Al-Mar, it didn't strike me as such a terrible fate. And really, who knows what made Alvin's friend sick that time? It could just as easily have been the company or too long a look at Alvin's fingernails or a stomach bug of some sort or something else entirely unrelated to the quality of the food at the Denny's up on route 21. We decided to take a chance.

It turned out to be a big mistake, but at the moment it seemed a reasonable enough decision.

Since there was basically only one road that passed through town, it wasn't hard to find our way. We passed a feed store or two, then a supermarket with a plastic sign in front advertising the price of milk, then a 7-11. By the time the country opened up, we were halfway there. The whole trip took about ten minutes. We were both starving, having not really eaten anything since our snack at the Land O' Donuts back in Regina. For a kid who barely spoke, Dave was being particularly quiet. To tell you the truth, I wasn't in too talkative a mood either. I guess we were both wondering what surprises the salad bar might hold in store at a Denny's that wasn't even in downtown Endoz, Saskatchewan.

The building, like every Denny's I've ever seen, was this freestanding brick and phony wood sort of affair in the middle of a parking lot. There were a couple of cars and a blue Ford pick-up in front. Towards the back of the building on the near side, I noticed a puke orange coloured Volkswagen beetle that I took to belong to one of the employees. For a whimsical moment, I wondered if Denny himself might not around this evening, maybe paying a surprise visit to an outlying outpost of his kingdom just to check that standards weren't slipping when people thought he wasn't looking. It seemed unlikely, however, that King Denny would drive a VW beetle. As we drove into the parking lot, however, I banished whimsy and turned to the matter at hand.

"We're here."

"Wow."

"You ever think about how no matter where you are, you can never be lying when you say the words "we're here" or "I'm here"? I mean, no matter where you are, that's where you are when you say that you're there."

"What?"

"Nothing. Let's go in."

"Sure."

There was no maitre d' hovering at the door, but there was a sign inviting us to seat ourselves. We chose a window table and waited for somebody to arrive. It took a few minutes, but eventually a waitress did show up.

"You guys ready?" she asked, presuming (I imagined) that context lent her question all the clarity it could possibly need to discourage whatever vulgar responses especially clever patrons like myself might otherwise have come up with.

"Can we see a menu?"

"I dunno. Can you?"

It took me a minute to recognize this as a joke, but once I did, there was no mistaking it. And not only had the waitress made a joke, but she was actually waiting for us to respond to it.

"Thank you for pointing out our error of usage, Darlene," I responded semi-politely, using the name embroidered onto her uniform right over her left breast. "May we see menus? If you have any, I mean. If you do, may see them? Please, Darlene? May we see a menu?"

Darlene was a dream come true. "Just one?" she asked, pleased as punch to have thought of another clever retort.

"My brother is blind," I answered without skipping a beat.

"Can I touch your breasts?" Dave asked almost immediately, displaying an unexpected ability to adapt to a new routine as he stuck his hands out into the space in front of his face in the manner of a blind person trying to feel who or what was in front of him.

"I dunno," Darlene responded, apparently delighted to have encountered such clever repartee on a slow weekday evening shift, "can you?"

I won't bore you with the rest of the conversation, which even strikes *me* as flat now that I'm trying to recreate it. Anyway, the basic idea is that Dave ordered the fish and chips and a small salad bar and I ordered a tuna melt and a large salad bar. We both ordered coffee. We would order dessert eventually, we assured Darlene, but only after we had eaten our meals. She seemed to accept this as reasonable and departed. Dave made a point of watching her behind swish back and forth as she vanished into the kitchen, but I found myself unwilling to be so overtly vulgar. Instead, I pretended to peruse the dessert menu Darlene had left on the table while watching her retreat into the kitchen.

The owners of the other cars in the lot were fairly easy to connect with their vehicles. The two guys wearing John Deere hats seated almost directly across the room from us were, I figured, the guys from the pick-up. A pimply teenager wearing a western shirt that looked to me like it came from Zeller's or K-Mart rather than from some fancy western emporium and a girl that looked more like his sister than a date ought to were, I thought equally obviously, the people who went with the tan Camry, which was probably the kid's mother's car or something like that. A lone gentleman with a long moustache and chipmunk cheeks was, by default, the driver of the bottle-green Bonneville, which I took to be at least twenty years old.

The waitress returned with glasses of ice water, plates for the salad bar, a basket of rolls and a little silver dish filled with pats of frozen butter. In fact, I had just managed to balance one of the little squares of butter on my knife when....

There were three guys, two of them brothers. (I'll include some background information that only came out later here and there if it doesn't interrupt the flow of my narrative.) Anyway, the two who were brothers—which was funny, since the one who wasn't a brother actually resembled Terry Dunn far more than his real brother did—so the two brothers rushed into the centre of the room while the third one—Jack Newell, the one who looked like he really could have been Terry's brother—he stood guard at the door in case some new patrons showed up for dinner while Terry and Clarence were still inside.

"Everybody stay calm," Terry yelled out to us all in a choked, high-pitched voice that was anything but calm. "Everybody stay calm and nobody's gonna get themselves hurt." I can still remember that voice, but that's mostly because it went so poorly with the body that it came out of. I mean, this guy must have been 220 pounds, about six foot two or three, goatee, moustache, pony tail—you get the picture—and he had this high-pitched little girl voice that sounded like it should be coming out of some talking Barbie doll or something.

Anyway, he honestly told us to stay calm "and nobody's gonna get themselves hurt." Can you imagine? I get caught in one stick-up in my whole life and the guy doing the talking has to sound like he's learned his lines from reruns of Hawaii Five-O, if not worse. But I figured it was more important to obey the gunman's order than to comment on its literary worth, especially since all we had been told to do was to stay calm and I figured we could manage that best by not pissing the people with the guns too severely off.

I actually *was* pretty calm—the whole scene was just too weird to take all that seriously, even though Clarence Dunn's gun looked pretty real, at least to me—anyway, I was calm, but not as calm as the guy I had connected to the Bonneville who slipped his hand in his pocket, touched the power button on his cell and—this is the really impressive part, if you ask me—managed to dial 911 with his hand still in his pocket as Clarence began to make the rounds of the few of us in the restaurant to relieve us of our wallets and wristwatches. Anyway, the really, really good part is that the connection to the 911 people got made precisely as Clarence was standing in front of the guy telling him to stop wasting time and to hand over his cash and his watch.

I guess the police figured out what was going down right away once they heard Clarence barking his orders at the guy, but they didn't know where Mr. Bonneville and his cell were at that precise moment. That wasn't the problem it would have been on television, however. And later we learned that it really wasn't any more complicated for them than tracing the call to his cell number, getting his home number from the phone book, calling his house and having his wife tell them he was having dinner at Denny's because she was having—I love this part—because she was having her mah-jong club over and he couldn't stand trying to think over the clicking of those damn tiles.

Anyway, the bottom line is that Terry was emptying the cash from the register into an Adidas bag and Clarence was asking Darlene if she wouldn't like to come along with them for the evening to see if she couldn't try to earn some of the money back precisely when the police arrived. It must have been a disappointing moment. First of all, Dave didn't even have a wallet or a watch. My watch, which had cost me about four dollars at the K-Mart in Surrey about four years earlier, wasn't exactly a Rollex. And I had left my wallet locked in the car and only had about forty dollars in my pocket, twenty of which I gave to Clarence along with half a pack of Marlboros and a plastic thing of Tic-Tacs. Question: how stupid was Clarence Dunn? Answer: stupid enough not even to realize that if I didn't have my wallet with me (which assertion he apparently took at face value) and I was driving around in a car, then I probably could be ordered at gunpoint to get my wallet from the car where it probably was. At any rate, Clarence actually thanked me for the Tic-Tacs when he took them, which was entirely okay with me since his breath stank and I was glad to see them go to such a good cause. How much cash they found in the wallets of the John Deere guys or the teenager and his date, I don't know. But I don't imagine it was much.

Anyway, at the very moment that Clarence was making his lewd suggestion to Darlene—I had been thinking of inviting her back to the Al-Mar to spend some time with Dave and me later on that evening and was actually interested in hearing what her response to Clarence's proposal was going to be—that's the precise moment the police arrived. Jack Newell, the look-out, was apparently looking out for his own ass rather than for his pals: at the precise moment the policemen were walking into the restaurant, we could all see a car driving past the patrol car onto the open road. Of course, only Terry and Clarence recognized the car and understood that they had been abandoned. But we all figured it out soon enough anyway.

I don't know what kind of police force the good people of Endoz think they maintain, but if they think they have purchased adequate protection against the villains of this world, they have a major surprise coming. The two officers, who looked more like television parodies of overweight, hayseed policemen than real-life cops, sort of burst into the restaurant with their guns drawn but without any clear plan of action.

When Clarence saw the cops' drawn guns, he released Darlene, who ran into the kitchen. Somehow Clarence's gun went off—probably because he inadvertently pressed down on the trigger—but, whether it was on purpose or not, the gun went off and shot out the window just behind the John Deere guys, who jumped out of it and ran for their truck. We were all so surprised by the shot that no one noticed Darlene running for the kitchen, but we all saw the orange VW tearing out of the parking lot a second later right behind the Deere guys' pick-up and that made it pretty clear that the captain—to the extent that Darlene appeared to be the only living employee of Denny's present aside from whoever was working in the kitchen, I like to think of her as King Denny's own personal ambassador to the paying public—anyway, it was clear that the captain had abandoned her ship. If she had taken the cook along with her, which she had, we obviously had no way to know at the moment.

That left the pimply kid and the girl who looked like his sister at one table, Dave and me at another, the Bonneville guy at a third, Clarence and Terry standing next to the cash register in the centre of the room and Toody and Muldoon at the front door. For a long moment, no one moved. I had a few things I thought of saying, but I didn't feel like I really had the floor. I mean, I don't know what the rules are in situations like this, but I figured that Emily Post would say that in a situation where some people are waving loaded guns and others are sitting at flimsy formica tables trying not to dump a load in their pants, it's the guys with the guns who are usually considered to have the floor until they relinquish it formally. Always sensitive to the norms of etiquette, I kept my peace. Dave, whom I was guessing knew more felons than I did, did likewise.

"Okay, boys, drop the guns." The taller officer must have learned his lines from the same Hawaii Five-O script the criminals had.

"Kiss my ass!"

"Look, you're basically screwed here. This is a small town with only two roads leading in and out and the RCMP is already sitting on both of them waiting for you. You can try to escape on foot, but you won't get far…it would take you at least four hours to get to another town that way and there isn't a town between here and Regina that's big enough for you to get lost in. You've made a mistake even starting this, but you can make it a lot easier for yourselves if you give it up right now. Now put down the guns and let's figure out how we can put this whole unfortunate incident behind us."

It was a good speech, better than I had expected. Clarence appeared more impressed by its logic than Terry, however. Indeed, Clarence began to lower his weapon when Terry turned to face him.

"Give up now and I'll blow your chest open and eat your heart," he said, giving no hint in his voice that he didn't mean every word.

"Look, you said the cops couldn't get here before we'd be gone," Clarence said quietly and, I thought, rather pointlessly.

"Well, I guess I was wrong. Who knew they'd be coming by for a snack in a shithole like this just when we were doing the place."

"I like Denny's."

"Well, then, let's see if we can avoid getting sent somewhere for a very long time where they don't have Denny's."

"We don't even have a way to get out of here." A slight whimper in Clarence's voice.

"That's another thing—we have to get out of here so I can find Jack's kids and kill them."

It was a good line, but it was also a bit chilling in that nothing suggested that Terry was kidding or even exaggerating. If I had been one of Jack Newell's kids myself, I'd have been heading for Antarctica on the next Greyhound.

Anyway, this whole conversation didn't take more than half a minute. The cops seemed unsure of their next move, as did the Dunn boys, but the Bonneville guy showed more nerve (or stupidity) than either of them. He just got up, slipped his bill into his pocket (no doubt to mail in a cheque to cover the cost of his meal to the Denny's head office somewhere) and, since no one said anything to him, just walked out of the restaurant while everyone watched. We all heard the car starting up and we all looked on as the car drove out of the lot. Now we were eight.

Dave started to get up from our table, but Clarence wasn't making the same mistake twice and he whacked Dave with the barrel of his gun so hard that he drew blood from the side of his head. He wasn't bleeding badly, but it was obviously an awful blow and I felt genuinely sorry for him. He sat back down and took a napkin from the dispenser to mop at his wound. I considered my options, then resolved to wait and see what would happen next.

XI

I guess this could have played itself out in a dozen different ways, but what actually did happen next was like a scene from one of my worst nightmares. Terry came up to me, ordered me to stand up, then twisted my arms behind my back and tied my wrists together with duct tape. Then he told Clarence to do the same to Dave. At the moment I was pissed as hell, but in retrospect I realize it was their only logical course of action. They needed hostages to get past the police. They needed a car to get away in. They would be committing a marginally less awful crime if they seized adults rather than children as hostages—and the teenager and his date really didn't look like they were much over fifteen or sixteen. And they really, really needed to get the hell out of there if they didn't want to spend at least the next decade in jail for armed robbery. At any rate, the die was cast. We were elected. Things were not looking good. I thought for a second about little Lena and hoped she'd remember me fondly if I ended up getting my ass shot off in what the CBC would undoubtedly call "a bizarre hostage-taking incident in a small town in rural Saskatchewan." I hoped she would. How Helene would break the news to her ("Honey, you remember that guy we used to live with?"), I shuddered to think.

There wasn't much time to think. Terry marched me out to the car—I don't know how he figured out which car was ours, but if he was guessing, he guessed right—and pushed me into the back seat while Clarence came around the other side and waited for Terry to reach in and open the door so he could shove Dave in next to me. Up until we were in the car, there was the barrel of a revolver jammed into the side of my head, so it was sort of a relief to get into the car…but not too much of one. The cops watched on grimly, but they didn't do anything. I made a mental note to describe their immobility in detail to whatever newspaper wanted to hear about it if I got out of this thing alive. I mean, I was feeling screwed by the world, but not precisely suicidal enough to hope I was going to get myself killed. And even if I had been considering suicide, the whole point of killing yourself is that you kill yourself, not that you get killed by somebody else in the middle of *his* docudrama. I mean, if you're going to die any-way, then you certainly don't want people to end up wondering if you meant it or not. What would be the point of that?

Terry fished my keys out of my jacket and off we went.

"Pretty low on gas," I observed.

"Shut up."

"Yes, sir."

"Don't call me sir, you understand?"

"No, not really. But I'll call you whatever you want. What's your name?" Was he really going to be so stupid as to tell me his real name? I held my breath in anticipation of finding out.

"Terry," he said almost immediately, as though the question had been put to him by the guy on the next barstool. "Terry Dunn. And this is my brother Clarence." That settled it—this Terry wasn't only an armed criminal, he was also a dumb-ass Baby Huey type who didn't want to pass up a chance to make a new friend.

"I'm Will Robinson," I said easily. "And this is my boy, Billy Jr."

Dave looked at me like he couldn't believe how clever I was to have made up two realistic sounding names on the spot. He gave me this little conspiratorial grin, but the real question was if he was going to be able to remember the names I'd made up for more than ninety seconds. Well, I remember figuring, I'd find out soon enough.

I won't bore you with the details of our trip together, although the part where Clarence had to take Dave into the men's room at the Esso station we stopped to gas up at was pretty good, although neither as good as the analogous scene at the beginning of *The Crying Game* nor as the one that ensued not too much later when *I* had to go to the can, which fascinating story I will relate presently. Anyway, the basic idea is that they were probably going to let us go right after that, except that this was precisely when the cavalry arrived. We weren't two minutes away from that gas station when we first heard the sirens and it wasn't thirty seconds after that when we realized there were no less than six police cars chasing us. Terry stepped on the gas. Clarence looked nervous. Dave looked scared, but sort of pleased the cops had only shown up after he had gotten into the men's room of the Esso station. I was preparing myself for the worst. I mean, this wasn't Hawaii Five-O anymore—it was F-Troop.

We ended up barricaded in some deserted farm house about ten or eleven miles north of Denny's. And that's where things stood for quite some time—with the cops drinking coffee out front and the four of us, two hardened criminals and two hostages, holed up inside. Slowly it dawned on me that Dave and I could easily end up dead as a result of either stupid pride on the part of our captors or stupid bravado on the side of the police, but I hadn't noticed a particular lack of stupidity on either side so far and I wasn't precisely expecting anything much in the way of intelligent negotiation from either the police or the Dunn boys. The fact that I might get killed somehow failed to move me too much one way or the other, but I felt sad for Dave. Well, I told myself, if he does die, at least he got himself laid the night before.

By now it was almost midnight and it was my turn to need the toilet. I gave Terry the good news.

"Hold it in, man," came the measured response.

"I can't hold it in, man," I said back, trying to sound like a regular guy. "If you don't give me a hand, I'm gonna crap in my pants."

Terry seemed to weigh his options for a moment, then signalled me to get up (by waving his gun at me) and told me to get into the john. I went gladly.

"You gonna help me with my pants?"

Terry looked like he hadn't thought of this before—he had apparently missed *The Crying Game* when it was in the theatres—but, to his credit, he could obviously see my point and he didn't make me beg. He put his gun down in the sink and pulled down my jeans and my shorts as far as my ankles.

"Sit down," he said unnecessarily, gesturing with his hand towards the toilet bowl.

I sat. "You gonna wipe my ass too?" I inquired cheerfully, looking forward enormously to his response.

"I'm gonna lick it clean," he said almost immediately. I was impressed!

He stepped out of the bathroom while I emptied my bowels, but he kept the door open. When I was through, though, he took out a knife and freed my hands. Then he assumed this sort of half-kneeling half-crouching position he must have seen on television somewhere and aimed his gun directly at my head while I wiped myself clean. When I was done, he let me pull my own pants back up, then retaped my hands. All in all, a successful interlude. I had the strangest sense that we were bonding, just like on TV. It was more than just slightly exciting to see life imitating art so precisely. In fact, it was thrilling.

In the meantime, the cops were completely inert. They called in a few times and ordered our captors to give themselves up, but neither Terry nor Clarence bothered to respond and the cops didn't appear to care that much one way or the other. The people who lived in this particular house were either on a very long vacation or else dead altogether. Indeed, aside from the electricity being on, there were no signs at all that anyone had lived there any time recently. Even the door had only been closed, not really locked. Dave fell asleep shortly after our interlude in the toilet and I must have dozed off not long after that myself.

Our captors said they were going to take turns sleeping, but I'm sure they were both out of it before long. Was that why they hadn't responded to the cops earlier, so that it wouldn't seem necessarily to be the case that they had fallen asleep if they didn't respond later on in the night when they both really were asleep? I doubted they had the brains to figure out such a clever plan, but it still worked a charm and although I don't really know if the cops did or didn't yell into the house during the night, the bottom line is that morning came and no one stormed the house to rescue us or anything dramatic like that. The cops were probably asleep out in their patrol cars too for all I know. In fact, I'm sure they were. That's for sure where I would have been if I was an Endoz cop stuck spending the night outside a farm house in the middle of nowhere.

At seven o'clock the next morning, Terry got everyone's attention by squeezing off a shot into the ceiling, then called out to the cops that they were going to shoot one of the hostages—I was sure he meant me for some reason—if they didn't provide some hot coffee for us all, a car, a couple of jerry cans of gasoline, two thousand bucks in cash and a promise that we could leave the place unmolested. He and Clarence would leave Dave and me off on a public highway somewhere once they were on their way, he said. We'd be fine, he insisted in that high-pitched candy-ass whine of his...but only if their demands were met.

I was outraged. I mean really—two grand? The thought that I was being held hostage—and could still end up being killed—by some dunce whose idea of a fortune is less than I paid for my first car was just too much to handle and, for the first time, I felt myself really getting steamed. And the hot coffee was an even better touch—here was a guy facing life imprisonment if he doesn't manage to get away, but what he really had on his pathetic Baby Huey peanut brain was the fact that he could manipulate the situation to get the cops to bring him a free cup or two of hot joe. On top of all that, I was finding Terry's Tiny Tim voice more than a little irritating—it wasn't as high as the late, lamented Tim's, but it really was almost that high and it had this annoying lilt to it that made him sound like he was a child talking to other children no matter what he said. I had had just about enough of the whole situation, but I was afraid to provoke them for fear that little Billy Junior might get hurt. After all, he wasn't just my son in their eyes, he was my namesake!

Miraculously enough, the coffee arrived. Even better, it came from Denny's. One of the cops left it on the porch of the house and Clarence went out to get it. No one shot him while he was outside—which half surprised me—but I was sure I heard some shutters clicking in the cool morning air during the eight seconds he was out there. When he came back in with the coffee, however, our male bonding thing was complete. Clarence actually asked if we took sugar or milk—the tray had some packets of sugar and—this killed me—some little pink Sweet-N-Low envelopes and a couple of those little plastic things of 10% cream. Clarence made us our coffee, then undid our hands so we could drink it. No one seemed worried we might escape. The sick thing is that they were right—I didn't know what Dave was thinking, but I was happy to sit where I was and enjoy the java. I think that to this day, it was still the best cup of coffee I've ever had at a Denny's.

"This is boring," Clarence said to Terry.

"Next time, we'll hole up somewhere with cable," Terry answered so pleasantly that I couldn't tell for certain if he had meant his response sarcastically.

"Saul…my dad can tell us a story," Dave said unexpectedly. Just what I needed, I thought—to entertain our captives with a little story. I wondered briefly if they'd like to hear my version of Rapunzel—the one in which the witch ends up spending eternity with hell rats gnawing on her intestines for holding her own daughter captive in the tower—but I thought better of it. Why make people with guns mad, I figured, working on the slightly unlikely assumption that our captors might possibly have had the brain power to comprehend irony. It was a long shot, but why take any chances?

"That's okay, li'l Billy," I said quickly. "I'm sure no one wants to hear a story just at this moment."

Clarence, however, was intrigued. "Really good ones?" He turned to face Dave as though he were deathly interested in hearing the answer to his question.

Damn, I thought.

"Yeah, great ones." Dave was apparently really getting into the idea of me telling a story. I was partially flattered and partially irritated, but I didn't want to piss anybody off, least of all either of the guys with guns, so I just sort of smiled at the compliment and hoped they'd decline.

"Go ahead." Clarence was still looking at Dave, but it was obvious he was addressing me.

"You really want to hear a story?" I asked, playing for time.

"Sure."

"You too?"

Terry looked over at me like he couldn't understand the question. "You mean me?" he asked, his voice somehow even more grating, I thought, than it had been even a few minutes earlier.

"Yeah."

"Sure."

It was just then that the police officer called in to say that they could have the gas and the cash, but they'd have to leave the hostages—us—behind if they wanted to be allowed to leave unmolested. It took Terry about three seconds to accept, although I couldn't imagine why he thought he'd be safe without us in the car with them.

The cop sounded delighted. The cash would be there as soon as the bank opened, in about an hour. And they were going to look after the car and the gas. Until then, we were to stay calm and no one would be hurt. Why it wasn't obvious to Terry that the cops were going to arrest or shoot him and his brother as soon as they came out without us, I don't know. But the bottom line is that he didn't seem to realize that and I guess the reason was that neither Terry nor Clarence was exceptionally bright. These were two guys, after all, who were prepared to sit and listen to a story during a hostage crisis of their own making instead of planning their next move.

Still, it seemed like a good idea to keep their weak minds busy, so I set to my story with as much gusto as I could muster.

"Okay," I began as genially as possible. "Listen up and I'll tell you a story that happened a real long time ago."

Dave moved closer to me and sat down on the floor next to my legs. He sort of leaned over and pushed the side of his head up against my right leg while Terry and Clarence both put their guns in their laps and sat down on the coach facing my chair. It was like story hour at the Jumbo Dumbo Junior Library, I thought, as I collected my thoughts and began to speak.

XII

"Well," I began, "once upon a time, there was a mighty king named David who ruled over the entire Land of Israel."

I looked around to see if everybody was following me so far and I was semi-delighted to see that I had the rapt attention of all three of my listeners. Dave pressed up a little tighter against the side of my leg. Terry stuck his hand in his pants and appeared to be adjusting his testicles for comfort. Clarence just stared at me, apparently awestruck by someone who could tell a story without three and a half weeks of intensive preparation. I wondered for a moment what he would say if he knew I could read too, but thought better of interrupting myself to ask. Besides, I asked myself yet again, why piss off the guy with the gun if not absolutely necessary?

"Anyway," I began again, "there was this king named David and he was a just and wise ruler. I mean, he had his shortcomings just like everybody does—he once got a guy killed just so he could do the guy's wife, for instance...."

"Our dad did that too once," Clarence interrupted me to observe. For a moment, we all contemplated this remark, but no one actually responded to it. I found myself believing it, however. And I could tell from the fact that he was squeezing my legs even tighter, that Dave did too. I wondered what else I didn't know about Clarence and Terry's dad, but I could tell that Dave was as scared as I really should have been myself and needed us to get the hell away from there as quickly as possible. Well, if drawing my story out until the cops came was going to help accomplish that, I was all for it.

"Anyway," I began a third time, "he was basically this good king who ruled over the country with a strong, but just hand…but not everybody saw it that way. There were, for example, outlaws who were pissed to hell that they weren't free any longer to ply their murderous trade on the countries' highways and to stick up whatever gas station or restaurants they wanted without having to worry about the police or the army getting in their way. And there were all sorts of other types who weren't precisely prospering under the firm hand of a strong central government. Anyway, there were plenty of people who couldn't stand David and who resented his successes…and then there was this whole contingent of people who had been big supporters of King Saul, the guy David replaced on the throne. They had been at war for years when Saul finally died—not at David's hands, mind you, but still…dead is dead—anyway, Saul was a madman, but he was a beloved madman for most of the time and he left behind a lot of friends. And dying in battle against his country's main foes didn't exactly hurt his reputation either….

"Anyway, the country hadn't been all that unified in the first place. The tribes in the north basically couldn't stand the tribes in the south and the feeling was entirely mutual. And nobody could stand the snobs who lived in the capital city of Jerusalem, so the country wasn't exactly this happy kingdom of happy citizens working together to resolve their differences and stay together in one happy family like we all do in Canada. So all it took was one guy to start things rolling and his name was Sheva ben Bichri. That means Sheva, son of Bichri. Bichri was his dad's name."

"What was his last name?"

Terry looked proud to have asked a question, so I figured I'd better answer. "They didn't have last names in those days, Terrence," I explained slowly, hoping he'd understand what I was saying. "They just used their fathers' names to distinguish between people with the same first names. So this Sheva was Sheva ben Bichri, but some other Sheva would have been Sheva ben Dick or another could have been Sheva ben Harry or something like that. So the guy's name was Sheva ben Bichri and that's what people called him. And he was one mean son of a bitch too…a real Dirty Harry type who knew how to get things cookin' when he wanted to.

"So he declared a revolt against David. And he did pretty good too, at least at first. Lots of people liked the idea of a change of regime—they were sick and tired of nothing but David's songs ever getting any radio time and they couldn't stand living in a state that actually had laws that were actually enforced and all that kind of stuff. David had some loyal followers, but the whole state was in this major uproar and certain people thought it would be a good idea to take advantage of the situation to…to deal with some situations that hadn't ever really been resolved properly in the past."

"You mean to settle up with people who had screwed them over in the past while everybody was looking somewhere else?"

Clarence's question betrayed a certain ability to listen I hadn't expected in somebody that dumb, but I wasn't quite sure if I should answer honestly or not. "Sort of," I said vaguely after a moment's silence.

"Cool," he said, openly pleased.

"Anyway," I went on, "there was this guy named Amasa who was actually the king's nephew, the son of David's sister Abigail. Anyway, Amasa—this is a little complicated, but I'll try to say it clearly—anyway, this Amasa had previously supported one of David's sons, the one named Absalom, who had tried to revolt against his father and make himself king. Now David had another sister as well. Her name was Zeruiah and she had some sons as well and it was one of them, this guy named Joab, who ended up finally killing Absalom. Amasa had supported Absalom and Joab had killed him, so you'd think David would be thrilled with Joab and pissed as hell at Amasa, but it turned out just the other way—David was enormously pissed with Joab for killing his kid—and it didn't seem to make much difference that his kid was trying to steal the kingdom from him—anyway, he was enraged at Joab for killing the kid and he pushed him—Joab, I mean—he pushed him out altogether and fired him and made Amasa head of his army in his place.

"Anyway, it was this Amasa that David sent out to round up the army to do battle with this Sheva guy. Only he took a little too long to get himself organized, so David sent out Joab after him. Well, that was all the excuse Joab needed—he ran into Amasa in this place called Gibeon and he rammed his switchblade into the guy's belly so hard that his intestines actually spilled out onto the ground after just one thrust and he died there like a dog on the ground, whereupon old Joab set off in pursuit of Sheva."

"What happened to his body?" Terry asked.

"He just lay there on the ground drenched in his own blood until they dragged him off the road and pitched him into some ditch somewhere. But that's not the point—the point is that Amasa was dead and Joab was off in search of Sheva, who was the problem in the first place. Anyway, in the meantime, Sheva had gotten himself holed up in this placed called Abel and it was Joab's job to figure out how to get him out, preferably without having to burn the whole place down and kill all the innocent people inside the town."

"That would have been bad," Dave noted.

"I guess," I agreed slightly. "But there was this really smart lady in the town of Abel known as the Wise Woman of Abel."

"How smart was she?"

I wondered what the precise range of wise women Clarence had encountered in his life could possibly have been, but I decided not to approach his question from that precise angle. "She was really, really smart, Clar," I said. "She was the town doctor and the town lawyer and judge. She taught elementary school and high school and she was the junior varsity basketball coach. She published the local newspaper and she spoke at all the town's funerals and weddings. She even wrote the local advice column in her own newspaper and she used to preach regularly at camp meetings held on the outskirts of town. She had won a Nobel Prize and a couple of Pulitzers and a Grammy or two and a Tony and she had even been on that creepy English guy's best dressed list once or twice."

"Wow."

"Anyway, she had an idea. She snuck out of town one night and approached Joab and told him that if he'd lift the siege of her city and let them bring in some food and some fresh water, then she'd pitch old Sheva's head over the town wall before dawn the next day."

"That was smart." I was clearly impressing Clarence, which I hoped was making it marginally less likely that he would feel okay about shooting me if it came to that.

"It was smart."

"So how did she do it?"

For a moment, I tried to remember if the Biblical account suggests how precisely the wise woman of Abel managed to detach Sheva ben Bichri's head from the rest of him, but I couldn't quite recall. I didn't want to sound like I didn't know the details of my own story, so I decided to give a plausible answer. Only I had to think of one first.

"Well," I began, "the basic idea is that the wise woman had a daughter…."

"What was her name?"

"Her name? Her name was…Bina."

"Like String Beana?" My, my, wasn't Clarence the clever

punster!

"Yes, Clar, just like String Beana. Only it was just Bina. Anyway, Bina wasn't as wise as her ma, but she was pretty great looking."

"What did she look like?"

"Well, she had long black hair and a pretty face with these red, pouty lips and a long neck and huge breasts and wide hips. And nice feet with exceptionally long toes and painted toe nails."

"Sounds like Cher."

"Does Cher have such wide hips?"

"I dunno. Maybe. But she's got big boobs and long black hair."

"I guess," I guessed, having not seen Cher in much of anything since Moonstruck. For a moment, I could tell that both Clarence and Terry were contemplating Cher's breasts. Dave seemed distracted, perhaps uncertain what any woman older than Courtney Love looked like. I'd have to fill him in later, I told myself, assuming without any real reason that we weren't going to be shot in a botched police effort to save us any time soon.

"Anyway, this girl…."

"String Beana."

"Yes, Clarence, that's it precisely. This girl named String Beana made straight for the house Sheva was bivouacking in and she knew just what she was doing. She invited him to dinner, leaving open the question of what might be for dessert."

"He probably thought she was dessert."

"Good, Terry! You've caught on perfectly. He definitely thought she was for dessert, so he went right to her house and sat down to a really, really good dinner. Even better than they serve in Denny's."

"Wow."

"Wow is right. And lots of wine. Lots and lots of wine. White wine. Red wine. Rosé. Champagne. Riesling. Muscatel. Mogen

David. Valpolicella. Every kind of wine there is. Anyway, he got so pissed that he was passed out on the floor long before they even got to dessert. And that's when she did it."

"Did what?"

"Ran to the kitchen, got a long, sharp knife and cut his head right off his shoulders."

"She must have gotten a lot of blood on her carpet."

"She had tiles in her dining room."

"Wooden ones?"

"Ceramic."

"Oh."

"Anyway, she got his head off easily enough. And then she sent her servant lad to run for her mother, who showed up a little while later. They pitched the body into a latrine ditch behind the house, but old Shev hadn't been dead for an hour when his head was suddenly flying through the night sky over the city wall of Abel right into Joab's hands."

"He caught it?"

"Yes, Terry, he caught it. They all saw it coming real nice and gentle over the wall and it just sort of flew into his arms and he was so pleased to get it that he lifted the siege of Abel and went home instead."

"He was happy?"

"Deliriously so."

"So what happened next?"

"So nothing happened. That's the end of the story. Sheva ben Bichri got his head lopped off and pitched over the wall, Bina was still a virgin so her mom wasn't out any cash she might otherwise collected as her daughter's bride-price when she got married some day, Joab got to bring Sheva's head to David as proof of his good intentions in case the king was still pissed about him knifing Amasa in the belly and letting his guts spill out onto the ground, the Wise Woman saved her city and David got to hold onto his throne. End of story."

"That was great, man."

"I'm glad you liked it, Terry."

"Where'd you hear it?"

"It's in the Bible. You should have listened better in Sunday School and you'd know it too."

"No way."

"Really."

Pleased at how attentive my audience had been, I was just about to embark on a second story when one of the cops outside called in to say that the car, the gas and the cash would be there in about five minutes. For the first time, I was slightly touched that Terry and Clarence apparently cared enough about Dave and me not to want to add the theft of our car to the various other crimes they were going to have to answer for if apprehended. The only reason, in fact, to have asked for a car was because they wanted to leave us my car to continue our trip instead of stealing it and I found myself unexpectedly encouraged by this strangely friendly gesture. It felt good to feel good about people for a change and I recall wondering if I hadn't perhaps been a bit hasty in damning humanity as basically useless, hopeless and cruel. It was a new feeling for me…and I enjoyed all eight minutes of it.

XIII

The rest of story is pretty awful. I should have been smart enough to see it coming, but I wasn't. And Terry and Clarence died because of it.

How it all happened is like this. The cop called in a little while later to say that they had the car and the cash ready and that Terry and Clarence should leave us inside the house and come out and get into the car. They were going to be allowed to drive away and all they had to do was to leave the cash they had taken from the restaurant with us in the house. Now that I think back on the whole thing, I can hardly believe that I really thought the cops might let them get away, but the truth is that that's precisely what I thought. I mean, they were releasing their hostages, they were returning the cash they had stolen, they weren't stealing our car to get away in…it sounded to me—and there's no need to rub it in now because now, after the fact, it sounds idiotic to me too—but anyway, it did sound to me at the moment like a reasonable solution to what had become a difficult situation.

Anyway, we were told to sit next to each other on the couch and Terry gave me the plastic bag with the money, wallets and wristwatches they had taken from the restaurant and its patrons. What happened next is hard to say since I wasn't at the window to watch, but what I *think* happened is that they exited the house and made directly for the car. When they got about ten feet away, one of the cops jumped out and called out something incredibly derogatory about the boys' mother and what he had personally thought about her skill as a professional fellatrix. Both brothers immediately pulled out their own guns to defend their mother's honour, whereupon every other policeman present pulled out his gun and that was basically that. They both died instantly. When we came out of the house, Dave almost tripped over Clarence's body and we both felt this weird sadness come over us. I mean, Terry and Clarence had been dodos who had attempted armed robbery, threatened our lives and taken us hostage. On the other hand, Terry had let me wipe my own behind and both boys, Clarence especially, had listened pretty attentively to my story about Sheva ben Bichri. So it hadn't been that awful an experience and it didn't need to end with the death of one of the best audiences I've had for a story in years. I hadn't precisely liked our captors, but I hadn't loathed or despised them either. In fact, I would have liked to travel with them a bit, maybe to pick up some girls with them or get something eat or something like that. My life wasn't going to be dramatically diminished by their passing or anything like that…but I was sorry they were dead and I was irritated with the police for basically having executed them in cold blood. That, I now understood, was how things were done around those parts, but I wasn't from those parts and it wasn't my way.

Anyway, after it was all over, Dave and I got into my car and drove off. We promised to stop by the police station before leaving town to record formal statements about what had happened to us and how the Dunn boys had confined us against our will and threatened to kill us if we tried to escape. It all sounded so horrible when they put it that way, but what was really killing me was knowing that it was all basically true and that I was such a pathetic candy-ass that I wasn't even capable of getting pissed-off at a pair of villains who had taken me hostage just because they were borderline retarded and liked listening to stories.

We should have gone straight to the police station and left as soon as possible after that, but we somehow managed to waste almost the whole day sacking out at the old Al-Mar and doing some laundry at the laundromat and by the time we actually got to the police station, it was after four in the afternoon. We were there for about two hours and probably ought to have given up any plans of leaving that day, but by the time it got dark, we had had enough of Endoz, Saskatchewan, and were more than ready to leave. I wasn't tired since I had slept more or less all day, so we ate at the Denny's again, where I sort of thought they'd at least give us a free meal since we were taken hostage and held at gun point in their restaurant. All we got, however, was the same lousy service we had gotten the previous night. The place was pretty empty. The window near where the John Deere guys had been sitting had somehow gotten fixed. The whole place basically looked like it had the night before. I don't know if it was Darlene's regular night off or if it was regular Denny's policy to give waitresses the night after armed robberies off as a kind of combat bonus, but she wasn't around and we were served by an elderly black woman who spoke with a Caribbean accent and whose name tag read Benny.

"Maybe they get ripped off like that all the time," Dave suggested.

"I guess."

"I mean, no one seemed to amazed that it happened."

"I guess."

"You think the police just sort of shoot armed robbers when they can around here? I mean, without any trials or stuff like that."

"Maybe."

We ate our lousy meals in relative silence after that. Dave had a hamburger and fries and I had a Greek salad, which tasted like it might have actually been imported from Greece sometime in the last several decades, and we washed it down with some tepid, weak coffee and that was basically that. Endoz was already just a dream as we pulled back onto the road south and headed on a bit further. Dave was tired—we both were—but basically okay. He was looking a little less lousy, I thought, than he had when I had first picked him up, but he was still troubled—I could see that clearly—and he still didn't really look like he was in such great shape.

"So tell me about your mother dying and all that," I said cheerfully as I opened a package of Marlboros, pushed in the lighter and turned for a moment to look into his eyes as we drove on into the night.

"You really want to hear?"

"Sure."

"Like what part?"

"Well, what was her name?"

"Her name was Gloria."

"Nice name."

"I guess. She was a nice lady."

We drove into the night.

XIV

You'd think driving across the prairies at night would be no big deal, I'd guess. I mean, it's not like you can see anything in the dark, so what would be the difference between driving on flat land and driving through the mountains? I guess that makes sense—but it just doesn't correspond to what it's really like. I don't know, maybe it's the sense that you're driving across this endless black sea that extends in every direction as far as you can see (or rather, as far as you could see if you could see anything at all) and you're driving on this perfectly straight, perfectly flat black road you can't see either except for the couple of feet your headlights are lighting up. And there's this black sky all around that looks like this incredibly dark helmet set down on the world. I don't know—it's basically impossible to explain what it's like to drive on the prairies at night and it's even worse in the summer when the windows are down and you can occasionally smell the manure without being able to see any of the cows. It's like being some piece of dust floating around in outer space, if you want to know what it's really like. And when it's late enough for there not to be any other cars on the road, then it's even better than that. It's really hard to describe…sort of like being smothered by the dark, except that instead of choking to death you can breathe even better than you could if you were out driving in the daytime. Except, of course, that there aren't any cows in space. That we know of, I mean.

"So tell me about your mom. Her name was Gloria."

"Right. Gloria."

Endoz was an hour behind us. I figured we'd get to the Manitoba border in a few hours and hit Houghton sometime around six. With any luck, we'd find some place open for breakfast, get a room, sleep a few hours and then head into Winnipeg in the afternoon. I'd drop Dave at his grandmother's, get some dinner, crash with one of my friends for the night and be gone first thing the next morning. I didn't know what the hell I was doing—aside from running away from Wil's ghost and my demented parents and the wreckage of my miserable marriage—but I sure as hell wasn't making a pilgrimage to Winnipeg. Of all places.

Mind you, Winnipeg has a bad rep. I mean, it's incredibly ugly and seedy and the winters really are the nightmares you've heard about and the place is overrun with these enormous mosquitoes all summer, but it's also this really cool place with very hip people all over the place and a nice feel to it. It's friendly too—not like Regina or Edmonton maybe, but it's like the absolute, polar opposite of Toronto, which is the least friendly place in the world with no exceptions whatsoever of any sort. I mean, you could drop dead on the street in Toronto and they'd give your corpse a ticket for littering, but in Winnipeg someone would probably call an ambulance. And they'd probably revive you too, at least long enough to find out if you're covered by some provincial health plan somewhere. I mean, it's a nice city, but it's still Canada and all.

Anyway, the night was black, Dave and I were both fairly well rested, the air was cool and Houghton was hours ahead of us.

"What kind of a woman was she?"

Silence.

"Was she nice to you?"

"She was my mother."

"Not all mothers are nice to their kids."

"I guess. But she was really nice."

"Tell me about when she was nice to you."

"Well, she was really pretty. And she had black hair and really big…she had a really nice figure."

"Go on."

"And she could sing really good. She had a great voice."

"Like who?"

"Like who what?"

"Like who did she sing like? Did she sing like an opera singer? Or like Madonna? Or like what's that chick's name, the big singer from Quebec?"

"Celine Dion?"

"Right. Like her?"

"No, not like that. She just had a nice voice." Long pause. "Like Madonna a little bit, but only like she sounded in Evita. Not like when she just sings sings. Like in the movies when she sings."

"Got it. Go on."

Long pause. "She got raped when she was twenty."

"No way. Who did it?"

"My dad."

"Were they married then?"

"No, that's the whole thing. They were at this company picnic the place my dad worked in used to have each June. And she worked there too back then. It was a door place."

"A door place?"

"You know, where they make doors."

"Okay, so your mother worked in a door factory when she was twenty. How old was your dad?"

"Twenty-one."

"And what happened?"

"What do you think? He kept asking her out and she never went because she thought he was creepy and she didn't want to get mixed up with him and then he had this idea to make believe he was drunk and see if he couldn't get to her like that and it worked. He sort of went off into the forest with his pal as though he was trying to sober up with a hike before he had to drive home and then his friend came back all excited and told my mom that he was really sick and could she bring him some food to put in his stomach while he—the friend, I mean—while he went back to the cars to get some medicine or something. I don't really know what he told her exactly, but she was probably feeling guilty that he had asked her out so many times and she had always turned him down, so she took some sandwiches or something and headed down the trail to where my dad was waiting. And when she got there, he jumped her."

"How do you know all this?"

"My mom told me."

"And they got married?"

"Of course, they got married. She was too embarrassed to admit how stupid she had been, especially after she found out she was pregnant and I guess she figured the only way to make it right was to marry him. I don't know—my mother was pretty smart, but she wasn't smart enough to see that she should have run as fast as she could away from that son of a bitch…and that's the truth even if she was pregnant. Anyway, it was a wonderful courtship—all thirty-five seconds of it—and when he got his pants up, he slapped her around a little bit for being such a loose bitch and because—I can't decide if it's weirder that he told this to her or that she told it to me or that I'm telling it to you—anyway, he slapped her and called her a bitch because he knew for sure—this is a precise quote, by the way—that he knew for sure that she had liked it at least enough to make it her sin instead of his. Then they went back to the picnic like nothing had happened, but they were wrong and I was born nine months later. They were married by then, though."

"So at least you're not a bastard."

"Go to hell."

"Oh no, I insist. *You* go to hell."

"What?"

"Nothing."

There's nothing to report about the scenery as we drove across the prairies, because the whole point is precisely that it never changes. You move forward, but there isn't anything at all to see: just endless blackness on all sides and in every direction. The wind was actually rather sweetly scented in this part of eastern Saskatchewan and, almost despite myself, I was getting caught up Dave's story.

"So what happened?"

"When?"

"After that."

"Well, they basically spent the next fifteen years like that. She kept house and cooked for him and gave it to him when she had to or when he made her and he worked at Linden's—that's the door place—and beat the crap out of her when he figured she needed it. They had my brother. He used to whack us too, if you honestly want to know all about what the Cleaver family was really like when the cameras weren't running."

I did want to know, as it happened. "And what about your brother? What happened to him?"

"His name is Kevin, but I haven't seen him in years."

"Where'd he go?"

"Who knows? But wherever he went, he never came back. I used to think he still would, but now I think he's gone for good."

"You think he's okay?"

"Maybe. Probably. I think he calls my grandma every so often so she doesn't worry, but she only said something once to me and nothing at all to my mother, so I think she had to swear never to tell. I'll have to ask her."

"But he never called you?"

"Not one single time. Not once."

Another long pause in the conversation.

"There's a story like that in the Bible, you know."

"Like what?"

"Like the story of your parents."

A flicker of interest. "So?"

"So you wanna hear it?"

"Sure."

"What's the magic word?"

"Just tell the story, will you?"

"Okay, then…this is about two kids of King David's."

"How many kids did he have?"

"I don't know. A lot."

"Three?"

"More than three. I think it was more like fifteen. In fact, I think that's right—he had fifteen sons and one daughter.

"Cool."

"Anyway, he had this one wife named Maacah who was a royal princess herself from a different country and she was the mother of two of his kids, a girl named Tamar and a boy named Absalom. And then there was this other wife named Ahinoam and she was the mother of David's oldest son, this guy named Amnon. Anyway, Amnon fell for Tamar—she was only his half-sister, but it was still pretty kinky. Mind you, later on in the story Tamar herself says that she thinks that David would have gone for it if Amnon had had the decency to ask him straight out for her hand, but who knows if that's really what she thought or if she was just trying to talk Amnon out of sticking it to her. But I'm getting ahead of myself…."

Dave looked over at me in the dark. In the dim glow of the dashboard lights, I could see him brushing his hair up over the top of his forehead and I remember getting the distinct impression that he was actually interested in what I was saying. Could being interested in something conceivably have been such an unusual sensation that he actually enjoyed it independently of the larger experience of hearing my story? I shuddered to realize it, but that was exactly what I thought. I pulled over to the side of the road and got out to have a pee in the darkness. I thought Dave would take the same opportunity, but he said he was fine and we left it at that. Still, I remember asking myself what kind of guy passes up a chance to take a leak?

"Anyway, Amnon has the hots for his half-sister and he's all confused about how to go about getting her alone. I mean, it was all chaperons and stuff and no one was really ever able to get anyone else alone, especially not unmarried girls. So he's all confused about the whole thing until his cousin has the idea that he should pretend to be sick and then ask his dad to send Tamar over to cook him some dinner or something."

"Did it work?"

"Yeah, like a charm. David hears his kid is down with the flu or something and he comes to see him and ask what he needs and Amnon says he's basically okay, but he's starving and could David send old Tamar down to fry up some pancakes for him. So David's probably relieved he doesn't want anything worse than that…."

"Like something that would have cost him money or something like that?"

"Precisely. Anyway, David is thrilled all the kid wants are some flapjacks, so he goes back to the palace or wherever and sends Tamar down to fry 'em up for her sick brother."

"Only he's not really sick?"

"Good, David…you've caught on perfectly. He's not only not sick, he's great. And randy as a goat…."

"Randy?"

"Horny."

"He really wants it?"

"More than most guys ever do. Anyway, he's consumed with

wanting it. He's been totally aroused ever since Jonadab—that's the cousin's name who thought up the whole scheme—ever since Jonadab told him what to do and he began to think that he at least had a chance to bang Tamar, a chance which he hadn't previously considered even to exist. Anyway, he's hot to trot and he's just sitting up in his bed naked under the sheets and trying to look like he's really sick and he's got his knees bent and the back of his ankles pressed up against his bum so she can't see the evidence of his desire poking up through the bedsheets like a tent pole. Anyway, she has no idea what's going on and she just sets to making the pancakes, but after she's got them ready, he's got other plans. He gets rid of all his servants and whoever else was hanging around and jumps her. I mean, he's up front about it all and everything. He says what he wants and she tells him to buzz off—that she's a virgin and that it's not what decent people do—that's the best part of the story, if you ask me, where she tells him all this information seriously in case the problem was that he thought that people rape their sisters all the time and now that he knows that you're not supposed to do it, he's just going to forget the whole thing—anyway, it's pathetic that she even bothers to say it to him, but she does and he just ignores her and he pushes her down and rips off her skirt and before she ever realizes what's happening, he's inside, but he only lasts a few seconds and then he's done. And she's in shock…but the worst is still coming, because now that he's finally given it to her, he discovers that he doesn't love her at all like he thought he did. Just the opposite—he realizes that he can't stand her. She's not this noble princess that he thought, just another bitch to savage and pitch in the trash afterwards…and he especially hates her for putting on airs and parading around like she's this virginal ice maiden when all along she's just been another piece of ass waiting for someone with enough nerve to give it to her good."

"And what happens then? Does she turn out to be pregnant?"

For a moment, I had forgotten that this was at least slightly parallel to Dave's mother's story. "No, she doesn't end up pregnant. And Amnon doesn't end up marrying her—who ever heard of a prince of Judah marrying a his own half-sister?—anyway, they don't marry. But Tamar has this brother named Absalom and he knows just what to do once he gets wind of what Amnon did to his sister. His full sister. His whole, not-half sister."

"What?"

"Well, he waits. And waits. And then he waits a bit longer and then, one day a couple of years later, he's out shearing his flocks out in the country somewhere and he's a bit shorthanded, so he goes to his dad and asks if David would let him take his brothers and half-brothers along with him to give him a hand. It's not such a crazy request—and by this time, the whole business with Tamar is old news—anyway, it's not obvious that Absalom has anything sneaky up his sleeve, but David still refuses to send the boys along."

"Why?"

"I dunno. Maybe he…I don't really know why he doesn't send them all out. But he doesn't. And that gives Absalom his chance. He asks if David would at least send old Amnon along. They're old pals, he's stuck without enough help to get the sheep shorn, he really needs a hand…so what can David say? That he can't have any help at all from his family? That's too much…so he says sure, Amnon can go. And that, basically, is that."

"And he kills him?"

"That's the good news. They get out into the country at dinnertime, so they can't really do any work that day. Absalom has the mess guys cook up some supper and serve more than enough wine for the two of them to get royally pissed, except that Absalom has been pouring most of each cup into this pit he's had dug right by the base of his chair in the mess hut. Anyway, he might have gotten caught, but Amnon is so relieved that he's back to being friends with Absalom that he doesn't even notice and he's drinking and getting more and more snookered until he can barely stand up...."

"And that's when the other guy kills him?"

"Well, not precisely. First he has about thirty-five of his servants line up to give Amnon the reward he had earned by jumping Tamar in the first place. I mean, Absalom himself has been commuting back and forth to Jerusalem each day—I mean, he's the son of the king of Israel, so he can hardly live in the country with the sheep—but the rest of these guys have been out with the sheep for a year, some of them for two or three years. And they haven't seen a woman in as long as they've been out there and they're so sick and tired of doing it with each other and with the sheep when they can get them to stand still long enough that they're more than ready to mount anything novel that gets in their way without giving the whole matter too much thought. Anyway, they're all lined up and it doesn't take much to get these guys in the mood. Absalom ties Amnon's wrists to his ankles and they all give it to him good, just like he gave it to Tamar—I mean, more or less the same way—and then, when number thirty-five is finished, that's when Absalom lops old Amnon's head off with this big sword he's got hidden behind one of the wall hangings in the mess tent, then goes outside into the moonlight and drop kicks it into some nearby ravine like he's O.J. trying out for the Bills and that pretty much is that. Except that he's screwed himself pretty royally with David now and he has to go hide out for a while in his grandfather's kingdom which isn't that far away, but he still doesn't have any certainty that he's ever going to see his father or his palace again...."

"And does he? Ever get back home, I mean?"

I know it must sound like I'm remembering it different than it really was. But I'm telling you, Dave's voice was quivering. He knew the story well—he had lived through it mostly, except for the part where he arranges for his father to get gangbanged and then decapitated—and now we had finally gotten to the crux of the matter: does the revenge-taker pay for his pleasure with his life—not with his life in the sense that he dies, but with the life he knows and likes, with his home life, with his family life, with the life he's come to cherish in his own digs with his own people and his own girlfriend and his own servants and all that crap—anyway, does he pay for his sin with the life he loves or does he eventually get to come home again anyway? I hadn't realized that Dave was going to take this story to heart so intensely—if I had, I probably wouldn't have made up the part about Amnon getting savaged by three dozen of his half-brother's men and then having his head cut off—but, all that being as it may, the truth is that we had reached some sort of crossroads in both our relationship and, I sensed, in our lives.

It's not like we knew each other, after all. Dave was just some kid, some boy I had picked up somewhere between Barrymore and Stanhope back in B.C. whom I hadn't ever seen previously and whom I would undoubtedly never see again once I dropped him at his grandma's in Winnipeg. Who was I to play any role at all in his life, let alone the one I sensed I was standing on the threshold of playing? I wasn't anything to him and he was even less to me—we weren't any damn thing to each other, and yet we had somehow come to a crossroads in one of our lives—I was wrong about that, it turned out, but there's no need to get into that just right now—anyway, I knew we had come to a crossroads in *at least* one of our lives and that we were about to take one fork in the road or the other. I mean that's the whole thing about crossroads, you know—you can't do nothing because even not choosing is doing something. I knew that when Helene told me that she couldn't stand the *duplicity* involved in servicing the gardener's brother behind my back and that one of us was going to have to make some adjustments—I guess she thought that spreading her legs for her new little friend was her contribution to this new era of adjustment we were about to embark upon, so all that remained was for us to find out what mine was going to be—anyway, I knew that I was standing at a kind of crossroads at that moment and that the rest of my life was going to go one way or the other depending on the very next sentence I spoke aloud. It was an upsetting moment, but it was also cool in its own disconcerting way and I'm at least slightly proud of the fact that I recognized that as it was happening. Anyway, I've stood at other thresholds in my life too, but this was the first time in a while I had stood so clearly at someone else's. It turned out that I was wrong about that too…but I'll get there.

Anyway, there was a question hanging on the cool, dry air in my ancient Camaro as we moved through the prairie night along a ribbon of a road between Endoz, where we had seen men die, and Houghton, where the future awaited us. I know that sounds trite as hell—I mean the future awaits you when you go into the crapper in some Italian restaurant to take a leak too, for that matter—but there are moments when the present really is suspended between the past and the future in a way that's slightly more profound than the theoretical sense that it always is. If you haven't been there, you probably won't know what I mean. But maybe you can catch some glimmer of what I'm talking about anyway. And so, grasping the steering wheel with my left hand while I jammed my right hand in between my thighs for some warmth, I answered the question, more than aware that there are times when saying the truth is also a kind of a lie.

"Yes," I said, regretting my words even as they were coming out of my mouth, "he gets to go home again. It takes a while and it doesn't really end up too good for either of them, but Absalom does indeed get to go home again."

"Because his father forgives him?"

I sighed, then hesitated and feigned this big yawn. "Yeah," I said after slightly too long a pause, "because his father forgives him. Eventually."

"Wow."

"But only eventually."

"Even so, man. Even so…."

XV

I had been wrong about the distance and we ended up pulling into Houghton just after five in the morning. Now Houghton isn't too lively, I don't suspect, in the best of times, but there's *really* nothing going on at five A.M. If there were truckers who went through there in the early morning hours having early breakfasts, they must have been eating somewhere else. If there were enterprising teenagers delivering early copies of the Winnipeg papers, then their routes must have taken them along side alleys and back streets rather than along the section of route 17 rather pompously—for a town with only one shopping street, I mean—called Main Street. If there were shift workers winding their tired ways back home after a long night's work in the Canadian Bible Shredding Plant (or whatever CBSP stood for on the immense puke-green building with the tall crematoria-style smokestacks we passed about two miles west of town), they must have been shy to show themselves along their delightful town's only street at such an ungodly hour. We found parking easily enough—or I did, since Dave was fast asleep—since there were no other cars at all lining the street (and, even more amazingly, no street signs prohibiting overnight parking), so I pulled over and turned off the ignition. I rolled down the window, pushed my seat back as far as it would go and closed my eyes. When I opened them, it was about ten after eight in the morning.

Dave hadn't fallen asleep immediately after I finished my story about Amnon and Tamar, but it had been equally clear to me that he didn't want to discuss the obvious parallels between his parents' story and the tale of the randy prince and his woe-begotten half-sister in more detail than we already had by the time I got to its semi-encouraging denouement. Now the story wasn't precisely parallel to his parents', at least (I should add) not to the part I had heard that evening that we drove from Saskatchewan to Manitoba, but it must have been close enough for discomfort. And I sensed plenty of that emanating from Dave's side of the car…and not just discomfort, either. There was a kind of electric interest in the story that I was fascinated to notice Dave trying his best (and failing pretty utterly) to conceal. It was like the story had suddenly taken a bunch of disparate ideas that had come to him intermittently over the years and given them a frame that brought them together and juxtaposed them against each other in a way that cast them all in a slightly differ-ent light than the one that emanated from each of them when considered individually. I don't know—maybe I'm reading more into Dave's silence than anyone should, but I had the sense that he was deep in thought as he sat there saying nothing at all, his eyes wide open in the cool air of a summer's night on the prairies.

And now it was morning, take two, in Houghton. There were another four or five cars parked on Main Street now, one in front of the Dairy Queen, one in front of the Pharmasave and the others in front of Eve's Kitchen Table. Dave was awake when I opened my eyes, but he was still sitting there staring straight ahead like he had been just before he had finally fallen asleep. I didn't say anything at all, just got out of the car. He followed as though this had been the plan all along and simply wasn't worth the effort of confirming out loud.

Eve's Kitchen Table was your average small-town eatery, I guess. We headed into the men's room, emptied our bladders at adjacent urinals and went back into the main room to get some breakfast organized. I asked for oatmeal and tea, which came almost immediately. Dave ordered three fried eggs, sausage links, hash browns, rye toast and coffee, which took a few minutes to arrive at our table. We sat there without saying much—all I could think to say other than what I really wanted to talk about was to comment on the way my young friend had folded his hands backwards behind his head when we were in the men's room and cracked his knuckles one by one while taking his leak—but it was clear that he wasn't that interested in small talk. That was fine with me, but once our waitress—not Eve herself, but a very short, pretty native woman with the name Betty embroidered on her excessively starched, vertically striped pink and white blouse—brought Dave's meal, it seemed like the right moment to have the conversation we were obviously going to have sometime that day.

"We're about two, three hours from the 'peg."

Silence.

"You know your grandma's address."

"No."

"Well, how can I drop you if I don't know where she lives?"

"I know where she lives. I just don't know the address."

"But you can get me there?"

"I guess. She's in the North End near this big church."

"I can get to the North End easy enough, but you're going to have to navigate from there."

"No sweat."

"She expecting you?"

"No."

"What if she's not there?"

"Why wouldn't she be there?"

"How should I know? Maybe she's off in some cabin on Lake Winnipeg helping one of the priests from that big church near her house find out what he's been missing all these years. Maybe she's in Paris taking cooking classes at the Academie Française de Cooking. Maybe she's in Burma trying to buy up cheap opium for the Manitoba market. Maybe she's wandering naked through the forest trying to find God…."

"What are you talking about?"

"Nothing."

Long pause.

"What are you really going to do in Winnipeg?" It was my question to him, but it was, of course, also my question to myself. I remembered vaguely having a reason to drive from B.C. to Winnipeg, but I couldn't for the life of me recall what it had been. Was this supposed to be some pirsigian journey of self-discovery across the continent in which I would find meaning in my parents being crazy, my brother being dead, my career being in the toilet, my daughter being gone from my life and my wife living non-*duplicitously* in California with our former gardener's brother? It sounded likely, but I really couldn't remember. Or was this just something to do to get away from having to deal with the reality of my sorry life? That sounded both less likely and far more cogent, but I decided to ignore the larger picture for as long as I could. I tucked into my oatmeal, signalled Betty for some more tea and waited for Dave's answer to the question I actually had asked. The answer to the unasked one, I told myself firmly, would have to wait until I had the strength to pose it openly and he had the courage to address it honestly, two hurdles we would not necessarily clear simultaneously.

"I don't know. Visit my grandma. See my friends, I guess."

"You have friends in the 'peg?"

"Not really. But the family that lives next door to my grandma has a kid my age in it. He was arrested two years ago and sent to some youth ranch place for hitting his mother, but he might be back by now."

"They usually don't give you two years for hitting your mother," I observed cautiously.

"It was with their car."

"Oh."

"But she was okay and everything. That's why it wasn't, you know, murder or anything. And he was in youth court, so that meant he couldn't get more than two years."

"I think it's three."

"That's in B.C. Maybe it's different in Manitoba."

"I don't think so."

"Whatever."

Dave tucked into his meal like he hadn't eaten in days. Dinner at Denny's the night before hadn't been great, but I had come away more or less satisfied. Dave had only eaten a hamburger and some fries—although he had finished up with two decent-sized pieces of pie (one raisin-apple, one strawberry-rhubarb)—and was apparently ravenous. He ate everything on his plate, then slightly pathetically asked me—we had long since stopped discussing who was going to pay for everything whenever we went in anywhere to eat since there wasn't really anything to say—anyway, he finished his meal, then asked if he could have another order of toast. I held up his toast plate, caught Betty's eye and mouthed the word "more" to her. She appeared to understand instantly and it wasn't more than twenty minutes after that that she appeared back at our table with a plate of cold, greasy toast.

I had plenty of things to say, but something told me to wait for Dave to speak. He buttered one of the pieces of toast—it had actually come buttered, but he opened one of the little pots of margarine on the table and rather assiduously set to buttering it, so to speak, again. He then applied a thin layer of strawberry jam to the toast as though this were a difficult task that needed to be carried out with precision and grace. I thought briefly of that scene in that movie—the one Robin Williams remade—where that French butch homo guy tries to teach that French fairy homo guy how to butter toast like a man, but the idea only skirted through my head without really taking hold and before I could ask myself why that was—which, by the way, why was it?—anyway, before I could get involved in asking myself whether that particular thought had any bearing on any aspect of the fact that I was apparently driving across half of Canada with a boy only slightly more than half my age who was travelling with no baggage at all, who wore the same clothes every day and whom I had somehow come to know could crack his knuckles behind his head and pee at the same time, Dave had something of his own to say.

"You believe in hell?" he asked, apparently seriously.

"You mean other than this one we're living through right now?"

"What?"

"Nothing. You mean like with devils and pitchforks and the eternal fire of damnation lapping at the heels of sinners too late repentant of their repulsive deeds?"

"I guess."

"No."

"No what?"

"No, I don't believe in hell like that."

"But you do believe in it?"

"Yeah, I guess so. I think that there's something after the grave. Something that sort of evens up the score you leave behind. So like if you're this great guy who always does good things for everybody and you get cancer and die while your wife is pregnant with your first child or if you're this unbelievable creep who's mean and cruel to everybody and you end up fabulously wealthy anyway and live in the lap of luxury and you make it to ninety-nine and die in bed immediately after—not even while—giving it to your twenty-three year old wife—I think there must be some system afterwards for evening things up and getting the good people some return on their uncompensated goodness and the bad people a chance to suffer for all the bad things they did."

"Even that guy who killed all those kids in B.C.?"

"Especially him. Hitler too. All of them…."

Long pause. "How about guys who rape women?"

I hesitated before answering, but I knew that I owed Dave an honest answer. He was, after all, being honest (I thought) with me. "Them too," I said, speaking a bit excessively clearly.

"And who beat kids?"

"Yeah."

"I don't."

"Don't what?"

"Believe in any of that stuff. I think that when you die, you're dead and that's that. I mean, if there's a God, then why would any kids get hit?"

I couldn't think of anything to say, so I didn't respond.

"I used to hear them all the time, you know," Dave continued, apparently taking my silence for an admission that a fatal flaw had been uncovered in my theodicy.

"Who?" I knew who, but I thought I was supposed to ask.

"My folks. I used to lie in my bed in our bedroom—my brother and me, we had bunk beds and I was on the bottom—anyway, he used to fall right asleep—or maybe he just said he did afterwards, but he always did say that he never heard anything—anyway, he said that, but I didn't and that's because I really didn't fall asleep, almost ever. I'd hear him slapping her around and I'd hear her whimpering and begging him not to hit her anymore and then I'd hear them thrashing around on the floor and his grunting and her crying and then it would be quiet for a long time and then either the TV would go on or he'd put on some Beatles records—he had this real thing for the Beatles, like they were this really great band instead of a bunch of English creeps who couldn't even play their own instruments—and she'd clean up and he'd head off to bed as though they had just spent a pleasant evening watching some favourite program on television and he needed to get to bed so he could be rested for another busy day of making doors and raping people the next day."

"And how long did that go on?"

"From as far back as I can remember until the day before my mother drowned herself."

"Tell me about that.

"Well, there isn't too much to tell. It was a day like all the rest. My father had come home drunk from some party—he was a violent son of a bitch, but he didn't really drink too much and I hardly ever remember him being really polluted, at least not at home. Anyway, this time he did come home drunk. Really drunk. And he wasn't in a great mood. My mother had dinner ready—it was after midnight, but she knew what happened if dinner wasn't waiting whenever the hell he came home—anyway, she had his dinner waiting, but it wasn't what he had wanted—not that he ever told her what he wanted, but she was somehow supposed to know anyway. So she had made hamburgers and mashed pota-toes and a salad and he had wanted something else, so he threw the plate of hamburgers and a jar of relish on the floor and then told her to clean up the mess. We were in bed already—this was when I was seventeen and Kevin was sixteen—and he went really nuts, kicking her and screaming at her and then he must have knocked her down and did her right there on the mess of broken glass and hamburgers and relish and I guess the smell must have really gotten to him—unless it was the sight of all the blood from the cuts on her back all over the hamburgers—well, it must have been something because after he finished raping her, he puked all over the floor and got some of the puke on her—she must have still been lying there on the floor—and then he started yelling at her to clean up the whole goddam mess or he'd goddam kill her."

"And you and Kevin were awake?"

"Look, this is what it was all about. We should have come out and just killed him ourselves, but we didn't. Kevin was this little guy not more than five foot four or five and really skinny and frail—we thought he had some bone disease when he was a kid, but it didn't turn out to be anything really bad—anyway, the two of us were lying in bed listening to all of this—maybe Kevin really was asleep like he always said, but I think he was up and I know I was…but we were just too scared to come out and do anything. I mean, Dad wasn't just drunk, he was completely nuts. And he would have killed us if we had come out. That was one of the big rules in our family—that you weren't supposed to come out of your room after you went to sleep ever. I mean, we weren't supposed to drink anything after seven o'clock so we wouldn't ever have to pee in the middle of the night—that's how sick the situation was. But we should have come out this one time, but we didn't. And we both have to live with that…."

"Then what happened?"

"Nothing too much. He must have passed out on the couch or on his bed or somewhere and things quieted down. My mother cleaned the house really carefully, including the mess on the floor. Then she took a long shower—I could hear the water running for maybe twenty, twenty-five minutes—and then I thought she went to bed, but she didn't. And then a few minutes later, I heard the front door of the house open and close and the ignition get turned on and the garage door open and I heard her drive away. I thought she was just going out to get something—I know it must have been almost two in the morning—that's another thing, we weren't allowed to have a clock in our room for some reason—anyway, it must have been at least two and I thought, well, she's going out to get something or maybe—I hoped—to go to the police or maybe to the hospital if he really hurt her."

"But she didn't go to any of those places?"

"She went to the Oak Street Bridge and jumped into the river is what she did."

"You're sure it wasn't an accident?"

"She left a note. I told you."

"Where did she leave it?"

"Well, she didn't really leave it. She wrote it and put a stamp on it and mailed it from the corner. To me personally. It came two days later."

"And what did it say?"

"You don't think I know it by heart?"

"I'm sure you do."

"You wanna hear it?"

"Sure."

"'Dear Darling Boys,' it said, 'Don't hate me for doing this. I love you and I think you'll both be okay. Love, Mommy.'"

"That was it?"

"That was it."

"Shit."

"You said it. Kevin was gone a few days after the funeral. I stuck it out, but I was hardly ever home. My dad wasn't ever there either, although I'm not sure where he ever was. Porking some lady from the factory some of the time, but the rest of where he was, I don't know. Anyway, we had this home, but no one was ever there. My father sort of calmed down, but weeks would pass without me seeing him. I don't even think he realized Kevin was gone for more than two or three weeks after he left. I screwed up school, then stopped going. I started working a little, but it didn't really work out real good. This was all more than two years ago, by the way. I eventually took a course at some place that the government pays to train drop-outs to do something useful and I actually got a job selling computers. It was okay for a while, but I later realized that the manager was robbing the place blind and I was afraid I'd get in trouble if I stayed, so I finally said to hell with this and off I went onto the on ramp of the Trans-Canada and I got a lift to Hope, then to Barrymore, then a little further. You picked me up right after that. And here we are…." His voice trailed off.

"That was the Monkees, by the way."

"What?"

"The ones who couldn't play their own instruments. You said it was the Beatles, but they were real musicians, more or less. And they really did make some good music although a lot of what they put out was only fair."

"They were really big though in the sixties, right?"

"Huge."

"Bigger than Arrowsmith?"

"I'd like to think so."

XVI

We didn't end up staying too long in Houghton. We had each drunk at least three or four cups of coffee at breakfast, but either Betty had inadvertently poured us decaf or we were just so completely bushed as to be unable to respond normally to the caffeine, but for whatever reason, we both really needed to rest up a bit before heading south to Winnipeg. As luck would have it, there was a provincial park just south of town with public washrooms—Betty had made a special point of mentioning the washrooms as though this were a point of exceptional municipal pride among the Houghtonians—and a parking lot that was usually empty until afternoon where we could sack out for at least a couple of hours. We were both anxious to get to Winnipeg, but we didn't want to kill ourselves in the effort. We headed for the park.

The Bob Staley Provincial Forest turned out to be just as described, or at least its parking lot and public washrooms did. We pulled in, pushed back our seats and slept until noon. By the time we awoke, there were a few other cars in the lot, but if anyone had paid us any attention, they hadn't done so loudly enough to wake either of us from our beauty sleep. When we did wake up, I made a big point of taking a full change of clothing from the trunk and offering Dave at least some clean underwear and a new shirt. My stuff would be big on him, but this was the trunk of my Camaro we were talking about, not the Bay, and I couldn't offer what I didn't have. I told him he could pay me for them some day if he really wanted or he could just take the stuff as a gift or he could donate them to some thrift shop somewhere when he had the dough to replace them and we'd call it square. I could see that he was tempted, but that something was holding him back. I didn't push the point.

We headed into the washroom. I brushed my teeth with my toothbrush, while he smeared toothpaste on the index finger of his right hand and attempted to brush that way. While he did, I stripped down and got dressed in my fresh clothing. I could see that he was still debating whether or not to take me up on my offer of some clean jockeys and a new T, but in the end, he didn't say anything at all and I decided not to push the point. After all, this was his grandma we were going to drop in on in a just a few hours, not mine. And if he wanted to be wearing the same clothing he had worn for the last week when we got there, then in what sense was that my business? I made a point of brushing my hair and washing my face as slowly as possible in case he did end up changing his mind, but he apparently didn't and I didn't force him to explain himself. Who knows? Maybe he was just afraid his grandma was going to take one look at him and ask him whose briefs he had on and he didn't want to have to start in with her on the precise nature of our admittedly unusual relationship even more than he would have liked to get out of underwear he had been wearing (as far as I could tell) since I met him.

The drive south was as uneventful as I had expected it was going to be and we were in Winnipeg just before four in the afternoon. We stopped at a Petro-Canada station for gas and to check out Dave's grandmother's address in a phone book, but she wasn't listed. Still, he was certain that if I drove into downtown and then took the main road up into the North End, he'd know where to go. It had been more than six years since he had been there, he admitted, but he wasn't worried. The whole city, he insisted a bit more hopefully than reasonably, wasn't that big. And if we could find this big church near her house with a red brick facade and a sign in some language Dave thought might be Ukrainian in front, then he was going to be able to find his way to grandmother's house in jig time.

I was highly dubious, but it turned out the kid was right. We headed into the North End, drove around in circles for about twenty-five minutes before we found ourselves in front of St. Pyotr's Ukrainian Cathedral of the Holy Trinity with its facade of red brick and its bilingual signage. Grandma lived just three or four blocks up the road and, amazingly enough, Dave was able to say with certainty which of the two or three thousand identical homes that lined the street was hers. I had intended all along to drop Dave in front and be on my way, but now that we were actually parking in front of the house, I found myself oddly—and entirely unexpectedly—reticent to part company with my travelling companion of these last few days.

"You wanna come in?" Dave's voice was flat. Did he hope I'd agree or did he expect me to thank him for his offer and then get gone as quickly as decency would allow? I wasn't sure.

"I'll wait in the car until you see if someone's home. But thanks."

"It don't matter—I can just sit on the porch and wait if she's out."

"What if she's out of town?" Or dead, I thought to myself.

"Look, man, I'm not your problem. I mean, I appreciate the lift and I know we've had a couple of pretty intense days together…but you don't owe me anything. I needed to get to here and now I am here. So you're very welcome to hang with us for a few days if you want, but you're also free to get moving to wherever it is you were going when you picked me up. Okay? I mean, it's not like I'm wearing your underwear or anything."

So that was it—borrowing anything like underwear or a t-shirt from me would have created the context an ongoing relationship Dave wasn't entirely sure he wanted to undertake. I got the point and was…somewhere between irritated and relieved. On the other hand, there didn't seem to be any point in mentioning just at this particular moment that I had embarked on a major journey with a suitcase of underwear and t-shirts in the trunk and no particular destination in mind, so I didn't say anything at all for a while. And when I did speak, it was in a distant voice that, I hoped, concealed the sudden panic I was feeling at the prospect of being alone. "Sure," I said. "Whatever." Then, as though the idea had just occurred to me. "Go see if she's home and then we'll figure out what comes next."

Dave didn't say a word as he got out of the car. He walked up to the front door and pushed the doorbell. I couldn't hear anything, but the way I could see him straightening up his body and pushing back his hair onto the top of his head made it clear that he could. In a moment, the door opened.

I couldn't quite see who was in the doorway, but Dave was clearly speaking quickly now, his body hunched over in the manner of someone sharing secrets with somebody a good deal shorter than oneself. When he finally straightened up and stepped away from the door, I could see a teenaged boy of about eighteen standing next to him. The boy was scrawny—he was wearing torn-off denim shorts and white athletic socks, but no shirt or shoes—and less fair than Dave, but I somehow knew intuitively—and absolutely—that this had to be Kevin, Dave's apparently no longer long lost brother. I got out of the car and came towards the door from the outside just as the boys' grandmother approached from the inside. It was an awkward moment. She hugged Dave and didn't seem to notice me, but Kevin did and we shook hands and exchanged names. His voice was thinner than Dave's, but there was something cocky, almost belligerent in his stance and it was clear to me that he had been through a lot. His hair was so short that I had to look twice to see if he had any hair on his head at all and he had a Chinese character of some sort tattooed on his left shoulder. He also wore a tiny gold ring in his left nipple—which, for some reason, attracted my attention almost immediately—and a matching one in his right ear. Kevin wasn't anywhere as good looking as his big brother, but he did have a certain raw vitality to him that was as distinct and different from his brother's placid demeanour as it was attractive in a vaguely threatening sort of way.

Grandma turned out to have a name, which was Abigail Kleist. And she turned out to be lovely, hospitable and kind, all of which were very welcome to me at this particular juncture in my life's journey. We all stood for a long moment in the doorway, but once she seized the fact that her second grandson had appeared unexpectedly on her doorstep in the company of a man who, for obscure—or at least unstated—reasons, had taken it upon himself to drive him from B.C. to Winnipeg, she insisted that I stay for dinner, which she was just making. I could stay the night too if I needed or wished to. I couldn't say that I really, truly, needed to, but I found, slightly to my surprise, that I did indeed wish to spend a night under Abigail Kleist's roof. She was friendly and pleasant and even before I brought my suitcase in from the car, I found myself wondering if it was as obvious to her as it was to me that we were going to spend the night together, she and I. But I'm getting slightly ahead of myself....

Dinner was a great feast of home-made fish and chips washed down with beer and followed by coffee, apple pie and Breyer's vanilla ice cream I myself had been sent by Abigail to purchase in the corner store. We all helped to clear the table, but Abigail send the boys in to watch some TV right after that while "the big people" (as she called herself and me) washed the dishes and finished up in the kitchen. Kevin, it turned out, was working for some big construction firm at a site a few miles east of town and needed to be in bed by ten if he was going to wake up early enough the next morning to get to work on time and Dave, despite our snooze that same morning in the parking lot of the Bob Staley Provincial Forest, appeared to be almost as bushed as his brother. They watched a show or two on TV, then headed off to bed. I could hear the water of the shower running and wondered what two brothers who hadn't seen each other for two years would talk about once they were finally alone. Did Kevin ask Dave who exactly I was in his life and why it was that I had ended up staying with them? Could the topic of their mother's death have come up already? Or would it swim around safely beneath the surface for a while—if that's not the wrong metaphor to use given their mother's self-chosen method of suicide—and take its time before eventually deciding to come to the surface? Was there mistrust between the brothers? Love? Uncertainty? Friendship? Suspicion? Were they both naked together in the bathroom while one showered and the other waited his turn or was one waiting in the bedroom while the other one finished up in the john on his own? Or had they just stepped into the shower together as they probably had done when they were little boys? Did Kevin ask Dave about their father? Did Dave ask Kevin where he'd been for the last two years? Did Dave ask about the tattoo? As little as any of these questions were even remotely any of my business, I found myself occupied by them as I stood next to Abigail Kleist and dried her dinner dishes while she wrapped up the left-over fish in plastic wrap, then in tin foil. She took a roll of masking tape from a drawer, pasted a piece of it on the tin foil and wrote the words "Fried Fish" across its length. I remember noticing that she wrote exclusively in capital letters, except for the e, which she for some reason wrote in lower case. The few left over chips, she dumped into the garbage disposal unit in the sink.

Slowly, the house quieted down. The shower stopped running. The boys stopped talking and were either whispering or sleeping, probably the latter. The neighbours' Patsy Cline recording came to an end and was not replaced with a different one. The dog—Abigail had a standard poodle named Ruth—whimpered for a while, then finished her dinner and curled up on a blanket left for this purpose at the back door. The dishes were done, the fish was stored in the freezer along with the leftover ice cream. I felt somewhere between nervous and foolish, but Abigail was a good looking woman and I felt myself responding as much to the situation as to her personally. You know, when Dave had mentioned his grandmother, I had assumed that she would be in her sixties or seventies and would look like my own grandmother had looked when I was Dave's age. But now that I was alone with her, it struck me that she couldn't be much older than fifty-five and was possibly even less than that. She was zoftig in a very appealing way with fleshy, rounded hips, a large, slightly freckled bosom (she was wearing a kind of ribbed tank-top with a floral design on it that showed more than enough cleavage for me to have been able to make this observation almost immediately upon meeting her) and long, blond-and-black streaked hair pulled back into a pony-tail that hung halfway down her back. She looked like the kind of woman who would like making love to a man in a field of corn or on a boat or maybe in the back of a pick-up. I wasn't sure I was up to romance, but I felt myself rising to the occasion anyway.

"You sure don't look like my grandma used to," I began, hoping to break the ice with a compliment.

"And how did she look?"

"Well, she was about five feet tall, wore her white hair in a bun and had boobs that drooped down to her knees."

She laughed. "Just give me a few years."

"How old are you actually?"

"Does that matter?"

I paused for a moment. "No, not really."

"But you'd like to know?"

"Only if you'd like to say. Otherwise, forget the whole thing."

"Fifty-three."

"Wow."

"Well, are you going to do the math or shall I do it for you?"

I felt my face reddening. "If you want," I croaked out, suddenly more than aware that I was doing this entirely the wrong way.

"Well, if I'm fifty-three and Dave is nineteen, then that would mean I was thirty-four when he was born, right?"

"I guess."

"Well, let's see then. How can a thirty-four year old woman have a grandchild? Oh, I know, when she was raped by her father's best friend when she was fourteen. Then when Dave's mother ended up pregnant when she was twenty, that made me a thirty-four year old grandma. And now Dave is nineteen and I'm fifty-three. And how old would you be? Now that we're having truth night in the North End, I mean…."

"Thirty-four."

"Really?"

"You mean I look older or younger than thirty-four?"

"That would depend on whether you're fishing for compliments or insults."

Something told me not to pursue this particular line of reasoning and, for once, I obeyed my inclination. I liked this woman, but I wasn't quite sure how to proceed. I pretended to wipe a plate that was already bone dry, but what I was really doing was trying to figure out if I had ever slept with a grandmother before. It seemed unlikely, but really who knew? In the meantime, my hostess was leaning against the kitchen counter watching me.

"So," she said finally, as thought this were the result of some prolonged internal deliberation, "what do you think?"

"About what?"

"About spending the night with me. In my room. In my bed."

"You mean without getting married first?"

"Well, maybe just this once…."

XVII

G randma Abigail turned out to be one of the greats. She wasn't just energetic, although she was certainly that as well, as much as driven—and the results were spectacular. We had finally retired to her bedroom at about midnight. She had listened to the CBC news while I washed up in the bathroom and then left me to monitor the sports—she was particularly interested in knowing how the Red Sox had done that afternoon for some reason—while she brushed her teeth and washed her face. When she came back into the bedroom, she was naked except for a pair of black panties and I was still wearing my trousers and my shirt. She signalled me to stand up, paused for a moment to turn off the radio—and to ask for the Boston-New York score—then set herself to unbuttoning my shirt and pulling my trousers down to around my ankles. I stepped out of them and shucked off my open shirt as she put my hands on her breasts, which were even larger and more impressive than I had expected, and kissed me…and those were the last few experiences I had that evening that were even remotely similar to anything I could recall from my past.

Abigail wasn't an especially tall woman, but I felt dwarfed by her as she pushed me back onto the bed and, after bringing me to a state of total arousal in a variety of ways I don't think I'll mention just right here, lowered herself onto me for the first time that evening. It wasn't even so much that it felt wonderful to be inside a woman who wasn't charging by the hour as much as it was that it felt liberating and deeply satisfying, maybe even thrilling, to be part of the world again. I know that must sound more than slight-ly pathetic for me to admit, but there you have it: when all is said and done and the need to espouse only politically correct atti-tudes is blissfully absent, what man really feels that he belongs to the world when he has to pay someone to get laid?

Anyway, she rode me like a cowboy, then begged for more. I completely forgot the boys were in the house—which I don't regret for a second now, since neither of them stirred until morn-ing—and gave myself over entirely to desire. It was an incredible evening in the technical sense of the word—one that I wouldn't have believed possible had anyone described it to me in advance and that I don't really expect anyone to believe from my pale, accurate but totally inadequate description of it. We did it in a dozen different positions, failing only at one she showed me in a volume of erotic Indian miniatures she kept in her night table that required me to penetrate her while the soles of my right and her left feet were pushed up against one another and our other legs were snaked around each other's behinds. I've thought of that position often—I actually found and bought a copy of that same book in a second-hand shop on Pender Street in Vancouver six months later when I was in town to look in on my parents—but aside from that single failure to fulfill that single one of Abigail's fantasies, which I still think you'd need rubber knee joints even to attempt, I think I can accurately say that neither of us experienced any disappointment at all in the course of the entire evening. I know I didn't…and it's also worth saying that the passage of time hasn't done anything to make me feel differently.

By a quarter to three, we were done. I was totally exhaust-ed—as I flatter myself to think she almost must have been—and I would have gladly turned out the light and gone to sleep, but Abigail was too keyed up to end our evening on such a prosaic note. She had her bedside lamp on some sort of rheostat which allowed her to turn it down real low, which she did. Then, nestling up against my back so that I could feel her breasts pressed up against me, she reached around and began to stroke the hair on my chest.

"Davie says you tell good stories," she said unexpectedly.

"He did? When?"

"When you went down to the store for the ice cream."

"What did he say?"

"Just that, that you tell good stories. Weird ones, he said, but good. And you claim they're from the Bible."

"What else did he tell you about me?"

"That you're kind."

"Anything else?"

"That you admire men who can crack their knuckles and pee at the same time."

I couldn't quite think what to say to that, so I said nothing at all.

"So do you want to tell me a story?"

"What kind of story?" I was dog tired, but I owed this lady too much to give in to my own fatigue when even one of her desires was unfulfilled. Does it sound corny to put it that way? I guess it must, but that's precisely what I was thinking. And, even worse, I really didn't want to disappoint her. "A fairy tale? Or maybe a fable?"

"How about something sexy?"

"How about something about the first Abigail?"

"The first Abigail? Who was that?"

I widened my eyes in feigned amazement. "King David's wife. Who else?"

Now it was her turn to widen her eyes. "King David in the Bible?"

"That's the one."

"His wife's name was Abigail?"

"One of them."

"One of his wife's names? Or the name of one of his wives?"

"The latter."

"Tell me!"

I drew myself up into a kind of sitting position in bed. The comforter was tucked into the foot of the bed—we had spent most of our evening on top of it, but now that we were beneath it, it held fast and when I sat up, I was suddenly only covered to the top of my thighs. Abigail sat up next to me, her breasts supported from below by a pillow she was clutching to her chest, but otherwise as exposed as I was, although somehow distinctly less vulnerable.

"Well," I began, trying to recall how the story in the Bible begins, "there was this guy named Nabal. A real villain. Mean. Ornery. Not too smart. But rich as Croesus. Anyway, he had this wife whom he didn't deserve. Smart. Clever. Beautiful. Generous. Her name was Abigail…."

"Abigail what?"

"Not Kleist, that's for sure. They didn't have last names in those days like us. She was just Abigail, wife of Nabal…."

"And before she got married?"

"Then she was Abigail, daughter of whatever her father's name was. But we're getting off track. She was lovely and bright and he was nasty and stingy and then it happened one day that he was out shearing his sheep and his goats—he had thousands of animals, so he wasn't doing it himself, but he was out supervising the shearing of his flocks in a place called Carmel."

"Like in California?"

"Precisely. Only this wasn't in California because there wasn't any California yet. Or I guess there was, but no one called it that. Anyway, he's out there in Carmel getting his sheep and goats shorn and suddenly ten of David's men—David was the future king of Israel, but at this point he's still living like an outlaw in the wilderness trying to keep King Saul from blowing him away before he could replace him—before David could replace Saul, I mean—before he could replace him as king. So anyway, he has this protection racket going…."

"No shit."

"Not a lick. Anyway, he sends his guys around to find Nabal and tell them that he's already anted up his part by not attacking Nabal's shepherds while they've been out with the sheep and that now it's old Nabal's turn to come up with some cash. They tell him they'll take whatever he can give, but the message is clear enough: either make it worth our while after the fact not to have attacked your flocks and stolen your sheep or don't count on that kind of forbearance next time."

"So what happens?"

"So Nabal tells them to go to hell."

"Good for him!"

"I think so too—although the Biblical storyteller sure doesn't think so—but anyway, the guys go back and report what Nabal said to David. And David is pissed. He's *really* pissed. And this time, he comes himself to see Nabal…and he brings four hundred men, all girt with swords."

"And does that get his attention?"

"Well, it surely would have, but that's where Abigail comes in. She hears about what happened and she knows that her husband has really screwed up. I mean, she knows what David is capable of and that he's not going to just forget the whole thing and go put the screws on somebody else. And she knows that if she doesn't act, they'll both be ruined."

"So she married David?"

"Not so fast. She rummages around the house and puts together as good a gift as she can muster in the time she's got to work in. She doesn't do too bad—judging from the story, their pantry must have been the size of a Safeway—anyway, she puts it together and heads out only to run smack into David and his men on their way to put the screws to Nabal. So she's all my husband is a huge scoundrel—his name even means scoundrel in Hebrew—and he's too stupid to know what he's doing and he didn't really mean anything and here's the damn protection money anyhow and just take it and leave us alone."

"And what does David say to that?"

"Well, one thing about David—he knew a good looking woman when he saw one. So this beautiful woman is standing in the road in front of him wearing denim shorts and this ribbed tank top with flowers all over it and enough of her cleavage showing for David to get a good look at her freckles and she's offering him this amazing set of gifts and things—if I remember, she had something on the order of two hundred fig cakes alone—anyway, this stunning woman with really, really sexy long blond-and-black streaked hair pulled back into this fantastic ponytail is standing in front of him bearing just precisely the kind of supplies he needs—fig cakes and wine and bread and licorice and a thousand salamis and a couple of cases of decent single-malt and about a hundred cartons of cigarettes…."

"What kind?"

"Benson and Hedges. Menthols."

"Wow…that is a good gift."

"I told you she was smart. Anyway, she practically throws herself on the ground in front of him and begs him to take the damn presents and go back wherever he came from, but by then, it's too late. I mean, he doesn't give a damn about Nabal anymore, but he's in love."

"With Abigail?"

"With who else?"

"So what happens then?"

"Actually, the end of the story is the best part. She comes home and she's all thrilled about having saved her husband's ass and she finds he's not only not worrying about David and what might happen next, but he's giving this ridiculous party and all his friends are there and everybody is drunk and there are dancing girls and even a few dancing boys and hot and cold hors d'oeuvres and in the middle of the whole thing, Nabal himself is so looped that he can't even stand up. So Abigail announces that the party is over and everybody goes home and she somehow gets Nabal undressed and in bed—he's basically unconscious the whole time—and then goes to sleep herself wondering what in the world she's going to do with this stingy, hard-ass drunk she's gotten herself married to."

"And when they get up the next day?"

"Well, that's just the thing. They do get up and he's hung over like a horse, but she tells him what happened anyway and he gets the picture. The Bible says that his courage died and he became like a stone...."

Abigail's eyes twinkled as she reached down between my legs. "Hard and smooth? Like a stone like that?"

"No," I answered, leaving her hand where it had landed, "not like that. Cold and silent and incapable of action. And that was just the beginning. Ten days later, he was dead."

"Wow. And what happened then?"

"Well, you can just guess, can't you? David hears that Nabal is dead—he must have been real sorry to hear that—anyway, he gets wind of Nabal's death and he send his boys on down to propose marriage."

"And she accepts?"

"Well, she has to wait for a decent interval of mourning before she remarries, so she holds off for about twelve seconds, then agrees."

"And they marry?"

"They do."

"And do they live happily ever after?"

"Well, they have a kid, so they must have been okay."

"And does having a kid mean you're happily married? My

daughter had a kid, two actually…."

The text of the note Abigail's daughter had mailed to her sons before jumping into the Fraser passed through my mind. Had she really signed it Mommy or did Dave just wish she had? And where was that note now, I suddenly found myself wondering. Did Dave save it as some sort of gruesome souvenir? Had Abigail ever seen it? Was it perhaps tucked away somewhere in the back of a drawer in the very room I was in at that moment? All these pointless questions flitted through my head in a matter of seconds, but not so quickly that I couldn't register them and promise myself to work them through at a more leisurely moment. "No," I answered, thinking suddenly of the way Lena looked through the window of her mother's car as the two of them drove off into their new life and left me on my own, "it doesn't. But David and Abigail were okay. It wasn't perfect, but what marriage is?"

"Actually, my parents had a pretty good marriage."

"And you?"

"And me what?"

"And you, what was your marriage like?"

"I'll let you know if I ever get married…."

"You've never been married?"

"It's not that easy for fourteen-year-old mothers to get a date."

I was suddenly exhausted and I couldn't think how to respond to that anyway. "You want to get some sleep?" I asked.

"Sure."

"You don't want to hear another story?"

She didn't answer, merely turned out the light, slid under the comforter and kissed my cheek.

"You too," I responded wittily.

"Sure," came the reply. And then the room was completely still and she was asleep.

XVIII

The Kleist household woke up earlier than I would have thought possible for two teenagers and a woman who had made love like a truckdriver in training for the triathalon. Kevin had to be at work at a quarter past seven, which meant him getting into the shower around six and his grandmother having his breakfast on the table for him no later than twenty-five minutes past the hour. Since Abigail had no intention of serving breakfast three separate times—and since she appeared to feel that she had to get up to serve Kevin his breakfast, which (if you ask me) was the main point—she saw no reason not to rouse Dave and me to join them at the table. I don't know—I must have been so tired that I didn't even ask what time it was, but somehow there I was with three hours of sleep behind me sitting at Abigail's kitchen table at six-thirty in the morning eating—this is the best part—eating flapjacks with real maple syrup, oatmeal and toast.

"A little heavy on the carbohydrates, don't you think?" I asked as delicately as possible.

"I think most people could do with considerably more starch in their diets than the conventional diet books recommend," she answered, sounding for the life of me like she meant it entirely seriously.

I was too tired to argue. I ate half a flapjack and a piece of rye toast and washed them both down with two cups of Earl Grey tea. I was impressed that Abigail served real maple syrup not that sickening table syrup crap they always try to pass off as the real thing in family-style restaurants. I was also impressed that she knew how to make a decent pot of tea, another lost art. Most of all, however, I was impressed by the way my balls felt, which was like they were floating on a sea of cool lime jello. I'll tell you, I hadn't been that devoid of any tension down there in months. Maybe years. Come to think of it, maybe never. I had some more toast and decided to be awake.

It struck me as odd, but not at all unappealing, that Abigail didn't make even the slightest effort to camouflage the previous evening's sleeping arrangements. The boys had gone to sleep before us, but I had somehow managed to run into both of them upstairs that morning already: Kevin, when I was going out from Abigail's bedroom to get to the bathroom at the end of the hall, and Dave when I was going back from the bathroom into the bedroom. Neither boy seemed shocked or even surprised to observe that I had apparently spent the night in their grandmother's bed. I thought I should probably say something, but nothing handy came to mind and I ended up not saying anything at all. This was, after all, Abigail's house and I supposed that made the precise way she organized her house guests' sleeping arrangements entirely her business.

By seven-thirty, Kevin was long gone to his construction job, the dishes were done and Abigail had returned to bed. I was, she said, welcome to join her if I wished. I was so tired my eyes were stinging, but I wasn't ready to go back upstairs just quite yet. I sat down with the morning paper, poured a third cup of tea and waited to see what Dave was going to do.

He must have had the same set of thoughts, because when I peered over the paper to check on him, he was just standing there.

"Are you going back to bed?"

"No."

"Were you surprised your brother was here."

"No."

"But you didn't expect him to be here, did you?"

"No."

I saw Dave wasn't in an especially communicative mood that morning, so I decided to take another tack.

"Got any plans for today?"

"No."

"Wanna get laid?"

"Sure."

"Good luck."

"Thanks."

I folded the paper again, making a big show of trying to line up the various sections neatly. Then I peered over the top of the paper again. He was still there.

"You want to talk about something?"

"Yeah."

"Go ahead."

"Not here."

"Where?"

"I don't know."

"But not here?"

"Right."

"Want to go downtown?"

"Okay."

I could tell something was up. Dave hadn't been this taciturn since Alberta, but I could sense that he was anxious to say something or tell me something or ask something. I don't know how I knew this—although I was completely right, as you'll see in a moment—anyway, I don't know how I knew it, but I could tell something was brewing in him and he needed for it to come out.

We set off on foot and an hour later we were seated in the Peg O' My Heart Cafe ("Smokers 'R' Welcome") on Portage Avenue downtown. No one seemed especially friendly, which suited both of us, and after we ordered our second breakfasts—black coffee, poached eggs, toast and a pack of Benson and Hedges menthols—it was clearly time to get down to business.

"You want to wait for the food to come?" Before telling me what this is all about, I meant.

"No."

"This isn't about me spending the night with…in your grandmother's room, is it?"

"What?"

"I mean, you're not pissed that I hit it off with your grandmother, are you? She's a great lady and I know she doesn't need your permission to run her life however she wants, but I don't want you to think that…."

"To think what?"

"To think that it was somehow..that it was wrong for me to get so friendly with your grandma so quickly. Like I somehow betrayed you by…."

"By what?"

"By I don't know by what. By something."

Dave looked at me like he truly had no idea what I was talking about. I decided to leave things be.

"So what's up?"

Dave paused for a moment, then looked around to see if the waiter was lurking close enough by to eavesdrop. Then, when he was satisfied that no one was anywhere nearby to overhear, he leaned over the yellow formica tabletop and spoke in a quiet, determined voice I hadn't heard before.

"I want to…I want to deal with my father." Dave's face looked drawn and oddly pale, almost as though he wanted to draw my attention to the seriousness of what he was saying.

"Deal with him? How?"

"I want him to pay for what he did to my mother."

"So phone the police."

"Yeah? And what will they do? Arrest him for a murder he

didn't commit?"

"If he didn't commit a...."

"Don't hand me that crap—I can't stand even listening to it. He killed her. He didn't pitch her off the bridge himself, but he might as well have. He tortured her and he hit her and he made her so miserable that she couldn't carry on even one more day. She wasn't a bad person, but he made her weak. And then he made her dead. And if that isn't murder, then I don't know what is."

"So what are you going to do? Shoot him?"

Silence.

"Are you crazy?"

"That's a weird question. I mean, if you are, you'd say you're not because you wouldn't think you were. And if you're not, you'd also say no because you also wouldn't think you were. I mean, who thinks he's crazy? Not not crazy people, but not crazy people either, right? So whatever you say, it doesn't mean squat...."

These two outbursts—about his father's extra-legal culpability in the matter of his mother's death and about the nature of the question I had asked about whether or not he was crazy—were the longest speeches Dave had made since he told me the story of his parents' marriage in the car on the way to Winnipeg. I had no idea what he was talking about, mind you, at least in the matter of the second issue, but his answer did sound impressive. "Cut the *pilpul*, son," I responded after a moment. "I'm asking if you're crazy or if you're not crazy?"

"Not crazy."

"And you want to kill your father yourself? Sort of do the job the cops won't have the balls to do and the courts won't have the balls to do and God in Heaven won't have the balls to do, but only you—just you and nobody else in the world except you—you are going to have the *cojones* to pull off?" Mentioning balls made me think, unexpectedly, of the previous evening, but I forced myself to focus on what Dave was saying instead of slipping off into that entirely tangential reverie.

"Yeah."

"And when you say that you want to kill your father, do you mean that you really want to kill him or just that you want to talk about how great it would be if he were dead? Or do you want to kill him by letting him know what a terrible parent he was?"

"Is your problem that you're crazy or is there something else?"

I was babbling, but at least I was prepared to own up to it. "The former. But let's get back to your father. You really want to kill him?"

"Why not? It's what he deserves. He killed my mother as sure as if he had shot her with a gun."

"Not precisely."

"Why not precisely? She's dead and he's responsible. He made her dead. That's got to be the bottom line…."

It was precisely at this moment that the waiter arrived with our meals. He unloaded his tray, accepted a tenner for the cigarettes (which he had had to run out to the Shopper's Drug Mart on the corner to buy for us) without even making a pretence of trying to return the change, and—this is the best part—sort of chucked the back of Dave's head with a loose fist as he left. What precisely that chuck meant, I couldn't even begin to guess. Even more interesting was the fact that Dave didn't even appear to react to it—I suppose strange men touched his head so regularly that he had long since stopped even pausing to take formal notice—or to respond to the experience either favourably or unfavourably. I was impressed.

As we began to eat, I heard Dave's words ("he made her dead") echoing through my consciousness. Somewhere in B.C., there was a man who had been so mercilessly cruel to his wife that she had been driven to suicide. This man hadn't suffered when his wife died, hadn't been remorseful, hadn't made even a cursory effort to explain his role in his wife's death to his sons or even, I presumed, to himself. Of course, I reminded myself, I only had Dave's version of that story to go by. Was there another? I told myself that it would only be reasonable to assume that there was, but I found I didn't really think so. Not for a second.

And now the whole story of Dave's mother's death became confused in my mind with the story of Wil's. He hadn't exactly been killed by someone who ought to have loved him, but the reverberations of his death were just as consequential as those of Dave's mother in the lives of the people he had left behind. Gloria Kruger—did I mention that Dave's last name was Kruger?—anyway, Gloria Kruger had left behind two children who had needed their mother's love desperately and a mother who had needed her daughter, while Wil had left behind two parents who had needed his support no less desperately (even if they didn't become truly gaga until after he died) and a brother who had truly loved him.

Did Gloria Kruger have any thoughts on what she wished to be done with her body after death? I supposed not, since she had probably intended for her body to be washed out to the sea by the Fraser and eaten by the fish. Did she wonder if one of those fish might not end up on the dinner plate of someone she knew, perhaps even as a meal one of her sons might consume someday? I dismissed the line of thought as pointless, but something of it lingered in my consciousness as I returned to thinking about Wil.

He was my brother and my best friend. And he knew he was dying and wanted his head to be preserved against the possibility, slim but real, that cloning might someday become so advanced that his body could be reconstructed from the neck down, his AIDS cured and his life restored to him. It was a silly pipedream, but it was real to him and I, who had promised not vaguely or symbolically, but in so many words and with full understanding of what he was asking of me, I had allowed myself to be talked out of it by people who hadn't promised him the right to fart on Sunday.

All of these thoughts came to me as we ate. Why were these stories connected to each other? Wil and Gloria were both dead, but they really didn't have much in common. Wil was my brother, Gloria, the mother of some kid I had picked up hitchhiking between Barrymore and Stanhope, B.C. My failure to carry Wil's wishes through was one of the great failings of my life, but I hadn't even ever heard of Gloria Kruger until the day before I was having a second breakfast in the Peg O' My Heart Cafe with one of her two sons. Wil hadn't wanted to die—he had wanted so desperately to live that he had conceived on his own of this loony plan to have his head frozen and then made me promise to follow through on it—but Gloria had taken her own life. On purpose. In public. With a letter guaranteeing that she had been acting intentionally to follow in the mail a few days later.

"You serious?" As long as we were both eating, the conversation was held in abeyance. But now that we were finished and were both smoking and sipping cold coffee, it started up again.

"Yeah."

"How do you want to do it?"

"I don't know."

"You don't really want to kill him, you know."

"I don't?"

"No, you want to hold a gun to his head and hear him crap in his pants when you release the safety. You want to hear him beg for mercy. And then you want him to acknowledge his full responsibility for your mother's death. And then you want him to beg you for forgiveness. For killing her. For ruining your home. For depriving you of growing up with your brother—who incidentally what is that nipple ring thing all about?—and your mom. For making you into a kid hitching a ride halfway across Canada when you should be in high school dating cheerleaders and hoping to make it into the honours science programme. For ruining

MARTIN S. COHEN

your whole damn life. Isn't that right, Dave? Isn't that what you really want?"

For the first time in our admittedly very brief relationship, he stared directly into my eyes. "No," he said simply, even elegantly, "it isn't."

"You won't get away with it."

"Who says so?"

"I do."

"How do you figure?"

"The RCMP has homicide guys who spend all day everyday figuring out murders. They're going to be a lot smarter than you."

"How about you?"

"How about me what?"

"How about do you think they're all going to be any smarter than you?"

"That's crazy."

"You really think that you are dumber than every single RCMP officer in the whole country?"

I felt myself being sucked into something I knew I didn't want to be part of, but I still had the strength to resist at least formally. "I don't know. But I'm not helping you on this. I have enough problems. And I have a daughter who is going to need me someday and I don't want to be in prison forever when she does. And it doesn't matter if I'm smarter than any of them. I'd have to be smarter than all of them to figure out a plan you could get away with."

Dave smiled. "No one's going to prison so fast," he said affably. "Look, let's head back to B.C. and we'll see what happens. We'll go see my dad and you can help me figure out what to do then. He's a real nice guy. You'll like him. And I'll help you."

"Who says I need your help?"

"You never know what could happen, Saul. Shit happens all the time."

I couldn't argue.

XIX

The rest of the day sort of passed uneventfully. It was Winnipeg. It was August. It was twenty thousand degrees in the shade and I could hardly breathe. The locals didn't seem too bothered by the heat, however. I attributed this to the fact that they were probably mostly all still thawing out from the winter that had only really ended in May and could therefore probably not even feel the heat, much less be oppressed by it. Anyway, the city was an oven. We walked around a bit, drank a few cold Cokes from vending machines we came across, then played the slot machines in some run-down casino on the top floor of some dingy hotel where they actually made us wear these ratty, puke-orange one-size-fits-none sports jackets lest a gambler from one of the Lower Classes sneak in and sully the elegant air of the gaming floor by appearing underdressed. Eventually we lost our—or rather, my—last quarter and decided to call it a day and head back to Gloria's place.

We didn't speak much as we walked through the heat back to the North End. It took about an hour, which suited me fine—I had all sorts of things to think through and doing it in Dave's company but without having to discuss every single point with him out loud was just what I wanted to do. He wasn't so much a friend—although he was probably a little of that by this point as well—as much as he was company that didn't talk too much, which was just what the doctor ordered. I hated being alone like poison. But I hated having to pay for the antidote with endless small talk even worse.

I expected to spend the afternoon thinking about Wil, but I ended up thinking about Lena instead. Helene and I had more or less shared custody of her—an informal arrangement that we had worked out on our own, since we weren't divorced or even legally separated—until June, when Helene announced her plans to go south. With Lena. Which event, I now realize, is what pushed me over the top and sent me on this peculiar voyage to nowhere I was undertaking.

Where Helene and Lena were at that precise moment, I didn't know. Helene promised to write me with their address and phone number as soon as she got them settled in California so we could discuss the new custody arrangements—which was complete garbage since there wasn't any legally binding arrangement between us and we both knew perfectly well that the reason she moved down south in the first place was to get Lena away from…from Vancouver, from me, from my parents…from her life. Helene's mother—another piece of work, by the way, so don't get me started—was from St. Louis, so she—Helene, I mean—she was an American citizen and didn't have to get permission to move or to work down there. Eventually, I knew I'd find my way down and reconnect with Lena, but just the thought of having to fly a thousand miles to spend a long weekend with my kid instead of living with her and putting her to sleep at night and taking her to the movies on cheap Tuesdays was enough to make me want to break down and cry. I didn't—cry, I mean—but I wasn't happy. And that's what I thought about almost the entire way back to Abigail Kleist's modest home in Winnipeg's lovely North End.

I guess I was thinking about Lena—which I knew would make me crazy—because I didn't want to think seriously about Dave's apparently sincere suggestion that I drive him back to B.C. and help him murder his father. It was just too much even to think seriously about—I couldn't do it and he couldn't do it and we'd get caught anyway and the father might well have his own side of the story anyway—not that I didn't trust Dave, but you never know—anyway, there were a million reasons just to say goodbye, get in the Camaro and leave Dave in the able hands of his grandma. Thinking about her able hands gave me a slight shiver of arousal, but I willed my libido down and walked forward without letting on to Dave that I was thinking about his grandmother. Was he waiting for me to mention a second time that I had spent the night in her bed? I didn't think so—he didn't raise the matter, even obliquely as far as I could tell—but who could be sure? I wasn't especially anxious to discuss the matter, however, and I certainly wasn't going to raise the issue a second time if he didn't.

By the time we got to Abigail's house, we were both completely enervated by the heat. He told me I could have the first shower—Abigail herself was nowhere to be seen—because he wasn't really that hot. But when I came out of the bathroom, Dave was sitting completely naked on a stool in the hallway waiting his turn like a naughty schoolboy waiting on a bench in front of the principal's office for his turn to get yelled at. He was a goodlooking boy with his clothes off, but what I found myself focusing on was a fairly long, jagged scar on his right buttock which I noticed when he walked past me. I thought of asking about it—it must have been the result of an exceptionally deep wound to have created such a prominent scar—then decided to say nothing. In a moment, he was in the bathroom and I could hear the water running in the shower.

When he came downstairs afterwards, I had a pot of coffee on the stove and was washing a few dishes Abigail had left in the sink. We sat for a while and drank the coffee, each of us wanting and not wanting to have the discussion that was looming, so far mostly un-had, between us.

Anyway, we didn't have the discussion. We drank the coffee

and washed the pot and our cups. I found a note from Abigail asking me to get dinner started—she was at some art class downtown and would only be back around six—so I found the chicken she had left thawed in the fridge and set to rubbing it down with lemon juice, garlic and paprika and put it in the oven to bake. Dave set to washing his grandmother's kitchen floor, which he did with surprising skill. I was impressed.

When dinner was well underway, I found a Yellow Pages and checked the listings for synagogues in the hope of finding a place to say Kaddish for Wil.

My parents were both born in Canada—my mother in Montreal and my dad in Toronto—but their parents came from Europe. No one seemed to know (or care) where precisely it was they came from, or even from what specific country they hailed, what language they spoke as children or why precisely it was that they had emigrated. In fact, both my parents always seemed to me as eager as could be to forget the fact that their families had ever lived anywhere but Canada...and that certainly included not wishing me to become interested, let alone obsessed, with tracking down our families' roots. As a teenager, I had done a bit of work on the matter and I had more or less concluded that my father's family came from Warsaw and my mother's from Odessa, but even that information, gleaned mostly from phone interviews with my grandparents' surviving siblings in the various nursing homes in which their ungrateful children had dumped them to avoid having to care for them in their own palatial residences, even that information failed to impress, or even really to interest, my folks.

Their attitude towards their Jewishness was part of their feelings about that vast, dark, unspecified place ("Europe") from which they sensed themselves to be completely divorced.

My folks weren't ashamed of being Jewish. Just to the contrary, they chose to marry each other, to produce two Jewish children. They gave—not much, but something—to the Jewish National Fund from time to time and they occasionally spoke about going to Israel, although they never actually went. They both used some Yiddish expressions now and then in their speech, but only at home and only when no one other than the four of us was present. I guess that the sense that there is a certain basic incompatibility between Canadianism and Jewishness that requires that strong feelings about one impinge on one's ability to feel strongly about the other was probably so basic to the world view of that generation that there's no point in singling out my parents in any of this, but it still seems odd to me that so many people freely and entirely voluntarily embraced an approach to their own ethnicity which was as illogical as it was, at its core, intensely self-deprecating.

Anyway, we grew up in a Jewish home almost completely devoid of any Jewish observance. I think my father actually fasted on Yom Kippur, but he always made a point of lying about it to the people he worked with lest they take him for a religious man and, therefore, somehow less of a citizen of the country in which he was born. My mother made nice meals for us on the eve of Rosh Hashanah—the Jewish New Year—and on the first night of Passover and we ate fried *latkes* now and then on Chanukah, but that was basically it: Judaism scaled down to its gastronomic bottom line.

It was with all the more surprise, therefore, that I found my parents so involved with the concept of doing things "the right way" when Wil died. I don't want to go through all that again, but I somehow ended up resolving to say Kaddish for my brother since my parents had no intention of doing it themselves, but still wanted it to be done. At first, I thought I'd go every day. I actually did go for a week or two, but I just couldn't bring myself to get up at six-thirty every morning to go to synagogue and so I started saying the prayer less and less often in public and then, finally, only on Friday nights. That much, I figured I could handle. And, for quite a while, I kept it up pretty faithfully.

At first, I hated the whole thing. I hated standing up when everyone else was seated. And I hated having strangers come up to me afterwards and asking me who I was saying Kaddish for. And I especially hated having to feel that I was this living example of faith in the face of adversity for all these old men in Arnold Palmer trousers and Zeller's shirts who seemed to find it moving that a man my age would undertake to say Kaddish for anyone, let alone for someone other than a parent, for more than three days.

And another thing: you're only supposed to say Kaddish for a brother for thirty days. In fact, you're only supposed to say Kaddish for anyone for thirty days except for your parents, for whom you say it, for some obscure reason, for eleven months. I had my own system, however: thirty days times three services a day yields ninety Kaddishes. I couldn't bring myself to go every day. I even missed plenty of Friday nights when I was out or doing something and couldn't get to synagogue. But I was keeping track pretty carefully and I was damn sure I would eventually say all ninety Kaddishes.

Anyway, by the time I was washing the dishes in Abigail Kleist's sink in Winnipeg in the middle of the first August since Wil's death, I had said Kaddish for him precisely eighty-seven times. I was close…and something appealed to me about pursuing the matter while I was staying at Abigail's. And it was a Friday to boot, which had been my traditional night for adding a Kaddish to my score if I could. And it couldn't be that difficult to find a *shul* where I could say Kaddish for my dead brother in Winnipeg, of all places.

Anyway, the phonebook yielded the names of a dozen synagogues. I had noticed a map of Winnipeg on the shelf over the sink with the cookbooks on it and I took it down and tried to locate some of the addresses. I didn't want to go to an enormous place where I'd feel like an ant in a cathedral, but I didn't want too small a place either where people might speak to me. I needed…I didn't know what I needed precisely, but I wanted a place that I could walk into, say Kaddish and leave without feeling any worse than I already felt, without inspiring anyone with my indomitable faith in the face of loss and pain, without anyone talking to me at all. And I wanted a place I could walk to, which would make it slightly easier to discourage anyone from wanting to come with me. I spent a good twenty minutes perusing the Yellow Pages listing of synagogues and finally selected one that had a nice sound to it: The Brick Street Synagogue. I liked that—it sounded solid, basic, unadorned. I phoned and got a recorded message. The office was only open from Monday to Thursday, but there were Friday evening services scheduled for eight o'clock that evening. All, the recording said, were welcome. Judging from our walk downtown and back, Brick Street itself looked like it was about a fifteen minute walk from Abigail's house. And eight o'clock was perfect—more than late enough to have dinner at home without having to rush and early enough to get back long before Abigail might think of going to bed without me. I knew I was a temporary thing in her life, as she was in mine, but I certainly wasn't going to pass up another evening in bed with her if I didn't have to. And who knew? Maybe we'd get that sole-to-sole thing working yet, I figured. I was certainly game to try. I resolved to do some deep knee-bends before Abigail got home to limber up my knee joints as best I could.

Dinner was low-key. Kevin showed up back from work about four-thirty and didn't look any the worse for wear. He was a strong boy with a cocky attitude that looked about skin-deep to me, but he was a polite grandson to Abigail and, when he came down from his shower, I was impressed to see that he applied himself to setting the table immediately as though it were his regular responsibility.

Abigail herself came home a few minutes after five. She still looked good to me and I think she could tell I thought so. Anyway, she was pleased the table was set, pleased the chicken was in the oven and pleased that the salad and the dressing were made. She went upstairs to change into a sundress, the came back, opened up a few bottles of beer and served dinner. It was a pleasant meal. We all told about our days. Kevin's friend Jerry had been taken in an ambulance to hospital after he dropped a hammer on his foot and probably broke his toe. Abigail's girl-friend's father, a dentist, had had a sudden heart attack and had died in his office with his drill in his hand. Dave and I told about our walk downtown, but without mentioning anything about the precise topic of our discussion. By seven-thirty, the meal was over. I announced that I had to go out for about an hour or so, but no one seemed especially interested in my plans and I didn't need to say where I was going or why I was going there. Dave volunteered to clear the table and help with the dinner dishes. Kevin announced a date for later that evening. Abigail said something vague about having to phone "a friend" and about there being some movie she had missed in the theatres on CTV at nine. I excused myself and walked out the door, the map of Winnipeg folded neatly in my pocket. I lost my bearings for a moment, but then I noted the sun setting in the west and, in just a few minutes, I was on my way to Brick Street to say my eighty-eighth Kaddish for Wil.

It was a very warm evening and the streets were filled with people. I noted that the presence of all those people didn't make me feel any less lonely, however. And I also noted that my unexpected, if certainly temporary, membership in Abigail Kleist's slightly extended family was something I had craved since Helene and Lena vanished from my day-to-day life, Wil died and my parents moved into the home. It felt good even to be part of something I didn't truly belong to, I realized. I dwelt on that notion, playing it over this way and that in my mind until I was a block or two from Brick Street and could feel Kaddish looming before me not so much as a task to be accomplished as a challenge to be faced. I hated saying Kaddish, but it somehow kept Wil from being entirely dead, from being entirely missing from the world, my world. I'm not the kind of guy who only found out that he loved his brother after his brother died. I knew I loved Wil my whole life. I loved him and I valued him and I held him in more esteem, generally, than I held myself. But it was the depth, not the basic nature, of my feelings for him that I was able to own up to only after we buried him.

I told myself that I was feeling guilty because I hadn't insisted that we obey his wishes with respect to the disposition of his body, but, as I walked slowly, if not quite inexorably, towards the Brick Street Synagogue, I allowed myself to understand—if not quite to accept—that I was using my guilt as a shield to protect myself from the crushing sense of loss I ought to have been feeling. And that Wil's head wasn't the problem in all of this—mine was.

There was more to work out about the way Wil and I were going to have to get along with one of us alive and the other one dead, but in the meantime, I was already on Brick Street and I could see the synagogue looming before me. I found the front door, pushed it open and stepped inside.

XX

The outside of the Brick Street Synagogue was this horrible combination of greenish stucco and cheap brick, but inside the atmosphere was entirely different. For one thing, it was cool. Even at eight o'clock in the evening, the streets were sweltering, but the interior of the synagogue was dark and slightly musty and I had the sense that I had entered a cool place rather than one in which I was just going to be shielded from the heat. I don't know if that really makes any sense, but it was precisely how it felt as I stepped inside.

There weren't many worshippers. Maybe twenty. Maybe twenty-five. And they were all seated in the front of the sanctuary. It was already after eight and the service had begun. In front of the room, a guy wearing green Dockers and a black polo shirt was leading the service. I could see his wallet bulging in his back pocket. He had a fair voice, but I wasn't interested in following the service. Like I always did, I just sat there and thought about Lena and Wil and how I missed them both in a way I could barely admit even to myself. It must have been eight-five degrees outside, but I felt chilly, even a bit cold, in the sanctuary. The lights were down low and the others appeared to be wrapped up in their prayers. It was just me who was alone and disconnected, a sailor in a holy place, an ant crawling through the queen's pudding fully aware what happens to bugs who get caught where they aren't supposed to be.

The congregation was singing a hymn I recognized as part of the Friday night service from the synagogue back home I had gone to a few times to say Kaddish for Wil right after he died. It was one of those minor key tunes that somehow managed to be upbeat and merry, but it didn't cheer me up. Just the opposite. I mean, there was something profoundly wrong with this picture. I had just had a great meal. I had had sex the night before with a great lady who wanted me to try it one last time while the soles of our feet pressed up one against the other. I had every reason to expect a repeat performance that evening when I got back to Grandma's house. I was in a cool place on a very hot evening. I had clean clothes on—I had run a couple of washer loads while I was getting dinner ready and had had time to dry the first one while the second was still in the washing machine—and more neatly laid out for the next day. So what the hell did I want?

I don't know, but I was suddenly so upset that I thought I would have to leave. But it was already too late to escape. The preliminary part of the service was over and the rabbi—or rather, the guy I assumed was the rabbi since he was sitting up front and was carrying himself like a rabbi in his own synagogue—anyway, this guy I took to be the rabbi was already standing up and getting ready to say a few words. I wasn't surprised. This was the place in the service where the rabbi spoke in that synagogue back home I was just mentioning.

Given the fact that I make my living—or I used to make my living—teaching the Bible, it always amazes me how there can be people like rabbis and priests and ministers who have devoted their entire lives to religions based on the Bible and yet who display no particularly keen interest in actually reading through the book from beginning to end. It's almost as though they're afraid of what they're going to find and they somehow have this sixth sense warning them away. Mind you, they're not entirely crazy.

Anyway, this rabbi gets up and he starts talking about the story about how the Israelites got warmed up for their conquest of Canaan by conducting this war of extermination against the

Midianites. It's at the end of the book of Numbers and it must have been part of the reading from Scripture they were going to do in the morning, but it's possibly the worst story in Scripture and definitely one of the most painful. I couldn't wait to hear what the rabbi was going to say about it.

I should have known that I was going to have a stroke when I heard what this guy was going to talk about, but somehow the actual experience of hearing somebody that proud of the degree to which he was willing to lie about Scripture for the sake of giving everybody pleasant dreams made me even more upset than I would have normally expected. But I'm getting ahead of myself. So the guy gets up and starts telling the story. The Midianites, it turns out, had inspired this mass apostasy in the desert by inspiring the Israelites to worship Baal Peor, the special god of Midian. So that's their big sin—they existed and the Israelites were so drawn to their form of worship—did I mention that the worship of the Peor involved the delightful custom of ritual defecation?—anyway, the Israelites were so delighted to have a god who understood the value of a good dump that they joined up in droves. Anyway, it didn't end well—God sent along this big plague that killed something like twenty-four thousand people, for one thing—but the fact that the Israelites were the ones who had abandoned their own religion for the sake of shitting on somebody else's altar didn't mean that the Midianites were entirely off the hook.

So the Israelites go off to war and they basically kill everybody except the women and children. They kill the five kings of Midian. They kill off the entire army. The members of parliament. The judges. The bowling alley attendants. The gas station guys. The whole damn thing gets blown to kingdom come and everyone in it ends up dead except the women and children. And then they come back to camp and Moses, instead of being impressed, is royally pissed. How dare they keep the kids and the women alive he says? Anyway, he's got this great plan to make things right with God—they should kill all the boys and all the adult women who aren't virgins and that will just about do it. Mind you, Scripture doesn't say in so many words how they were supposed to know which women were virgins, but I guess they could just sort of tell. Anyway, they're supposed to kill all the little boys and all the grown-up girls.

And now the rabbi is telling the story and he's really getting into it. It's true, of course, that Scripture doesn't precisely say what happened after that, but it's pretty clear. In other words, we don't get to hear the innocent little Midianite boys screaming as the Israelites cut their heads off, but we do find out afterwards that there were exactly thirty-two thousand virgins among the womenfolk and that suggests pretty clearly that they did what they were told.

So the rabbi is clearly not pleased with this story and he starts making this enormous big deal out of the fact that Scripture leaves out any reference to the Israelites actually doing what Moses said. He doesn't have a reasonable leg to stand on—and I can't believe he didn't know it—but he's suddenly making this enormously big deal out of one missing sentence as though there must have been this general uprising in the ranks with tens of thousands of soldiers laying down their weapons and just refusing to murder babies. As though the Bible just somehow forgot to tell about how the Israelite nation discovered the existence of an extra-divine sense of morality that made some things just wrong no matter who—or I should say, Who—commanded them to whom. As though the same Bible that thinks that death by stoning is an appropriate way of dealing with the kind of human scum that gathers sticks on the Sabbath would just somehow manage to forget about a mass decision on the part of the rank and file of the Israelite Fighting Force to ignore the commands of its commander-in-chief.

The basic idea is that the story is horrible. The antithesis of human morality. The single story in the part of Scripture Jews revere as the quintessentially sacred part of Sacred Writ that basically endorses genocide. The story that all by itself provides proof that no one will ever be able to find God by slavishly following anybody's version of The Rules. It's a horrible story, but it's also a great one and I've taught dozens of very successful classes on it. And now this rabbi—who must have weighed at least three hundred pounds, by the way—now this morbidly *obese* rabbi is standing up in this cool sanctuary on a hot August evening and he's telling us all that it never happened. That they never did it. That Moses was raving. That no one took him seriously. That his instructions are included in the Bible precisely to garner some serious praise for the people who didn't follow them. It was all complete bullshit—apologetic, stupid, one hundred percent devoid of any basis in the text itself and deeply self-serving in the worst sense of the word.

I couldn't stand it. I had already said one Kaddish, the one that comes after the preliminary part of the service, and I figured that was going to have to be enough. I got up just before the rabbi finished and walked out. Not a head turned. Not one person got up to ask if I was okay. No one approached me. In a second, I was out in the heat again on Brick Street. Twenty minutes later, I was back at Abigail's. The boys were out at some movie and we had, she said, the house to ourselves until after eleven. She was wearing a sun dress with, as far as I could see, no bra underneath. The house was neat. The television was on. I didn't want to be rude, so I watched the end of some rerun of Picket Fences and only then suggested we retire to her bedroom.

I vaguely heard the boys come in a eleven-thirty, but neither of them called to us and I supposed they simply must have assumed that we had gone to bed. As well we had. Sex was different that night than it had been the night before. Abigail hadn't displayed much reticence the previous evening, but where there had perhaps been a slight smidgen of residual shyness the night before, there was now none at all. She was everywhere, stroking me, licking me, kissing me, enveloping me in every available orifice or fold of skin she could think of. She made me take her over and over until I couldn't imagine being aroused again for a month and then, when I thought I was completely through, she brought out a whole new set of positions and postures that she wanted to try and I found myself responding yet again.

She wasn't precisely an acrobat, but she must have been at least some sort of a gymnast once and she was certainly not letting that training go to waste. But it wasn't only gymnastic stuff that made her different from any woman I had ever slept with—there was a certain passion, a certain fire driving her, pushing her, forcing her forward to yet another orgasm, to yet another level of intimacy, to yet another level of intensity, to another level of hunger, to another level of lust.

It was as though she wanted to consume me…and not merely emotionally, but really consume me, eat me, ingest me, swallow me, put me inside of her in the absolute way, not just in the schematized way everybody does it by putting a little piece of the man—well, not that little, but you know what I mean—by putting a part of the man inside a little part of the woman. She liked the idea, but she wanted it all. And, to the extent any woman can, she wanted me her totally, absolutely and thoroughly.

By one o'clock, I was done. Through. Spent. Finished. I actually ached. My skin was sore. My knees were tender. (I had been on them for hours, it seemed.) My lower back hurt. But I was a happy man. I had found the one woman in the world who was able to make love to a man without holding anything back at all, something I hadn't even known for sure to be possible, let alone expect that I might ever actually encounter. I had never had such an intense sexual experience in my life—certainly not with

Helene, whose ability to make love spontaneously evaporated sometime between the wedding ceremony and the reception, but not really with any other women I could think of either. I was a happy guy who had had two amazing (and consecutive) nights with a woman who was attractive in a way few women truly ever had been to me previously. She was passionate and lovely and had just the kind of body that, I thought, was made to make love to mine. I'm not even sure what I meant by that thought when I first had it, but there was something distinctly special, maybe even magical about our union. It wasn't just special in the sense that it was intense, it was different in terms of its basic nature from any other act of lovemaking I had ever participated in. Maybe I should say that it wasn't so much coupling as it was joining. But even joining isn't the right term—it was more than that as well. There was a certain aspect of union to it—the coming together not just of this piece of me into that piece of her, but of man and woman, of male and female, of yin and yang. I don't know what I'm talking about, but let me tell you one thing I know for sure: giving the time to Abigail Kleist was the most thrilling sexual experience of my entire life.

I left at seven the next morning and never expected to see her again.

XXI

Don't ask. Or ask if you want to, but I'm telling you up front that I don't know. I loved everything about Abigail, not just her unbelievable ability at sex. She was generous, she was pleasant, she could cook. She had nice hair. She kept a tidy home. She had taken in her grandson when he had no place to go and kept him for years without suggesting even one single time (she told me this herself) that he go home, go to school, get a job, do any one of the various things any outside observer could reasonably have expected her to hock him about forever if he wanted to live in her house. He came on his own, he got his job on his own, he gave her $35 a week towards the groceries on his own. And he was free to leave on his own if he wanted. He was allowed to smoke, to bring girls back to his room, to conduct his life as he saw fit with his grandmother's presence guiding him precisely by not insisting that he be any older or more mature than he really was. And it was working: Kevin was growing up in his grandmother's house in a way he never could have in his own parents' home and that meant a lot to me. Abigail was, even to this day, one of the kindest people I've ever met. And she was as good a parent as she was a grandparent, which is rare enough, I think, to warrant me noting formally.

So what happened? So I already said I don't know. When we were finally finished for the night—and let me tell you, 'finished' doesn't even begin to describe what we were (or at least what I was) when we finally turned off the light and hit the hay—anyway, when we were finally done, she kissed my cheek as she had the night before, turned over and went immediately to sleep. I fell asleep right away too, but it didn't last and I was up an hour later, thinking, wondering and worrying about things. Where was Lena? Where, for that matter, was that bitch Helene? How could I have left my parents in Stalag 65+ for this long without even phoning to see if they were still alive? I mean, it hadn't been that long, but still…you'd think a guy would phone his parents from time to time to see if they were any more gaga than the last time he spoke to them.

But mostly I thought about myself. About what I was doing in Abigail Kleist's bed with sore knees and such a heavy heart. I kept thinking about Wil and remembering this and that about our childhood. The time he won this swimming race at summer camp and everybody cheered and he was so proud that he actually burst into tears as soon as he was alone with me and my folks—this was on visiting day in the middle of the camp season—and how he told me after that that he never wanted anyone to cheer for him again. The time he got caught at the border with his friend's brother trying to smuggle a carton of Marlboros back from the States in *our* dad's car and how my dad had to go down to Blaine to bail him out, pay the duty and pay some exorbitant fine to get the car unimpounded. The time my mother found a pair of girl's panties under his bed and, instead of realizing that he had been bringing his girlfriend up to his room during their lunch break from school, she actually asked him if he ever had the yen—that's the exact word she used, by the way—if he ever that the yen to dress up in girl's lingerie and that it wasn't anything to be ashamed of and that they could just talk it out if Wil wanted. He had been too floored to laugh, but we all did laugh afterwards, all of us—my parents and him and me—and we considered it a treasured family story even if none of us, I don't think, ever told it to anyone else. Wil had been fourteen at the time, incidentally.

Anyway, I lay awake for a while and thought about things

and then, when the clock by Abigail's bed said it was 5:45 in the morning, I got up, threw on my clothes, got my stuff together and headed out into the dark street. I got into the car and drove a few blocks to an all-night Subway and had the worst cup of coffee—and I include the coffee at Denny's in that thought—anyway, I had the worst cup of coffee I had ever had and half of a breakfast sub and read a copy of the day before's Globe and Mail that they had lying around. At seven, I was back at the house. Kevin was gone to work and Abigail had gone back to bed. Dave was doing the breakfast dishes.

"Was your grandma surprised I was gone when she woke up?"

"She didn't say."

"Were you curious where I was?"

"I thought you were sleeping."

"I went out for breakfast. At Subway."

"How was it?"

"Awful."

"You should have eaten breakfast here. We had oatmeal."

"Now you tell me."

I went over to the sink, picked up a dishtowel and started drying the dishes Dave had already washed.

"I'm heading back to B.C."

"Cool."

"Today."

"Can I come?"

"You should stay here with your grandma. She's a good person and she'll look after you. And you're not too old to need some looking after, are you?"

Silence.

"Well, are you?"

"Look, you're not exactly my parole officer, so you don't have to be so interested in my wellbeing. I know my grandma is a great lady and I'm going to live here. But first there's something I have to do back home. And if you're driving back there and you'll take me, that would be good. If not, I'll get the money somewhere and take the bus back."

"Where would you get the money?"

"Why would you care? I'll get a job. Maybe at Kevin's place if they need anyone."

"Maybe sucking off guys downtown for five bucks a pop so you can get AIDS and die."

"Maybe I'll go to medical school and become a brain surgeon. I hear they make good money."

"Not as good as in the States."

Our conversation went on in this vein for quite some time. He wanted to go and didn't want to go and I wanted him to come and didn't want him to come. I wanted my privacy and wanted his company and he wanted his privacy and wanted my company. He knew he'd have more fun—not to mention more pie—with me than he'd ever get on the Greyhound, but there would be a price for all that pie and it was going to be having to talk to me. I figured he was getting the better end of the bargain—or at least that it would be easier for me to pick up another hitchhiker to keep me company that it would ever be for him to find another ride to Vancouver—but that wasn't as important to me as the fact that I knew that the reason he wanted to go back to Vancouver was to whack his father and that gave me some vague sense of responsibility towards…I don't know towards what. Not towards his father, that's for sure. Towards Dave himself, I guess. Because I knew that he'd get himself caught and end up in some prison for slightly underage parricides and if I could prevent that and end our relationship with him safely under Abigail's wing and with a job, maybe even at the place his brother worked, then I wanted to do that. I don't know. He wasn't my problem. And he certainly wasn't my responsibility. But I liked him and—this is where the reasoning gets a little hazy, so don't think I don't know that—but I did like him and there was some small way that I was going to atone for having failed Wil by keeping young Dave from screwing himself so completely that he'd never really get over it.

Does this all sound like I was some sort of pathetic Albert Schweitzer wannabe who picks up troubled youths and tries to set them straight before releasing them back into the world? I guess…but that's not at all how I felt. Not like Albert and certainly not like some Jewish male version of Mother Theresa, but just like a guy with a sin to atone for who suddenly saw a way to undo some of the wrong in some tiny, insignificant way and wanted to take it: Wil wasn't going to be any less dead if Dave managed to avoid committing a crime he would never really put behind him, but I would be. I know it sounds even screwier now than it would have then, but I really was dead in those days, at least in a certain sense, and I thought that keeping a skinny teenager who could crack his knuckles behind his head while he peed and whose grandmother was one of the greatest sex partners of my life, I thought that keeping him from ruining his life by icing his dad—after which, of course, his mother was going to still be as dead as Wil—if I could keep him from doing that one thing and get him back to Winnipeg and back to his grandmother's home, then maybe I wouldn't have screwed up as royally as I thought I had with the whole Wil thing. And, more to the point, there might be some peace for me yet.

I finished drying the dishes and went into Abigail's bedroom. My stuff was already in the car, which she must have known, but she had just gone back to bed and had fallen asleep. If she was secretly hysterical about my unexplained and unexpected departure, she was doing a really, really great job of hiding it. In fact, she was not only asleep, but she was snoring lightly when I went into the room. The comforter was pulled down to about her waist and I could see one of her breasts—the right one—peaking through the front of her nightgown where she had missed a button. I couldn't see the nipple or anything, but I could see the white, freckled flesh and I was suddenly overwhelmed with desire. I loved making love to that woman. And I would gladly have spent the rest of my life doing whatever it took during the days for me to have the right to spend my nights in that bed next to that woman. She wasn't just sexy—although she certainly was that as well—she was...I don't know what the word is...voluptuous, carnal, sensual...something like that. She was just great and she was friendly to boot. I don't know how I found the strength to leave, but I guess part of it was that I knew that if I spent a third night in her bed it would either kill me altogether or else I'd never leave. Not for the rest of my life. And I wasn't ready for that. Not yet.

I slid in next to her, still completely dressed. She didn't stir, with my front pressed up against her back. I pulled her close and reached around to cup her breasts in my hands. They had a certain weight that I found enormously attractive—Helene's always felt like they were filled with those styrofoam chips they use to pack up dishes when you move—and, for just a moment, I pulled myself close to her. She didn't stir, didn't say a word..and it was then that I knew that she was awake—I don't know how I knew, but I did, absolutely—and I realized that she didn't want to discuss the matter, didn't want me to give her this long, drawn-out goodbye speech, didn't want to hear promises I wasn't going to keep or even, probably, promises I did think I might keep. She didn't want to hear anything now that she knew I was going—I guess my missing clothing must have been the big tip-off—and just wanted me to go and leave her with some good memories and no phoniness. I don't know how I understood all of that just from feeling the weight of her breasts in my hands—I'm not usually anywhere near insightful enough for stuff like that—anyway,

I don't know how I knew what she wanted, but I did know it and I knew it absolutely.

I granted her unspoken wish. I slid out of bed without saying a word. I closed the bedroom door behind me quietly and went into the kitchen. Dave was still there. He was sweeping the floor and he had this real sad look in his eyes, like he knew he should stay and he knew that the best decision for him was to stay and he knew he was going to go anyway. For the first moment, it dawned on me that he must have felt towards Kevin something like what I felt towards Wil and that we (probably) shared the weird experience of looking up to a younger brother. I felt close to Dave in that moment, closer to him than I had felt up to then including when I had watched him banging that Patsy chick back in Alberta with his jockey shorts stretched out between his ankles and this look of strained ecstasy on his face.

Anyway, there wasn't much to say. He didn't have any gear, but his grandmother had given him a fifty to buy some clothes and that was basically all he had—the fifty, not the clothes, I mean—so there wasn't any real reason not to go if that was the plan. We both stood there for a long moment as though each of us was waiting for the other one to talk us both out of leaving. But, in the end, neither of us said a word and when I walked out the front door, he just followed me.

By this time, it was almost eight o'clock. I wondered if he wanted to spend the fifty before we left, but there was no way I was going to hang around in Winnipeg until the stores opened up and I figured if we left right away, we could get to Regina in time for him to do some shopping there. And if we missed it, then there would be a chance soon enough somewhere else.

And that, basically was that. We got into the car and drove off. Twenty minutes later, we were out of the city heading west. The sun was behind us. Abigail and Kevin were behind us. The past itself felt like it was behind us. The day was clear and bright and I found myself feeling slightly optimistic. I turned on the radio. Dave fell asleep. I stopped for gas and bought two Cokes and two Sweet Marie bars for myself and Dave (if he ever woke up), then kept driving. The prairies were green and lovely. My knees felt a little less sore. I ended up with tears in my eyes thinking about Wil and I was just as glad Dave was asleep. The Sweet Marie bars began to melt. I ate mine. And then I ate his as well—it was already half melted and I was just going to end up throwing it out if I didn't eat it before it got any softer or more disgusting. The sun rose in the sky. I stopped the car by a field with horses in it to pee by the side of the road. The news came on the radio. There was a report on the radio about a big fire in Kenora, Ontario. Some big economic summit was poised to begin somewhere and Canada either was or wasn't participating. The Pope had gotten himself involved in asking for clemency for some Italian drug smuggler the Saudis were about to behead in some big public execution. I drove on.

XXII

The trip back was basically boring. We drove. We ate. We drank coffee in the morning and Coke in the afternoon and beer at night. We got to Regina that first day and to Medicine Hat the second. For two people on their way to commit and prevent the same murder, we weren't in much of a hurry. We spent the third night in Canmore, just outside of Banff, then entered B.C. the next morning and drove as far as Kelowna. In Kelowna, I sprung for a decent place with a nice pool and we swam and ate fried fish in one of those all-you-can-eat places they have along the shore of the lake. Some girls approached us later that evening when we were finishing off the evening with a couple of beers in this lounge just a hundred yards or so from the hotel, but neither of us was interested. They both looked like they were maybe sixteen anyway. The best part was that even Dave thought they were a little young….

Anyway, that was our trip. We stayed up late each night and Dave slept most of the morning away while I drove. That wasn't as awful as it sounds, though, and I actually sort of liked having the time to think about things. I was dwelling less on Wil than I had been and was focusing my thoughts on Lena. I hadn't heard a word from her since Helene took her to California, but I knew that I was going to have to figure out how to be a long-distance dad one way or the other if I didn't want to lose her entirely. Helene was supposed to phone with their new address and phone number, but she hadn't up until I left and I didn't really expect to have a message waiting for me on my machine with the required data when I got back home either. Of course, I knew that she'd be in touch eventually, if only because she'd want me to know where to send my child support payments if we ever really got divorced (and if I ever got another job), so it wasn't like I was really afraid that I might never see my kid again—or, unfortunately, like I wouldn't ever see her *duplicitous* bitch of a mother—but I still felt pretty lousy about the whole situation.

I don't know…I guess the simple way to put it was that I truly loved that kid and I knew that the best possible scenario I could come up with for the future of our relationship was pretty pathetic. I'd send birthday cards and gifts and we'd talk on the phone whenever Helene was in the mood not to hang up on me and she'd even probably even come to visit in B.C. when she was a little older. But the part of the relationship in which each of our lives was totally, absolutely interwoven with each other's—that's the part that was over. She had just turned six about a month and a bit before we were spending the night in Kelowna eating fried fish and not having sex with sixteen-year-olds. For all I knew, Helene had probably tried to convince her that her life with me was just a dream she once had and that Gary Hey-*She*-Seduced-*Me* Bouvier had been her daddy all along. Could she remember when we all lived together as a family? I guessed she probably could if she wanted to no matter what Helene tried to tell her, but whether she really could—or if she even wanted to—was something I had no damn way to know.

We left Kelowna early, stopped for breakfast in a greasy roadside place a little past Penticton, then headed into Vancouver. We stopped twice after that, once to get some gas and once to buy some cold pop, as a result of which we didn't end up arriving in Vancouver until about five in the afternoon. It's funny, but I don't even remember discussing with Dave whether or not he was going to stay with me. I mean, he could have gone wherever he wanted, but he seemed to take it for granted that we were in this—whatever "this" ended up being—together and that I would naturally want him to stay with me. I did actually want him to stay with me, but I wasn't prepared to insist. Whether I was his best or his only option, I didn't ask. I'm still not sure, by the way. But he did end up staying with me in my parents' house, now my house. It turned out all for the best.

I had been living alone in the house for about two months when I left on my trip to nowhere. Mom and Dad had gotten more or less used to their new digs at the Brier Home—if that's the right expression for two people who basically had no idea where they lived or why they were living there—anyway, they had gotten used to the routine of their new lives and I had gotten used to the routine of mine. And now I was home.

All the time I was away—which was only about ten days—I hadn't had a worry about the house or about whether things were safe at home. I hadn't given a moment's thought to paying any bills that might have come while I was away and I hadn't even bothered to get the post office to stop delivering my mail while I was away. I hadn't even really thought of myself as going away, I guess…just stepping outside my life for as long as it was going to take to get myself straight about…about everything, about Wil and about my parents and about little Lena and about that faithless bitch Helene and about being unemployed and about my funds rapidly dwindling to close to nothing and about the books I never quite got around to writing ("because at Corlingham, teaching always comes first") and about every other damn thing that was making me into a wreck who could barely remember how to blow his nose without looking it up first, let alone how to teach college courses.

So we came back to my folks' house, now my house. I found myself a little nervous as I turned into the street, but everything looked calm and the house looked okay. I got my bag out of the trunk and Dave got his—he had spent his fifty on t-shirts, underwear, socks, a pair of shorts and, for some inexplicable reason, a jock strap in some strip mall in Medicine Hat and I had chipped in another fifteen for him to buy a nice gym bag to carry his worldly possessions around in—and in we went. The house was fine. No one had broken in while I was away. The world had resisted one final assault on my wellbeing. I was impressed.

There was a mountain of mail on the floor under the mail slot. It was mostly bills and flyers from the Bay and Eaton's, but there was also a postcard from California. It had a picture of the Golden Gate Bridge on it and it was from Lena, although I figured Helene had picked it out because you could see Alcatraz pretty easily in the background and I knew that she would have thought that was a real scream. She was, Lena wrote in her childish (but totally legible) hand, having fun. The had driven a lot. Gary (at least it wasn't Daddy) had bought her a doll in Oregon. She missed me. Mommy says hi. (Right!) It was signed with the words "love, Lena" surrounded by a dozen x's, which I took to stand for kisses. That was all I needed to see. She loved me. She was gone into a new life with a new man in her mother's bed, but she loved me. She didn't know when she'd see me, but she still loved me. She didn't blame me for ruining her life, even if I was the one who moved out, because she truly loved her old man and she knew I loved her back. As big as the world, as Lena used to like putting it. Was I reading a lot into a circle of x's? I guess…but I was sure that we'd never lose track of each other and that, somehow, we'd always be father and daughter. It turned out I was right, but I obviously had no way to know that then.

Anyway, we settled in. I knew it was a mistake, but I put Dave in Wil's room. My parents' bedroom was the largest bedroom and had its own bathroom, and although I had originally thought it was going to be creepy to sleep in my parents' bed, I knew it would be even worse for me to move back into my old room. Getting used to sleeping in my parents' bedroom had been one thing, however, but seeing Dave unpack—which didn't take too long, since his worldly possessions consisted of half of a gym bag's full of stuff—in Wil's room and put his underwear and socks into the top drawer of Wil's dresser was something I hadn't anticipating being so upsetting. It's not like Dave was exactly doing something to Wil, but he was….I don't know, he wasn't so much taking his place as much as he was taking up his space. It's a weird concept, I guess…but I didn't want anyone to be in Wil's space and, although I only came to this realization after it would have been pathetic for me to do anything about it, I certainly didn't want anybody sleeping in Wil's bed.

Still, I gave it my best shot.

"This is my brother's room, you know."

"The one who died?" I had told him most of the story on the drive home.

"I only had one."

Dave nodded, as though this were fascinating information he was now going to set himself to digesting.

"He died of AIDS, you know."

"I thought you said he hung himself."

"Hanged."

"What?"

"Nothing. He did hang himself, but he would have died of AIDS if he hadn't."

More silence.

"This was his bed. You don't mind sleeping in it?"

"Why would I mind?"

"I don't know. You know, because of him having AIDS and all that."

"Can you get AIDS from sleeping in someone's bed after they're dead?"

"No."

"So why would I care?"

I gave up. Dave appeared not to even realize that I was trying to discourage him from sleeping in my brother's bed. (This was possibly because it had been me who had installed him in Wil's room about twelve seconds before I realized how much I didn't want him to sleep there.) He finished unpacking, then sat down on Wil's bed.

"Was he gay?" The first flicker of interest in Wil I had detected in Dave.

"No."

"You hungry?"

"I'm always hungry."

"You wanna get something to eat?"

"Sure."

We went out to some greasy Korean place on Fraser. I ordered this big wok thing of mixed vegetables with peanut sauce, but Dave thought it would be really funny to order fillet of dog, which basically resulted in them giving us the cold shoulder for the rest of the meal. The food—Dave finally ordered something on the menu, but I forget what—anyway, the food was cold when it came and the portions were about half the size of the meals being served to the people at the other tables. I would have ordered some beers, but I was afraid they were going to piss in them before serving them to us, so we had Cokes and hoped for the best. We ate some of what they served us, then got out. Dave was chagrined.

"No sense of humour, those chinks."

"They were Koreans, not Chinese."

"Like there's a difference."

The evening progressed. We walked down Fraser for a bit, then went in to some pseudo-Cuban place for coffee, then played some pool at the "Pool Guys" Cue Club & Lounge, then went home.

When we got home, there was a certain something in the air.

It wasn't precisely tension—Dave and I had no cause for tension between us that I could think of—but there was definitely something. Some electricity. Some sense that we were about to make a decision of some sort. I went upstairs for a shower, leaving Dave in front of the television. But when I came out of the bedroom, I saw him standing in the hallway stripped down to his underwear waiting to go into the other bathroom for his own shower once I finished running the water in mine. While he was in the john, went downstairs to put up a pot of coffee. When he came down, he was dressed in the same clothes he had been wearing all day and was drying his hair with a towel.

"You wanna go out?" he asked.

"Out? It's eleven o'clock at night. And we've already been out. All evening. You wanna see if we can find somewhere to have an even worse meal?"

"I'm full."

"Good. You want coffee?"

"I thought we might go see my dad."

"Your dad?"

"Yeah."

"Why?"

"I wanna tell him something."

"So call him."

"I wanna tell it to him in person."

"What makes you think he wants you to arrive unannounced at his place in the middle of the night to tell him something you can't say on the phone. Maybe he'd prefer some notice."

"Who cares what he wants?"

"Well, if you want to have any chance of a relationship with him, you might."

"Might what?" A tone of genuine confusion rather than cockiness.

"Might want to care at least a little bit about what he wants. That's how people develop relationships with each other. One person makes believe he cares about what the other wants and that stimulates a parallel desire in the other party to make believe that he cares about what the party of the first part wants. That's why it's called reciprocity. It's also called being nice to each other and not being difficult with people from whom you want something."

"Who says I want anything from him?"

"You want to tell him something that you can't say on the phone."

"That's not the same as wanting something from him."

"What if I call him? You know, just say that you're in town and I have to be going out in his direction and would he mind if I brought you over for a little visit. I could say we're leaving tomorrow and that this is the only chance he'll have."

It was an idiotic idea, but Dave seemed to be taking it quite seriously.

"You'd do that?"

"I guess."

"And you'd tell him that we're leaving tomorrow....for where?"

"I don't know. China. Chile. Guam....someplace."

"You could say we're leaving for Mexico. That you're a Mexican guy and you've hired me to...to work for you...to work in your house for you in Mexico...you've hired me to work as your...no, you could say that I'm marrying your daughter. That's even better. I'm marrying your daughter because she's pregnant...because I got her pregnant when she was up here last year working as an au pair or something. That she was here in the spring and I had a date with her and now she's pregnant and you are taking me back to Mexico to marry her and you don't know when or even if I'll ever be back, but you know how much I want

179

to see him before I go and that you'd like to meet him too because…because he's going to be your daughter's father-in-law and you'd like to meet him. How does that sound?"

Dave was becoming more animated by the moment. I was suddenly a little afraid of what I had started. "And what's my daughter's name?"

Dave thought for a minute. "Evita."

"Evita? He'll never believe it."

"Why not? It's a real name."

"Can you think of anything else?"

"Chiquita?"

"We'll go with Evita. You think he'll find it suspicious that I don't know any Spanish and that I don't have a Spanish accent and that I won't be able to answer even one single question about life in Mexico? That I can't name a single brand of Mexican cigarettes? That I can't name the city in which I was born?"

"Say you're from Rancho Burrito and he won't ask anything else. He's not like really very swift, my dad."

"He's going to have to be a lot dumber than just 'not like really very swift' not to catch on that I'm not a Mexican."

"So say you're an American."

"And what's my daughter's name?"

"Chloe."

XXIII

I couldn't think of anything else to say. Dave wrote down the phone number on a piece of paper and handed it to me. By this time, it was almost twenty past eleven. The whole concept of phoning this guy up and inviting ourselves over was pretty loony, but the idea of doing it in the middle of the night and asking if we might drop over around midnight so Dave's dad could say goodbye to him forever was just insane. Still, I was having difficulty thinking of another plan of action. And I was afraid that Dave would just go over there on his own without me if I didn't insinuate myself into the story that was apparently unfolding around me one way or the other. I picked up the phone and dialed.

One ring. Two. Three. I was feeling relieved. He wasn't home. No machine. Just hang up and try again some other time. Five. Home free. Six.

"Who is it?"

"Is that Mr. Kruger?"

"Who wants to know?"

"My name is…Heidigger. Martin Heidigger."

"Yeah?"

"I know it's late and I'm real sorry to be phoning at this hour…" My Southern drawl was becoming more pronounced by the syllable. "…but your son David and I are planning to leave Vancouver first thing tomorrow morning and he would like to know if it would be possible for us to drop by and get a few of his things. And he has something he wants to tell you, as well.

Something he says he wants to tell you in person."

"What did you say your name was?" A slight slur in his speech, but I couldn't tell if he had been asleep or if he was slightly drunk. These were, of course, not mutually exclusive possibilities.

"Heidigger. Jefferson Davis Martin Heidigger. My friends just call me Jeff."

"And what does my son have to do with you?"

I took a deep breath, then plunged in. "David is marrying my daughter, Mr. Kruger. Chloe was up here in your lovely country last spring working as an au pair girl and she met your son. They…she…well, you know how kids are…anyway, she got herself in the family way and…well you know that we would never consider an abortion, being Republicans and all…anyway, she's going to have the baby and we wanted to have the wedding before she was too big to fit into her mother's wedding dress, God rest her soul. So I flew up to help him get this things together and we're flying…."

"He ain't here. He left a week ago. I don't know where…."

"But Mr. Kruger, he's right here with me. We've just spent a nice week together up at Whistler getting to know each other and now that we do…know each other, that is…anyway, now that we've become such close friends, we're flying back to…to our home…in the South…we're flying back to our home in Georgia tomorrow morning. It's such a lovely house, ours is. And large! Very large and very lovely. Did you know that Georgia is the largest state east of the Mississippi? It is and our house, well it certainly isn't the largest home in Georgia, but it is…it is very commodious and very lovely. Your son will be very happy with us, Mr. Kruger." I was raving and I knew it. But having started, I found myself almost unable to stop. "So would it be alright if we just stopped by right now so David can gather up some of his things?"

A long pause. I could hear Dave's father breathing, so I knew he hadn't hung up. For a while, the breathing was so regular that I thought he might have fallen asleep, but when he spoke, he sounded as though he had only been momentarily lost in thought. "Sure," he said easily. "Come on over. Dave will show you where the house is. Do you have a car?"

"Of course, sir. I rented a lovely car when I arrived and we'll drive over right away."

I hung up the phone. I had come to Vancouver specifically to prevent Dave from doing anything to his father that he would regret for the rest of his life and so far what I had accomplished was arranging a midnight rendezvous with the man under entirely false pretenses without the slightest concept of what Dave was planning or what it really was he intended to do when we got to his home. I was doing great!

We got into the car and drove off. My folks' home is in the part of Vancouver called Kerrisdale, but Buddy Kruger lived somewhere off Forty-Fourth Avenue in East Vancouver. And so we drove off into the night. I could practically feel our evening at the Filet of Seoul and the Pool Guys Cue Club receding into the distant past as we drove. It was cooler than it had been for a while and I was sorry I was wearing shorts. I guess I should have put on a white suit and grown a moustache for my new role as genteel Southerner, but there wasn't time. I'd have to do my best. And Dave was going to have to do his best as well. About me, I was worried enough. But about Dave? Forget about it.

It was almost midnight when we pulled up at Dave's father's bungalow. There was hardly any traffic at all on the main streets we had been driving on and the specific lane Dave's dad lived on was completely still. The house was dark. There weren't any signs of life at all, not a stray cat, not a smoldering cigarette in the ashtray on the front porch, not anything at all to indicate that anyone was home or ever had been at home. Was this where Dave had grown up? I could see him hesitating at the curb as I walked towards the front door.

"You're coming or you're not coming?"

"I'm coming."

"You want to just skip it and go home? That's cool. I don't have any business here of my own, so you don't have to do anything except say you want to forget the whole thing and we'll go home."

"I have to do this."

"You don't have to do anything. But if you want to say goodbye to your father and get your clothes and let him think you've moved to Twelve Oaks to marry Scarlett when you're really going to live happily every after with your grandma in the 'peg, that's up to you. I'm just a prop here, not a player. So what's it gonna be?"

"Ring the bell."

It somehow seemed too late to ring a doorbell, so I knocked. Three times, sounding (even to me) as though it were some sort of signal. Silence. Three more knocks. Nothing. Not a footfall, not an eye (as far as I could see) peeking out from behind an only almost drawn set of drapes. No sign of life at all.

"You sure this is the house?"

"What am I? Stupid?"

"I just meant…."

"He's in there. He was home and this is where he is. Knock again."

I did knock again, then held my breath and listened. Someone was coming towards the door now. I could practically feel the footsteps as they became more pronounced. It wasn't that big a house, but he seemed to be taking an awfully long time to get the door. The porch light went on. I noticed Dave clenching his fists. I took a deep breath. The doorknob began to turn. The door opened….

Buddy Kruger was, to my surprise, a slight man. I had imagined him like some sort of Hulk Hogan type who could beat up his kids with as little effort as most of us need to swat a fly, but he was a small, wiry man that couldn't have been more than five foot five or six. He was slender and balding and he looked more like a worker in a door factory than a cop or a professional wrestler. He was wearing a pair of gym shorts and a yellow tanktop and he was surprisingly polite.

"Come in," he said, stepping back to allow us to enter. "You are Mr. Davis?"

"Mr. Heidigger. Davis is the first of my middle names." Or had I said my name was Something Something Jefferson Davis? Well, too late now.

"Well, come in, Mr. Hydinger, and let's have us a visit." Then, turning to face Dave. "You come in too, son."

The front door opened onto the living room, where we all sat down. Dave took the only arm chair in the room and I sat down on the couch. Buddy Kruger sat on what looked like a piano stool, although I couldn't see a piano anywhere to go with it.

"So can I get you something to drink?"

"I'm okay, thank you."

"Dave?"

"No."

For a long moment, none of us was sure what was supposed to come next. Were we alone in the house, the three of us? There was no indication of a fourth party, but I had no idea if Buddy had been in bed alone when we phoned or not. And whether whoever might have been there when I had phoned was or wasn't still there was obviously something I also did not know. But it felt like we were alone.

Eventually, Dave spoke up. "Okay if I get some of my stuff, Dad?"

Buddy looked surprised by the question, almost as though he hadn't really understood it. "Your stuff?"

"You know, my clothes and stuff like that."

"They're yours, son. Take what you want."

Dave got up and walked out of the living room through a narrow hallway to the back of the house. Buddy and I were alone.

"What's your daughter's name?" he asked, almost as though this were a normal conversation.

"Chloe. And she's a lovely thing, if I do say so myself. Your son has excellent taste."

"And he knocked her up?"

"Yes, sir, he did. Mind you, we're not mad or anything. It always takes two to tango, after all. She wasn't attacked and she's never claimed that he forced himself on her. They were just two kids in love showing each other just how much they loved each other." I couldn't have sounded less like the father of a teenager who had come to Canada to work for a few months as an au pair and ended up pregnant, but I wanted at all costs to preserve the calm. And who knew, I asked myself—maybe Dave and his father would end up saying goodbye to each other and shaking each other's hand and Dave would be free to go to Winnipeg and get on with his life. "Anyway, she came home and only discovered she was pregnant once she got back. She phoned him and he has behaved, sir, like a real gentleman. I might almost say, like a real Southern gentleman. He proposed marriage on the spot. And she accepted. He invited her to live up here, but, well, you know how it is, Mr. Kruger. We are so fabulously…well, let's just say that we are very comfortable people and there didn't seem to be any reason not to bring David down to live with us. We're giving the children the east wing for their own. That's where the nursery is, right down the hall from the billiards room and the sauna."

What was I talking about? I had no idea.

"And how is my boy going to get permission to work in

the…."

When it happened, it happened so quickly that he was actually dead before I realized I was still waiting for him to finish his sentence. Dave had known what he was doing all along, I suppose, but I still think that I didn't really believe anything was going to happen at all. Dave, at any rate, hadn't packed a thing, but had returned with a gun and shot his father in the back. Death, as far as I could tell, was instantaneous. Was that his father's gun that he had used? It must have had some sort of silencer on it because there hadn't been a loud gun shot, just a sort of whoosh that I hadn't even realized was the sound of a gun being shot until I saw the blood spurting out of Buddy Kruger's chest. And when I looked to Dave, there was indeed a black gun in his hand.

I looked around to see where the bullet had gone, but it was either lodged somewhere in Buddy Kruger's chest or else it had harmlessly passed through him and embedded itself somewhere else. I'm not sure how to explain what happened next. I was somehow giddy and clearheaded at the same time, somehow able to think carefully about what the best way to proceed was going to be and also entirely incapable of really taking in what had just happened in any truly honest way. I was both there and not there, both aware that a dead man was lying on the floor in front of me and completely oblivious to that fact. The only thing I can say for sure is that I was there when Dave shot his father and I think that he died instantly. Or at least that he appeared to.

Dave looked like he was in shock. He started to shake, then told me he was nauseous. He went into the bathroom and kneeled over the toilet bowl, but in the end he didn't puke. And then, when he stood up, he looked slightly better and distinctly less green.

"So now what?" What an idiotic question, even for me!

"Well, we could phone 911 and confess so they can send us to jail for the rest of our lives. Or we could just get in the car and go."

I wasn't sure what to do. I couldn't see calling the police, at least not from the scene of the crime. But it just didn't seem possible to get in the car and drive away as though we had spent a pleasant evening visiting a dear friend and were now ready to head back home.

"What do you think?"

Dave appeared, in fact, to be thinking carefully about the right way to proceed. "Go sit in the car."

"You want me to get in the car?"

"That's what I said."

Dave was calm now, but I could hear the heat—if that's the right word—I could hear the heat in his voice. He was in control, but he wasn't the same kid I had picked up between Barrymore and Stanhope a week earlier. He was more self-assured than I had pictured him, more self-assured and far more mature in his bearing. It was almost as though he had grown up in the time between pulling the trigger and seeing the bullet enter his father's back. I wasn't sure precisely what I should do. I didn't want to leave him, but this was, after all, his business, not mine and it didn't seem quite right for me to be telling him what to do now that he had committed the very murder I had fantasized I was bringing him to Vancouver to prevent. Had I done even one thing to prevent this from happening? Off hand, I couldn't think of any I'd bother mentioning in a court of law.

It seemed odd to me that I was still sitting on the couch, but, of course, it hadn't been five minutes since I had been describing my plantation to Buddy and indicating which wing was to be his son's once he married my lovely daughter, Chloe. I got up from the couch without saying anything and walked out the front door. I got into my car, stuck the key in the ignition and turned on the radio to the all-news station. It was entirely irrational, but I was vaguely surprised that they weren't switching live to police head-quarters downtown for an up-to-the-minute update on the investigation into the murder of Buddy Kruger.

I lit a cigarette, then leaned back and closed my eyes to wait for Dave.

XXIV

"Pop the trunk, will ya?"

I opened my eyes instead. Dave was standing by the driver's side window and bending over to see me. "Just open the trunk, okay?" He sounded self-assured, in control, like a man (not a boy) who had been waiting for something to happen for so long that he knew what to do and what to say like a kid in some school play who had memorized his lines and was just reciting them aloud without having to worry about getting them straight. I got out of the car and opened the truck. Then I got back into the driver's seat. I had expected Dave to put something in the trunk once I opened it, but he just watched me and then headed back into the house.

I noticed my hands were shaking. I jammed them in between my thighs—I was still wearing shorts—for some warmth, but it didn't much help. I wasn't chilly—I was more freaked out than I had ever been in my life. Including when Constable Wu came to tell me about Wil, I might add.

It seemed to me that a long time had passed since Dave had asked me to open the trunk. I didn't want to attract attention, however, and sitting in a car on a residential street in the middle of the night with the trunk wide open was, it struck me, a fairly suspicious thing to be doing. I got out to close the trunk, but just as I did so, Dave exited from the house.

He looked calm as he carefully locked the door, but whether he had had his own keys with him or if he had taken his father's, I obviously had no way to know. At least, I supposed, he didn't

190

expect me to shove his father's body into the trunk and dump it somewhere. As I watched him hurry down the walk leading up to the front door, I could see Dave was carrying three things. In his left hand, there was a suitcase. In his right hand, he had two things: something that looked like a bowling ball carrier case and a black plastic garbage bag. He didn't hurry, didn't jog the last few steps as though he couldn't wait to get into the car and get gone. Instead, he carefully put all three things in the trunk, closed the top and got into the car. I got in too and we drove away. It was just after twelve thirty. We had visited with the late Buddy Kruger for about ten minutes before his untimely death and Dave had spent another twenty minutes or so in the house. I couldn't believe it still wasn't half past twelve—when I looked at my watch, I expected it to be hours later. To my surprise, I found I was hungry. Starving. Ravenous. I had to get something to eat, but I wasn't sure I wanted to encounter anyone who could identify either of us later on. I decided to wait until we got home to eat.

I was suddenly very tired. I drove slowly, figuring that the very last thing we needed was to get stopped by a cop, but I wasn't really able to control the speed of the car in the normal way—I kept decelerating to ten or fifteen clicks beneath the limit, then accelerating up until I was really speeding. I was driving like a drunk, although without the weaving part, and I was afraid of getting pulled over. I resolved to put every ounce of concentration into controlling the car. I did a bit better, but it still wasn't great. By the time we turned into my street, I was a wreck. My hands were really shaking and my back was covered with sweat. I felt a sudden wave of nausea come over me, only to be replaced with a kind of vertigo that really made driving almost impossible. I don't know how I managed to do it, but I did eventually get back to my house without killing us or crashing the car. We got out of the car.

"You gonna leave your gear in the trunk?"

Dave smiled. "No."

"You want me to open the trunk?"

"Yeah."

"You wanna tell me what you took out of the house?"

"Sure."

"Well what?"

Dave looked amused to be having this discussion in the middle of the night on a public street. "Well," he began, "in the garbage bag are my father's bloody clothes and the gun."

"You took your father's clothing with you? Why?"

"I dunno. I sort of liked the idea of leaving him lying there naked. Sort of something to confuse the police a little bit. Like make it look like he brought this hooker home and got himself undressed only to have her rob him and kill him."

"You took his wallet too, I hope."

"Obviously. And his watch. They're in the garbage bag too."

"Okay, then, what's in the suitcase?"

"My stuff. Some jeans and some shirts and a pair of Reeboks and a framed picture of my mom and Kevin and me. And this blanket my grandma knit when my mom was pregnant with me."

"Your mom's mom or your dad's."

"My dad's."

"And what's in the bowling ball case?"

"Guess."

I swear I had no idea at all what was in the case. I know you'll find that unlikely, but I swear it's true. I had no idea what was in the case.

"A bowling ball?"

"No."

"What then?"

Dave looked at me as though he couldn't believe I was asking for real. "His head," he said calmly, as though he were simply cataloguing his belongs for some customs officer at the airport after a holiday in Hawaii. "What do you think took me so long in there? I tried to get it off with a steak knife, but it wasn't long enough. And then I tried this big knife my dad used to clean fish he caught, but it wasn't sharp enough."

I wanted to ask him what he used to hack off his father's head, but I found that although I had formulated the question clearly enough in my mind, all I could do was make some unintelligible gurgling sounds in my throat.

Dave had apparently seized the essence of my question anyway. "Then I had the idea to use this saw he had in the tool shed out back. It worked really good, but it made even more of a mess. I was smart to get him undressed before I started, but it wasn't that bad really…."

I began to regain my composure. "You cut off your father's head?" I asked, sounding as though he hadn't just said precisely that.

"Are you stupid? I just said that."

"And what are you planning to do with it?"

"I dunno…." Sounding as though he hadn't really considered that was going to have to do something with it now that it was in his possession. "Get rid of it somewhere, I guess. You wanna see it?"

I meant to say no, but I heard myself saying that I did. Was I crazy? Or was this some sort of self-imposed penance for not having had the nerve to have Wil's head severed from his emaciated body so that it could be frozen and then thawed out and cloned into a full person after a cure for AIDS is perfected one day? Or was I just curious what a severed head would like up close? I had seen plenty of pictures of Salome contemplating the severed head of John the Baptist, of course. And I had had that dream about the heads of Ahab's seventy sons stacked up in those pyramids at the gates of Samaria dozens of times. So I knew what I thought one would look like, but it was hard to know for sure. I contemplated the situation, wished I had just said no, but didn't retract my answer. And, if you want to know the absolute truth, I didn't want to retract it either. I wanted to see what Buddy Kruger's head was going to look like as Dave lifted it out of the bowling ball bag.

Suddenly, a new thought. "So where's the bowling ball?"

A sly smile. "I stuck it on his neck."

"Oh."

We went inside. The evening had turned cool, but the house was warm and inviting. Dave went upstairs with the suitcase of his clothing, which I had carried inside, and left me downstairs with the garbage bag and the bowling ball case. I wasn't too happy to be alone with the head and the bloody clothing and the gun—I tried to remind myself not to forget about the gun—but there didn't seem to be too much choice. And Dave was back in a moment anyway.

He picked up the bag with his father's head in it and put it on his lap. "You sure you wanna see?"

"You sound like you're not sure you want to show me?"

"Hey, if I could get it off his body, I can show it to you, man. That was a bloody mess—this is just show-and-tell."

"So let's see."

Like he was the initiating priest in some ancient mystery cult, Dave unzipped the bag. He looked in for a moment. I thought he was going to be sick—or do I mean that I thought I was going to be?—anyway, I thought he was probably going to be sick, but he didn't say anything at all, just reached in and pulled out his dad's head by its thinning—although I guess it was as thinned as it was going to get—curly hair. The human head, I remember reading somewhere, only weighs about eight pounds. I don't know why that surprised me—I guess it seems like it should weigh more. Anyway, Dave lifted it up and put it down on the newspaper I had been reading the morning I left on my trip while I drank my coffee and which was still where I had left it.

Buddy's head didn't look as sickening or as scary as I thought it was going to be. I felt a little ill when I focused for a moment on the jagged tears of flesh at the neck where Dave had apparently sawed it off his father's body, but when I forced myself to ignore the neck and just to look into the eyes, it looked…okay. Like a really life-like bust of someone rather than like a real person's head. So this was the head of a man who had beaten a woman, then raped her on a floor covered with hamburger relish and broken glass and the mess of a dinner she had made for him, then puked all over her. This was a man who used to whack the crap out of his own sons and then calm down by listening to the Beatles' White Album. For a pointless moment, I tried to conjure up that scene. Did he hit them with his hands or with his belt or with something else? Dave hadn't ever said. And did he have certain specific songs on the album he liked to listen to or did he just start from the beginning and listen to the whole thing. And if he did listen to the whole album, did he make a point of always listening to the first record first, or did he just put on which ever one was in the sleeve of the jacket he reached into first?

I had other questions to ask as well, although I didn't hear myself asking any of them out loud. Aside from raping her and beating her up, had Buddy betrayed her in other ways as well? Was he faithful to her, for instance, or did he have other women on the side? And did he beat her because he had this insane idea that she needed the punishment for whatever sins he thought she had committed or because it just felt so good to him that he couldn't hold himself back? Was doing her afterwards an afterthought or the point of the whole exercise in the first place? And would he have acted differently if he knew that his boys were awake—or at least that one of them was—or was that part of the thrill, knowing that he had an audience of terrified little boys?

I had no call to ask these questions out loud for several reasons. For one, the head wasn't going to answer them anyway, so it would hardly have been worth the effort. For another, I wasn't sure if I wanted to make Dave think about the very demons I knew he was trying his best to exorcise. I mean—don't misunderstand—I was completely appalled at what he had done. But I also understood it and, at least in some sick way, I esteemed him for having had the nerve to avenge his mother's death in a way he was absolutely correct in believing that the courts never would. Was taking justice into one's own hands such a sin, I asked myself. And my answer? Only when (a) there's the alternative of bringing in the police and (b) when you aren't absolutely sure you're right. If those were my criteria, then Dave passed. And besides, Buddy Kruger was already dead so the question to ask wasn't really whether or not he deserved to die, but what I was going to do about it right now. Was I going to turn Dave into the police so they could put him away for twenty-five to life? Was I going to forget the whole thing? Was I going to put Buddy's head out with the trash the following Tuesday morning (maybe in front of my neighbours' place) and hope that the bag ended up in some landfill site somewhere without anyone ever opening it? I thought I should wash the bloody clothing and then leave it at the nighttime drop-off box behind the Salvation Army Thrift Shop down on No. 3 Road in Richmond. The gun, I could either keep or just pitch in the trash at the Burger King just up the street a bit from the thrift shop. The head…I didn't quite know what I thought we should do with the head.

And now a new set of thoughts.

"When do you think they'll find your father's body?"

"I dunno. Maybe never."

"Well, they will. At least eventually."

"Why?"

"Well, because someone is eventually going to realize that something is wrong. The postman will realize that no one is picking up the mail, for one thing."

"There's a mail chute, so it'll take a while before anyone notices."

"And the garbage men will notice that no one is putting any trash out."

"You really think that they report which houses don't put out trash?"

"And all his bills will go unpaid."

"They'll just send second bills the next month. And then third bills the month after that."

"And he won't show up for work on Monday. They'll notice. And they'll phone."

"So he won't answer. They'll think he's too drunk to come to the phone. Or they'll think he's with some chick somewhere and can't be bothered getting out of bed long enough to call in sick."

"Well, he must have some friends. They'll call a few times and he won't answer and someone will eventually call the police. They'll break in the door and find his body with the bowling ball instead of a head on its shoulders."

"So what? No one saw us. And no one can connect me with him. My stuff is gone, or at least some of it is, but they have no way to know when I took it. I can always say I had it with me all along, if it comes to that. But it won't. It'll be days before anyone thinks to phone the police, or more likely weeks since his friends aren't mostly the kind of people who look forward to having unnecessary contact with the police. They may never call…."

"Well," I countered, feeling truly exhausted, "eventually if he doesn't pay his property taxes, they'll seize his house. And they'll find him then."

"When do you owe your taxes?"

"July."

"You mean next July?" It was still only August.

"I guess."

"Well, then, that doesn't sound too serious now, does it?"

"And then there's the smell. The neighbours will smell his body rotting and they'll phone the cops. And they aren't necessarily the kind of people who won't want to be in touch with the police."

"Who cares?"

It was a good question. In the end, I thought, no one would care. A man would be found murdered. He had no parents, no wife, no locatable children. If Buddy had any siblings, Dave hadn't mentioned any. There wouldn't be any clues (I hoped) and no one would be able to identify the car. And even if someone did see a blue Camaro parked on the street, there must be hundreds, maybe thousands, of cars like mine in B.C. alone. Would anyone have taken down the licence plate number? That sounded unlikely—why would anyone have? Would Dave be questioned? Undoubtedly. But he could either get his grandmother and brother to say he was in Winnipeg the whole time or else he could just say he had nothing to do with it. There wasn't any sort of obvious motive anyway that would make him a suspect. He didn't stand to inherit too much, I didn't think. And the beatings he and his brother got had never been made public. And neither, I presumed, had Buddy's treatment of their mother. He would be seen as an orphan and a victim, not as a suspect, I told myself. And they would be right in the end—he *was* an orphan and he surely *was* a victim. And if the man who was responsible for an innocent woman's death had been executed, then that wasn't such a bad thing either.

I excused myself and went upstairs to bed. I heard Dave shuffling around in Wil's room, then going to sleep himself. The house was still. Buddy's head was still on the coffee table. I thought I wouldn't be able to fall asleep, but I did, almost immediately. I had the dream about the heads of Ahab's sons at the gates of Samaria, but it didn't scare me particularly. And none of the heads was Wil's this time. Or Buddy's, for that matter. I woke up at seven and felt pretty good about things. We'd ditch the head, launder the clothing, lose the gun and get Dave back to Winnipeg. Things were looking up already.

XXV

The head was gone when I came downstairs, but Dave was in the kitchen trying to figure out how the percolator worked. He was dressed in fresh clothes and his hair was still wet from the shower. I was in such a weird state of mind that I found myself wondering how he could have showered without me having heard the water running instead of focusing on the fact that I was about to have coffee with a boy who had executed and beheaded his father the previous evening. I showed him how to make non-instant coffee—and found it charming that he needed to be taught such a basic skill of adult living—then took out some waffles from the freezer and popped them into the toaster. It was a warm Thursday morning. The regular sounds of an urban summer's morning were easily audible. It was a normal day….

"So what do you have planned for today?" As though we were old pals looking forward to a few pleasant hours in each other's company.

"I dunno. I guess we should ditch the head and the rest of the stuff."

I nodded gravely. "I guess we should. Any ideas?"

"Let's wash the clothes and take it from there…."

I had all my clothing from the trip that I wanted to wash, but it didn't seem right to put all the stuff in the washer together. I should have made Dave do it himself, but I didn't want to for some reason—and, besides, if he couldn't figure out the percolator, why would I think he could dope out the washing machine? I found the black garbage bag where he had left it by the front door and took it into the laundry room.

I opened it, expecting…I don't know what I was expecting, but when I turned it over to empty its contents onto the floor, I was surprised not by the awfulness of what I saw, but by the banality of it all. On the floor at my feet were a yellow tank top, a pair of blue gym shorts, a pair of white jockey underpants, two grey athletic socks, two sneakers, a wallet, a wristwatch and…this was the only real surprise…a hearing aid. Had Buddy been wearing the hearing aid during our brief encounter? I couldn't recall. I certainly hadn't noticed it, but that wasn't too conclusive—I was hardly focusing on his ears during our time together. Still, I was surprised I hadn't noticed.

Other than the shirt, the clothing was distinctly less bloody than I had expected it was going to be. The tank top itself was soaked with blood, now mostly dried to a dark red, and there were bullet holes in both the front and the back, but there wasn't too much blood anywhere else and, at least as far as I could see, Buddy's gym shorts and his underwear were almost completely unstained.

I put everything except for the gun, the wallet, the hearing aid and the wristwatch in the machine, put a little plastic shovelful of detergent and a little bleach into the machine and turned it on. Then I opened the wallet. In it, I found what anyone would consider the boring record of a boring life. A driver's licence in the name of Robert Arnold Kruger. A social insurance card. A B.C. health plan Care Card. A Sear's credit card. An Esso card. A Bank of Hong Kong Mastercard. Three Canadian five-dollar bills and nine American dollars, all singles. A torn off piece of newspaper with a telephone number with a Calgary area code written on it. A credit card receipt for a meal at the Hunan Garden, a place on King George Highway in Surrey where, oddly enough, I had eaten with Helene once or twice even before we got married. I put the wallet's contents in my back pocket, then put the empty wallet in my front pocket and looked for a moment at the watch. A Seiko with a frayed imitation leather band. The time was correct, as was the date. I put the watch in the same pocket as the empty wallet, then sat down to read the paper while the machine washed a dead man's clothing. The gun, I wiped down carefully to get rid of fingerprints (just like in the movies!), then wrapped in a dishtowel and put in a plastic Safeway bag. The hearing aid, I just threw in the trash.

The rest of the day passed quite uneventfully. The machine finished washing the clothes and I put them in the dryer. The dryer dried them, whereupon I replaced all of them but the tank top in the plastic bag. Dave sat still during all of this, declining a look at the paper and indicating with a casual nod backwards of his head that he had no wish for any stimulation other than his own memories of the previous evening. There really wasn't any point to belabour the point—I suppose I would have felt the same way. I cut Buddy's shirt up into little yellow squares and divided them into two piles, the two with the bullet holes on the left and the rest on the right. I put the piles of yellow fabric in separate pockets.

We went out. As I had planned, we drove into Richmond and left the bag with Robert Arnold, a.k.a. Buddy, Kruger's clothing at the clothing drop-off bin behind the Salvation Army Thrift Shop on No. 3 Road. To make it look slightly less like one single outfit of clothing, I had added in some old underwear and some old t-shirts of my own plus an old pair of running shoes and an ancient pair of ice skates I had been meaning to replace for years. If anyone ever connected that bag of clothing with Dave's dad, I never heard about it.

The parking lot at Burger King was filled and there were cars waiting to get in, so we decided to change our plans for getting rid of the wallet and watch. The Salvation Army shop was open, so we headed back there and bought bathing suits and two towels.

Then we drove into Vancouver—for some reason, I didn't want to go home until this was all taken care of—and headed for the public pool at Kitsilano Beach. We swam for about an hour, then changed back into our clothing, locked Buddy's empty wallet and watch in a locker and got back into the car. We drove to a 7-11 where I bought two containers of Tropicana orange juice. We drank the juice, put the key to the locker at the pool in one empty container and the contents of Buddy's wallet in the other, then jammed both into an overflowing garbage container at the rear of the store's parking lot. It was just plain fortuitous that Vancouver was having a garbage strike at the moment, but I just couldn't imagine anyone ever going through that much trash with no reason to do so and I imagined that whatever happened to all the rest of the garbage—and there was a ton of it—whenever it was eventually hauled away would happen to our two orange juice containers as well. That took care of the wallet, the clothing and the watch and left us with the gun, the head, the pieces of Buddy's shirt and the bowling ball case to deal with. Dave's own clothing, we decided we didn't need to deal with at all—it was his size and belonged to him and in the unlikely event that anyone ever needed or wanted to know how he had come to have it with him, he would just say he had taken it with him when he left in the first place.

By this time, it was already the middle of the afternoon. We stopped into a Chinese place on West Broadway and ate dim sum for a while, then headed to Oakridge and went to a Julia Roberts movie, which I actually disliked less than I expected I was going to. I put the pieces of Buddy's shirt without the bullet holes in the trash in the men's room of the theatre, then flushed the two pieces that did have bullet holes in them down two separate toilets. When we came out, it was already evening. We went home and retrieved the bowling ball bag with the head inside. I had half expected it to be emanating the foul odour of rotting flesh, but there was no smell at all…or at least none that I could detect. Dave put the bag—or actually, I must have thought, the bags, since we had put the head in three or four different Safeway bags, each one separately sealed with a twist-tie, and then jammed the whole thing in the carrier bag—in the trunk and we headed off for some bowling alley Dave said he had once been to with some friends.

The place turned out to be quite far out on the Lougheed Highway, but we found it and went inside. Dave carried the bag and set it down on one of the plastic seats behind the lane we were assigned. We played a few games. He was terrible, but I was worse—between the two of us, we managed to play three full games without either of us getting even a spare, let alone a strike. We drank a few Cokes and Dave ate two orders of chips with vinegar. And then, when we were through, we put the bag with about four dozen other, almost identical bags—it was a league bowling night and almost every lane was in use—against the back wall of the place, then played another game and walked out. No one called to us, no one seemed even to notice us. No one, certainly, was watching anywhere nearly closely enough to notice that we had left our bag with the others. Another party took our lane almost immediately. Dave stopped into the men's room in the Arby's at the other end of the strip mall. I bought another Coke at the grocery store between the bowling alley and the Arby's, then wasted some time looking at the selection of dirty magazines until Dave came to get me. We got in the car and went home. The gun in yet another Safeway bag was still in the trunk of my car.

We watched the local news that evening at 11:30, but there was no mention of Buddy's murder and neither was there anything about an unidentified man's head being found in a bowling alley on the Lougheed Highway. We were both pleased and disappointed at the same time, or at least I was. Was it really this easy to get away with murder?

The next morning, a Vancouver city policeman came to my front door and asked to speak to Dave. He didn't ask who I was or what my precise relationship to Dave might have been. What he surmised, I can't imagine—or rather, I can—but he didn't say or ask a thing. Instead, he took me aside before I had a chance to get Dave (who was upstairs, I hoped, making the beds) and told me the sad story. Dave's father hadn't gone to work the day before and a woman he had been seeing off and on over the last few months phoned the police that she had gone over to his house last night and found his body. There was no question that he had been murdered, the officer said—without giving away any details of the event that were still classified, he could assure me that there was no question that the man had not died a natural death. The woman—Buddy's girlfriend—had thought that Dave was living at home and had no idea where he might be, but she knew that the other boy, Kevin, was living with his maternal grandmother in Winnipeg. How Buddy had known that, the officer didn't say and I didn't want to ask. I assumed—as I still do—that Kevin must have let his father know where he was once he was settled in and that his father, for his own reasons, must have chosen not to share that information with Dave. Yet another reason to think ill of that lowlife, I thought—he didn't only deny Dave a mother, but he denied him a brother as well.

The police had found an address for Kevin in Buddy's address book and the Winnipeg police had gone there to tell Kevin the awful news. While they were there, they had learned that Dave had recently been in Winnipeg for a visit and that he was probably at this address—I had left Abigail my address and phone number in the hope she might want to be in touch with me later on—which was why the constable had come to my door: to tell Dave the awful news of his father's death and to ask him if he had any idea who could possibly have wanted his father dead. If the officer, whose badge gave his name as D. Singh, suspected any connection between Dave and his father's death, he didn't let on, I thought, even obliquely. Of course, I reminded myself, it was hardly in his best interests to let such suspicions be known at all, least of all to the suspect himself.

I kept feeling that I ought to explain who I was in all of this, but Constable Singh didn't ask and I somehow found the discipline not to say. (Partially, this was because I myself had no idea why precisely it was that I had allowed Dave to become part of my life, to stay in my home or to involve me in a criminal deed for which the punishment was certainly, I imagined, decades in prison without the possibility of parole.) I went to get Dave.

"There's a policeman downstairs."

"No way."

"Take this seriously, David. He's here to tell you about your dad's death. He's going to ask you if you have any idea who would have wanted your father dead. Listen to me carefully, Dave: say nothing at all. Tell him you have no idea, that your dad must have surprised a burglar, that he was involved with drugs off and on and that he may have forgotten to pay his cocaine bill or something like that. Don't mention your brother, don't mention yourself and, of all things, don't mention your mother. Your future depends on how shocked you can look when he tells you the news. Now go, before he wonders what we're talking about."

Dave put down the pillow slip he had been holding and went downstairs.

Constable Singh spoke clearly and to the point. Dave looked shocked, then stunned, then amazed. It was a wonderful performance, a true tour de force. He didn't cry—which would have been too much for someone receiving such stunning news—but he also didn't sound as though he fully believed the awful news. He was excellent in every way, I thought. And I saw no indication—and believe me, I was watching carefully—I saw no indication at all that Constable D. Singh considered Dave anything more than the victim-by-extension of an awful example of the kind of urban violence to which even a city as peaceful as Vancouver was becoming more and more used with every passing year.

There was an autopsy scheduled for the next day, Constable Singh informed us. That would last a few hours, but if Dave wanted to arrange a funeral for any time after that, there would probably not be any problem. When we were through hearing these details, Dave asked how precisely his father had died, quite as though the thought had just that moment occurred to him.

"He was shot," Constable Singh stated in as matter-of-fact voice as he could.

"My father owned a gun," Dave volunteered.

"He did?" Constable Singh sounded very interested. "What kind?"

"I don't know. It looked like a revolver, but I don't know what brand or anything like that. Just a gun. A black one."

"Do you know where he got it?"

"He always had it."

"We haven't found a gun in his house."

"Maybe he didn't have it anymore. He never mentioned that he had gotten rid of it, so I just sort of assumed he still had it. But maybe he didn't…."

"And when did you see the gun last?"

Dave actually furrowed his brow as he appeared lost in thought. "I dunno," he said after just the right pause. "Maybe three or four years ago."

"You saw it three or four years ago, but not since?"

"That's right."

"We're going to need to find out about that gun. Do you know where he kept it? In the house, I mean."

"I don't know. In his bedroom, I think. In the closet some-where, maybe in some box. I never saw him take it out or put it away."

"Do you know if he had any ammunition? Bullets, I mean. Or cartridges. For the gun, I mean. Did he have any stuff like that?"

Dave shook his head. "I dunno. He would have, I guess. But I never saw any."

A long silence. And then, a painful question asked so com-pletely guilelessly that even I managed to forget for the moment that Dave knew the answer to his question perfectly well. "Do you know why anyone would have killed my father?" he asked, his eyes almost miraculously welling up with tears.

"Well," the policeman said, "we don't know that. But there have been other instances…."

"Other instances of what?"

"Look, son, I haven't mentioned something you're going to find out anyway soon enough, so I might as well say it to you now. Your father was killed with a gun, but whoever killed him also…he also beheaded him. Your dad's head is missing and we haven't been able to locate it. We will, but we just haven't quite yet."

Dave somehow knew that the ticket was to look more as though he simply couldn't take this all in at once than outraged or angry.

"His head is missing? Where is it?" Asked perfectly, without even the slightest nod to the fact that Constable Singh had just said ten seconds earlier that the police had no idea where Buddy's head had ended up.

"We don't know. But there have been three other murders in the last four years in B.C. in which the heads of the victims were cut off. Two were here in the Lower Mainland and the other one was up in Prince Rupert, but we're investigating them all again to see if there's any relationship between them all or even between one or two of them and your father's…and what happened to your father. It could be some weird cult thing or it could just be a coincidence. I know it's tempting to start spinning out elaborate conspiracy theories, but I wouldn't jump to any conclusions just quite yet if I were you. Better just to let us do our job and see what happens. It might take a while, but they'll release the body once the autopsy is complete and you can proceed with a funeral."

The rest of the interview went by quickly. Constable Singh shook both our hands, still without asking what the nature of my relationship to Dave was. Did he assume we were older and younger gay lovers? Or did he just imagine I had rented a room in my large house to a tenant? Or had Abigail told the Winnipeg police that I was a friend of hers so that it must have seemed that letting Dave sleep for a while in my house was a favour I was doing for her rather than for Dave himself? All of these were plausible, but none of them came to the fore. Constable Singh told us again how sorry he was for Dave's loss, then went off into the bright morning.

As soon as he was gone, Dave turned to face me. "Shit," he said.

"Shit what?"

"Shit I hadn't thought that I was going to get stuck making a funeral if I don't want it to look like I hated the bastard. I mean, he was my father. How much do you think that's going to cost?"

"Cost who?" I asked. It was one thing to buy him a few meals and a gym bag, but I certainly wasn't going to underwrite the expense of his father's funeral.

"Cost anyone. I'll call Kevin. We'll sell the house and pay for the funeral from the proceeds."

"You're going to need the money before you could possibly sell the house."

"Why? We'll schedule the funeral for a week from now and we'll sell the house before then. I'll call a real estate agent and get it looked after. You only have to pay them after they sell the house, you know."

I knew, but I was semi-surprised Dave did. "Okay, but what if it doesn't sell? In a week, I mean. What if you need the money before you can get the house sold?"

"I'll borrow it from my grandma if I have to."

"You think she's going to front you the money to bury the man who caused her daughter's death?"

"She hated him so bad I think she'd pay anything to get him underground."

I thought about this for a moment. "You're probably right."

"You know I am." Then, a thought. "Do you even have to have a funeral?"

"No, I don't think so. But you have to do something with the body."

"Can we cremate it?"

"I guess. Why not?"

"And then what do we have to do with the ashes?"

"I have no idea. I don't think you have to do anything. You could sprinkle them somewhere. Or keep them. Or bury them."

"Could we put them out with your trash on Wednesday morning?"

I smiled, but wearily. "It's Tuesday morning in this neighbourhood."

"Even better."

XXVI

The autopsy, I later realized, was being carried out Friday morning while Constable Singh was talking to Dave at my home. The newspapers were filled with the story of Buddy's murder, but for all the space they devoted to the story, it was still clear that no one knew too much about what had happened. The police, I read in the Friday papers, were looking for a gun that was missing from the home of the deceased. The paper didn't say how the police knew he had owned a gun, thereby giving the impression that he had possessed a licence for it that the police had tracked down. For all I knew that may well have been true, but the fact that the gun was in the trunk of my car was making me very nervous indeed. Dave, for his part, seemed oddly uninterested in all the excitement and barely glanced at the papers.

Around noon on Friday, I phoned the coroner's office and learned that the autopsy was complete and that the family was free to claim the body. I didn't respond one way or the other, just got off the phone and relayed the message. At my insistence, Dave phoned his grandmother's house to speak to his brother. They were, Dave had assured me, their father's only living relatives and, at the very least, it would look odd to the police if they didn't appear to care enough about their father's death even to claim his body. They were on the phone for about twenty minutes, after which Dave came in from the study to speak with me. He looked a bit pale, but otherwise okay. He seemed more confident than grief-stricken, almost as though he was slightly ashamed of feeling as proud as he did feel that he had managed to do something he had hoped to accomplish for a very long time.

"So are you going to have a funeral?"

"No funeral. My grandma says to have the body cremated, then to collect the ashes and sprinkle them somewhere."

"Where?"

"She said in the nearest cess pool, but I think we'll go for something less gross. How about we go across on the ferry to the Island next week and we can pitch the whole thing overboard?"

"That sounds reasonable."

And that's how it happened. I phoned a funeral chapel and had them pick up Buddy's body and get it cremated. The charge was, I thought, reasonable—$400 for the whole thing, pick-up, cremation and post-cremation packaging included. I stopped by later in the day with a cheque and that, more or less, was that. Buddy was cremated on Saturday, I think. We picked up his ashes early Monday morning, then headed for the ferry terminal in Tsawassen. We parked the car and went on as foot passengers. About halfway through the trip, I went into the men's room, pried open the urn, checked that the ashes only filled up the bottom third (as the man at the funeral chapel had mentioned), then took the gun from the gym bag I had bought Dave in Regina, jammed it inside and went back to join Dave at the railing.

"So are we going to have a funeral?"

"What?"

"I mean, are you going to deliver a eulogy?"

"A what?"

"A speech about the deceased. About what a tragedy his death is for his beloved family and how the gaping hole he has left in all your lives will never be closed entirely."

"What are you talking about? The gaping hole in his chest is what will never be closed entirely, at least not in my memory. But if you think we should have a funeral, go ahead. But you'd better be quick if you want to pitch this thing in the river before we get too close to Swartz Bay."

"It's a strait, not a river."

"Wow…is it great to be so smart?"

"Actually, it's idyllic."

I opened my Bible and read the twenty-third psalm. I wasn't sure that was an entirely appropriate choice, but the part about walking through the valley of the shadow of death somehow struck me as not entirely inappropriate. When I finished, Dave solemnly took the box from my hand. To keep our little project safe from inquisitive eyes, I had wrapped the urn in a Safeway bag and fastened the top with one of those super-long twist-ties you get with the really big kind of garbage bags. Dave looked as though he were going to take it out of the bag, but I stayed his hand.

"Not a good idea."

"You sure?"

"Yes."

Dave didn't seem in the mood to argue. He seemed, oddly enough, subdued and filled, if not with remorse, then with regret. This was, for better or for worse, what was left of his father. It was, therefore, also what was left of whatever hopes he might have had for his life as a son, for what might ever have become of his relationship with his father, for what home life he might ever have been able to reclaim. In a white plastic bag with an oversized S on one side and a long green twist tie holding it closed was Dave's father—or what had become of him—and that, more than any of the details of the man's life or death, was what occupied his son, I thought, as he prepared to pitch the package into the dark blue water. That the gun Dave had used to murder his father was in the urn only made the scene more piquant, not less tragic.

I thought he was about to change his mind, perhaps even to refuse to go ahead with the plan altogether, but then, just when I was thinking he was going to ask me to figure out some other way to get rid of his father's cremains, he leaned over the rail and dropped the bag into the water.

"Go to hell," he said in the direction of the white bag, which disappeared almost immediately beneath the surface.

"I wish you a long life," I said to Dave, uncertain where that had come from or what precisely I had meant by it.

"Thank you. You too."

"Thanks."

We went inside into one of the larger lounges. I gave Dave a five dollar bill and sent him for coffee while I sat down and contemplated the events of the last few days.

As far as I could figure, we had covered all our bases. If anyone had seen my car parked in front of Buddy's and noted down the license number, we'd have been arrested already for sure. The gun was, I thought, unretrievable even if the police did ever get some tip about where to look for it. The autopsy had only proven what the police had probably already suspected and what Dave and I knew for certain, that Buddy had been shot in the chest from the back and then decapitated posthumously. His clothing was probably lost in a sea of old clothing the Salvation Army receives in its thrift-shop drop-off centre every single day. The wallet was long gone as were the watch and Buddy's driver's licence, credit cards and hearing aid. Dave's own clothing was in my house, but I couldn't think how anyone could ever prove whether or not he had taken those specific articles of clothing with him when he left for Winnipeg or not.

The only mystery left, I thought, was why there hadn't been any mention of Buddy's head being found in that bowling alley on the Lougheed Highway out in Burnaby. Could they not have found it? I supposed it was possible—we had only left it there the day before and it didn't seem that impossibly unlikely that the people who ran the place would just leave a forgotten bowling ball bag where its owner had set it down it without bothering to check inside. The more I considered the matter, in fact, the more likely that seemed—what could they expect to find in a bowling ball case other than a bowling ball that would have prompted them to bother checking in the bags their regular customers left along the wall? Probably, lots of the league people left their bags in the alley between games. And even if they had practice sessions between tournament games, those sessions would be in the bowling alley as well, so why would they bother carrying their bowling balls away just to have to bring them right back? Perhaps it would be days, even weeks, before anyone noticed that one bag was just sitting there day in and day out. Perhaps no one would ever notice. And, even if someone did notice it, who was to say that it would be the management? Maybe a regular bowler would notice it and steal it before anyone who worked there even knew it had been left there in the first place. These were the issues that occupied me as I sat and waited for Dave to come back with the coffee. And then he did come back and I stopped considering the matter entirely, at least for the moment.

We still had about forty minutes before docking on Vancouver Island. Although it was August, the ferry was nowhere as crowded as I had expected it was going to be. We weren't quite alone in the lounge, but there was nobody seated anywhere near us. Dave looked his age for once—a teenager with no parents, a brother and grandmother in a different province, no girlfriend or, for that matter, any male friends I could detect other than myself, but with a lifetime of abuse behind him which would, I suspected, haunt him for the rest of his days.

"You got any more stories?"

The last thing I expected him to say. "Stories?"

"You know, like the ones you told me when we were driving to Winnipeg."

"You liked those stories?"

"Yeah."

"Well, did I ever tell you the story about Gideon and the generals of Midian?"

"No."

I had had Midianites on my mind ever since listening to that idiotic sermon in Winnipeg, but I hadn't expected them to pop out of my mouth right here. Still, having begun, I felt I might as well finish. "Well, it's not that long, but it should just take up enough time until we land. The Midianites were attacking the Israelites every which way and it was time to kick some Midianite ass, so Gideon—he was the leader of the people at this particular time—Gideon gathers up this mammoth fighting force to go to war against the nation of Midian."

"How many is that?"

"Well, that's a good question. About 32,000. Only God doesn't want that many people in the battle, because it won't be obvious enough that He has delivered the enemy into Gideon's hand if there are too many soldiers on the battlefield. So Gideon announces that anyone who is a little nervous about going to fight can just go home."

"And nobody went?"

"Nobody? 22,000 people went. Just up and left for home. I mean, the man said to go home if they weren't entirely sure that they were willing to die for their country, so off they went and that knocked the number down to 10,000."

"And that was the right number?"

"Still too many. So they devise this test. They go on a twenty mile march, all ten thousand of them. It's summertime. It's hot, so hot they are dying they're so hot. And they didn't take anything along to drink with them, so they're like *dying* of thirst. And the sun is just relentless, beating down on them and they don't have hats on and…well, you get the picture."

"It was hot out."

"Right. Anyway, they come to a cool spring where there's plenty of cold, flowing water. And that's the test, except that no one knows it's a test."

"So what was the test?"

"Well, the test was that Gideon didn't say a word, but the group divided down into two smaller groups. About three hundred men scooped up water in their hands and lapped it up the way dogs drink with their tongues, but all the rest—all 9,700 of them—they all got down on their knees and stuck their tongues in the water like…"

"Like what?"

"Like rats. Like the kind of water rats you see sometimes scurrying around along the banks of polluted rivers."

"And what happened to them?"

"Nothing happened. Gideon sent them all one home as well."

"So he started out with 33,000 people and he ended up with 300?"

"32,000. Otherwise correct."

"And what happened then?"

"Well, from there on in, it was just a piece of cake."

"What kind?"

"Angel food cake. With chocolate icing on top. He gathered the troops and divided them into three groups. Each guy got a clay jug and a ram's horn—the hollowed out kind you can blow into and make sound with—and a torch. The torches, they lit and put in the jugs so no one could see them. And the rams' horns they kept ready…."

Dave was like a little kid at bedtime. Here was a grown man, more or less, who had singlehandedly avenged his mother's suicide by shooting his father in the back and hacking off his head with a saw, but who was also capable of being enthralled by a Bible story. The loudspeaker crackled to life and the captain announced that we would be docking at Swartz Bay in about fifteen minutes. I offered to postpone the end of my story until the return voyage, but Dave wouldn't hear of it.

"Just finish it now. You have fifteen minutes."

"Okay, it's really over anyway. The approached the Midianite camp in the middle of the night. The hundred men with Gideon acted first. They smashed their jugs and blew their horns. That scared the hair off the enemy, but then when the other two columns of guys did the same thing, they all just ran away as fast as their little Midianite feet could take them."

"Then what?"

"Then nothing. The Israelites pursued their enemy until they were so dispersed so as not to constitute much of a threat any longer to anyone. They captured their two generals, Oreb and Zeeb, and brought them back to this guy named Purah who was Gideon's chief aide-de-camp. He looked at them and they looked at him. They were bad men, men who had exerted themselves mightily to thwart the will of God and who had wished only ill to Purah's people. So this guy Purah was overcome with loathing and even though he didn't have any specific instructions from Gideon about what to do with them if they were captured, he drew his sword from its sheath and ran it through their hearts, then hacked both their heads off for good measure. Mind you, he couldn't get them off at first, but when one of his servants produced one of the saws the army travelled with in case it had to chop down an asherah or an illegal maypole or something and he tried with that, they both came right off."

"You're making this last part up, right?"

"Not at all. Anyway, he sawed their heads off—they were already dead, of course, because he had run his sword through their chests—anyway, *after* he got their heads off, he put each on a nice silver platter and covered it with a nice piece of green silk he had brought along just on the off chance he might have a chance to behead any Midianite officers and he had his men bring Oreb's and Zeeb's heads directly to Gideon as a trophy."

"And what did he do with them?"

"He had them stuffed. And mounted on these low flag-pole things they had around Gideon's private chapel at Ophrah, where he came from. And then when his people finally captured the kings of Midian—Oreb and Zeeb were bigshots, but they weren't royalty or anything like that—anyway, when they finally managed to capture Zebah and Zalmunna, the kings of Midian, they brought them to Gideon as well. He—Gideon—wanted his oldest boy, whose name was Jether, he wanted Jether to kill them, but he was really young and he didn't have the nerve...."

"How young was he?"

"Nineteen."

"And he didn't have the nerve to kill these guys even though his father wanted him to?"

"Right. Anyway, the best part of the story is that these two kings start giving Gideon a hard time for being too tough on his kid. 'Let him be,' they tell him, 'and you kill us yourself. For strength only comes with manhood....'"

"So did he?"

"Did he what?"

"Did he kill them?"

"Slit their necks open like chickens and stuck their heads on poles in Ophrah just like Zeeb and Oreb. And that's where they stayed for the longest time, right there on those poles. Everybody who came to worship at the shrine had to walk right by them too...it was quite a scene, but you've got to admit it was a cool thing to do. Stickin' them right up there like lanterns in front of a Chinese restaurant...."

"Are they still there?"

"Nah."

"Well, what happened to them?"

"They shrunk and shrunk and shrunk until they were the size of grapefruit. And then someone batted all four of them out of the stadium during one of the softball games they used to have on Saturday afternoons and no one ever saw any of those heads again. The shrine at Ophrah didn't last for too long after Gideon's day anyway, so it wasn't such a big loss."

"And what happened to that kid, the boy who didn't have the nerve to kill the kings?"

"Good question. He got murdered himself later by a half-brother, this guy named Abimelech who was the son of Gideon and some concubine—sort of a cross between a whore and a wife—he picked up later in life. Abimelech wanted to be king and he figured a good first step would be murdering all his half-brothers, of whom there were a good seventy. He managed to be a kind of king too, at least for a little while…."

"And what happened to him?"

"A few years later he was laying siege to a little city called Thebez and some lady dropped a millstone off the top of the city wall onto his head while he was trying to set fire to the city gates."

"Why did she do that?"

"She was pissed that he was trying to burn down her city."

"Did he die?"

"His head split open like a coconut."

"I guess that means he died."

"Good guess."

By this time, we were already disembarking at Swartz Bay. We took the city bus into Victoria and spent most of the day wandering around, then took the boat back to the ferry and went back to the mainland. Dave slept almost the entire way on the return ride, which was just fine with me.

I went for a coffee, then came back and sat down beside him. My head was filled with a million things—my failure to honour Wil's last request, what I was going to do about my parents (whom I swore I would phone the very next day), how I was going to go about finding Lena somehow in California, the chances of my being indicting of complicity in the murder of Robert Aaron Kruger, the odds that Indian guys really can make love to women with the soles of their right feet pressed up against the sole of their women's left feet. These were all important issues for me to consider, but I couldn't keep concentrated and before I knew it, I was asleep on Dave's shoulder.

I woke up just before we docked. We disembarked, got into the car and drove home. On the off chance the police had phoned in an indictment for murder, I checked my messages.

There was only one and it wasn't from the police...it was from Helene.

XXVII

It wasn't much of a message, just Helene's voice—I thought it was charming that she felt the need to say who it was, as though I might not recognize my own wife's voice on the phone—anyway, the whole message was just her giving me a phone number and asking me to call her there whenever I got in. The number had an Oregon area code and a room number extension to ask for, so I presumed she was in a motel somewhere in Oregon. Why she was calling me, she didn't say.

It was only about ten o'clock at night. I could, of course, have waited until the next day to phone. She had no way to know if I was even in Vancouver, so she could hardly have been sitting by the phone waiting. And I hated her thinking that she could get me to do anything merely by asking, even something as ultimately inconsequential as returning a telephone call. I know it must sound petty—hell, it *was* petty—but I still was in no mood to let her think she could get me to do any damn thing. On the other hand, I started to wonder and worry about Lena. Maybe something was wrong. If they were in Oregon, then maybe Lena wasn't well and they were coming back to the Land of Socialized Medicine before anything got worse. Or maybe Lover Boy found some other family to wreck and Helene was coming back with her tail between her legs to throw herself on my mercy and beg for another chance. Maybe Helene herself had been diagnosed with cancer of the liver or something equally terminal. That line of thinking cheered me considerably and I decided to return her call and see what, precisely, was up.

I dialed.

"Valley Forge Inn, Ashland," the voice said.

"Room 275."

"Just a moment."

Helene's voice came on the line immediately, almost as though she really had been sitting there waiting for me to call.

"Thanks for calling me right back." She must have left her message just before we got home, I realized.

"No problem. What's wrong?"

"Why do you assume something is wrong?"

"No reason. What's up?"

A long pause. She's setting me up for something amazingly bad, I thought. I had some ideas what she might be gearing up to say—aside from the liver cancer theory—but I knew it was wisest to say nothing.

Eventually, she spoke. "Look, Saul," she opened, "there's no easy way to say this so I might as well just come out and tell you. I want a divorce. I'm going to marry Gary as soon as I have one…."

I cleared my throat as though I were going to respond, but she cut me off.

"Wait, there's more. He was born in Vancouver, but his folks are from Australia and we're going to live there. We thought we were going to try to live in California somewhere, but he's been talking to his folks and his grandparents have a sheep farm and he's going to manage it for them now that they're too old to do it themselves. But the point is…the point is that I'm not going to ask for custody, Saul. Lena can live with you, but you'll have to let her come to Australia at least once a year to spend a month. If that's okay, we can just get this done with…."

Her voice sort of trailed off, leaving me to wonder what she expected me to think of a woman who would dump her own kid so she could go off to Australia to sleep with some loser she picked up somewhere who hadn't *even* been a full-time janitor. I decided to say nothing at all to dissuade her from her plans, however.

"Well, you gotta do what you gotta do," is what I finally came up with. It wasn't too original and it certainly wasn't too clever, but Helene must have been so anxious for me to agree to take Lena back that she wasn't bothering to listen to the subtext of my response.

"So you agree?"

"Sure."

"Great. Look, we're in Ashland already and we're coming as far north as Portland. Can you meet us there?"

"For the hand off?"

"It's just that we got a really cheap flight from there and Vancouver is another six hours north and there and back would be twelve and if you could come down—I know it will be the same twelve hours of driving for you, but we're coming up from San Francisco and Gary wants to stay in Portland long enough to sell the car and we're only going to get there tomorrow late in the day...." Tomorrow was Tuesday.

"And when is your flight?"

"Friday morning."

"Where are you going to stay?"

"I'm not sure."

"Well, stay where you want, but I'll meet you in the coffee shop of the Highland Motel just north of the city at the Quintsillup exit. Wednesday afternoon. One o'clock. You want to write that down?"

"You don't think I remember the Highland Motel?"

We had spent a weekend in Portland when we first got married and had spent most of our time in that very motel. Why we had wanted or needed to drive all the way to Oregon to lock ourselves in a motel room, I can't remember.

"Okay, then…be there Wednesday at one. I'll be gone very early in the morning, so you won't be able to get in touch with me if you want to change the plan."

"It won't change."

"Then I'll see you then."

"Not if I see you first."

"Okay, Helene…I'll see you Wednesday."

The phone went dead. I remember thinking that there was a certain odd combination of playfulness and regret in Helene's voice, almost as though she didn't need to feel defensive or guilty about leaving me now that she had made a decision that would basically end the life she had been living and enable her to begin a new one in New South Wales with Gary Hey-I-Only-Stepped-In-When-Your-Marriage-Was-Falling-Apart-Anyway Bouvier on his grandparents' sheep farm. What were my initial reactions to her phone call? I don't know…I guess I felt mostly relief that Lena was okay and this intense sort of happiness that she was going to come home to live with me. That was all I wanted and now it was to be granted to me. It bit the bird big-time that it had to be Helene, of all people, who was granting me what I wanted, but even that aspect of the situation, galling though it certainly was, failed to dampen my spirits. My bitch of a wife was running away to as far away a place as God made on this sick planet and my baby was coming home. And what else mattered, really? Let me tell you: not one damn thing.

I told Dave the general gist of my conversation with Helene. He listened thoughtfully, then asked if he could come along to Portland. For the drive, he said. To keep me company, he also said, but I recall wondering if he wasn't just a little bit jealous of little Lena. After all, Lena really was my child and I think Dave must have understood just from listening to my end of the conversation and watching my face as I spoke just how much I loved that child. Did he want me to love him the same way? As a son?

As an offspring? As an heir? Had he been talking about going back to Winnipeg to be with his grandmother because he really wanted to or because he was hoping I would try to convince him to stay in Vancouver with me? He could live in my house, finish up whatever coursework he was missing to graduate from high school, do some odd jobs around the house or whatever I needed done to cover some of the expenses connected with having him around. I wouldn't have to adopt him formally of course—I wasn't even sure if you could adopt a kid his age—but simply allow him into my home and my life. He was a handsome boy and a clever one, I remember thinking. And he wasn't going to be around forever—he'd get a job or go on in school and start a career. He'd get himself married one way or the other one of these days the way we all somehow do eventually and that would be that. It wasn't a long-term commitment, I figured. But I wasn't really ready even to broach the topic. Not yet. Not until…I'm not even sure how to end that sentence. What was it I was waiting for? Was my mind made up? I don't think so…but it wasn't not made up either. I knew that I wanted Dave to stay on in my home, but I wasn't ready to say that to him or, I guess, to myself. Instead, I changed the topic.

Tuesday was a busy day. We needed to be on the road at six in the morning on Wednesday, so we had to do all the laundry and buy whatever we needed for our trip the day before. I had to go to the Brier home to look in on my parents and I wanted to pack up some of Lena's favourite stuffed animals so she would have some familiar friends in the car on the way home. I was smart enough to phone the lawyer to get a letter from him stating that I was Lena's custodial parent—I could just imagine what it was going to be like at the border back into B.C. without such a letter when the kid told the customs guy that she had been living with her mommy in California and now Daddy was taking her back to Vancouver to live with him forever—and I had a million bills to pay and stuff like that.

My trip to see my parents was the worst part of the day. The doctors were still insisting that my parents didn't have Alzheimer's or anything like that, but I don't know what difference that made because they were just almost completely gaga anyway. They had a double room they both slept in, but whether they knew (or cared) why that was, I couldn't say. They recognized me when I came in, I think, but it was clear that they hadn't missed me or even realized that it had been more than two weeks since I had been around. The conversation was almost normal for a while, then Mom started asking why Wil never came around. I didn't have the heart to tell her that Wil was dead, so I told her he was on a post-doc at the University of Tibet and that he would be back in Canada sometime around 2010. She seemed quite satisfied by this information, as though all she had wanted in the first place was to be assured that he hadn't been around for a reason rather than for no reason at all.

Can you imagine a worse hell than losing a son and then having to be told of his death over and over and over a million times without you being able to remember from day to day that he was dead? I can't. But that was the world both my parents lived in. I could have told them Wil was dead—I probably should have—but I just couldn't bring myself to. It was like that movie with Bill Murray where he lives the same day over and over until he gets it straight. Only, in the movie, it was okay because you knew he would eventually get Andie MacDowell in the sack if he just did that same day enough times over. But my poor parents weren't going to sleep with Andie MacDowell if they finally managed to assimilate the news that Wil was dead into their meagre, beleaguered consciousnesses. They weren't going to get to sleep with anybody, not even each other probably...all they were going to do was to live out the experience of hearing of Wil's death over and over and over until they died themselves of the grief.

My visit was brief. They were happy to see me, but I could see that the thrill of my presence only lasted about fifteen minutes. After that, they seemed bored and listless and I could tell it was time for me to go. My dad came over to me and told me quietly that Mother got very anxious if she missed her afternoon program on television. I was surprised that he had enough insight into things even to know that she liked a certain program on TV.

"Which program?" I asked.

"Perry Mason," he answered in all seriousness, leaving me to wonder if she was watching television in 1957 or if there was possibly some remake on television that my mother had become fond of. I recall thinking that I would do better not to ask and not to know. I nodded gravely, as though my father had just shared with me some information of inestimable value and left them to their afternoon of television.

We woke up at five. Or rather I did. I went into Wil's room to wake Dave up and found him sleeping naked on top of the blankets. It was pretty hot out and I didn't blame him for wanting to be cool, but somehow the image of him lying there completely bare-ass naked and fast asleep on my brother's bed made me feel even more strongly that bringing Dave into the family was, in some convoluted way, an act of betrayal of Wil's memory. I shucked that thought aside—not knowing what it was all about anyway—and awakened him. I made a pot of coffee while he showered and we were, amazingly enough, in the car pulling away from the curb at precisely six in the morning.

By twenty-five past the hour, we were approaching the border. I sensed Dave had something to say.

"Look," he began a bit sheepishly. I had no idea what was coming. "Look, there's something I didn't tell you."

"Yeah?" I felt the hairs on the back of my neck standing up.

"Well, it's not that big a deal."

"Good."

"Aren't you going to ask what it is?"

"No."

"Well, if you must know, I didn't tell you that…that the…what I didn't tell you is that my dad's head…that it wasn't in the case we left at the bowling alley."

My eyes widened. "It wasn't?"

"No. I knew you wanted me to get rid of it, so I went along with leaving the case there. I wanted it to feel right, so I stuffed it with some of the books I found in your brother's room."

So that was why the newspapers hadn't reported the discovery of a murdered man's head in a bowling alley in Burnaby.

"And where is the head right now."

"In the house."

"Where?"

"In another Safeway bag. I was going to keep it under your brother's bed, but I was afraid it would begin to smell while we were away."

"And where is it now?"

"In that big freezer thing in the laundry room."

"Your father's head is in the freezer trough in my laundry room."

"Right."

"And why are you telling me this just right now?"

"Hey, man…I thought you should know."

I could feel the colour draining from my face. "You can go to hell."

"You don't have to get all steamed. I mean, it's not like I'm hiding it from you or anything. I just wanted to let you know in case…I don't know, in case you opened the freezer when we got home to get your kid an ice cream or something and you found it before I could mention it. And I figured you wouldn't want me to tell you while the kid was in the back seat…"

"Who says she's sitting in the back? Maybe you're going to sit in the back."

"Whatever."

"We have ice cream in the freezer?"

"A tub of Lucerne. The kind with pieces of marshmallow in it. I had some the other night."

"How was it?"

"So sweet you could puke, but otherwise okay."

By this time, we were at the border. I suppose I should have been grateful that Dave hadn't put his father's head in the trunk when I wasn't looking—that would be just the thing to have some customs agent find in my vehicle—but I was more pissed than I was grateful. He hadn't lied to me…but we both knew that I had thought we were ditching the head in the bowling alley and we also both knew that Dave had misled me. And that not every lie has to be spoken aloud…

Anyway, the rest of the trip was uneventful. We passed customs easily and headed south. We stopped for coffee in Mount Vernon, then for gas in Everett. We had some breakfast in some greasy dump in Centralia (loose, runny scrambled eggs and whole wheat toast for me, waffles and sausages for Dave) and were at the Highland Motel in Quintsillup at a quarter to one. We sat in the car until one precisely, then got out. I told Dave to buy a six-pack of Coke, some magazines and a couple of bags of chips at the gas station just down the road from the motel, then to wait for me in the car. And then, girding my loins to encounter the single female I hated the most in the entire world and the single female I loved the most in the entire world, I opened the phoney oak door to the motel and stepped inside.

XXVIII

D o I have to describe my reunion with Lena? I guess if I wasn't shy about some of the other stuff I've been writing about, I can tell you what it was like to see my Lena for the first time in three months. And it wasn't only that I hadn't seen her in three months—it was that I hadn't had any idea when I was going to see her again. Yes, of course, I had known that some sort of custody and visitation arrangement would have to be settled when Helene and I finally did get around to arranging a divorce, but who knew when that was going to be? But in the meantime, Helene was in California with my kid and no plans, at least as far as she had shared them with me, to return to B.C. or even to Canada. Did I mention that Helene was a U.S. citizen? I think I did—but I don't think I wrote that Lena had an American passport as well. I didn't know if that was going to affect things one way or the other, but the point is that although I knew I would see Lena eventually, I hadn't known when that was actually going to happen.

And then suddenly—and it did seem sudden, even if it wasn't really—anyway, all of a sudden there I was walking into this seedy motel outside of Portland with every expectation that my kid, the single fruit ever to have been plucked from my loins, the daughter I made with my own sticky stuff, the sole heiress to the Jacobson fortune (or what I feared was going to be left of it after some judge somewhere gave away eighty-five percent of it to her mother, that is)—this person was going to be standing on the other side of the door.

And, amazingly enough, she was. The scene was…wonderful, chaotic, unbelievably moving, overwhelming, all of the above. She hadn't really grown too much since I had last seen her—she had only been gone for three months—but she somehow looked more mature and she did look older and, if it isn't silly to say this about a six-year-old, wiser. She was wearing blue denim shorts and a white t-shirt with that stupid Nike swoosh thing on it and her hair was tied back in a ponytail. She was holding a little stuffed bear I don't think I had ever seen before and, for some reason, a pencil. She didn't see me at first, but I saw her. And then I came closer….

She was standing right there, but she was looking in the other direction. I saw Helene standing just behind her, but I couldn't take my eyes off of Lena. I was…I don't know what the word is…overwhelmed to see her.

"Leeny?"

She turned towards me.

"Leeny honey? It's me. Dad."

Her eyes widened just in all those Shirley Temple movies when the little moptop finally finds her long-lost parents and they turn out to be these multizillionaires who adopt all the other kids in the orphanage. She looked confused, then dazed.

"Daddy?"

"Leeny."

It sounds pathetic, but I couldn't say anything other than her name. I reached out for her and she ran into my arms and we just stood there for a long minute hugging each other and crying. I was just as glad Dave was in the car drinking Coke. I kept trying to speak, but I just couldn't get a word out. Not hello. Not how was California? Not did I mention your mother is a filthy adulteress who is about to abandon you for a farm full of Australian sheep? Not even I love you. Nothing at all. Not one word.

She didn't say anything either. Eventually, the moment

passed. I set her down and she took my hand. As though we had been rehearsing it for months, we both turned at the same moment to face Helene.

She looked, I must admit, great. She was tanned. Her hair was pulled back just like Lena's in a pony tail. She was wearing this black stretchy top that showed just enough cleavage to be interesting without being truly trashy. For the briefest moment, the picture of the Indians doing it with the soles of their feet pressed up against each other passed through my mind, but I banished it as inappropriate and refused to get caught up in any sort of recollective musing that might conceivably have made me hate Helene any less.

"Hi." What a brilliant opening line! I must use it in a play someday if I ever write one.

"Hi."

"Has Lena eaten?"

"Half a grilled cheese sandwich and a few French fries. And a glass of milk."

"She knows?"

"Not yet."

I was floored. I mean, I didn't like Helene. And I certainly didn't think much of her as a moral person. But even I would never have expected that she would be capable of bringing her six-year-old kid to the place she was about to say goodbye to her for a full year—assuming she managed to come up with the airfare to Australia the following summer, since I was certainly not about to contribute one solitary dime to sending Lena down there to live with her adulteress mother and the former janitor her mother was destroying her family for the treat of sleeping *unduplicitously* with—I would never have imagined she would be capable of just dumping her kid like that without having made at least some attempt, even a pathetic, useless one, at explaining why this was the best decision for both of them in the long run. I mean, Helene was an immoral jezebel who deserved to fry in hell for what she did to me and our family, but she wasn't a complete idiot and I remember thinking that she could certainly have come up with something if she had put her mind to it.

I must have looked at her like I thought she was crazy, because she suddenly became defensive. "I didn't want to upset her," she said, as though this were a cogent thought.

"Well, you're upsetting her now. So why don't the two of you have a little talk while I go over and use the men's room for a few minutes." I looked down at Lena. "I need to use the washroom, honey. Stay here with Mommy until I get back."

"Don't go away."

"I'm not going away. I'm going into the men's washroom to pee. I'll be back before you're seven."

"Daddy, I'm not going to be seven until next July. On Canada Day, don't you remember?"

"I was kidding, honey. I'll be right back."

I went quickly away in the direction of the coffee shop. I looked at my watch. I was prepared to give Helene one single minute to tell the kid that she was abandoning her. If she couldn't do it within the allotted time, I would do it myself.

I went into the washroom. It was thirteen minutes after one. I went into a stall and sat down with my pants still up. I watched the second hand on my watch go around one full revolution. I walked out of the stall and through the washroom into the lobby. Helene was down on one knee talking earnestly to Lena. Should I interrupt? I hesitated, then walked on over.

As soon as I got there, Helene stopped speaking.

"You finished?"

"Not really even started."

"Probably all for the best. Where's Leeny's stuff?"

"In the trunk of my car. Are you parked in the lot?"

For some reason I can't remember just right now, I was not

anxious for Helene to meet Dave or even, for that matter, to learn of his existence. I'm not sure why this mattered so much to me, but it did. At least for the moment.

"I'm having the guy at the gas station rotate my tires while I'm in here. I'll just take her stuff with me and walk over there with it." It was an idiotic story. Why I would have chosen to have somebody in Oregon rotate my tires when I could just as easily have it done at home on some occasion when I didn't need to get back on the road as soon as possible, I couldn't even have begun to explain if Helene had pressed me on the point. But she was apparently so used to lying and making up stories to suit the moment that she didn't even notice that my remark lacked cogency.

"No problem."

Was she going to recognize my car in the lot? It suddenly struck me that she would. It had been her car too, for God's sake. And even with Dave sitting in it, she would certainly notice the B.C. licence plate that used to be hers. Could she be that oblivious to her surroundings? I didn't know, but I supposed we were about to find out.

In the end, nothing happened. Whatever Helene had told Lena didn't seem to have upset her terribly. The three of us went out of the motel into the parking lot. Helene led us to a white Grand Prix on the far side of the lot around the corner from where Dave was sitting in the Camaro. For a minute, I was afraid that the sheep heir was going to be in the car, but he was nowhere to be seen. For a moment, I almost asked where he was, but I caught myself in time. As far as I was concerned, he was a nightmare I had already had and was in no need of repeating. He was probably off wrecking somebody else's marriage while Helene was busy ditching her kid so the two of them could live happily ever after. I wished them both cancer of the pancreas. Him first, so Helene could be alone when she died.

Anyway, Helene opened the trunk and lifted a brown leather suitcase out which I vaguely recognized as a wedding gift we had received and never used. I took the suitcase in my right hand and Lena's little hand in my left. Now for the hard part.

"Helene, I phoned my lawyer and he said I should ask you for a letter stating that Lena has your permission to come to Canada with me."

I expected her to react poorly to this request, but she seemed almost to have already thought of it. "No problem," she said easily. She took a pad of paper out of her purse and wrote on it that her estranged husband—that's the phrase she used too—that her estranged husband had her permission to bring her daughter, Lena Marie Jacobson, into Canada to live with him in Vancouver. She signed it Helene Kaufman Jacobson as though using her maiden name lent the letter some shred of dignity. If it did, it was too minuscule for me to detect. Still, it was a kind of a kindness that she wrote the damned thing at all and I was, to the extent I was emotionally capable, grateful to her.

Now it was time to clear this all with the kid. "You know that you're coming home to live with me in Grandma and Grandpa's house. They have a new apartment in a special hotel and I live in their house now. And now that you're coming home with me, it's going to be your house too."

Little Lena looked absolutely thrilled the way only a six-year-old can when she finds out that she's going to live in her grandparents' home. "Wow," she said. "Where are all my toys?"

"Whatever you and Mommy left behind is in boxes in the basement. We'll find it all as soon as we get home." I had moved into my parents' house about a month before Helene and Lena had left, but the apartment the two of them had lived in with the sheep heir—my apartment, our apartment—had been in my name and Helene had simply dropped the key into the mail for me when she left. Not knowing what else to do, I had packed up everything in the apartment once they were gone and moved most of the stuff other than the furniture myself to my parents' basement. The furniture I sold to a second-hand guy, but I packed every shred of Helene's stuff that was left in the place into black garbage bags and drove them personally in a pick-up I rented expressly for the occasion to the landfill site in Delta. Where her stuff was now, only the mayor of Delta might have known. But I doubt it.

My reference to boxes in the basement seemed to ring a bell of sorts for Helene. "What about my stuff?"

"I'll send it all along just as soon as you give me your address in Australia."

"I have it right here." Helene pulled an index card out of her purse and handed it to me.

"No problem," I said half-affably, taking the card. "If you want to reimburse me for the postage, you can. And if not, then there's no problem there either. Why can't we all just get along?"

"I'll send you a cheque in Canadian once the packages come."

"Fine."

XXIX

A fter I took the suitcase from Helene, none of us knew quite what to do. It didn't seem like a good idea for Helene and Lena to have this long, drawn-out farewell scene—and I certainly wasn't about to mention to Lena how long is was likely going to be before she saw her mother again—but neither was it possible for Helene just to wave good-bye and be done with it. So since she didn't want to make a big or a little deal about saying good-bye, she said nothing at all and we all just stood there for a long couple of minutes.

Finally, she knelt down and pulled Lena close to her. "Mommy has to go away for a little while," she said, her lie all the more pathetic for sounding so plausible.

"Why?" An entirely reasonable question.

"It's the kind of thing only big people understand," Helene answered her six-year-old, omitting the fact that the vast majority of big people in the world would be entirely incapable of understanding how she could do what she was apparently intent on doing.

Lena looked confused. "When are you coming back?"

"Soon." A stern look from me. "I don't know, honey. One of these days." Another look. "I guess I'm not really sure, Leeny honey. I'll write and I'll phone and if Daddy ever figures out how to work e-mail, we'll write back and forth that way as well."

"What's e-mail?"

"It doesn't matter. The point is that I won't be right around the corner, but I'll always be right here." Helene actually extend-

238

ed the index finger of her right hand and touched the centre of Lena's forehead, just like the alien in E.T. did with that little kid. It was even the same line, which I found partially hysterical and partially so deeply pathetic that pathetic isn't even the word for it. Of course, Helene and that alien had plenty in common: they were both incapable of saying anything other than what others had written for them and they were both made of plastic and metal. Especially Helene.

Lena, who hadn't seen the movie, appeared actually to be moved by this gesture. "Right here?" she asked, touching her own head.

"Yes, honey, right there."

I could sense that Helene, to her credit, was about to break down. Mind you, she wasn't anywhere near sufficiently upset to cancel her plans and not abandon her kid, but she was at least unhappy enough for her voice to be breaking and the first glimmer of some tears to be visible at the corners of her eyes. Maybe she wasn't from outer space after all, I recall thinking briefly. But I also knew that, in the long run, getting Lena out of her mother's adulterous, disloyal clutches was probably the best thing that could happen to her.

It was right here that I stepped in. "I think it's time we hit the road," I said, trying to defuse the emotion of the moment.

Helene, uncharacteristically sensitive to somebody else's feelings for a change, agreed. "Okay, then," she said bravely, "it's time for you and Daddy to get going if you're going to get back to grandma and grandpa's house before bedtime."

It was already hours too late to get Lena home before bedtime, but I wasn't going to argue. Besides, what difference did it make?

Lena said nothing. I was afraid she was going to make a major scene about leaving her mother, but she didn't say anything at all. She just stood there with her hands clasped around her mother's neck for a long minute—Helene was still kneeling down to speak to Lena at face level—and then let go. I found the letting go deeply symbolic, but I doubt it was meant that way. Lena wasn't crying. She didn't even look all that upset, to tell you the truth. Who knows? Maybe it had dawned on her that getting rid of her mother also meant getting rid of the sheep heir, whom I hopefully imagined she loathed. I knew better than to quiz her on the spot about her emotions, so I also said nothing and we all just stood there for another long moment.

Finally, I couldn't stand it any longer. "Okay, honey, time to go."

Lena looked around almost as though she had forgotten I was standing there. "Okay, daddy," she said agreeably. "Let's go."

And so we went. I wasn't sure if Helene was or wasn't actually staying in the motel and I didn't want to ask. I took the suitcase in my left and Lena's little hand in my right and turned to go. "Be in touch," I said over my shoulder.

"I will," Helene said, her voice steady and calm now.

And with that, we left. Lena and I walked around the building to where the Camaro was parked. Dave, to his credit, was sitting in the back seat. I reached in and took the keys from Dave, then put the suitcase in the trunk. I opened the door and Lena got into the car.

I went quickly around and got into the driver's seat.

"Lena, honey," I began, "this is my friend, Dave."

She turned around in her seat to see my friend, but she wasn't big enough to see over the headrest thing, so she unbuckled her seatbelt and got up on her knees to look into the back seat.

"Hello," she said with what sounded to me like uncommon maturity for a six-year-old.

"Hi."

"You're my daddy's friend?"

It was an interesting question and I was quite looking forward to hearing Dave's answer.

"Sure. And he's mine."

"Do you live in Vancouver?"

"I'm staying with your dad until I go to my grandmother's place in Winnipeg. I'm staying in your uncle's room."

That seemed to satisfy Lena, who found nothing at all unusual in the concept that I would let a friend of mine stay in my house until he was able to go wherever it was he was going. As well, I thought to myself, there wasn't....

I pulled out of the parking lot. Dave had gassed up the car and bought a couple of bags of chips, some cans of pop and a few Fifth Avenue bars. We shared a candy bar or two as I headed back to the interstate. It was almost two in the afternoon.

The trip back was uneventful. We stopped for a coffee break in Olympia, then for dinner in Bellingham. The border was a zoo and we were lined up for almost forty minutes just so I could tell the customs guy that we hadn't purchased anything in the States. I told him we were all residents of Vancouver, which we more or less all were. He didn't ask who Lena was or where her mother was and I didn't even have to produce my lawyer's letter or the one I had gotten Helene to write. It was probably all for the best.

By the time we got home, it was after ten in the evening. The house seemed fine. Everything was where we left it. I carried Lena inside—she had slept most of the way between Olympia and Bellingham and had then fallen back asleep after the border—and put her in my old room upstairs. I was sleeping in my parents' bedroom and Dave, of course, was in Wil's room. I didn't want to risk waking her, so I just took off her shoes and socks and let her sleep in her t-shirt and shorts. She looked peaceful and happy in my old bed. I didn't have any reason to think she had really hated her vacation—as she called it—with her mom and the sheep heir, but I hadn't wanted to press the point unnecessarily. She was, at any rate, in a deep sleep. The rest, if there was anything left to say or ask, could wait until morning.

Dave and I had driven for more than thirteen hours in one day and we were both wrecked. He opened a can of Coke and sat down at the kitchen table to look at the sports section from that morning's newspaper which had been waiting for us at the front door. I went upstairs and took a warm shower, then came down and made a pot of coffee, then went into my study—I had taken to thinking of the downstairs den as my study since installing my computer there and filling the bookshelves with my own books—to get something to read.

The shock was too great for me to capture in words. The window was open and there were shards of glass on the floor. The computer, an expensive Toshiba laptop I had bought for myself a few weeks before my former life ended, was gone. The television was gone. The CD player was gone. My papers were all over the floor. The door had been closed, which is why I hadn't felt a cool breeze when I was making coffee in the kitchen, but I was now suddenly freezing. The night wasn't that cold either, so I guess it must have been the realization that I had been the victim of a burglary that was chilling me. But whatever, I was frozen. I went into the living room and found more things gone. Mother's silver candle sticks. The chest with all the sterling silver flatware my parents had gotten from my maternal grandparents as a wedding gift. The silver trophy my father had won a million years ago for getting a hole in one in some tournament somewhere.

The living room was uncommonly neat. Nothing was out of place. There was no sign that anything but the greatest care had been taken in ripping us off. There was no sign of anything at all except for the things that were actually missing. The only mess was the broken window in the den, and the thieves had closed the door to make it at least possible that their forced entry wouldn't be discovered immediately, as well it hadn't.

I called Dave and he came running. At first he didn't realize what had happened, but then, when I called him into the den, he saw right away that the house had been burgled. I went through the house. Upstairs, I hadn't noticed anything missing, but now that I went back into the master bedroom, I noticed that the drawers had been gone through. Mother's jewelry, of course, was in a safety deposit box except for a few relatively inexpensive pieces she had with her in the home. My dad's watches were gone from the dresser drawer where I had left them, as were all three pairs of his gold cufflinks and a few out-of-date tie tacks and tie clips. The room looked perfect, but now that I was searching, I was finding more and more missing things. When I looked more closely, I could see that they had been in my old room too, but there had been nothing to steal. Or at least nothing struck me as out of place or missing.

I went back down to the kitchen to phone the police. For years, people had been telling me that the police do nothing about B&Es, that they usually don't even bother dusting for fingerprints or looking around for clues that might lead to the identification of the thieves. I guess I had been watching too much television, but I just couldn't believe the police wouldn't care that a citizen's home had been violated and I therefore, naively, fully expected a major investigation and, with any luck, some arrests. I wanted my stuff back!

I phoned 911. A woman operator listened politely to my story, then promised to send a police car over right away. Since no one was in any danger, she wouldn't flag the call as urgent, she said. But the police should arrive within the half hour nonetheless, she assured me. I wasn't to touch anything—that sounded promising—and I wasn't to worry.

Dave was standing by me as I spoke to the police. Our relationship had changed subtly in the course of the previous few days. He was still a friend, still a young man who had somehow come into my life and who was apparently going to stay there until our paths parted as mysteriously, and perhaps as unexpect-edly, as they had crossed in the first place. There was a certain warmth I felt in his presence as I spoke on the phone with the police and he stood next to me. It's hard to explain—he wasn't a son and he wasn't a friend—at least not in the normal sense of the word—as much as he was presence in my life that symbolized hope in the future. I know that must sound completely loopy, but there you have it. Maybe that's what a friend is, come to think of it. Who knows?

So we had about a half hour to kill until the police arrived. I wasn't wild about the police coming to call, but there really had-n't been any way to avoid phoning them and there really wasn't anything to hide in the house. Old Buddy's wallet, clothing and wristwatch were long gone and the clothing Dave had taken from his father's home the night Buddy died was upstairs in Wil's room. It was mixed in with the stuff he had bought in Regina and half of it had been laundered since it got here and it wasn't like it wasn't his in the first place.

It suddenly dawned on me that there wasn't any reason for Dave to be around when the police arrived. He wasn't anyone to me—not my brother, not my son, not anyone at all. And having a nineteen-year-old house guest whose relationship to me I was unable to articulate precisely would only invite the suspicion of the police. And when he mentioned his name and the constable asked him if he were related to the man who was murdered in East Vancouver the other night....

"Maybe you should go?"

"Go? Go where?"

"I dunno. Out. Go to a movie."

"This late?"

"Go for coffee somewhere. Go downtown and get laid. I just don't think you want to be here with the cops get here. You'll have to say who you are, they'll ask if you're your dad's kid, they'll ask why you're living here…they'll ask all sorts of questions you don't really want to have to answer. And if you go, you can avoid the whole thing. If anyone notices the stuff in your room, I'll say it's all Wil's and no one will know you've ever been here."

"There's nothing wrong with me being here."

"No, there isn't. But you really don't want to start in with the police, do you?"

Dave thought for a moment. "They sometimes have late movies down on Granville," he said.

"Go. Here's a fifty. Take a bus down and a cab back. I can't go get you because I won't want to leave Lena alone in the house. Or take the car…."

"It's okay," he said, pocketing the bill. "I don't know where I'll go, but I'll be back in…I'll phone in an hour and you can tell me if the cops are still there. Then I'll phone again an hour after that if they are."

"Okay."

"Fine."

He got up and walked out. I admired that in Dave, his ability to move about in the world unencumbered by things. I would have spent twenty minutes thinking about what I should take along, but Dave just stood up, stuck the bill in the pocket of his jeans and went out the front door. Lena and I were alone in the house.

The police would be there in five or ten minutes. I went for a broom, then remembered that I had been told not to touch anything. I went out into the garage to get a piece of plywood I thought I could use to board up the broken window after the police left. They were going to arrive any moment.

It was only after I heard their car actually pulling up in front of the house that I remembered the head in my freezer. I was aghast at my own stupidity—had I really phoned the police on my own to invite them to step into the house where a murdered man's head was being stored in a Safeway bag in the freezer? I hadn't meant to, but, I suddenly realized, I apparently had.

I heard the motor turn off. It would take them a few seconds to check the address and then come to the front door. I ran into the laundry room. The freezer looked as it always did—a long, low white chest with a chrome handle. I flicked on the light and lifted the lid of the freezer.

No head. I looked again. There were some frozen chickens and a few bags of frozen milk, but definitely no head. Had it been stolen? Do thieves generally bother looking in the freezer troughs in the houses they hit? It didn't seem likely, but what other explanation could there have been? Could Dave have been lying to me about the head being here in the first place? He certainly hadn't sounded like he was lying, but what did that mean? But if Buddy's head actually had been in the bag we left in the bowling alley on the Lougheed Highway, then that still left unexplained why it had never been found. Unless it had…and the police had suppressed the information and kept it out of the media for some reason I didn't understand….

All these thoughts passed through my head in a few seconds as I stood holding the top of the freezer open. And then I heard a loud knocking at the door and I knew the police were standing on my doorstep.

I closed the lid—the pointless thought flitting through my head that the freezer trough looked oddly like a large coffin—and hurried to open the door.

XXX

I can sum up the rest of the evening pretty quickly. There were two policemen at the door, a Constable Ng and a Constable MacDonald. They were pleasant enough. They exuded concern. They took a statement from me. They looked around. They noted the damage to the window and they made a handlist of all the things I could think of that were gone. I was pretty honest about that—except that I upgraded the laptop dramatically and said it had been Wil's, then threw in about three hundred CDs, a Rollex watch I said my dad had given me when I got married and about $250 U.S. in cash I said I had stashed in my laptop's carrying case. Whether they believed me or not, I can't say, but most of what I told them was true and I figured that since the premiums my parents had been paying all those years were as high as they were precisely because there are so many fraudulent claims, it wasn't really stealing to get a little back on the side as compensation for all those years of paying for other people's larceny.

Anyway, Constables Ng and MacDonald stayed for about an hour. They gave me the number of the report they were going to file—this was the whole point of the entire exercise, I realized: to give me a file number I could submit to the insurance people, not to gather any information that might actually have been used in any sort of serious criminal investigation—anyway, they gave me the number and then off they went.

About twelve seconds after I closed the door, Dave called. He was downtown and had just been hanging around eating pizza and playing video games. If the coast was clear, he wanted to come back. No problem about me not picking him, up, he still had most of the fifty and he'd take a cab. What was the precise address of the house? He'd be there in twenty minutes.

And he was. By this time, it was just after one thirty in the morning. We boarded up the broken window, swept up the broken glass and went to bed. The next morning, I was up early, but Dave slept in. Lena and I had our breakfast together in the kitchen and discussed our new life.

"So you're starting grade one in a few weeks, right?"

"You know I am, Daddy."

"We'll have to register you again, I think. This house is probably in a new district and you'll probably go to a different school than last year."

I expected this news to be slightly, or even seriously, upsetting to little Lena, but she took it in stride. "That will be fun, Daddy," she said easily. "The old school had a bad smell."

"It did? What did it smell like?"

"It smelled like Mrs. Volochek."

There didn't seem to be much pursuing this particular line of thought. I had met the formidable Volochek once or twice at kindergarten open school night and hadn't come away with a sense that she had a peculiar or even a particularly strong odour. Still, Lena seemed quite certain that she not only possessed a specific smell, but that scent was sufficiently strong to have given the entire school building a distinctive aroma. I liked that Lena remembered things like that, taking it as a sign of intelligence that I rarely saw in children her age.

When Dave came down, Lena took it in her stride. He was wearing a t-shirt and pair of jockey shorts.

"There's a lady present, Dave," I said pleasantly.

"There is? Oh, yeah," he said, completely oblivious to the point of my observation. He moved to pour himself some coffee.

"Do you think you could put some pants on?"

"Oh, yeah. Sure." He continued towards the coffee.

"Now?"

"Sure." He turned and headed back upstairs. A moment later, he was back downstairs wearing a pair of shorts. Was this the beginning of family life? I thought it might be, but the thought was too absurd to entertain and I dismissed it almost as quickly as it had popped into my head in the first place.

The rest of the day passed uneventfully. We had the Doctor Hour Glass ("For Pane Relief In Hours, Not Days") people in to fix the window. I phoned my parents' insurance agent, then a claims guy from the insurance company itself. He came over that same afternoon and took a list from me of what was missing. He told me he would get approval as quickly as possible, whereupon I could start replacing the items that were stolen at the company's expense. When he left, it was still not even one in the afternoon, so we all headed downtown for some lunch. We ate in some dive on Dunsmuir that indicated on the menu how much each sandwich cost both in Canadian cash and Salvation Army chits, then hung out for a while at MacLeod's bookshop, one of my favourite places downtown. We ate some pizza at one of the 99-cents-a-slice places, then headed back to the house. By the time we got home it was almost seven. We were all tired, but I felt especially drained. Still, it was a good day. We had made big progress on the insurance claim, the window was fixed and, most important of all, Leeny's first day with me in her new home had been a big success. Who she thought Dave was in all of this, I had no idea. I could have asked, I guess, but I didn't want to plant ideas in her head where there may well not have been any in the first place. Besides, kids are very accepting of the world as they encounter it. If Dave was my friend and was staying for a while in my house before he headed off to his own grandma's in Winnipeg, then why should Lena find that odd or inexplicable?

I made some dinner for us all. None of us was all that hungry since we had eaten all that pizza, so I scrambled some eggs and toasted some onion bagels I had bought on the way home and we ate fried egg sandwiches and drank milk for dinner. It was a nice atmosphere in my little house that night, I thought. I don't know…it was somehow different than when Helene and I had been together. There had always been some tension in the air in those days, tension about money or about sex or about something one or the other of us had said. We were in love, we said over and over, but when you come right down to us, there was more peace—and a lot more, to tell you the truth—in the kitchen as Dave, Lena and I ate scrambled egg sandwiches on onion bagels than I could ever recall there being in my married home. I did the dishes, put Lena to bed and percolated a fresh pot of coffee, then turned to the evening's main topic.

"So let's talk about the head."

Dave was sitting at the kitchen table reading an old Newsweek. "What's there to say?"

"Well, it isn't in the freezer and I can think of only three ways to explain that fact. One, it flew away on its own and the thieves found the window already broken because your dad's head had flown through it on the way out. Two, the thieves took the head. Three, it wasn't there in the first place."

Dave's eyes widened. "You think I was bullshitting you. In the car, when I told you that I had put the head in the freezer?"

"I didn't say that. All I said was that…."

"Was that you think the head might not have been there. Which means I was lying. Come on, man, why would I lie to you? I mean, what would be the point of lying?"

"I don't know." And I didn't. The truth was that I had no idea what could possibly have motivated Dave to tell me the head was in the freezer when it wasn't really so.

"Well, it was the truth. Look, I'll tell you what happened. You were upstairs closing the windows just before we headed out to the bowling alley. And I suddenly had a bad feeling about ditching my dad's head out there, but I was…I dunno, I was embarrassed…well, not really ashamed, but embarrassed to tell you that I didn't want to go through with it. I mean, that was the plan and you were really so good about not giving me a hard time and you were so unbelievably helpful that I just didn't want to bail out of what we had said we were going to do. But I had this really, really bad feeling about just leaving the head in the bowling alley.

"So I put a few layers of plastic wrap on the counter and lifted the head out of the bag. It had shrunk a little, I think…or maybe it hadn't, but it looked a lot smaller than it had when I had first…when we first saw it together the night we came back here with it. Anyway, the bottom had sort of congealed or something, but there wasn't anything leaking out of the bottom, but since I didn't know if the brains would turn to liquid eventually or if they wouldn't, I figured the smart thing would be to freeze the whole damn thing. Then it wouldn't smell *and* it wouldn't leak. So I put it down on the Saran and wrapped it up as best I could—this only took a few minutes and I figured I'd for sure hear you flushing upstairs when you were finished with your dump—anyway, I wrapped it up and put it in one of the Safeway bags in the broom cupboard, then put it in the freezer. I even sort of buried in under the chickens, but it wasn't, you know, invisible or anything, just not completely right there on top for anyone to see. Anyway, I got the head in the freezer and some books from your brother's room into the bowling ball case just in time. You must have been reading up there or something—you were in there a really long time, you know—anyway, you eventually came out, but by then I was all finished. And away we went…."

"So where's the head right now?"

"That a good question. It's the best question. Hell, it's really the only question that needs an answer right now, isn't it?"

"I agree. So what do you think?"

"Well, it didn't fly out of here. And it was there in the first place. So the only one of your options that makes any sense is that someone took it. And since we know there were people stealing in here while we were in Portland, then it must have been them."

"It's like having coffee with Perry Mason."

"Who?"

"This really smart lawyer on TV from a million years ago. My parents used to watch it when I was a kid."

"Oh."

"So these are the questions. Where is the head? Who has it? And how are we going to get it back?"

"Well, that's easy. I don't know. I don't know. And I don't know."

Dave sat back in his chair as though he had said something truly witty. I didn't think he was being all that clever, but I also had to admit that he had a point. I also didn't know, didn't know and didn't know. So what were we going to do? I didn't know that either.

A few minutes passed in silence. But when Dave spoke, he sounded as though he hadn't even taken note of the lull in the conversation. "We could do nothing," he said.

"How zen of us!"

"How what?"

"Nothing. What would doing nothing get us?"

"Nothing at all. The head is gone. The cops don't have it or we'd have heard from them already. The thieves either took it because they're going to try to sell it back to us, in which case we'll find out where it is and who has it and how we're going to get it back right away, or they took it and pitched it when they realized what it was and freaked out in which case someone will eventually find it and report it to the cops. They'll investigate, but the investigation won't point to us because we aren't the ones who dumped it wherever whoever finds it is going to find it. They'll either find the guys or they won't. If they don't, we're home free. If they do, the guys will either tell them they stole the head from here or they won't. If they don't, we're still home free. And if they do, the cops will either believe them or they won't. If they don't, we're still okay, in fact, we're in great shape. And if they do, then it's still only their word against ours. So I think we're in pretty good shape. I say we don't do anything at all."

Since I had no idea what we even could do about finding the head, I was forced to agree. There's nothing like feeling virtuous about taking the only path that you can see stretched out in front of you. "Okay," I said, trying to sound as though this were a concession I was making rather than an admission that I couldn't think of any approach to the missing head issue other than the one Dave was suggesting. "We'll do nothing."

Dave took a long sip of coffee. "What if the head tells them who cut it of my father's neck?"

I took a long look at Dave. "Are you crazy?"

"No, really, man. I mean, what if the head somehow talks, like the head in your dream. You remember the dream where your brother's head is in the pyramid with the other ones, the heads of the sons of that guy, what was his name?"

"Ahab."

"Right, Ahab. Anyway, remember they have the sons of Ahab's heads stacked up in these two pyramids at the city gates and your brother's head is one of them somehow and you pick it up and it talks. Remember?"

Of course, I remembered. "It was only a dream, David. It wasn't real."

"Yeah, but what if it was? What if that kind of stuff sometimes really does happen?"

There was an audible level of panic in Dave's voice I wasn't accustomed to hearing. "Hey, calm down, man. This is crazy.

That kind of stuff doesn't really happen in real life. It's just a dream, just a way of me working through my guilt over not having done to my brother's head what I promised him I would. It's just a way of dealing with all that guilt, man, not a real story. Heads can't talk. You know that."

Dave looked half-mollified to hear that decapitated heads can't talk and half-embarrassed to realize that he had given voice to the kind of deep-seated fear about things that most people have the common sense to keep to themselves. "I guess," he said, his voice calmer now.

I poured him some fresh coffee and took a package of vanilla cookies from the cupboard. "Eat some cookies. I think your blood sugar level must be getting a bit low if you are seriously wondering about whether your dad's head is going to rat on you to the cops."

Dave looked a bit chagrined to hear things put that baldly, but he didn't say anything. Instead, he ripped open the cellophane and took a stack of seven or eight cookies. He set to eating them one by one, interrupting his chomping only to sip some coffee. When was done, he wiped his mouth, then went to the sink to wash out his coffee cup and mine. I put the cookies away. We both went upstairs. We brushed our teeth—it was already almost midnight—and said goodnight. I heard him rustling around in Wil's room for a while, then it was quiet and I presumed he had gone to bed. I stayed up for a while reading. Then I decided to brush my teeth again. I finally got into bed around one in the morning. The bed felt cool and the sheets were fresh and nice. I felt at home in my place and secure that we had pulled off a very serious crime and had, as far as I could tell, gotten away with it. If worse came to worst, I was just an accomplice to murder, but I knew that being party to a crime like that could end a citizen up in jail for life anyway. I refused to dwell on that possibility and had almost convinced myself that the whole incident was completely behind us when the phone rang.

Not wanting the ringing to wake Lena, I rolled over quickly, reached for the phone on the night table and picked up the receiver.

"Hey, man, you know you give really great head," a voice said into my ear before it dissolved into cackling and guffawing as though this vulgar attempt at humour were the single most clever thing anyone had ever said to anyone else. I wasn't laughing, however. Not even slightly.

XXXI

Eventually, the laughing died down.

"Who is this?" I asked pointlessly. No matter how stupid the person on the other end of the line was, he couldn't be stupid enough to tell me his name.

"You don't need to know my name." The voice dead serious now. I took it for a young man's voice. Maybe early 20s. Maybe a little older.

I told myself to concentrate, to listen for anything that could conceivably constitute useful information for me later on. The voice sounded totally at ease in English and his accent was certainly North American and probably Canadian. There weren't any background noises I could identify other than the occasional roar of a truck or a car passing by. Was my caller phoning from a phone booth? That seemed likely, in that he might not have stopped when he was in the house to notice if I had that call display thing that shows the number of whoever calls your house.

"Well, what can I do for you?" Playing dumb seemed like the right approach. He might get irritated with me sounding like I thought I was even marginally in charge and I desperately didn't want to piss him off if I didn't have to. He was, after all, holding the cards and I needed to win this hand.

"I got your head."

"It's not my head."

"Don't get smart. You know what head I mean. It wasn't me who hit your house, it was some pals of mine. So after they finished loading your crap into their car, they decided they were hungry. There wasn't dick in the fridge, but they thought maybe you had some ice cream or something in the big freezer." I remember thinking that "the big freezer" was probably what his own mother called the freezer trough when he was growing up and he had never stopped to consider that this was not its formal title. "So they opened it up and there isn't any ice cream, but there's this head in there. Get it? Dick in the fridge, but a head in the freezer...." More paroxysms of laughter. I said nothing. After a long thirty seconds, the voice stopped laughing and continued where he had left off. "Now a man's head is not what you find in every house to knock over, you know. You do find pretty weird stuff—believe me, I could write a book—but a head is really something special. Only it isn't any head, is it? It's a special head. Someone's head. Someone who's dead's head. And maybe it's someone's head who was in the paper last week about getting knocked off in his own house and then having his head cut off and ripped off by whoever did it. I don't know if that's whose head it is, but I bet the cops could find out right away."

"You can bring it to the cops if you want, but you'll have to admit where you got it."

"Yeah, smart man, maybe I'll just mail it to them. That will get you good at the same time it leaves me out of it completely."

"So why would you waste your money on the postage? There's no advantage to you is doing that, is there?"

"Are you stupid? I'm willing to sell you the head back if you want. Otherwise, off it goes to the cops. In the mail. Nice and neat."

"I'll just deny it. I'll say I have no idea what you're talking about. I'll tell the cops you tried to blackmail me into giving you money and I refused which is why you're trying to involve me in this."

"Well, that would be a good plan except for one thing. The head really was in your house, pal. And that means that there has to be something that connects you to the guy whose head we're talking about. Some way that his head really did end up in your deep freeze. So maybe the cops will figure it out or maybe they won't. Maybe they'll just take your word that this doesn't have anything to do with you or maybe they'll tear your house apart looking for clues. Maybe you'll get off or maybe you won't. But if you have the head back, you're on easy street. Look, this is up to you, pal. I gotta go."

The phone went dead. My caller, whoever he was, had spoken a lot more than I had expected him to, but he hadn't really said much. And he had hung up very quickly, almost as though someone had come into earshot that he didn't want to hear what he was saying to me. I would have to ponder that later on.

In the meantime, my options were extremely limited and, for all I hated to admit it, he was really right about the two central points around which this whole mess rotated: he had the head and I wanted it back. Refusing to deal with this creep could risk Dave spending his entire life in prison. Not to mention what they'd do to me as an accessory-after-the-fact, which was probably the best light a good lawyer could cast on me if the story ever got out. But mostly, this was about Dave and I knew he would have to be part of the discussion.

I went into Wil's room. Dave was asleep, as seemed to be his normal practice, on top of the bedspread. He was wearing a pair of jockey shorts this evening, but nothing else. He looked peaceful in the white moonlight that was streaming in through the open window. I could hear the almost, but not entirely, inaudible rasp of his breath drawing in and out. His eyes were flexing, but without him actually opening his eyes, and I took this for a sign he was dreaming. I wondered what his dream was about? Was he reliving the experience of lying terrified in his bed and listening while his mother was raped on a mess of hamburgers, green relish and glass? Or was he remembering what it had been like to hear the postman open the mail chute in the front door of his father's home two days after his mother killed herself and push through a letter from her addressed specifically to her darling boys? Or was he dreaming about living in Winnipeg in a nice house near a Ukrainian church along with his brother and grandmother in a semi-normal family setting? I hesitated to wake him, but I knew it was the right thing to do. There was, after all, no way to know when the phone would ring a second time.

I shook his shoulder, then again a second time a bit more vigorously. He turned over, then over again. He seemed to be in a deep sleep and I regretted having to wake him, but I knew he would approve of my decision once he heard about the phone call. Finally, he woke up and sat up. He drew his knees up towards his chest and put his arms around his shins.

"Are you cold?" I asked. He looked cold, although the room was really quite pleasant.

"Yeah."

I went into the hall and came back with a blanket. He draped it around his shoulders and looked a bit more comfortable.

"Were you dreaming?"

"Yeah."

"About what?" It wasn't any of my business, but I was too curious not to ask.

"About doing that chick back in Alberta. What was her name?"

"Patsy."

"Right. So is there something else? Or did you just want to know what my dream was about?"

"Someone called a few minutes ago who said he had the head. Your dad's head."

"You don't think I knew which head you meant?"

"Sorry. Anyway, he was giving me this whole song-and-dance, but the short version is that he has it and he wants us to buy it back."

Dave's eyes widened. "What are you going to do?" he asked, exhaling like a smoker as he spoke.

"Me? It's your head."

"Yeah, but it's your ass if they connect it to this house, isn't it?"

He had me there. "I suppose."

"You suppose?"

"Okay, it's my ass if they connect the head to this house. But it's yours as well."

"Well, my ass happens to be worth a whole lot less than yours. And the bottom line is that I don't have any money at all. If anyone buys the head, you'll have to."

"Well, don't say that too fast. Assuming you aren't arrested, tried and convicted of your father's murder, you're going to have some income from the estate. The house is worth something. Hell, the lot is worth more than the house. And eventually it will get sold and you and Kevin will split the proceeds. I think you can count on at least eighty or ninety grand. Maybe more. And your dad might have had some money too…."

"I don't think so."

"Believe me, pal, you never know."

"So you're saying you won't pay this guy off?"

I don't know where this came from, but I suddenly knew—and knew absolutely—that this was something Dave had started and that he had to finish. "Let's see what kind of dough they're asking. If I have it, I'll lend it to you. Hell, I'll give you one quarter and lend you the other three. When the house gets sold, you can pay me back. That sound fair?"

Dave looked up at me and, for a moment, I could see the little boy that once lived behind those eyes. He looked almost ashen in the white moonlight, but there was a certain innocence there as well, a certain insouciance that spoke well, despite everything, for the way in which Dave had been raised. I could hardly believe that our relationship had progressed from hitchhiker and lift-to-hitchhiker-giver to something beyond friendship, something approaching a son and father relationship. There wasn't anything sexual about my feelings—or at least nothing overtly sexual, Dr. Freud—but there was a deeper sense of caring about another individual that I could recall ever feeling about anyone else in the world other than Lena and Wil.

I think Dave had the same depth of feeling in that moment towards me. I've never asked him and he's never said, but things changed in that moment and they changed on a dime.

When he spoke, his voice was soft and peaceful, almost as though an enormous burden had been lifted from his shoulders when I made it clear I was going to help him redeem his father's head from its captivity rather than just jump in and bail him out with my own money like a dad would a little boy. "Sure," he said. "That sounds fair."

There wasn't any real need for it, but we shook hands. "Deal?" I asked, superfluously, but with enough dignity to make Dave realize that I took his word as his bond.

"Deal," he said quietly.

And then he lay down under his blanket and turned onto his side. I tucked the blanket in around him—this was a nineteen-year-old semi-grown man we're talking about, but I tucked him in anyway and sat on the bed and watched over him while he drifted off to sleep. I felt good about our conversation. Good and principled and not as worried about the future as I had been just ten minutes earlier.

I got back into bed, constantly expecting the telephone to ring. I actually dreamt the phone was ringing at one point, but when I awoke, all was still. I slept fitfully and, as far as I can remember, without dreaming. And then, just when I thought the night was never going to end, it was morning and yellow sunlight was streaming in through the window and filling the room.

XXXII

In some ways, it was a day like any other. It was only half past seven when I awoke, so I figured I'd get dressed quickly and head on down to one of the big synagogues on Oak Street so I could say Kaddish Number Eighty-Nine for Wil. The last time I had bothered with Kaddish had been in Winnipeg almost two weeks earlier and I was feeling a bit guilty. I threw on some shorts and a t-shirt, scribbled a note to Dave asking him to give Lena some breakfast when she woke up and headed out. I missed the first Kaddish, then sat and contemplated the phone call of the previous evening for the rest of the service and said the last Kaddish instead. The whole thing lasted thirty-five minutes and, as it turned out, I was back home before either Dave or Lena had stirred. I put up a pot of coffee and made some oatmeal, the sat back to read the paper until somebody else in the house woke up.

I kept feeling that I was supposed to do something. Somewhere out there, somebody had Buddy Kruger's head and that somebody wanted to sell it back to me. I was prepared to deal—the more I thought about it, the more obvious it was to me that I needed that head back desperately—but it frustrated me that I couldn't contact them. The man hadn't precisely said he'd phone back, but I assumed that went without saying. He had gotten off the phone very abruptly, I recalled, almost as though he had been surprised by somebody whom he had definitely not wanted to hear what he was saying to me. For the three hundredth time, I catalogued what I knew about my mystery caller. He was a male. He was, I thought, in his twenties. He was a native

English speaker. He was not entirely on his own—the way he quickly ended our conversation implied that he either lived or worked or hung out with somebody he was anxious to keep unaware of his life as a felon—but then again he had said in so many words that there had been several people who had robbed my house. Needless to say, I didn't particularly believe that it had been buddies of his who had hit my house and that he himself hadn't actually been involved.

We went through the motions of a normal day. Lena woke up and ate some oatmeal. Dave eventually woke up and drank two cups of coffee. We drove down to Granville Island and had lunch in the public market. We did some shopping at Safeway on the way back. I set a nice table for dinner—it was Friday night and Helene, for all her faults, always made a point of making a nice dinner and lighting Sabbath candles on Friday evenings. I thought it was probably important to keep this up for Lena's sake and I was prepared to see it through. I ironed a table cloth and sent Dave back out to Safeway to buy some candles. We resolved to go over to the Brier Home in the morning so that Lena could commune with her grandparents for as long as it took for them to remember who she was. Dave surprised me by declaring himself willing, even eager, to come along as well. Did he really want to meet my parents? Or was he just anxious that Lena not usurp him totally in the structure of my family life? I didn't much care and the basic idea was that we would make a family day of it. First, we'd spend some time with my parents, then we'd head over to the cemetery to visit Wil's grave. I couldn't recall off hand if the cemetery was closed to visitors on Saturday or not, but I figured we'd be able to sneak in one way or the other.

The call came at midnight, pretty much precisely as it had the night before. I was in bed, also like the night before. I knew who it was as soon as the phone rang. I lifted the receiver and said nothing.

"You there, man?"

"Yes."

"You want the head back?"

"Yes."

"You prepared to pay for it?"

"Yes."

"Okay, then. Put two thousand bucks in tens and twenties in a paper bag. Drive out to Manning Park and meet me tomorrow at noon by the rowboat rental shack on Lightning Lake. It's right by the lodge and this whole thing should be real simple, man…you give me the cash and I'll give you the head and we're all out of there in ten seconds. And another thing: make sure you come alone. I see anyone with you, I'm gone. You know where Manning Park is?"

"Yes."

"You don't say much, do you?"

I hung up. Dave, who had heard the phone ring, came into my room and sat down on my bed. Lena, as far as I could tell, was fast asleep. I told him what the caller had said.

"So we gonna go?"

"What choice do we have?"

"Where's the park?"

"It's not too far. Somewhere near Hope, I think. I have a map in the car. If I'm right about where it is, it'll be about an hour's drive or maybe a bit longer. If we leave at ten, we'll have more than enough time."

"What will we do with Lena?"

"We'll take her. You can eat ice cream with her in the lodge while I head out to meet the guy. I don't have anyone to leave her with and I think she'd like the trip. And after we have the head, we can spend the day in the park. It will be okay, you'll see." Where this uncharacteristic optimism was coming from, I can't say. But it all sounded like it was going to work out and I was so relieved to have a plan of action that I was just not prepared to worry about this or that detail.

"Where will we get the money?"

"Don't worry about that. I'll get it. I'll get two grand and you'll owe me fifteen hundred back. That fair?"

"Sure."

Dave went back to bed and I turned off the light and got into bed myself. I lay there, thinking about the next day. I could get the money easily enough—I had a few hundred bucks in my own checking account and another four or five hundred in savings. The rest I could either withdraw from my parents' savings account—I had full power of attorney over their funds—or withdraw from a cash machine as an advance on my Visa card. No, the money wouldn't be a problem. All I had to do was get the money, put it in a bag, head out to Manning Park, buy back the head, ditch it somewhere and the whole sordid mess would be behind us and we could get on with our aimless, pointless, meaningless, goalless, directionless, jobless lives. I could hardly wait.

The next morning began innocently enough. We were all up long before nine. Lena ate some waffles with maple syrup. I had a bowl of cornflakes. Dave ate half an English muffin. We all drank coffee, even little Lena, who took hers with about three parts milk to one part coffee and five tablespoons of sugar. Everybody seemed excited about the outing.

"What about visiting grandma and grandpa?" Lena asked.

"We'll go tomorrow."

"But they'll be expecting us today?"

"They aren't expecting the sun to go down tonight, honey. They're sort of in this wait-and-see mode, so they're never disappointed when things they forgot to expect don't actually happen."

Whether this made any sense at all to Lena, I can't say, but she seemed quite content with my answer. I loved the way I could see her trying to work through the intricacies of Daddy's logic in her mind. Should I have just come out and told her that her grandparents had sunk to the point at which they could barely remember their own names, let alone how long it had been since their granddaughter had come for a visit? Or that I would have been impressed if they even remembered that they had a granddaughter? There didn't seem to be any reason.

We got our things together. I found the map and located Manning Park between Hope and Princeton, more or less where I had thought it was going to be. I left Dave and Lena to clean up the breakfast dishes and ran down to the bank to get some cash. I considered bopping over to the synagogue to say Kaddish—number ninety!—but there wasn't time since I had undoubtedly already missed the first Kaddish and I wouldn't be able to stay for the end of the service if we wanted to be in Manning Park by noon. I ended up doing the cash in quarters—one quarter from my checking account, one quarter from savings, another quarter from my parents savings account and the last quarter as an advance on my Visa account. I put the money in a paper bag and locked it in the trunk. When I got home the kitchen was tidy and everybody was ready.

I didn't own a bowling ball case, but I seemed to remember that my mother owned one of those big black patent leather carrying cases that ladies used to carry their hats in about a million years ago. I had the vague sense it might be in the garage somewhere, so I rummaged around in there for a few minutes and managed to find it. We had the money, we had a carrying case for Buddy's head and we didn't need to pack a lunch since there's a cafeteria at the park where we could eat. We were all set.

And away we went. The drive was easy, the day was clear, the mood in the car was upbeat. Lena was intent on telling us this favulously involved story about some miniature golf place she and Helene had been to in California and although it was almost incredibly boring to listen to, I think we—Dave and me, that is—I think we were both happy to have something to talk about other than the real reason we had planned this last minute outing to Manning Park.

We arrived around eleven-thirty. Everything seemed calm. The park was truly lovely: lush, green and, as far as I could see on the drive in, very well maintained. We found the lodge and the cafeteria. I took the bag of money from the trunk and we went inside. Lena was so absolutely thrilled to be there that you'd think she had never eaten in a cafeteria before. We ordered plates of spicy chips and Cokes and sat back to enjoy our meal. The crowd looked pretty typical—young families, middle-aged couples, a few obviously foreign tourists. There was a group of Japanese men seated at the table next to ours and a few German women sitting a little further on. I kept expecting something to happen, but nothing did. And then it was five to noon.

"Leeny, honey, you stay here with Uncle Dave and have some ice cream. Daddy has to see somebody about something for a few minutes."

"Okay, Daddy. Come right back."

"Okay, honey. Just a few minutes."

Dave looked up at me as though this were some sort of ominous prediction, but I shrugged it off and refused to be drawn into that kind of mode of thinking. I went out, the bag of money in my hand.

There were signs right outside the cafeteria directing visitors to the rowboat and canoe rental shack on Lightning Lake. I set off. There was no one around. By the time I was on the actual trail leading to the lake, I couldn't even hear anybody else.

I came up to the lake and saw the shack. Nobody was around. I clutched the bag and moved forward.

The rental shack was open and I assumed that there must be

somebody inside handling the boat rentals. But I didn't see anybody. My plan was to walk up to the side of the shack and wait for five minutes, then leave. I looked at my watch as I approached the shack; it was precisely noon. I walked closer.

What happened next came so quickly that I can hardly describe it fast enough to give you the correct impression of what it felt like. I heard somebody running behind me, but before I could turn, I was pushed to the ground and dragged off into the woods. When I tried to get up, I felt somebody kicking me in the side with what felt like steel-tipped boots. The pain was terrible, so terrible that I wondered if I would survive the experience. I remember this all as though I was an outside observer rather than the actual person being kicked in the side. I felt someone reaching down to pull my arms up behind my back. The bag fell and was immediately picked up. I vaguely heard people yelling to each other, but I couldn't make out what they were saying. Still, I had the sense they were speaking English and, strange though this will sound, I actually had the presence of mind to ask myself why it was that I couldn't understand their words.

And then they were gone. I pulled myself up and began to run back towards the lodge. But as soon as I had taken a few steps back towards the path, I saw Dave. He was about twenty yards or so into the woods on the other side of the path and he was sitting on somebody whom he had obviously knocked to the ground. The bag of money was on the ground by his side. You could hardly see their position from the path and there wasn't anyone around anyway. As far as I could tell, we were totally alone.

The man he was sitting on looked to be about six feet tall. He had very short blond hair and an earring in his right ear. Dave was, I thought, trying to figure out how to break his right arm. He kept pushing it back further and further until the guy he was sitting on actually puked on the ground from the pain. Then he went to work on the other arm.

I had no idea if Dave planned to continue with the guy's legs, but I thought we had had enough.

"Let's go," I said.

"Not yet," he answered calmly, looking up as though I was suggesting we leave a restaurant before he had finished his meal.

"How did you know to follow me?"

"I figured it couldn't hurt. A family with two little girls is watching Leeny. They said they'd be there for an hour and she could play with their girls for a while if I needed to go back to the cabin to use the washroom or something."

"You asked them that?"

"I was sort of hopping around and that's what they thought I meant."

"And you saw this guy running?"

"I got there just in time to see him knock you down from the back. I just stood off to the side until he was right in front of me, then I jumped him and dragged him over here. There was another one too, but he ran ahead. But neither of them had any extra heads with them as far as I could see. I think they were planning to cheat us, that's what I think."

"So what do we do now?"

The man Dave was sitting on seemed to think this question was meant for him, but when he raised his head to answer, Dave shoved it down onto the ground as hard as he could.

"He's talking to me, scumbag," he said.

Then, turning to me. "The rest is real easy."

The guy's right arm was, I thought, definitely broken. He looked to be in terrible pain—white as a ghost, facial features drawn and tight, lips dry, eyes wild. I was delighted.

"What do you want me to do?"

Dave looked down at his prisoner. "Hey, scumbag," he said, "what kind of car do you have?"

No answer.

Dave reached around for the man's left arm and grabbed it firmly in his right hand.

"Blue Tercel." The man's voice was faint, but I was certain this was who had phoned me two nights in a row.

"Okay, then." He looked up at me, now fully in command of the situation. "Saul, go to the parking lot and find a blue Tercel. It should have a man sitting in it. Tell that man that I'll swap him his friend's head, which for the moment is still attached to his shoulders, for the one he has. No money, just one head for another. Tell him to take it or leave it."

"One other thing…." Dave reached into the guy's pants and pulled out a key chain. "Take this. It might be useful."

"What if the other guy didn't hang around?"

Dave looked down at the man he was sitting on. "Then I'm gonna kill this guy."

I didn't know if this was adolescent bravado speaking or if Dave was really contemplating murdering a second time. I decided not to find out until it was absolutely necessary. I headed off to the parking lot, bruised but ambulatory and not really any the worse for having been knocked down and kicked. My ribs were sore and getting worse as I walked, but there was obviously no choice.

In the parking lot, I saw a blue Toyota Tercel that I thought was at least ten years old. There was a young man with a shaved head and uncommonly taut skin sitting at the steering wheel looking nervous.

I approached the car. I was trying to walk like Al Pacino, but I don't think I was doing such a hot job. Luckily, the guy in the car looked even more scared than I was.

"Do you have a man's head in your trunk?" I asked, as though this were a normal question one stranger might ask another in the parking lot at Manning Park.

"Who wants to know?"

"Well," I continued, "since the man who belongs to the head was murdered last week, maybe the R.C.M.P. would like to know."

"You can't pin that on us."

"Well, I can't pin anything on anyone. That would have to be the police's decision." Then, as though giving voice to an afterthought. "Say, you wouldn't be a friend of the guy whose arms and legs my little brother is breaking in the forest back there, are you? How about we make a deal? I'll get li'l Billy to stop breaking off bits of your friend's body and you give me the head you stole from my house."

"What about the money?"

"To hell with the money."

"But Brian said…."

So the guy's name was Brian. "Brian is full of it, pal. And he's about to be crippled either for life or for a real long time. Did I tell you that li'l Billy only starts with arms and legs. Why, he's got a collection of pricks at home that he's sliced off guys that have tried to doublecross him that would impress anybody. I know it impresses me when I see them all laid out. He keeps them in these little test tubes filled with formaldehyde. Of course, I'm sure he'll need a real big test tube for your friend, but we can get one of these, no problem. So what's it gonna be?

The guy looked like he didn't know what to do. He didn't look much older than Dave, maybe not even older at all. His chin was quivering and I could see he was beginning to realize that he was mixed up in something that could end up with real serious consequences. "I…I gotta talk to Brian," he said.

"Sure. By all means. I'll wait here."

The guy got out of the car and ran towards the path that led to the lake. As soon as he was gone, I opened the trunk and took out the Safeway bag with Buddy's head inside it, then threw the keys into the trunk and locked it. I ran to our car—Lena was still nowhere to be seen, thank God—and put it in our trunk without bothering to put it in my mother's hatbox. Then I ran as fast as I could towards the lake.

When I got there, the scene was incredible. Dave had gotten tired of breaking arms, I guess, and had moved on. In a flash of what can only be called almost telepathic prescience, he had pulled the guy's pants and shorts down around his ankles and had this big bowie knife—which I vaguely recognized as one Wil had owned—he had Brian's prick in one hand and the knife pressed down hard at the base where he looked as though he might seriously be contemplating cutting if off. Brian, for his part, was white with fear. He had vomit dribbling down his chin and his eyes were bulging out like a fish's. I had a momentary pang of sympathy for what he was going through, but I squelched it. This was, after all, the guy who had violated the sanctity of my family's home and no one is lower, at least in my humble estimation, than someone who would violate the sanctity of another man's home.

The other guy was standing at a distance trying to take it all in. I was standing behind him.

"You got it?" Dave asked me.

"Yeah."

"Take the money."

I moved quickly up to where they were standing and picked up the bag of money.

"Now should I cut off this guy's prick or not?"

"I don't know. What do you think?"

Dave pressed the knife down a bit harder and drew a little blood. Brian's bowel emptied audibly. Then he puked.

I came around to where Dave was standing. "Come on," I said, "let's go."

Dave looked up as though this were precisely the invitation he had been hoping for. "Sure," he said. "Let's go. Get the other guy's keys."

I approached the other guy. "I don't have keys to the car. Brian does," he said. "It's his car."

"Give me the keys you do have."

The guy was so disoriented and nervous that it apparently didn't dawn on him that all he had to do to avoid complying with my demand was to turn on his heel and run away. On the other hand, he really didn't have any reason to think that Dave wasn't about to maim his friend Brian with my dead brother's Bowie knife. Anyway, he fished a key ring out of his pocket and gave it to me. I didn't see a Toyota key—I didn't see any car keys, actually—but I figured that it's better to be safe than sorry. I left them all for a moment, walked the thirty yards or so to the lake, pitched the keys as far as I could into the water and came back.

"Okay, time to go."

Dave got up and released his prisoner. Brian looked a mess—his behind was filthy, his pants and shorts were still down around his ankles, there was blood smeared on the front of his thighs, the front of his shirt was covered with vomit and his right arm, I thought, was definitely broken. I remember noticing to my vague amusement that he had the beginnings of what under other circumstances would undoubtedly have been an impressive erection.

"Well, bye," Dave said in their general direction as we walked away. "And don't be back in touch. The next time, I'll kill you for real."

After that, it was all easy. We collected Lena and got back into our car. We didn't want to hang around in the park after all that, so we headed into Hope and had some ice cream at the Dairy Queen there. We sat there for a while, then got back in the car and headed back home. It had been a sunny day when we started out, but it had clouded up considerably while were in the park. Nonetheless, our mood was quite upbeat as we headed for the Trans-Canada and home.

XXXIII

"You got any more stories?"

I looked into the rear view mirror. Dave seemed to have shed his role as violent arm-breaker of extortionist punks and to have returned to being the adolescent lad who liked stories told to him that I picked up between Barrymore and Stanhope a few weeks earlier. As I looked at Dave's flat, round face, I wondered what Lena would think if she knew what precisely Daddy and Uncle Dave had been up to while she was playing with her little friends. For a moment, I wondered if I would ever tell her, then decided that I most decidedly would not. Dave would move on to Winnipeg and she would forget that he had ever stayed with us. We would get rid of Buddy's head one way or the other and this whole incident would be entirely behind us. I would get a new job—I was in too upbeat a mood to ruin things by dwelling on the fact that I had no idea where precisely to look for one—and Lena and I would live in my parents' house and be a family. Perhaps one day I would marry again....

These thoughts flitted quickly through my mind while Dave's question was still hanging on the air in the car.

"I got a million stories."

"So why don't you tell one?"

"Any particular one you want to hear?"

"One you haven't told yet."

I looked over at Lena and saw she was fast asleep.

I thought for a few moments about what story to tell. There were lots of plausible candidates, but I kept coming back to one single one that seemed especially apt. "How about the story of David and Goliath?" I asked.

"Okay." Dave's voice was flat now, as though he was already settling back to listen. His arms were clasped behind the back of his head and I noticed that he had closed his eyes. For a moment, I thought he might have fallen asleep, but when I said his name out loud, he opened his eyes and repeated that the story of David and Goliath would suit him.

Lena was in a deep sleep. I reached over and took her little hand in mine. It was small, even for a child's, so small that I was able to envelop in almost completely in mine. She smiled in her sleep and I felt my heart melting. I truly loved that child...and I wished to hell Buddy Kruger's head wasn't in the trunk. Well, I told myself, we would see about getting rid of the head as soon as we got home.

"Well," I began, "this happened a real long time ago, when Saul was king of Israel and David was a little boy. He was a cute little guy—red hair, big round eyes, the tanned skin of a shepherd lad—but he was also a decent musician and he was working as Saul's personal music therapist Whenever Saul got depressed, in fact—which was about every thirty minutes—they'd call for David and he'd shlep his lyre over to where Saul was camped and play a bit and sing for him and Saul would become marginally less depressed."

"And that worked?"

"It wasn't as good as Prozac, but it was still pretty effective. Anyway, Saul may have been this major depressive who could only snap out of it when cute little boys plucked their lyres in his presence, but he was also king of Israel and he had some other things to look after as well. The Philistines, for example, who were massing forces at the border and appeared to be poised to attack the Israelite kingdom. It was some scene in those days. The Philistines were this warlike people and they basically hated the

Israelites and spent years and years fighting with them. So all they needed to hear was that the king of Israel—the first king of Israel, since the country had only just recently traded in its judges, of whom Samuel was the last, for kings, of whom Saul was the first—anyway, all they needed to hear was that the king of Israel was generally too depressed to get dressed in the morning, let alone lead his forces into battle successfully, for them to get the idea that the time was right for them to embark on this major campaign of annihilation. So that's precisely when this story takes place, with the Philistines massing their troops on the border and Saul lying in his tent trying to find the courage to put his boots on."

"So what happens first?"

"Well, the armies are camped over and against each other and everybody is sort of waiting to see what is going to happen when this enormous guy named Goliath sort of just walks out into the space between the two camps. Now he was big. Really big. More than nine feet tall. And broad. And hairy. And very, very strong. He's carrying a sword the size of a flagpole and a shield the size of a tabletop and he's got this bronze helmet on his head that alone must weigh a hundred pounds. And this…this guy—if he was a man and not some other species of prehistoric creature that had somehow survived in Philistia—anyway, this person who looked like a man comes forward and put forward a proposal. All the Israelites have to do is send out a warrior to fight him one-on-one and that will do. If the Israelite wins, then the Philistines will become their servants. But if the Philistine—Goliath—if Goliath wins, then the Israelite nation is going to cease to exist and all the people will become the slaves and servants of the Philistines."

"No one is really nine feet tall."

"Well, he was. I mean, no one is seven foot nine either, but the NBA spends a fortune sending people around the world looking for these guys. And they find them, so why shouldn't this one guy have been nine feet tall. I mean, it's not like he was ninety feet tall, just nine. Or nine and a little bit, but still...it's not entirely impossible."

"It's pretty unlikely."

"Look, it was unlikely, but even the laws of probability allow for the occasional improbable event. So let's just say this guy really was nine feet tall and leave it at that. Anyway, he makes his offer, then walks back into the Philistine camp. So the Israelites are all shitting bricks and they are very, very unhappy. I mean, it would be this enormous act of national shame for no one to take up the offer to fight this guy, but who precisely is going to do it? Certainly not Saul, whose hiding from the demons in his tent. And not Saul's kids who were...who weren't up to this kind of combat...."

"What was wrong with them?"

"Well, they were...let's just say they were lovers, not warriors. And no one wanted them to die just because their father was king. So they needed someone else. But no one stepped forward. I mean, it's one thing to think that the national honour rests on somebody fighting this guy and another thing entirely to walk out and put your own life on the line. So they had the basic idea down straight, but no one wanted to go. Now David's older brothers were there and they weren't too anxious to go either. But when David's mom send him with some packages of food and stuff down to his brothers—and also a few gifts to their commanding officer just to make sure he didn't order the boys to take on Goliath, I think—anyway, when David's mom sends him over and he hears the whole story, he says he'll go."

"And they let him?"

"No, they don't let him. They think it's the funniest thing they ever heard. They're rolling in the aisles. Tears are coming down their faces. This little boy with red hair is going to take on this nine foot Philistine freak? They've never heard anything funnier. Only David isn't quite the little boy everyone remembers him as being. In the meantime, he's grown a bit. And he's had some experience fighting animals—when he was looking after his father's flocks, he once had to kill a lion with his bare hands and another time, he had to defend the sheep against a bear, which he also killed. So he only looked like a kid, but behind those kid-like features was a man who knew how to kill when the situation demanded it."

I looked back at my Dave to see if he was getting the message. His eyes were still closed, but I could sense that he was concentrating on what I was saying.

"Anyway, there's this whole big debate. The other guys can't believe Saul would let this baby go fight Goliath, but Saul sees something in David that the others can't or won't see. He sees somebody brave. He sees somebody with the courage of his convictions. He sees somebody who has the nerve to mete out justice when it needs to be meted out without worrying about his own safety. And he sees somebody that will do something—which is a hell of a lot more than anyone else seems to be doing. So he agrees. 'Go and may God be with you' is what he says to David. And then they get down to real business and Saul gets all this cool stuff for David to wear. A big bronze helmet like Goliath's. And a big breastplate, also bronze...."

"What's that?"

"Like a bullet-proof vest, except made of metal instead of kevlar or whatever they make bullet-proof vests out of these days. Anyway, it's like when 007 stops in to see whatever that guy's name is, the one who outfits him with all that neat gear, after M gives him his assignment. Only David doesn't get exploding cigarette cases and eyeglasses with atomic lasers built into the frames. He gets a shield and sword and a helmet and whatever other junk Saul can find in a hurry. Only there's one problem—the stuff weighs so much that David can hardly walk. I mean, he's completely immobilized by all the gear Saul has given him. So he takes it all off and approaches Goliath wearing....what do you think?"

"A tank top?"

"Okay, a tank top. Anything else?"

"Jeans. No, cut-offs. And sneakers."

"That's all?"

"A Canucks hat?"

"That's it precisely. So David approaches Goliath wearing a Vancouver Canucks hat, a tank-top, cut-off denim shorts and Air Jordans. And he's also carrying his slingshot and a few pebbles. And do you know what Goliath does?"

"He gives up immediately?"

"Well, not precisely. He takes one look at the sight of this redheaded boy in denim cut-offs coming close to him carrying a slingshot and he almost splits his sides laughing. I mean it, he's laughing so hard, he's crying. The tears are running down his cheeks and he still can't stop. He turns to his own people and mugs for them. 'I'm a tiny little doggie,' he says, 'and the big, bad Israelites are coming after me with a stick.' And then he actually gets down on the ground and starts crawling around on all fours as though he really were a dog. And all the while, David is watching this guy make a complete fool out of himself and just patiently waiting, biding his time, knowing that all he has to do is wait for the right moment to come and justice will be served after all."

I stole a look at Dave in the rearview mirror.

"Anyway, David waits until he stops doing his doggie impersonation and stands back up. He takes a step closer. And another. And another. Finally, he's only six or seven feet from Goliath and that's when he takes out his sling and puts a little white pebble in the leather pouch. He takes his stance. He aims. He shoots. And he scores. The little pebble lands right in the middle of Goliath's head and sinks down immediately into the outer flesh and pierces through the giant's skull into his brain. The guy reels this way and that. He tries to keep from falling over, but it's too late. A minute later, he's lying dead on the ground.

"But that's not the end of the story. David runs up to the body of his adversary just as the Israelites are coming out from their hiding places to see what happened. He hadn't taken the sword Saul had given him, so he takes Goliath's own sword and there, in the full sight of both the Israelite and the Philistine armies, he cuts off the villain's head. Now that's bad—not only to be beheaded, but to be beheaded by an unarmed teenager with your own sword!"

I looked in the mirror again and this time, Dave was smiling broadly.

"Anyway, the story goes on a bit longer. Saul is so gaga at this point that even though he is the one who sent David out to fight the giant, he's already forgotten about that and he actually asks Abner, his big general, to find out who the boy is who killed the giant. Anyway, Abner doesn't have time to do much research—and he's not quite sure how to handle a request from the king that if anyone knew about it they would think he was even more nuts than usual, which was already plenty as it was—anyway, as soon as David comes back to the camp, Abner shuffles him in to see Saul even though he—David—even though he is still carrying the head of Goliath with him. Anyway, he puts the head down on the king's coffee table and waits for the king to speak.

"'Whose son are you, my boy?' the king asks.

"And David answers, 'The son of your servant Jesse of Bethlehem.' And that's the end of the story."

I thought Dave would take advantage of Lena being asleep to ask me if I thought there was any resemblance between the story of how David beheaded Goliath and the story of how he had beheaded his father, but he didn't and I certainly wasn't going to raise the issue if he didn't.

"You might as well sleep too," I said after a long couple of minutes had paused. "You must be tired from all that arm breaking stuff."

"I'm actually fine."

"Not tired?"

"Well, maybe a little bit."

He closed his eyes and was asleep a moment later. I was pleased to have them both sleeping while I drove. I played back the scene in the forest and layered it over the story of David and Goliath and a million other memories I had. I thought about Buddy Kruger's head in my trunk and wished to hell it was Wil's instead. I resolved, not for the first or the last time, to phone the place in California Wil had been in touch with to see how important it was that the head be sent down to them immediately for freezing, the assumption being that if it were still possible to follow through on Wil's wishes, then I would dig him up myself and send his head where he had wanted it to go in the first place. I spent some time remembering my evenings with Abigail Kleist and trying to recall what precisely it had felt like to be totally satisfied with a woman for the first time in months. Or was it years? Or was it ever?

I usually hate it when my passengers sleep and I have to stay awake, but this time it felt good. And when we finally got home and I awakened my passengers, nobody was any the worse for the rest. It was after seven when we finally got back to the house. I was too tired to cook, so we sent out for pizza and I commissioned Dave and Lena to make a salad to go with it while I lay down to rest. I couldn't remember when I had been so weary. I knew it was silly to have a nap when we could clean up dinner and go to bed for the night, but I suddenly couldn't help myself. I lay down on the couch and fell immediately asleep. But when I awoke, the table was set, the pizza was hot, the beer was cold and the salad, created through the joint efforts of a nineteen-year-old arm-breaker-decapitator punk and a six-year-old angel, was crisp and dressed. My God, I remember thinking, this is just how real families must do it....

XXXIV

By the time the dishes were done and everything was finally put away, it was after ten. Lena was falling asleep at the table, so I left Dave to wipe down the counters and turn on the dishwasher while I put her to bed. But when I came back downstairs, Dave himself was asleep on the couch. The counters, however, were wiped clean.

My eye fell on the flashing red light on the answering machine. I asked myself how I could possibly not have noticed it before, but it was a foolish question since Lena had put her stuffed bear on top of the machine when we came into the house and had only removed it when I took her upstairs. There were three messages, all from women.

The first was from a woman named Allison Brague. I didn't know her, the voice said, but I should. (My God, I thought, how many women have said that to me before! The rest of the message, however, was not anything that any woman had ever said to me before.) She was, she said, the chairwoman—although it sounded so much like charwoman the way she said it that I actually rewound the tape to listen a second time—anyway, she was the chairwoman of the department of humanities at a college in Kenora, Ontario, and she was looking for a Bible As Lit teacher for the fall semester. She knew, she said, that it was short notice. Still, she was getting desperate (just what every teacher likes to hear from a perspective employer) and if I was interested, I should give her a call within a day or two. Needless to say, I was interested. But what was even more interesting, I surprised myself by acknowledging, was that the number she gave me had a Manitoba area code. Was that her home phone number? Could she live in Winnipeg? I couldn't quite remember where Kenora was, but it struck me that it might be one of those towns in the extreme western part of the province near the border with Manitoba. I resolved to check in the atlas before I went to sleep. Well, well, I told myself, maybe there is a God after all. Or perhaps a Goddess.

The second message was from Helene. She had survived her flight to Australia, she said, and wanted us to know that she had arrived safely in Sydney. I was disappointed her plane hadn't caught fire and plunged into the Pacific, but I reminded myself that Lena would be pleased her mother had survived the journey and I consoled myself with the thought that a sheep farm was still the perfect place for Helene to fall asleep by a campfire in the outback and be eaten by a wild dingo. I was, she said, to let Lena hear her voice on the tape. She then addressed herself directly to Lena and promised she would write soon. I wondered if Helene thought that Lena had perhaps learned to read in the last three days.

The third message was from Abigail Kleist. She was phoning for three reasons, she said quite quickly as though she were worried that the tape would run out before she got them all out. First, she wished to express her condolences to Dave on the passing of his father. She doubted very much that he was paralyzed with grief, but she wanted him to know that she was sorry...sorry for the way the man had lived and sorry for the way he died...and that Dave should know that he would always be welcome to live in her house for as long as he wished. Second, she wished to tell me that she missed me. And that she wanted to see me again. In fact, she said, she would like to invite me to a Labour Day barbecue in her backyard. To be held, naturally enough, on Labour Day. At noon. I could bring the beer if I wanted, but she'd get everything else. I could bring Dave too, which she'd especially like. I was not, she said pointedly, to bring a date. The third thing was that she wished to know if an Allison Brague had phoned. If she hadn't, I should phone Abigail immediately and she'd give me the phone number of a woman who could possibly be very useful to me. As a postscript no less quixotic than irrelevant, Abigail noted that Ms. Brague was the lesbian lover of Kevin's and her dentist and a professor of something in Kenora.

Here's the scene. Lena is asleep upstairs in my old room. She's wearing the cotton Beauty and the Beast pyjamas I wrestled her into after she was already asleep and is clutching a stuffed bear her depraved mother bought her somewhere in California.

Dave is asleep on the couch in the living room. He is wearing cut-off jeans and a t-shirt with the words "Kurt is God" on it. His left leg is up on the back cushions and his right leg is bent off the couch and is resting almost on the floor. His jaw is open slightly. He is breathing irregularly and, judging from the bulge in his pants, appears to be having some sort of erotic dream.

The kitchen is neat and clean. The faint aroma of salad dressing made with too much vinegar lingers on the evening air. The windows are open. It is the first slightly cool August night. I can hear the neighbours—also, coincidentally, a lesbian couple—playing one of their apparently enormous collection of Keith Jarrett CDs. Buddy Kruger's head is back in the freezer trough with the frozen chickens.

I am standing in the little hallway between the dining room and the living room by the table with the answering machine. I could go sit down in the kitchen over a cup of coffee or I could go upstairs to bed, but I find myself unable—I suppose I mean unwilling, but it *feels* as though I'm unable—to do either. Or anything else, for that matter. I sit down right there on the floor. I close my eyes and my life opens up before me.

There are always two ways. My mother used to say that to

me all the time and, although I don't think I ever stopped for half a second to wonder what she meant, it now strikes me that she was completely right. There always are two ways. The path through yellow wood is always diverging in front of you wherever you go and with every step that you take. This truth visits and revisits me as I sit on the floor by the answering machine and, for a few long minutes, I allow myself to contemplate its larger implications.

Just thinking about Abigail has given me an erection, so I unbutton my shorts and unzip myself so as to be slightly less uncomfortable. Unfortunately, this doesn't work—yet another disadvantage to being so almost amazingly well-endowed—so I take my pants off altogether and sit on the floor in my jockey shorts. I wonder who Dave is dreaming about. I wonder if his and my lives are going to remain as tangled together as they have become in just a few weeks since I picked him up between Stanhope and Barrymore or if this has been an odd interlude in both our lives destined to be recalled either fondly or indifferently as it fades slowly from both our consciousnesses. I wonder if Dave has really gotten away with murder. In the movies, thinking precisely that is just about always the prelude to being apprehended—this is what passes in Hollywood, after all, as The Supreme Irony—but I wonder how true this is in real life. Are the police actively working on solving Buddy's murder? Or did they basically focus on it for as long as the papers were writing about it and then file it away to be worked on again if anyone ever asks why no arrests were ever made. Or were they led off in the wrong direction by those other instances of beheaded corpses Constable Singh had mentioned when he came to tell Dave about his father's death? In the end, I come to this: why would the police give a fat rat's ass about who killed a useless lowlife creep like Buddy Kruger? Case, therefore, closed.

I think about life itself. I think of my aging parents sinking into an abyss of knowledgeless, emotionless, meal-to-meal existence devoid of love, self-awareness or hope. I think especially of my father and wonder how a man who was so intelligent and so clever could be reduced so quickly to a caricature. I remember how he used to beat the other dads at arm-wrestling when we had class picnics in elementary school and how proud I was of him. I wonder if he ever had memories of any sort any longer.

And then I broaden my spectrum and think about all of them—about my parents, about Helene and her sheep-farmer, about Miss Swee and Miss Petuchowski and Miss Sorensen and Nurse Sawlicki, about Morey the Masturbator and John Cassingham and Eduardo Bernardo Alfredo Bergmann, about Gene Zaremba, about Milton Schwinger, even about Constables Wu and Ng and Singh and McDonald and about the dead Dunn brothers…about the endless cast of characters in the play that is my life…but most of all, I think about Wil. My heart still aches for him and, for the first time in a long time, I allow myself to shed a few tears. He wasn't just handsome and athletic and successful with girls, after all—he was everything I had ever hoped I would ever be or become. And then he died and left me on my own without much reason to hope that I would ever be anything at all. And that's what it finally comes down to as I sit on the floor by my answering machine and consider what my life has become: one way or the other, I am either going to have to find hope somewhere in this sick, unfeeling world or else follow Wil into the pit. It must sound pretty melodramatic when I write about all this now, but it certainly didn't feel melodramatic as I was sitting there—it felt like somebody had put the poisoned tip of a sharp sword at my neck and dared me either to fall on it or to find the strength to push it aside. But let me get back to the moment as it actually was.

For some reason, I find myself thinking of old Abimelech, Gideon's evil son, beneath the walls of Thebez. How he somehow managed to summon up enough breath after his skull had already been smashed by a millstone to order his servant to stab him through the heart lest it be said of him that he had been killed by a woman. I've always liked that story, but suddenly a flaw in it presents itself to me where I have never seen one before. How, I find myself asking, did Abimelech know that it had been a woman who flung the millstone over the city walls? After all, millstones were heavy things, heavy enough to grind corn into meal by their own sheer weight. Surely if such a thing came flying over a city wall, anyone's initial assumption would be that a man was responsible—or, even more likely, that several men were. And the answer couldn't possibly be that he just saw the woman flinging the stone—if he had seen it coming, why wouldn't he just have stepped out of the way and saved himself? No, it had to have come as a surprise, yet his last thoughts were how to avoid the ignominy of being killed by a woman. How had he known?

You could imagine, I guess, that he hadn't actually known. That he just wanted his servant to kill him on the chance, no matter how slim, that it had been a woman who had somehow found the strength to throw the stone over the wall. But that's not what he says…and the stirring cadence—and it really is stirring—of the Hebrew comes back to me so strongly that I almost think I've heard someone saying the words out loud: *shlof harbekhah umoteteni pen yomru li ishah haragatehu.* Draw your sword and make me dead lest it be said of me that I was killed by a woman. And another thing—why precisely was that something Abimelech was so anxious to avoid? Is it worse to be killed by a woman than by a man? Maybe it's a bit of a come-down if you're wrestling with each other and you're some WWF guy who weighs two forty and your opponent is five foot two and weighs a hundred and eleven soaking wet, but if we're talking getting a millstone flung at your head, surely it doesn't reflect poorly on you if your skull cracks open and you die of your wound just because it was a woman who was doing the flinging!

And then, almost as quickly as all these thoughts assault me, I see a path of light opening up before me. I follow the path of light up towards the ceiling and there, I can see Abigail in the pale yellow light of the hallway. She isn't precisely a ghost, but she isn't the real woman either…something more like a apparition or a phantasm than a real spectre. She is lying on her bed—I can actually see through the spectral bed floating in the air beneath her—and she is completely naked. Her legs are open wide and in the centre, precisely where her thighs come together, I can see…something. Not Abigail or any part of her I can recall, but something else, something I can see but can't quite identify. I seem to recall that I've lost something somewhere and I wonder for a moment if that might not be where I lost it. Should I try to float up the path of light just to check what's up there on the off chance that it might be mine? I actually consider this for a moment as though it were a reasonable possibility, but before I can decide what precisely I should do, Abigail is gone and the bed is gone and the hallway has returned to its former, apparitionless state.

The moment has passed. I get up, put my pants back on and head into the living room to wake up Dave. He has rolled over, but he still doesn't look too comfortable and I imagine he would prefer being awakened to spending the night in his clothes on the couch. I touch his shoulder and, to my surprise, he awakens almost immediately.

"I fell asleep."

"I know. You've been sleeping for at least an hour. I figured you'd want to go upstairs…."

"Sure."

He gets up and goes upstairs. I hear him going into the bathroom and puttering around in there. I hear the toilet flush. I hear the water in the sink running. I hear the door to the bathroom open and I hear his footsteps as he walks across the hallway to Wil's room. I hear the bedroom door open and close.

I am alone again. I close up the house, turning off the inside lights and turning on the lights outside the front door. I make sure the door is double locked. I go upstairs and check on Lena. She is sleeping peacefully. I go into my bedroom, brush my teeth, take off all my clothes and lie down naked on top of my bed. The words keep plowing through my brain like a harrow through a farmer's field: *shlof harbekhah umotetêni pen yomru li ishah haragatehu.* And suddenly, I have the meaning behind my vision. A woman almost killed me—that would be Helene who robbed me of my…of basically everything. Of my self-respect. Of my manhood. Of my dignity. Of my family. Anything would be better than dying that way, it strikes me, and suddenly I have, if not quite respect, than at least a new kind of sympathy for that old fratricide times seventy, Abimelech. But just when I think my skull is completely crushed and that there is, therefore, no choice but to admit that Helene has done me in, a young man with a dagger appears in my life. Not a son. Not a friend. A kind of aide-de-camp, I suppose, but one who not only *can* offer me an alternative, but who *does.* I don't deserve it, but I am deeply, permanently grateful. And, as I lay naked on my bed in the cool August evening air, I know that God has answered my prayers and that no one would ever say that a woman had killed me.

The picture of those Indian lovers with the soles of their feet pressed up against each other materializes for a moment in my consciousness, but I will myself to banish it. Instead, I crawl under the blankets and close my eyes. I am asleep almost instantly. My last conscious thought is that I have won.

XXXV

I think the hardest thing about being a decent actor must be knowing how the play ends. You know, it's one thing to live your life in the way we all do—day by day by day with no certainty at all about what the future is going to bring—and another to go on stage for act one when you've already read the last act and know who dunnit and who didn't. Not to mention what your personal role in the larger drama going on around you is…because we generally don't know that either. I mean, we think we do. We think we understand, if nothing else, at least who we ourselves are in the play even if we have no idea who everybody else is. But the truth is that that's the most difficult thing of them all to know. To really know, I mean. Generally speaking, it's the one piece of the puzzle that no one ever finds out, I don't think. Not even after the whole damn hurly-burly finally does die down. Which, believe me, it does.

Anyway, that's what the next few weeks were like for me. I felt like an actor in a play I had already read through and Labour Day was opening night. I had, therefore, two weeks and two days to get things right. Now I have to admit that I didn't feel at all hampered by the fact that I felt certain that I knew how things were going to end up. I can't say how precisely I knew—or where that intense, entirely uncharacteristic certainty was coming from—but I can still remember those days so clearly that I can promise you it was so. Absolutely. I had this odd feeling that I had been manipulated into the particular situation I found myself in, but who was manipulating me and for what reason, I was totally unable even to guess. In retrospect I suppose it was just an illusion. But it was a splendid one the recollection of which I still treasure.

I phoned Allison Brague, Abigail's dentist's lover and the charwoman of humanities at Ross Head College in Kenora and we talked at length. I faxed her my resume and she phoned me a day later with a proposal. She didn't mention a second time how desperate they were to find somebody and I didn't tell her that I had never heard of her (or any of her several dozen articles on the use of Biblical sources in Chaucer) or her school. She mentioned a number, I haggled her up another six grand (by agreeing to supervise three honours theses a year) and we had a deal. She sent me a contract and I signed it.

I sold the house. I had had the brains to have my father give it to me clear and away before anyone even contacted the old age home, so the house was mine to dispose of as I saw fit. (Except for the contents of that savings account I had power of attorney over, the rest of their wealth was going to go to the home—which I begrudgingly admitted was probably fair—although the guy who admitted them promised me—I swear he said this in all seriousness—he said that if my parents were to pass on before they managed to spend everything, the home would forward the change directly to me. I figured that was about as likely as hell freezing over, but who was I to argue? Still, that didn't seem like a good enough reason not to lie about a savings account with a lousy four or five hundred dollars in it.) Anyway, selling the house turned out to be a piece of cake. I called Mrs. Eadie Yee ("Whose Name Sounds Like Initials"), a real estate agent whose signs I saw all over Kerrisdale, and told her she could have exclusive rights for precisely seven days to sell the house for the most money she could get for it. After that, I'd go elsewhere. She was out of joint about the seven days part, but once she realized that I had no intention of negotiating the point, she backed down and signed on. She sold the house within twenty-four hours to some people who were still in Hong Kong for precisely twenty-two times what my parents had paid for it in 1955.

I went to see my parents. My mother had no idea who I was. My father wasn't much better, although he thought I was his brother. Since my Uncle Morris died in 1964, I could have been Fritz the Cat and it would have meant about the same to my dad. I felt guilty telling them I was moving away, but not as guilty as you might think. I mean, what did it matter to them? They were fixed for life—if you can call that living—and no one could evict them. When their wealth ran out—assuming they didn't die first and force the home to refund the change—the province would take over. They weren't going to miss me because neither of them, as far as I could tell, had any idea that they had a son, let alone that they had once had two. I thought they could probably still recognize each other, but I wasn't sure. They hardly interacted when I was there saying goodbye, not even furtively. If I ever get to that state, I hope somebody shoots me. In the back, if necessary.

I went to Wil's grave. I went without knowing what precisely I intended to do when I got there and then I just found myself pouring my heart out to this little grey stone and crying and crying until my eyes were so sore that I could barely keep them open. This thing is already more than long enough, but if I wrote another ten thousand pages, I could never say how much I loved my brother. Or ten million, for that matter. Because, when it comes right down to it, he was the best part of me and that's basically all there is to it. But when I was through crying and the snot was running down the back of my throat and my eyelids were so puffy they actually hurt, I pulled myself away and stood back. You're not supposed to say the Kaddish without a full quorum of ten, but I said it anyway. Number Ninety. The whole enchilada. Over seven months instead of thirty days. At least once without the requisite quorum of fellow worshippers. Without the prayer being a function of any real faith in God or, even less so, of His eternal goodness or fairness. But even so, I figure God and I are even—I'll more or less believe in Him even though he killed my brother and He can forgive me for saying a prayer—which it's a miracle anyone believes in Him enough to say in the first place—He can forgive me for saying it with a bit of an attitude and, at least once, without nine other people standing around watching. And then, when I was through with my prayer and I couldn't stand being there even one second longer, I left. But I never got over it. I don't suppose I ever will. I've never been back to the grave. I just can't. I'm even crying while I'm writing this now.

I went to the lawyer to discuss the Helene situation. Getting a divorce was a simple enough proposition if neither party wanted to make a big deal out of it. The lawyer, an extremely thin woman by the terrific name of Moira L. Ork, was not thrilled that I had accepted the house from my parents while I was still married, but there was nothing to do about it if I didn't want the full value to go to the home. Losing half to Helene was the better alternative, I figured, although I can't tell you how much it bit my ass to think of half that money passing through her treacherous little hands into the pockets of the sheep farmer. Still, absent him she might never have relinquished Lena to me and I figured that was worth at least half the value of my parents' house. So if little Lena ever asks me what she was worth to me, the answer is the sun and the moon and the stars. And to her mother? Four hundred grand less the agent's commission. I remember hoping Helene took her share of the take and spent it on chemotherapy. For the both of them.

And that, more or less, was that. I told Lena that we were moving to Winnipeg because Daddy found a good job there. I expected her to pitch this major fit about moving, but she took it quite well. In retrospect, I suppose she had just been moved around so much in the then recent past that another move just didn't seem like any sort of big deal. But at the moment, I found her willingness to go along with the plan just another sign that I was following the lead of heaven in all of this and that her acquiesence was just another sign from God that I was doing the right thing.

I told Dave the truth, more or less. That I had a job in Kenora. That I was moving to Winnipeg instead of Kenora precisely because I was hoping to pursue a relationship with his grandmother. I wasn't asking, I said clearly, for his blessing. But I still hoped that he found the prospect of an ongoing relationship between her and me—and, by obvious extension, between him and me as well—to be as pleasant to contemplate as I did. He seemed surprised by my interest in his grandmother. I remember thinking that this was not so much because he couldn't see us as a couple as much as it was because he simply had almost no experience seeing sex develop into love. It was one thing, after all, for me to have slept with her a few nights when the opportunity arose. That, he found entirely reasonable. But to think that the seeds of love might have been planted in the course of those few nights was simply something he had had almost never seen before and, therefore, something he found surprising. Not upsetting or alienating, just unusual. In this, as in many ways, Dave had a bit of growing up to do even if he was six feet tall and could crack his knuckles behind his head and take a leak at the same time.

Emptying out the house was easier than I thought. The furniture, including all the pots and pans and kitchen stuff and bed linens and blankets and pillows and towels, I put into storage on the chance I might be furnishing a house in Kenora one of these days. (I was being hopeful about my relationship with Abigail, not insane.) Lena's clothing and my stuff, we packed into boxes and shipped to Winnepeg. My parents' stuff, or rather the stuff of theirs they had made a conscious decision not to take along with them to the home, I gave to the Salvation Army for their thrift shop. That was about it and whatever we didn't take or give away, I just left in the house for the Yips to keep or pitch as they saw fit when they arrived.

Wil's stuff was a different issue. I just didn't know what to do—keeping it all seemed pathetic, but pitching it out seemed like killing him a second time. In the end, I gave almost all his good stuff—his leather jacket and his collection of flannel boxers and his dead rock star t-shirts and his jeans—to Dave, who was pretty much the same size as Wil had been. The price I exacted for all that stuff was simple enough—Dave had to earn his haul by taking the rest of Wil's stuff out of the house when I was gone and getting rid of it. He could take it to a thrift shop or throw it out or give it to whomever he wanted to, but all I wanted was for whatever he wasn't keeping to disappear. To his credit, Dave understood why this was important and he did as told. I never heard another word about it and when I came back from the store with Lena a day or two after having my first and only conversation with Dave about the matter, Wil's stuff was gone and his room was entirely clean.

And so we left. Precisely eleven days after listening to the messages that were waiting for me when we came back from Manning Park. We drove to Winnipeg—I was hardly going to pay to ship the car and for airplane tickets for the three of us—but the drive was nowhere near as exciting as my previous journey that route. Because Leeny was with us, we took it easy. Kelowna. Banff. Medicine Hat. Regina. Winnipeg. Five days without having to drive more than six or seven hours a day. Motels with pools. Miniature golf. A drive-in movie or two. Ice cream. Eggs for breakfast. No smoking in the car. The Trans-Canada almost the entire way. I still regret we didn't detour off the highway to show Lena the dinosaurs in Drumheller, but I thought it would delay us unnecessarily and I told myself she was probably too young really to appreciate the place. Buddy's head was in a cooler in the trunk and Dave made a point of buying fresh ice whenever we stopped at a gas station that sold that kind of thing.

We got to Winnipeg the day before Labour Day. I can't say why, but I didn't want to arrive early. I sprung for an extra-nice motel—Lena was thrilled—about twenty miles or so west of the city and we stayed there overnight. More miniature golf. Another movie. More midnight ice cream. Then sleep and up late and back in the car at eleven. We got to Winnipeg in about a half hour and headed north. I stopped at a liquor store and bought a flat of Molson's. At five to noon, we were pulling up to Abigail's house. I could smell hamburgers cooking somewhere, presumably in Abigail's backyard. Had she expected us so promptly? I hadn't phoned her back—that's another thing I can't really explain, but I just didn't want to. I wanted to show up, to see if she was going to expect us. I know it sounds crazy, but she didn't phone back—which I fully understand—and I didn't phone and we sort of made this major adjustment in our lives based on one phone message I didn't return. Now that I think back on it, I must have been truly insane. But we were there. And I really could smell hamburgers being grilled somewhere....

We had been expected. Abigail had invited some neighbours with a daughter Lena's age to join us and within a few minutes of our arrival, the girls were off playing somewhere and the adults were, more or less, left in peace. Kevin was there with a girl he worked with, a woman at least six inches taller than he was who seemed as devoted to him as she was solicitous and pleasant towards us. Dave, for his part, seemed to segue into his new life almost effortlessly and was deep in conversation with his brother and his brother's guest in a corner of the backyard almost immediately. That left Abigail, her neighbours who had brought the girl

Lena's age, and me. Abigail looked lovely that September afternoon. She was wearing a tan sundress with red and black smocking across the front and had her hair pulled back in a ponytail just as it had been the first time we met. She still didn't look like a grandma to me, but perhaps that was part of her charm. And she was truly charming....

The day passed and evening fell. The neighbours left with Lena in tow to watch some Disney video in their house across the street. The air became cool. Kevin announced that he was leaving to take his friend home and that he would be back. I thought he meant that he was planning to spend the night with her and would be back in the morning, but I was wrong and he was back not more than an hour after leaving. Abigail spent a long time talking quietly with Dave while Kevin was gone and I tidied up. And when Kevin came back, she announced a plan. We were going to collect Lena and go for a end-of-summer nighttime drive out into the country.

It turned out that Abigail owned part of a cabin up on Chapman Lake with three of her girlfriends. They had bought it years ago when such things could be had for very little money and it had proven to be the investment of a lifetime. There was no one there that evening, she said. We weren't going to stay over, only drive up to take a look. It seemed like a long drive to nowhere for no reason to me, but when I saw Dave lifting the styrofoam cooler with his father's head in it out of the trunk of my Camaro, I suddenly understood where we were going and why.

In no time, Lena was asleep in the back seat of Abigail's ancient yellow Volvo wagon snuggled up against Kevin (of all people.) Abigail drove. I sat next to her. Dave was in the backseat behind his grandmother and looked slightly put out that Lena had chosen to lean up against Kevin instead of him when she was falling asleep. I doubted this had been a conscious choice, but something held me back from saying so in so many words. In some ways, Kevin looked to be the older brother now, I thought. He was muscular and mature and he had the way of a working man about him. His girlfriend looked like a grown woman, not a teenager—I later found out that she was all of twenty-one, three years older than Kevin was then—and they both carried themselves like adults rather than like children. Dave, on the other hand, looked like the teenager he was. He was more gangly than tall—although he was taller than me and significantly taller than Kevin—and he still looked like he had some maturing to do, especially in his face. They didn't much look like brothers, but they both bore some faint resemblance to their father.

We drove for about ninety minutes. At first, there was some attempt at conversation, but that didn't last. We were all tired, but there was also a certain air of excitement in the car. It was hard to describe—lassitude and an almost electric sense of anticipation in the same little space. For the last hour, at any rate, we drove in silence. Other than Lena, no one slept.

When we pulled into the cottage's driveway and Abigail turned off the car's headlights, everything was completely dark. I could barely make out the outline of the cottage itself and I could hear the loons on the lake, but otherwise, all was still. No one spoke. Abigail opened the trunk and lifted out the cooler. She handed it to Dave. Then she took out a flashlight and handed it to Kevin. Then she closed the trunk and took my hand.

I guessed that Kevin had been there recently, since he obviously knew his way around. He led us around the building, not into it. I could see the black lake in front of us shimmering faintly in the starlight. The moon either hadn't risen yet that evening or, if it had, was just not visible from where we were standing. If the neighbours across the lake were awake, they were laying low. There were, at any rate, no cottages other than Abigail's along this particular promontory. As far as I could tell, we were totally alone.

And now we were on a kind of floating dock. I could see a rowboat tethered to the dock and a canoe behind it. There were no motor boats, at least not as far as I could make out. I had the sense that a script was being followed, but I could not imagine who had written it or why. But nothing struck me as happening by chance. And Kevin was leading the way with a certain air of assurance that impressed me.

Abigail took my hand and led me to a picnic table on the shore. I could see the outline of the car not more than fifty yards behind us and I knew that I would hear Lena instantly if she woke up. It was just Kevin and Dave on the dock now, just the two of them and the cooler with their father's head in it. What was about to happen, I could hardly predict.

The boys were speaking in low voices at the end of the dock. They weren't arguing and they certainly weren't raising their voices, but I could hear them speaking and I could tell they were trying to make a decision of some sort. Finally, the speaking stopped. Kevin went to the back of the dock and disappeared into a tiny shed I hadn't even noticed up until that moment. Dave bent down and opened the cooler. For a long minute, he peered inside, then he undid the twist tie holding the Safeway bag closed and lifted his father's head out of the bag by its hair. All this was only faintly visible in the light of distant stars, but I could still see what was going on when Dave lifted the head to his own height and looked deeply into its eyes. As far as I could tell, he said nothing.

And then Kevin returned. He was carrying something that looked like a big fish trap of some sort, but I couldn't really make it out too clearly in the dim light. I saw him open the top and lift back the lid while Dave put their father's head inside. I could see that the sides of the trap, if that's what it was, were made of some kind of malleable meshwork. The head was a black space at the bottom. Kevin closed the lid and fiddled with it some sort of latch to keep it closed.

I could see Kevin undressing now, first pulling his t-shirt off over his head, then unbuttoning his cut-offs and pushing them and his underwear to the ground as he stepped out of his moccasins and stood naked on the dock next to his brother, but with his back towards us.

He took the trap from Dave and tossed it into the lake, then dove in after it so quickly that he was already well on his way by the time I even realized he was in the water. I stood up to see better what was happening, but Abigail held my arm and I didn't move any closer. By the light of distant stars, many of which had died in the countless millennia it had taken their light to reach earth, I fancied I could see Buddy's head bobbing up and down in the water inside the trap as it trailed behind Kevin's dark figure as he made his way to the middle of the lake.

And then he was back, hoisting himself up effortlessly onto the dock and standing naked in the dim light of a September night sky. He must have been freezing, but he didn't do anything for a long moment but stand there and talk quietly with his brother. And then he pulled on his shorts, slung his t-shirt over his shoulder and stepped back into his moccasins. In a minute, they were both off the dock and heading back to the car. Abigail and I followed.

As though we had agreed on it in advance, we all stopped for one long moment and looked back at the lake. The surface was dark, shiny, undisturbed. The spot where Kevin let go of the trap with his father's head inside was absolutely unrecognizable. One thing was completely clear, however, and I found myself moved beyond words by its various implications and ramifications: although neither needed to have done so, both Abigail and Kevin had joined themselves to Dave and his deed in an absolutely irreversible way. I considered it highly unlikely that the head would ever be found at the bottom of one of Manitoba's endless thousands of lakes. But this was no longer a rogue operation by a troubled youth—or at least that's not how it would appear to the police if Buddy's head was ever found in a lake that bordered on his mother-in-law's property. I knew that and I knew that both Abigail and Kevin—and certainly Dave—knew it as well. I felt a bit like an outsider who shouldn't have been there to witness something that would more properly have taken place in the closed bosom of a newly reconstituted family, but it was too late for me not to have been there and, although I had the sense that I ought to have finished the evening off with some sort of profound statement, I found that I couldn't think of one damn thing to say that wouldn't have ruined everything.

We went home. Abigail drove. Lena never stirred. Kevin and Dave spoke together quietly in the back seat, then fell asleep. Abigail took my hand and put it on the knob of the stick shift, then put her own hand over mine so that she could drive and hold my hand at the same time. I resisted my thoughts for a while, then surrendered to love.

XXXVI

That scene at the lake was twenty-one months ago. But even less than two years later, the whole saga sounds to me more like a fable or some weird, turn-of-the-last-century coming-of-age novella than an actual account of the couple of weeks that changed my life and made me into the man I've become. Maybe that's why I've bothered to write it down...and also so that an accurate account of the death of Buddy Kruger can exist on the off chance that Dave ever wants anyone to know.

I married Abigail about a year after we moved to Winnipeg. It turned out that Abigail's mother's mother had been Jewish—she confided this to me as though it was a great secret on the ride back from the cottage that same evening that Kevin towed Buddy's head out into the middle of Chapman Lake—and that made loving her even simpler. Indeed, by the time the stuff we shipped arrived about a week after we ourselves had, Lena and I were so well ensconced in Abigail's house—not to mention her life—that we could hardly recall not living there.

Lena took to Abigail from the start, which didn't surprise me at all, and also to both Dave and Kevin, which did—at least a little bit. Kevin, completely untrue to his tough guy pose, turned out to be a sucker for kids and loved the idea of having a little girl around the house. He took her to the movies and for pony rides at some stable nearby that his girlfriend's sister-in-law's father owned. For the first time since my marriage to Helene broke up, Lena seemed calm and happy and I think that she came to love all of them without reservation in about as little time as any child

303

could.

I sent a postcard to Helene with our new address and let her think that I had come to Winnipeg solely because of the job I had found. She wrote back after a month or so that she was pleased we were settled, that she was happy on the ranch and that she wasn't coming back. I forwarded her letter to my lawyer and nine months after that, I was a divorced man. I found a rabbi in Winnipeg who was willing to work with a friend of his in Sydney to arrange a *get*—a Jewish bill of divorce—and that got itself taken care of too. And so, less than a year and a half after she left me, I was a single man both in the eyes of the provinces of British Columbia and Manitoba and in accordance with the law of Moses and the people Israel. After I married Abigail, I let Helene know the good news. She responded with an invitation to her own wedding. I summoned up all my inner strength and sent her a note congratulating her on her good fortune and I haven't heard from her since. Lena gets letters every couple of months and I expect something special will come for her birthday. Helene's letters, which I read to Lena out loud, make occasional reference to Lena coming to Australia for a visit, but I don't think it will ever happen. It certainly won't if Helene expects me to pay for it.

Dave took the longest of all of us to get used to his new surroundings. He drifted from job to job, accepting Kevin's help at first and then refusing it for fear of embarrassing his brother if he screwed up, which he seemed to do regularly. I think I had been working with an overly romantic impression of him both as a result of our odd odyssey across western Canada and of his willingness to avenge his mother's honour in the only real way he could accept as meaningful, but now that I was able to observe him in the cooler light of a Winnipeg autumn, I saw something else: a troubled boy who was growing into a troubled man enormously less free of the heritage of both his parents than he fervently wished to think.

In the course of the first few months we were there, he went through a string of girlfriends none of us could stand. Eventually, though, he met a woman just a year his senior who seemed to understand him and genuinely to like him. She wants them to live together for a while, but he clings to our makeshift family life in his grandma's house and doesn't seem at all ready to strike out on his own. Kevin seems at peace with his older woman as well, but he also gives no indication that he's hoping to move in with her any time soon. What it comes down to, I think, is that neither boy had a real childhood and although they're now twenty-one and twenty years old, they're grasping at life with Abigail, Lena and me as a way of experiencing the great nurturing experience of family life before they have to try to invent it on their own with no working model at all to go on. For our part, we're glad to have them. And it continues to impress me that both girlfriends seem to understand what's going on, although I doubt either brother would be able to say in so many words precisely why it is they can't be pushed into moving out on their own just quite yet.

Although Lena is still the centre and hope of my life, Dave and I have established a deep relationship that feels permanent. In some way I can't even begin to explain, he's my big chance to make it all up to Wil and I'm not going to blow it a second time. It's funny that in all this thinking about the way I let Wil down, I've never seriously acted upon the one way I really could have made it up to him. I know that Jewish cemeteries are pretty negative about exhumation, but I could probably get a court order easily enough if I convinced a judge that I had somehow only now become aware of my brother's dying wishes. The whole idea of digging him up and lopping off his head so I could ship it off to California—assuming they don't require the head to be removed within a certain amount of time, presumably less than a two years, after death—is sort of daunting, but not so absolutely impossible for me not to have to ask myself why I've never actually worked on it seriously. I'd thought of it, but I never did phone the place in California to ask if it was still an option, either. I don't know, maybe the answer is that becoming Dave's friend and then his step-grandfather—although I admit that sounds ridiculous when a thirty-six-year-old says it out loud to strangers—maybe that experience has simply helped me move on from Wil's death so that the whole situation that was once so sorely in need of some kind of resolution was now not in need of resolution at all. What can I say? In his own artless way, Dave helped me realize that in the context of love, letting go and not letting go are more or less the same thing.

And so I've ended up, also more or less, on top.

I have a job.

I have a contract to put out a book of essays on Shakespeare's use of the Psalms and another to publish a novel I've been working on about the Biblical story of Cain and Abel. I'm talking to a publisher in Toronto about putting out a collection of violent, sexually explicit Bible stories for children whose parents want to protect them from the violence and sexual depravity of the Brothers Grimm. I've published a few book reviews and I've been talking to a few friends I've made at work about starting our own literary journal, one devoted to pseudo-scholarly articles about the Bible that are completely rooted in their authors' unfounded fantasies about various Biblical personalities rather than on any real information.

I'm married to the sexiest grandma on either side of the Assiniboine and I live in a house filled with love. I can't think of a single thing lacking from our marriage, except maybe the years I wasted with Helene.

Abigail, for her part, seems as content with marriage as I am. Her sexual appetites are basically insatiable and the things she hears of and wants to try continually amaze me. I do my best. She says that she likes the way her house feels now that we've finally managed to turn it into a home. I couldn't agree more. We keep trying the position with the soles of our feet pressed up against each other, but so far, no go.

Lena is almost eight years old. She's doing well in school and wants to be a Broadway actress or an astronaut when she grows up. Every now and then, she asks about her mother, whose letters come less and less regularly. I encourage her to phone if she wants to know what's happening with her other birth parent. Collect.

Dave and Kevin have blossomed in our home, both of them learning to trust and to love in ways I would have thought at best unlikely for either of them. I think they'll both end up being husbands and fathers and I think that Dave and I will always care deeply about each other. I can't explain who he is in my life or where he came from, but when I needed a friend to get me over the guilt I felt about being alive once Wil was dead, he materialized on the road between Barrymore and Stanhope and saved my life. I won't forget.

My parents are still alive, but without any recollective memory at all in either of them. I've been back to B.C. twice since I came out here and neither of them recognized me either time I came to visit. I feel guilty about not going more often, but not quite guilty enough to bother making any more pointless trips. They don't seem unhappy, mind you, although that only makes the situation weirder, not really easier to handle. I love them, but it's like loving a dream you once had, not like loving real people.

Wil, of course, is still dead. A day doesn't pass when I don't think about him, about what he looked like, about what his voice sounded like, about what it was like to have someone in my life that I cared about so deeply that even death couldn't deprive me of the succour I still derive just from having known him for as long as I did. His head (or what's left of it) is on his shoulders (or what's left of them) which is where it belongs, I suppose. I like it when I see Dave wearing an old pair of Wil's flannel boxers around the house or his leather jacket over one of his dead rock star t-shirts out in the street. I did let him down, though. I know that and I believe it and I live with that failure of nerve every day as well. I think I always will because the guilt will always be in my system, I guess. But, in the end, I found love and it set me free.

On Cain and His Brother

(*pages from an unpublished novel*)

Saul Ira Jacobson

You know, it didn't end up so bad for old Cain after all. I mean, Abel, for all his righteousness, ended up being the dead one…and Cain, for all his blood guilt and all his other tzuris, *ended up with a nice house in Afghanistan and became the father of Enoch (not the famous one begat by Jared who walked with God for three hundred years until the Lord beamed him up alive into heaven, but some lesser known* schlimazel *whose big—actually, whose only—claim to fame was that Cain founded a city and named it after him)…but I'm getting off topic here. Abel ended up with the reputation of having been the more saintly of the two brothers, but he was a dead saint and, in the end, Cain didn't end up so bad either—and that's the point I'm trying to make.*

I mean, sure God was royally pissed with Cain for killing his brother, not to mention for inventing murder and trying it out on his irritating little sibling, then for trying to bury the evidence in the ground—which is a nice touch in the story, by the way, because it was Cain, after all, who was the first farmer, the first guy ever who figured out how to make his living by putting things in the ground—anyway, it's true that God punishes Cain with that most quintessentially Jewish of all penalties: the penance of wandering endlessly through the earth, but it's also true—we sort of skip over this part most of the time—it's also true that God sort of forgets about His awful decree after a little while and Cain does settle down and get married, he does find happiness, he eventually does learn to forgive himself for the role he played in his brother's death.

But there's another part of the story, one no one knows, a part that only I know because…because I do. The day that Abel died, Cain and he had had breakfast together. Now Adam and Eve hadn't ever really mentioned that the girls they lived with—obviously, their intended—were actually their sisters. Even though they—the girls, I mean—had grown up with them in the same house, Eve and Adam had sort of just let their sons assume that the Lord God had made all of them out of the dust of the earth so as not to discourage the boys from figuring out about sex and then getting all turned off by the whole thing when they realized that the only single women in the world were their sisters. Anyway, the part the Bible leaves out is that it was that very morning that Abel—by all accounts, the smart one—that Abel had figured it all out and was sharing his discovery with Cain. Scripture omits the dialogue, but I've reconstructed it through a very sophisticated exegetical method I can't divulge just right now.

"But they're women." *A certain hormonal surge in the nineteen-year-old Abel's normally quiescent tone of speech.*

"But come on, man…they're our sisters." *Eighty percent outrage, ten curiosity, ten lust. Just enough of the latter in old Cain's voice to hint that maybe it wouldn't be that bad to get talked out of the former and be left with even amounts of lust and curiousity.*

"Look, there are only six people in the world: Mom and Dad, you and me and Diane and Sheila. So either it ends right here or we do it with Mom or…."

"You sick…."

"Okay, okay…but that's my whole point…we're obviously not going to do it with Mom and that doesn't exactly give us much choice here. In fact, I'm making my move. For Sheila. Today. Right now. I'm getting married."

"What's 'married'?"

Anyway, that's how it went. They had breakfast early in those days—Abel had his usual plate of lamb chops and Cain ate corn flakes—so everybody could get to work on time. And Cain did head off into the field, but Abel decided the time had come to make his move. And it didn't take much. Sheila was out back braiding Diane's long, brown hair when Abel called out to her and said she should come into the barn…that he wasn't feeling that well and could she bring him a pitcher of cool date beer from the cold room under the house. So she finished up her sister's hair, got the beer and headed into the barn.

I mean, it was a farm and all…and, even if they were a little short on people, they had plenty of animals hanging around so it wasn't like old Sheila didn't know what her brother was after when she came into the barn and found him with his loincloth down around his ankles and his nostrils flaring. To tell the truth, she sort of wanted it too…and the rest…well, the rest you sort of know from Scripture.

Sheila wasn't a bad looking girl, but she never could keep a secret—not that Abel had made her swear not to tell anyway—but she really couldn't keep her mouth shut, so she told Diane who told Eve who told Adam. And it really was only a matter of time—in this case, about twenty minutes—before Cain got word of what had happened.

"You betrayed our family."

"I didn't betray anyone. I got laid. I got married. Maybe I begat somebody. You can raise all the corn you want, but who's going to eat it if there's no next generation? I should get the freaking Nobel Peace Prize for saving the world, not a load of snot from you about how I did it. Felt pretty delightful too, since you haven't asked."

And Cain said to his brother Abel, "Yeah, you must be right. Let's forget the whole thing. Mazel tov and may you both know nothing but happiness. Let's go into the field for a minute, though…I want to show you some…some…I finally figured out what you do with corn and I want to show you. Get a pot and some kindling and a brick of butter and some salt and meet me out there in, say, twen-

ty minutes? I'll draw some water from the well…"

Abel was delighted that he and his brother were back on good terms, but he was a little too happy a little too soon. And twenty-one minutes later, he was a little too dead, his blood seeping into the ground in little red rivulets that wound their sickening way around the stalks of his brother's corn.

"Teach him to screw around with my sister," Cain muttered as he went back to the house, thinking that was that….

But that is never really that. Not in real life and certainly not in the Bible. Cain thought he was done, but there were still a few things left for him to deal with. His parents' endless, abysmal grief, for one thing. Sheila's endless, abysmal grief for another. And that's not even to mention the wrath of the Lord and all that stuff about having to wander around forever with this big black mark on his forehead that as much as said: Hated of God. But more than God, more than Eve, more than Sheila, Cain had to deal with his own demons.

He had avenged his sister's honour, but at what price? He had done the right thing, but he had ignored his brother's needs, his brother's wishes and his brother's entirely reasonable plan for the future. He knew what his brother wanted, but he couldn't stand letting him get it…and that, in the end, was the real story. Abel was always the better son. He was the handsomer of the two. He was the more athletic of the two boys. He was the one with the bluer eyes, with the curlier hair, with the bigger muscles. He was the one that exuded the kind of self-confidence that Cain could only dream of having one day. He was the one who looked right in his clothes, who never gained a pound, whose skin was always clear. And poor Cain—the other brother—was left being, well, the other brother. The gross one. The one with acne. The one with nose hair. The one Adam kept catching in the barn going at it with the cows. The one everybody felt sorry for. The one who looked like a man and worked like a man, but who somehow never really got over being a fat little boy. The one who loved his brother and envied his brother and, yes, in the end, also the one who loathed his brother for being everything he wasn't and, especially, for being so stinking genial about it all and for never lording it over him and for making him feel so unbearably lousy about it all precisely by never trying to make him feel lousy at all about anything.

And also the one who killed his brother. Not figuratively. Not indirectly. Not with kindness or with flattery. He got him out into the field and he whacked him over the head with a plow blade so hard that his head actually came off. The Bible leaves out that part, but it's absolutely true and that's why there was so much blood on the ground that it was able to call out to God on its own, so to speak, and to draw His divine attention to the fact that one of His beloved creatures had been deprived of his head and his life before his time was really supposed to be up. So okay, it's true God was pissed...but not pissed enough to wave His mighty hand and make dead Abel alive again. So even then, dead was dead, you see....

And so was Cain left holding the bag. He wandered for a bit, then ended up settling down with Diane and Sheila—the Bible leaves that part out too, by the way—and they lived out their very long lives more or less happily. Sheila never conceived—which was also a bit of a miracle since she and Cain basically went at it like bunny rabbits at least seventy times a week—but eventually, paradoxically, poor Diane (whom Cain only bothered with when, as the Israelites used to put it, Sheila was crossing the Red Sea) bore Cain a son, whom they named Enoch, a name Sheila liked because it sort of sounded like one of the nonsense words she screamed out while she was in labour since no one had invented obscenity yet.

He was a troubled guy, that Cain. He loved his brother and he loved his home, but he couldn't let his brother be, couldn't let him do what he thought was right and leave it at that...and because he couldn't let it be—just that once—his brother died. He suffered over that the rest of his life and that, if you ask me, was his real punish-

ment. I mean, he did know happiness in his life. He got married, he had a kid, he settled down. He and Diane just ignored their "other" relationship—that's what they called their siblinghood, by the way, their "other relationship"—and poor Sheila, who was really not much brighter than the cows, she never really understood the whole business about being siblings and spouses at the same time and how it wasn't the best arrangement but that there really wasn't any other way.

Eventually, Adam and Eve had more kids. As a result, siblings stopped marrying and cousins started marrying and even that was just for a while until there were enough people to date without charity having to begin at home. And eventually, when families spread out and forgot how they were all related to each other and descended from the same people—or rather, once people sort of agreed just to ignore their interrelatedness— everyone just sort of forgot about their "other" relationships and just began to concentrate on being husbands and wives.

So old Cain invented a lot of things—the furrow, the plow, corn on the cob, wheat germ, vodka, billiards (they played with those little red potatoes)—but what he really invented was just ignoring all the other relationships between people and letting sex beget love and love beget peace. And, in the end, nothing is more important that being at peace. With your parents. With your kids. With your bedmate. With your siblings, living and dead. With your memories. With yourself....